THE VISIONARY PAGEANT
AND OTHER STORIES

THE VISIONARY PAGEANT
AND OTHER STORIES

PAUL DI FILIPPO

WILDSIDE PRESS

For Deborah, who inspires visions

"Worldshifter" appeared from NewCon Press in 2021. "A Canticle for Ackerman" appeared in *Amazing Stories* in 2024. "Nine Hundred Grandmothers" appeared in *Multiverses* in 2023. "The Dream-Sculptor of A.I.P." appeared in *Reports from the Deep End* in 2023. "The Steam House at Innsmouth" appeared in *Shadowmen 20* in 2023. "I, For One, Welcome Our New Insect Litterateurs" appeared in *The Magazine of Fantasy and Science Fiction* in 2023. "Hivehead" appeared in *The Mad Butterfly's Ball* in 2024. "The Visionary Pageant" appeared from NewCon Press iin 2022.

Published by Wildside Press LLC.
wildsidepress.com

CONTENTS

CONTENTS

WORLDSHIFTER

PART 1
SHIPBREAKER

> If this was what death was, somebody ought to care.
> --*Earthblood*, by Keith Laumer
> and Rosel George Brown

A craggy, jagged mountain fell slowly through the sky.

Attended by a flock of Class D Hagfish pilot ships, their coruscant supportive fields overlapping the larger vessel, the dead hulk of another retired starliner descended toward the Shipbreakers' Yard on Asperna. Possessing no discernible symmetry, the machicolated and turretted starcraft was a conglomeration of protuberances and ports, pods and pavilions, so ugly it forced the viewer to concede new notions of beauty. Its space-pitted, many-textured surfaces bespoke millennia of interstellar service.

Occulting Asperna's Least Sun, the dropping starliner robbed each individual in the crowd below of a single shadow. A vast horde of ragged workers, the crowd featured one or two representatives from the Yard's management. Apart from their finer clothing and lack of visible cruft, these overseers could also be recognized by their attendant swarms of majestatics.

The workers and executives had arrayed themselves randomly along a wide sloping beach of firm-packed sand, facing the water. On either extreme of the gathering lay vast hard-surfaced staging areas for the upcoming deconstruction, dotted with tools and agravitic lifters and cradles which would soon receive components gutted from the newest salvage prize. The shoreline was stained with exotic industrial fluids that had killed off all vegetation and tinted in oily chromatics the waters themselves. At several docks bobbed scores of dirty utilitarian slab-sided watercraft used to ferry workers out to the ship-corpse, their lifting units deactivated.

Behind the onlookers stretched inland the nameless collection of hovels and shanties, shacks and huts, warehouses and refectories, barrooms and brothels, laced together by muddy paths, all of which the shipbreakers simply called home. At the very edge of the water and wading into the shallows, a vast system of tall baffles and shunts--a diamond labyrinth--stood poised to deal with the imminent surge that would accompany the ponderous settling of the starliner into the sea.

Now the descent of the falling mountain and its host of attendants slowed even more dramatically. The liner that had once cruised like a queen among the worlds of the Indrajal seemed to hover unmoving in the atmosphere. But ever so timidly the Least Sun emerged crescentwise from behind its upper rim, indicating a slight actual progress toward berthing.

The lower edge of the liner lipped the waves. The Hagfishes pulled their fields steadily upward from contact with the rising water, not wishing to dissipate power by lifting cubic meters of sea needlessly. As their fields shifted off the center of the big's ship's mass, the little craft had to strain to maintain the equilbrium of their prize. Soon, judging by the strobing moire patterns, they would have to let their capture go.

When the ocean had swallowed the bottom third of the liner, a dark architectonic iceberg, the pilot ships cut their fields entirely.

The resulting tidal surge whooshed shoreward, smashed the baffles, then dissipated in a chaos of foam and spume and a noise like the manifestation of a deva.

From the crowd ascended a lusty cheer. Here was work aplenty for the next several months. Fat profits, to be sure, for the Shipyard's owner--the enigmatic and seldom-glimpsed Horseface known as Bright Tide Rising--but enough scraps, at least, to sustain the meager lives of the breakers themselves.

And, as always, the dream--

Perhaps one of the breakers would even strike it rich, finding something onboard that earned its discoverer a bonus. Hefty by comparison with the regular day rates, these incentive payments represented the smallest fraction of what Bright Tide Rising would resell the prizes for.

But the breakers were in no position to bargain or complain.

* * * *

Klom turned to the woman at his side. Sorrel's buttery face was sheened with salty spray blown back from the collision of tide and baffles, and her auburn hair was damp. A smear of neglected grease grimed one hinge of her jaw; scavenged O-rings served her as bracelets, and a unredeemable chunk of fused gold circuitry spotwelded to a clasp hung from one small earlobe.

Klom lifted a blunt-fingered hand big enough to palm Sorrel's head like a gameball. The back of his hand was tessellated with the latest cruft, a mica-like substance that evolved out of Klom's epidermal cells and flaked off regularly. The cruft had come in on the Snuffler ship they had dismantled some months ago, and as yet the Yard's curanderos had no remedy for the exogenous affliction. With a forefinger large as the nozzle of a watercutter, Klom swiped moisture from the skin underneath Sorrel's green, horizontally slitted left eye and down over her sharp cheekbone.

"You got wet."

Sorrel glared up at Klom, who towered above her much as the floating ship now towered over the crowd, even at the remove of a kilometer. Her throaty voice registered exasperation. "Big news, you dumb two-strand! We all did."

"Oh." Klom raised the hem of his tattered coarse shirt, revealing a midriff packed with muscle and striated with more cruft. He dried his own rugged face. "I didn't even feel the spray. I was busy thinking about my mother."

Sorrel snorted. "Your mother! You haven't even seen the woman in ten years. I'm sure she would have forgotten that you even exist, if it weren't for the money you send."

"Maybe this ship will make us rich, Sorrel. Enough for you and me and my mother too. We could go back to my village and all three of us could live together. You'd like living in Chaulk, I know it. There's a lake there--"

"Oh, my deva! I've heard about Lake Zawinul so often I'm starting to develop gills! And what makes you think I'd go with you to your stinking little home village even if you were rich? I used to be a city girl, you know, before I had the misfortune to end up here. Can Chaulk compete with the Whispering Gardens of Lustron?"

Utter incomprehension transformed Klom's massive features into a mask of hurt confusion. "But Sorrel, we love each other."

"So you keep telling me."

Klom shook himself as if dispelling a cloud of the gnats that arose in the springtime from the stagnant marshes bordering the Yard. Then, forsaking words, he enwrapped Sorrel with one arm and hugged her to him. Her olive-drab shift bunched up on one hip. Klom's smile was holed here and there by missing teeth.

"Ow! Let me go, you big idiot!"

"Hey now, what's this? Assault on a lady? Shall I be forced to give you a good thrashing, you monster?"

Weaving through the throng came a lean man with coppery skin and sandy hair, dressed in what passed for finery among the breakers: clean, albeit ragged white blouse and trews. A wispy mustache draped his upper lip. Taller than Sorrel, he still seemed small in comparison with Klom. Closing with Klom and Sorrel, the newcomer began darting and feinting, tossing mild jabs at the giant.

Klom released Sorrel, and laughed in such a titanic manner that the nearest bystanders winced. "Airey! Where were you? You missed the landing!"

Airey ceased his shadowboxing and shook Klom's hand. "Deva bless you, Klom, that cruft's hideous! Don't you have any gloves?"

Klom examined his hands as if seeing them for the first time. "No gloves fit me."

"Nonsense! I'll get you a pair that fits somehow." Airey turned to Sorrel and briefly embraced her, bestowing a kiss on her forehead. "Any damage to the fleshy goods? No? Very well, but let me know if your reputation needs avenging." Sorrel laughed, her bell-like tones generating more pleasant notice from those nearby than Klom's robust guffaws.

"Airey, you make everyone laugh," Klom said.

"Too bad I can't convince old Right Tight Raisin to pay me for such services. Yard comedian, that's a role I could enjoy! Instead, I have to labor in the drainage pits like some unskilled kilobase. And if beauty were money, Sorrel wouldn't have to slave on the sorting line. Oh well, that's life."

Klom scratched his head through a thick mat of black hair. "Maybe this new ship will bring us all good luck."

"Ah, that's the very reason I sought you out, Klom. I did not miss the landing at all. I was standing as close to the overseers as I could get, while the ship came down. Those lousy terabases and four-strands are damnably suspicious of eavesdroppers, though! It was all I could do to avoid rousing their majestatics."

"You didn't take any chances, did you?" asked Sorrel, looking alarmed.

Airey patted her hand. "Not at all. I have no desire to be drilled through the heart by an angry busybee, believe me! But I was able to overhear the high and mighty ones discussing the origin of this ship. It's a Vixen craft. Most recently made the circuit among Bastiaan, Meuse and Greengage for centuries. But it's much older than that. Parts of it were decommissioned over a thousand years ago. That's where I'd head first if I were you, Klom. Deva knows what goodies you'll find there!"

Klom considered the information, ruminating over it in his slow, stolid fashion. Any idea introduced into Klom's brain met with a laborious reception, but frequently he ground a notion to a finer intellectual dust than the more quick-witted Airey ever could, with surprising results.

"I'll do that, Airey. Anything special I should look for?"

"Oh, I don't know... What about the Book of Forgetting?"

Sorrel laughed, but sourly this time. "Why not hope to find a globe of Mazarine isinglass, or a Ledan swanrobe or a map to the treasures of Mount Sumeru while you're at it?" Here she broke mockingly into a snatch of song: "'The fields of pleasure, the seas of love/Heavenly eyes that peer from above....' And how would anyone even recognize the mythical Book of Forgetting?"

"Oh, if half of what's said about it is true, I suspect the finder would quickly realize what he'd found. The legends are evocative, though not precise. The Book is nothing less than the universal anodyne for all our mortal suffering--"

Suddenly the crowd surged forward en masse, breaking around Klom's immovable bulk, which protected his companions as well.

"What's happening?" asked Klom.

"I assume the marabouts are about to invoke a deva to bless the proceedings," said Airey.

"Lift me up," Sorrel said, and I'll tell you what I can see."

Klom's hands encircled Sorrel's torso just as her O-ring bracelets encircled her wrist. His fingers and thumbs met across her span. In half a second she stood on his shoulders, her sandaled feet finding plenty of purchase on Klom's broad frame, while he braced her behind her thighs. Canopying her hands, Sorrel shielded her eyes against the triple sunlight.

"Yes, I see it all now. Several marabouts are riding a lifter out to the ship. Oh, how beautiful their robes are, billowing in the wind! Oops, one's lost his miter! They've stopped now, not far from the ship. They're making the sacrifice. I think they're using a Redskull ox." A tremulous bellow cut short drifted across the waters. "Now they're feeding power to the prayer wheels. Get ready for the boomtube--"

Airey covered his ears, as did Sorrel. Klom seemed unconcerned, but in any case did not cease supporting Sorrel.

If the might of the tidal surge hitting the baffles had produced a noise akin to the collapse of a small house, then the manifestation of the deva's boomtube generated a soundwave resembling the demolition of one of Voyle's cloudscraper towers. The whole crowd staggered backward, with some losing their footing. Klom barely rocked, while he kept Sorrel anchored.

Now above the floating ship hung the deva: a silvery distortion in the air, in which the minds of lesser beings discerned varying images, depending on both physiology and cultural conditioning.

The majority of sapients in the galaxy--Humans, Foambones, Weepers, Hyenas, Gadabouts, Crickets, Leatherheads, Cygnets, as well as a thousand others and all their miscegenous offspring--encoded their genomes in some variation of DNA: two helical strands of nucelotides on the order of three billion basepairs. But there were higher orders of natural beings as well, those whose longer evolutionary histories had achieved more. Their genomes consisted of four, six, or even eight strands, featuring trillions of basepairs. These terabase beings exhibited emergent properties, sophistica-tions of mind and body unattainable by the two-strands and gigabases.

The devas were sentients who had bootstrapped themselves entirely out of conventional spacetime thanks to their cellular complexity: decas-tranders, yotta- and zettabases. The subtle cosmic fields that supported life simply kicked the devas up to a different quantum level of existence.

Sorrel shivered atop Klom. "I see a Trundler Demon. This is a bad omen."

"Nonsense," said Airey. "I can plainly discern the smiling face of a Hovaness Lamb. Nothing could be a better sign. Klom, what do you see?"

Klom did not speak immediately. "I--I don't know the name for what I'm seeing."

"Can you describe it?"

"It's--it forgives everything."

Airey made a dismissive noise. "Oh, that's helpful, all right."

A bolt of silver energy lanced out from the deva and splattered across the ship: a token of beneficence. A joyous shout went up from the crowd at this blessing. Then the deva silently snapped out of their ontological plane.

"Okay, Klom, you can put me down now."

Klom complied effortlessly. Airey tugged straight his best white tunic, which had been disarrayed by the boomtube's blast, and said, "Well, I think this event calls for a drink. Shall we go to Thrash's for a flagon of toadc-hunder?"

"Who's paying?" asked Sorrel.

Airey clapped Klom on the shoulder. "Why, Klom of course. He's the one who saw the unknowable face of the deva. He's the one who's going to get rich!"

* * * *

The gangboss for Klom's shift was a Quetzal from Muntjac, named Rapaille. The amputation of Rapaille's wings necessitated by a clumsy curandero after a barroom brawl had long ago left the avianoform ill-tem-pered and unforgiving. As meager compensation for his lost wings, Rapa-ille spent every last spare taka and paisa to adorn his priapic cockscomb with a variety of gaudy baubles. Today, setting out for their first foray to the Vixen hulk, Rapaille wore several sparkling garnets and a lozenge of nightmare amber piercing his fleshy ruff.

Aboard one of the wallowing, unroofed ocean transports, still docked, Rapaille marshalled his workers, a motley pack of hard-limbed bruisers representing a dozen heterogenous races. Mounting one of the grimy seats to command more attention, Rapaille commenced a small speech. His beak clacked between syllables, and his narrow orange tongue stabbed the air.

"Listen closely, you scuzz-buckets! This ship has already been partially stripped by its former owners. They've taken most of the furnishings and fixtures. You won't find any old nesting materials to sniff, nor any dainty female undergarments to hug to your bosom."

An anonymous voice called out, "How about wings? Any chance of glomming a pair of those onboard?"

Rapaille scrunched his beady eyes and gurgled wordlessly, before regaining his self-control. "Quiet! The next wisecrack will earn someone a lost shift! Pay attention! It is equally unlikely you'll discover any valuable personal trinkets or artwork, although I don't rule out a few overlooked nanosculptures or parasite jewelry. So you might as well just forget about such easy booty. Any individual performance rewards will come from the neat and speedy accumulation of well-known structures. We're after control ganglia, matter-modems and entertainment nodes, for instance. Nexial splitters pay well too. Several teams have already been dispatched to handle the disentanglers and decoherers. Other groups have been assigned the bridge. But aside from those areas, we have free access to the rest of the ship. Our goal is to finish over the next few months at the same time as the others, so that we can all move on to breaking up the hull itself. Do you all have your downloaded ship schematics?"

Several breakers held aloft their industrial-grade readers, battered boxes good for little more than displaying pre-formatted audiovisual files. No ensouled devices were to be found on Asperna, at least among the lower castes.

"All right, then! Take your seats, and we'll be off!"

Before Rapaille could step off his own bench, Klom pushed forward through his fellows to confront the gangboss. Strapped across Klom's massive torso were various prybars, clamps, spreaders, holdfasts, desiccant packs and other tools. Slung in a holster at one hip was his bulky watercutter.

Even atop his seat, Rapaille found himself staring at Klom's chest rather than his face, until he raised his scale-rimmed eyes. "Yes, our big empty-headed man-ape from Chaulk. What do you want?"

"Are we allowed to go into the decommissioned areas?"

Rapaille let out a tweet of amazement. "The decommissioned areas? What are you interested in? Dust and bones? Faded signage and outmoded tech? Slavering senescent slop? That's all you'll find there!"

Klom blinked once, then said, "Are we allowed to go into the decommissioned areas?"

The Quetzal screeched in frustration, his wing stubs twitching beneath his embroidered shirt. "Go anyplace you want, you unreasoning curdled egg! But you'll never earn more than base pay if you persist in this foolish strategy. And my own bonuses will fall accordingly!"

Klom said, "I will be going into the decommissioned areas then." He sat down, occupying two seats.

Muttering, Rapaille signalled liftoff to the transport's pilot--a diminutive Melungeon with one tendril wrapped around a joystick and five others free for the separate controls. The transport lost mass until it floated half a meter above the waves. Surging forward through a channel opened in the baffles, the craft headed toward the Vixen ship. The Great Sun and the Lesser Sun raised the temperature of the air to a comfortable, shirtsleeve level. By the time the Least Sun arose, rendering the muggy atmosphere tropical, the breakers would be taking their lunch deep within the hulk.

The crossing of the kilometer of open water by Klom's craft and its mates resembled the engulfment of a school of minnows by a leviathan. The minor-city-sized disabled starcruiser--with the waterline halfway up its height, and its lower portions resting on the seabed--thrust out artificial pennisulas and lesser promontories. Once into its shadow and embrace, the transports assumed the insignificance of ticks on the hide of a Dominikono widestrider. Additionally, the ancient interstellar vessel seemed to be reradiating all the immeasurable chill it had accumulated over its millennia of high vacuum service.

It would take the gangs nearly a year to finish stripping the interior of the craft, and another six months to disassemble its hull. Of course, the whole process could have been accomplished in a fraction of that time by employing sufficient swarms of self-replicating majestatics. But such technologies--along with ensouled machines--were forbidden to anyone not at least a fourstrand. And the fourstrands and other galactic elites were both relatively small in number and disdainful of performing any such "labor," even distanced by layers of autonomic supervisors. With the fecund and subservient twostrands so handy, it only made sense to keep them profitably occupied.

The Yards at Asperna not only saw ships come in, but also go out, as salable constituent pieces. Brokers arrived and departed continuously, both from offplanet and from other parts of Asperna, leaving with cargoes for a hundred thousand destinations. Workers in the warehouse and sales end of the Yards felt their positions to be superior to the gritty, effortful tasks of the breakers and sorters, and a rough caste system existed, further fragmented into various levels according to the perceived crudity of assignments.

Klom's boat arrived at a sloping paw of the inorganic leviathan. Far, far above them, a different portion of the starliner formed a concave roof. A shoulder of the starliner constituted a distant wall running roughly parallel to the arm. A chaotic illumination came into this partial gallery as sunlight refracted from the bouncing sea.

The Melungeon shut down the lifting units, then secured the transport by a cable to a handy U-bar on the Vixen vessel. The breakers utilized the fractally porous surface of the starcraft's skin as handholds and toeholds to climb up several gently sloping meters of wall, their tools racketing against each other. Once aboard this small leg of the starliner--broad enough to host a ballgame--they waited for Rapaille's commands.

"Follow me, you wittolds! The nearest port is just a few minutes' walk in this direction."

The paw sloped upward, the roof sloped down, and the shoulder angled in, rendering the passage more tunnel-like the further the breakers progressed.

Klom marched at the head of the line, looking about with a kind of patient curiosity. He had taken apart a dozen ships so far in his career at the Yards, and he fully expected to take apart a few dozen more, before he got too old for the work. Each ship possessed its own personality. Klom assumed that by the time he was done breaking down this vessel, he would know good-sized portions of it as intimately as he knew his mother's house in Chaulk. Paradoxically, the ship would no longer then exist to be known. Such conundrums did not bother Klom.

Faded Vixen script, each character tall as a man, ran across this segment of the deck. Klom turned to the breaker next to him, a blue-haired, ice-skinned fellow named Nyerephar, a mixed-breed Human and Pinemarten from Frostholm. Nyerephar had a reputation as an intellectual, given his predilection for offshift downloading into his reader of novels of interspecies romance, many of which originated with the Vixens.

"What do these words say, 'Phar?"

Nyerephar smoothed his long jutting whiskers before replying. "It could be the ship's name. Yes, that's it, I'm sure. This is the ship's name."

"And what is the ship's name, 'Phar?"

"'Caution Discharge Zone'"

"Thank you for telling me this."

Soon the breakers arrived at the port. Standing outside in front of the entrance was an enormous matter-modem: a cube with one mirrored face.

Delivered earlier from the Yards, the teleportation device stood ready to receive any unliving object carved from the ship. Its mates, tunable at will, stood ashore, near the sorting lines. Very useful devices, integral to the functioning of most economies of the Indrajal, the matter-modems were subject to two major inconvenient limitations. They only operated over planetary distances, and they were death to anything living that attempted transit.

Now the matter-modem, sensing their presence, activated itself. Fed from the other end, a fleet of lifting sledges came thru the mirror face. Each breaker stepped up to take a floating sledge for carrying booty.

Rapaille triggered a Vixen wall control marked by a new slash of red spray paint, and the port hobermanned open. The black interior of the powerless ship beckoned like the afterlife. The breakers lowered their miners' lamps onto their foreheads and switched them on, flooding the scene with actinic light.

"Rendezvous back here at twenty-nine hundred hours. And remember! This was a luxury vessel intended to pamper its patrons, not a Scryer dreadnought bristling with weaponry. Nonetheless, you can die just as swiftly from a falling girder as you can from a antipersonnel wasp!"

One by one, with Klom leading the way, the breakers stepped inside.

* * * *

Klom grunted hoarsely as he completed his climb. Sweat riveted his skin, and a musty odor compounded of stale lubricants and malnourished organic units pumping out ketones made every breath an exercise in disgust.

The ship schematics on his reader had informed him that the ladder he had just topped ran for a kilometer and a half in a narrow shaft slicing through innumerable decks. The swiftest way to the closest decommissioned area, the ladder had seemed a gift when Klom stood at its base. But now, as Klom labored to catch his breath on a platform above 1500 meters of nothingness, the ladder appeared more like a poisoned fruit. Even Klom's work-hardened muscles quivered from the grueling ascent. Had his lifter fit into the narrow shaft, the ascent would have been trivial. Now, though, Klom was fatigued before he even began whatever labors awaited him.

Klom broke out his water bottle and a beancake. The water, sterilized by passage through a matter-modem, still retained the distasteful taints of decay and the metallic flavors of the marshes from which it was drawn. But this was the only drinking water available to the bustee-dwellers of Klom's caste. After so many years in the Yard, Klom was innured to the taste. But he still recalled the pure waters of Lake Zawinul with each sip.

After consuming the last crumb of beancake, Klom stood and faced away from the shaft. The door at the end of the platform presented itself as his next challenge. Klom looked for some control similar to the one Rapaille had used outside, but no such mechanism showed. It did not take Klom long to decide to cut his way through.

The watercutter hanging from Klom's belt was a simple pistol-shaped device with a second grip up front for two-handed use. Klom had wrapped tape around the butts for firmer purchase. He fitted a pair of scratched plastic goggles over his eyes, braced himself against a convenient strut, then triggered the cutter.

Out of its nozzle leaped a needle-thin jet of water possessing the destructive power of any stream of collimated subatomic particles, without any inconvenient radiation.

The closed end of the watercutter's barrel was a tiny matter-modem synced to another resting in a deep-sea trench where the water was at several dozen atmospheres of pressure. Only breakers of Klom's raw strength could handle this device, whose light weight and inexhaustibility were unmatched by any other cutting tool.

Klom inscribed a crude circle in the wall just big enough for him to crawl through. A salty mist enveloped him, making his footing and handholds tenuous. Practically at his elbow, the echoing drop into space awaited his first slip. But Klom coolly persisted. Finally finished, he kicked the circle of metal inward. Gaily colored fluids from severed conduits dribbled into the opening, where once, when the ship was under power, they might well have gushed. Klom squirmed through this mild dribble without concern.

On the far side, he found himself in a giant auditorium or ballroom or refectory, whose vast confines his headlamp barely illuminated. This room had been in active use right up until the end, but the decommissioned area lurked just beyond its remote wall.

Klom crossed the wide floorspace, the beam of his lamp picking out various columns and stubs of fixtures and some discarded artifacts which to a less ambitious breaker would have represented adequate salvage. But with Airey's tactics fixed firmly in his mind, Klom zeroed in on the mysteries of the long-sealed chambers.

A little searching revealed a door concealed behind a sagging arras that depicted the hunting of some spiny beast by a party of Vixens, the bushy tails of the hunters plaited with colorful streamers. The door--sealed with a blobby gasket of silicone--boasted a still-active glo-sign, but not in Vixen script. Half the letters in the independently powered message were dead with age, while the rest exhibited only a marginal brightness. But Klom could not have read the warning or advice even if active, so ancient and foreign was the script. So without any hesitation, he simply cut his way past it.

The space on the far side of the door, a corridor, was proportioned for creatures somewhat smaller than Klom. The big man had to hunch as he advanced. Dust lay thickly underfoot, and the air smelled of the slow disintegration of unnatural materials. The walls of the corridor were etched with shallow glyphs, as if the beings who had once traversed it had relied on tactile clues more than visual ones.

Some years ago, Klom had helped disassemble a Pingpank ship that featured similar carven icons, although much cruder. But the Pingpank had been extinct for five hundred years, and at the time of their disappearance had represented the degenerate offspring of a much more sophisticated race, the Marchwardens. If this were Marchwarden text, then the decommissioned segment of the ship had last been occupied over a millennium ago. Without any exo-inputs, even generations of invisible repair majestatics would be reaching the end of their preservation efforts.

Open arched doorways began to appear. Klom cautiously poked his head through each one. Most of the chambers were of moderate size, and easily scannable for booty. In one such, Klom found several crystal eggs harboring strange animated scenes flickering wispily in their centers. These he placed in a carrying pouch. But the majority of the chambers were utterly bare. Klom began to suspect that Rapaille's harsh words held more accuracy than Airey's optimistic encouragements. Nonetheless, he continued his search.

The corridor dead-ended at another door. Klom saltily sliced through it, the runoff from his cutter turning the dust at his feet to a thin river of mud.

Pushing the cut circle of metal clangingly inward, Klom was met by a gust of pungent atmosphere. He stepped warily inside.

Instantly Klom knew he had found a vivarium.

From the walls of the tall, extensive chamber hung a variety of suspensor-sacs, all of them, sadly enough, in various stages of decomposition. Klom walked over to the nearest such: the withered reticulated vesicle ripped apart easily under his big hands with a noise like shredding a few dozen thicknesses of paper, and a shower of skeletal fragments fell out, clattering noisily on the floor.

Klom kicked the bones in frustration. So far he had wasted nearly half a shift and discovered nothing to justify his efforts. At this rate, retirement with Sorrel to Chaulk seemed destined never to be more than a dream.

Wearily, Klom sat down and took out another beancake.

The majestatic that appeared hovering over his beancake resembled a thumb-sized golden bee. Klom jerked back, dropping the food. The majestatic levitated the cake and flew ponderously off with it.

Klom jumped up and followed.

Clinging to the far side of a massive pillar, a live suspensor-sac served as the focus of a thick swarm of shining majestatics. The agravitic attendants ranged in size from dust particles to hummingbirds. They wreathed the sac in a life-supporting cloud. Already Klom's lunch was being disassembled into its constituent nutrients to benefit the sac.

Why this one vesicle had survived, Klom did not know. Perhaps it had sent taps into the pillar supporting it, finding its necessary sustenance elsewhere, in the active portions of the *Caution Discharge Zone*. But whatever anomaly was responsible for extending its life beyond its mates, the sac represented a potential treasure.

Inside, a living mature being awaited rebirthing. For some unknown period, the metabolism of the concealed creature had been stepped down to nearly flatline levels, with interior majestatics tending to various cellular repairs as necessary. Given adequate resources, the upper time limit on sac containment had never been established.

Klom advanced on the sac, then stopped. He could not simply rip it open, he realized. How was he to get the vesicle to awaken and safely discharge its patient?

Filled with a fierce wanting, Klom hung his head and cudgled his thoughts for a solution.

Suddenly his vision was obscured by a shifting haze. A portion of the turbulent majestatic swarm had englobed his head.

"Please," said Klom aloud, "deliver your burden to me. This ship is dead. We are going to chop it up. Your charge will die."

Spinning in arcane patterns, the majestatics seemed to consider Klom's request, before rejoining the parent cloud.

Instantly, the vesicle began to undergo changes. Veins throbbed athwart its surface, swaths of livid color flowed across it like storms across a gas-giant planet, and a musky, urinous odor arose off it.

A split developed along the bottom ridge of the vesicle, widening quickly. The next instant clotted crimson and purple fluids gushed out, splashing Klom's workboots, followed by the plopping thud of a body hitting the floor.

Klom hastened over and squatted down beside the form, roughly one third as big as Klom himself. It resembled no sapient race he had ever seen.

The creature's head was an oblate boulder pebbled over with muffin-sized mounds. It had two eyes, now lidded, a blunt snout with flaring nostrils, and jowl-concealed jaws. A kind of skin-covered cartiliginous tuning-fork arrangment projected from its forehead. No ears were visible. Its keg-like body boasted four chunky legs, the paws showing blunt claws. Its hide was brown velvety skin wrinkled like a cortex. A pair of vestigal hands stuck out at its shoulders. No tail interrupted its hindquarters.

The being was struggling to draw a breath. Klom gripped it by the scruff of its neck with one hand, lifting its weighty head, then levered open its unresisting jaws with the other. He swabbed out a jellylike mass from its throat, then put his face to the creature's wet face and began exchanging breaths with it.

After a minute, the beast could breathe on its own. It opened its eyes, limpid gray pools. Klom fell into the creature's gaze, losing all sense of himself for a moment. When he had recovered, he asked, "Can you speak? Are you all right?" The creature said nothing, but tried to stand. Its legs gave way beneath it, however, and it collapsed back into its afterbirth.

Klom picked up the creature and set out to retrace his steps.

At the platform where the ladder began, he lashed the beast to his chest with a net of bungee cords, so that its head rested below Klom's chin.

Klom commenced the descent.

Halfway down, his muscles spasming, Klom thought he might not be able to complete the climb.

A giant tongue stropped his face.

Klom found the strength to go on.

* * * *

The interior of Thrash's shabeen was illuminated only by a few worthless lighting fixtures scavenged from a variety of ships, and powered off a rack of biomass fuelcells. The patchy, sputtering radiance formed many shadowy nooks where drinkers could sit and conspire, consumating the mingy deals that constituted the primitive economy of the bustee-dwellers in the Yard. The furniture of the dirt-floored barroom was similarly ill-sorted, a collection of spraddle-legged chairs and tables, and the occasional stained, bedraggled lounge for those customers whose anatomy precluded chairs. At the bar, the best-lit area, a row of stools with fragments of flooring still attached rested hard by the stacked packing crates separating Thrash from his customers.

Thrash's heritage included Slow Loris and Peluche genes, rendering him a shaggy ursinoid with huge eyes. All the tap-handles and liquor jugs had been customized for his broad paws. The mugs all sported wide grips as well.

Sorrel needed both hands to lift her glass. She raised her drink and sipped, then made a face before plonking the mug back on the rickety table.

"What sour piss this is! How I wish I had a glass of Tancredi nectar."

Klom drained his own dark brew with evident satisfaction, then wiped his mouth with the back of his crufty hand.

Sorrel winced. "Deva, Klom! I have to kiss those lips once in a while!"

Looking down at his flaking hand, Klom said, "But Sorrel, we know this cruft's not contagious. The curandero said so. Once it finds a host, it stops looking for others. It's worked its way right into me, though, adopting lots of my genes into itself. That's what makes it so hard to get rid of."

"That's no matter. I still prefer not to have those patches rubbed all over me, or to come in contact with certain parts of you. You're just lucky the cruft stopped at your waist."

Klom smiled dreamily. "Tonight we'll doublecheck its progress."

Sorrel stuck out her vividly pink tongue. "If you can spare a minute for me, now that you've got a new friend. Or if there's a centimeter of space left in your crib."

Klom looked down at his feet.

The creature from the *Caution Discharge Zone* lay peacefully sleeping, one forepaw folded over the other beneath its chin. Drool snailed down the side of its face to darken the dirt. Its unlabored breathing gently rasped the stale air within the shabeen.

Reaching down, Klom fondly skritched the beast's scalp around its fleshy forklike appendage. The rhythm of the creature's breathing deepened in a contented fashion. "Use his name, Sorrel, please. You know I gave him a name. Call him Tugger, please."

"Tugger! Ridiculous! Why 'Tugger' anyhow?"

"I found out he likes to play that way. You should see him pull on a rope. He can put up a real tussle."

"And why 'he'?" I certainly didn't see any ballocks on him when you trotted him around for everyone to admire."

"I don't know. I just feel Tugger's male."

Sorrel waved her arms about in frustration. "I give up! You get first crack at a potential treasure trove, and all you come away with is an ugly pet! This is so typical for you, Klom. You're just too dumb to grab the main chance, even when it's right under your nose."

Klom looked hurt. "There was nothing valuable in that decommissioned area, Sorrel. At least as far as I looked. But I stopped when I found Tugger. I had to get him out of there. The atmosphere was bad for him. And he perked up right away once we were outside in the fresh air. But I shared the money from the crystal eggs with you, didn't I? Ten taka and sixty paisa. That's something, isn't it?"

"Birdscratch! Someone with your experience should be hauling in much more. Tomorrow, I expect you to pick another decommissioned area and make a big strike!"

"But I already found something very valuable, Sorrel. Tugger! Just look at him. What a character! He makes me smile, just like Airey does. Who could ask for anything more? Anyway, I figure if I concentrate on ripping out the old Vixen equipment like everyone else, I can make a steadier pay. No, I'm not going back to any of the decommissioned areas. The odds are too slim."

"What's this, what's this? Abandoning my advice! I'm hurt! Truly I am!"

Airey dropped down onto an empty ladderback chair. He wore a shirt that proclaimed with glowing threads support for his favorite ballteam, the Alavoine Tumblers. His bronze face was slicked with sweat, rendering his mustache a limp strip of furze. Even hours after Final Sunset, the air retained a surplus of ennervating heat.

Signalling to Thrash for a drink, Airey resumed his chiding. "So, you're letting one little setback discourage you, Klom? I had thought much higher of you."

"Setback? What setback?"

Airey dug a toe of his sandal into Tugger's side, provoking a mild grunt and a shifting away by the beast. "This worthless thing! Now you have another mouth to feed. Have you considered that?"

Klom remained positive. "I can't get Tugger to eat anything yet. All he does is drink a little water. And he seems to do that just to please me. He just doesn't seem to be hungry. And even when he does decide to eat, I'm sure I can get plenty of scraps from Kirsh, over in Kitchen Number Twelve."

Thrash lumbered over, carrying Airey's mug and a plate of fried salicornia and quorn nuggets. "Snack's on the house," growled Thrash. "Your pet's brought in extra trade tonight."

"Thank you, Thrash."

Klom picked up a nugget and held it under Tugger's nose. Sniffing without opening his eyes, Tugger made a polite refusal by lifting his paws to cover his face.

"See? He's not greedy or any trouble at all. Tugger only brings happiness and good luck."

Exasperated, Airey blew air rudely past his fluttering lips. "I give up. Sorrel, can you convince him to abandon this worthless foundling and get back to some fruitful exploration of --what did you say the ship's name was?"

"Caution Discharge Zone."

"Hmm, a queer appellation. Well, Sorrel, go ahead. Lay your best arguments on our mighty yet stubborn friend."

Sorrel popped a nugget into her mouth. "Forget it, Airey. I'm sick of cajoling this idiot. It's like trying to teach a Tonshuan warthog to sing."

Airey pinched the corner of his mouth and rubbed a finger across his mustache. "Are we entirely certain this beast isn't valuable? After all, someone went to all the trouble of placing him in a suspensor-sac, however long ago. Klom, exactly what did our mighty overlord say when he inspected, ah, Tugger? And are you sure it was really him?"

Klom recalled.

At the foot of the ladder, Klom had exited the shaft and retrieved his sledge. He loaded Tugger onto it. The creature was alert, but still obviously weak and unsure from its long estivation. Klom had rested for a few minutes, refreshing himself with more water and cake, before setting out for the main port.

Out in the fresh air, Tugger visibly quickened. Rapaille, busy processing materials through the matter-modem, did not at first notice Klom and his living find. When he became aware of the rare discovery, Rapaille squawked with excitement and summoned one of his supervisors over his communicator. Harshly, the Quetzal pushed Klom aside and bent over Tugger.

"Please forgive the rude treatment you've received at the hands of this worthless drone, kindly sapient. You will soon be in touch with others of your kind, who will doubtlessly be overjoyed to know of your continued existence, and ready with a handsome reward."

In reply, Tugger laved Rapaille's face with his broad tongue.

"I don't think this one places so high on the sapient scale, Rapaille."

"Nonsense! Plainly an advanced being." Yet for all his blustering certainty, Rapaille regarded Tugger with a veneer of suspicion.

A personal lifter arrowed toward them in response to Rapaille's summoning. When it reached them, both Rapaille and Klom stared in disbelief.

The vessel held not a mere supervisor, but Bright Tide Rising himself. A sixstrand, the lanky Horseface was attended by a shimmering corona of majestatics that nearly concealed his head, yet remained recognizable by his strangely articulated build and various family sigils worn as a gorget. Rapaille dropped to his knees and bowed. Klom remained standing.

Without consulting either Rapaille or Klom, Bright Tide Rising directed a portion of his swarm to engulf Tugger. After a swift examination, the units reunited with their peers. Pausing an unnaturally long time, the owner of the Asperna Yard finally delivered his verdict in a rumbling voice.

"Minimal sentience. Germline not on record. No talents, no adjuncts, no discernible worth. Dispose of the creature as you see fit."

As soon as Bright Tide Rising left, Rapaille berated Klom for twenty minutes for wasting the time of both himself and their ultimate patron. Klom absorbed the tirade placidly, then announced he was ending his shift early and returning to shore on the next transport. This news elicited further incoherent screeches from the Quetzal.

Now Klom repeated the Yard owner's assessment to Airey. The words seemed to deflate the slight, capricious fellow, but he soon regained his usual jovial air.

"Oh, well, there are months of salvage ahead. You'll hit the mother lode yet, Klom, I'm sure."

"Thank you, Airey."

The trio passed a few more hours drinking and chatting, eating and joking. Numerous individuals came over to examine Tugger. Klom felt proud.

At last, in the face of another workday, their beds beckoned.

Once outside, Sorrel stumbled in the near-lightless mucky path leading away from Thrash's, but Klom caught her before she could land in a patch of redolent luminous vomit, seething with intestinal symbionts. Tugger trotted along fastidiously behind. The dank air weighed like a blanket.

"Sorrel?"

"Uh, what--?"

"When did you ever taste Tancredi nectar?"

"One night, Jess--Jess Badura--he and me--you were sleeping--"

"Oh."

Sorrel stopped and hung with both hands from Klom's bicep. "You're not mad, are you, Klom?"

"No. I just like to learn things."

* * * *

Three months into its disassembly, the *Caution Discharge Zone* appeared, from the outside, relatively unscathed. Here and there across its convoluted carcass, new holes gaped, broken open to facilitate the removal of the ship's guts when the nearest port was inconveniently distant and a matter-modem could not be manuevered inside. Cormorants and kingfishers wheeled above the Vixen starliner, colonies roosting in selected niches and staining the slopes with their guano. A line of goose-barnacles had formed just below the high-water mark; at low tide, the exposed barnacles craned their mouthparts around on long necks, questing for the gnats that swarmed above the waters, the gnats in their turn attracted by the floating mats of seaweed that now trailed outward from the hull.

At a definite point in the near future, the *Caution Discharge Zone* would be reduced to an empty shell no taller than the line of barnacles, all its superstructure dismantled. At this point breakers skilled in underwater work would cut up the remaining shell and float the pieces away. The ship that had sailed the starwinds for an eon would be no more.

But right now, much still remained to be taken from inside.

Klom and Tugger arrived with the rest of their crew and marshalled outside the assigned entryway. Rapaille paid no notice to the oddball pair: a marked contrast to the first day Klom had shown up for work with his pet.

Fixing his hard eyes on Tugger, Rapaille had demanded, "Klom! What's the meaning of this pointless complication of your duties? Why is this worthless mass of protoplasm not already ground up into raw chuck for Kitchen Twelve?"

Klom did not exhibit any anger. But something in his voice made Rapaille flinch. "Tugger is my friend. No one hurts my friends."

Rapaille retreated. "All right then. But why not leave the beast in your crib?"

"There are too many bad people in the bustee. Someone might break into my crib and try to steal Tugger. Maybe even harm him. He doesn't know when people plan to do him harm. And he's too gentle to defend himself. I need to keep him by me all the time."

Realizing when he was beaten, Rapaille angrily said, "Let the consequences of your soft-hearted stupidity be on your own head then! Tending to this monster will slow you down, and you'll soon be lying in a ditch with the Dungbeetles, begging paisa off the smart and sensible breakers who go about their work with vim and efficiency."

Klom made no reply, but simply marched inside the ship. Before they separated, Nyerephar and several other fellows congratulated him for standing up to Rapaille. Tugger came in for his share of the good will as well, accepting much petting and rib-thumping and shaking of his vestigal shoulder-hands.

Today, Klom and Tugger received no extra attention from anyone, so standard a part of the scene were they.

Half an hour's trudge through ravaged corridors and chambers, naves and apses, full of dangling cables and wires and sliced-open sheathing brought Klom and Tugger alone to the room where the breaker had left off work yesterday. The room was empty of furnishings, and only a scatter of devalued triptix littered the floor. The small personal data-palettes which had once carried routing instructions, dietary requirements, letters of introduction, shipboard credit-debit records, medical histories and other information needed by interstellar travelers now constituted nothing more significant than a drift of dead leaves.

One entire wall of this room presented a matrix of small doors inset with clear panels. Each door opened onto a long slim padded capsule plainly intended as a sleeping tube for members of some vaguely serpentine species. Each tube had to be disengaged from the matrix and stacked on the sledge. In one corner of the room squatted a large matter-modem. This deactivated cube, part of the intraship goods-transport system, presented no mirror face.

Klom fell to work, his head lamp casting all the illumination he needed. Tugger lay down peacefully on the hard floor and fell asleep. The puddle of drool spreading from his jowls caught glimmers from Klom's headlamp now and again.

In the three months Klom had owned his new pet, the man and beast had become inseparable, even off-duty. Sorrel had come grudgingly to accept the new arrangement, while Airey simply disdained to pay any more attention to Tugger than he would have given to a familiar rug or table.

Several hours of hard work with spanner and snipper and prybar resulted in a sledge piled high with tubes. Klom must run these back to an active matter-modem before he could continue. But first he paused to refresh himself.

He took out his water bottle. Stretching sore muscles, he braced himself with his left hand against the dead matter-modem. He tilted back his head to glug a liter of warm musty liquid.

Ceiling lights flared improbably to life. So did the matter-modem.

Off-balance, Klom plunged in the mirror face up to his shoulder.

The lights snapped off. As did the matter-modem.

Klom howled. His arm had been sheared off clean at the shoulder. Vast quantities of blood sprayed the room. He fumbled frantically for a bungee, thinking to tie off his arteries. But there remained no flesh stub to bind.

Klom crashed to the floor like an uprooted Salembier sequoia. Consciousness slipped away from him like a school of fish from a disintegrating net.

"Tugger--"

* * * *

Rapaille awaited the first of his crew to emerge with that day's salvage. He would key descriptions of the items into his reader, contributing to the vast inventory of parts being taken from the ship, then dispatch the parts through the matter-modem to the relevant disassembly stations and sorting lines. Meanwhile, he had nothing to do but wait and ponder the many injustices of his life. Standing in a shadow to escape the growing heat, he idly scanned the skies. A small Mlotmroz ship undoubtedly bearing buyers soared across his field of vision. Very good, the more customers the better for the Yard's business. All fortune to Bright Tide Rising! Rapaille's phantom wings itched, and he rubbed his wing stubs against the bulkhead. But the itching persisted. Life was unfair.

Someone burst crazily out of the port, jolting Rapaille out of his philosophical contemplation. That dumb man-ape, Klom, followed by his galloping worthless pet--

Klom bellowed. "Rapaille! Is there a crew mucking about with the ship's power generators?"

Rapaille boosted his haughty demeanor. "This is no business of yours! Get back to your wor--*urk*!"

Klom had gripped Rapaille's shirt with both his hands and lifted the avianoform off his feet, incidentally choking the Quetzal with a knot of fabric at his throat. Klom thrust his face within centimeters of Rapaille and spoke with calm precision.

"You will call the crew working with the generators. You will tell them to be extra careful not to turn them on by accident. Or someone might get hurt. Do you understand?"

Rapaille understood that the person most likely to immediately get hurt was himself. So made a squawk he hoped Klom would interpret positively.

The huge breaker set his supervisor down and released him. After massaging his bruised throat, Rapaille placed the call Klom had ordered. Once Klom was satisfied, he turned away and climbed into a ship-to-shore barge, Tugger heeling behind his master.

"Take me back in," Klom told the bored Melungeon pilot.

As the barge pulled away, Rapaille sought to reassert his dignity and status. "Don't bother coming back for three weeks! Not till after Festival! You're on probation. Do you hear me, you addled eggsucker?"

But Klom never even looked back.

He seemed too busy stroking his left arm.

* * * *

The long hot shed (its sides open for whatever chance breeze might arise) that housed Sorting Line Number Thirty-eight featured the following arrangement: ten parallel conveyor belts ran from one end of the shed to the other. The belts contributed a certain varying level of noise to the shed, depending on how dutifully a small army of oilers--mostly children--tended to them. At the head of each belt stood a matter-modem delivering the smaller pieces harvested from the ship under deconstruction. (Larger pieces not saved and sold as integral units went to disassembly stations first, then to the Sorting Lines.) Along both sides of each conveyor sat the sorters, staggered on three-legged stools at intervals of a meter or so. By the elbow of each sorter, mirror-face upward, was a smaller matter-modem with a keypad that allowed a choice of destinations.

Each sorter had his or her or its special range of components to watch for. When spotted, the component would be snatched off the belt and dropped into the matter-modem. Simultaneous with the grab, the sorter would key in the relevant warehouse station to receive the transmission.

At the end of the belt awaited a final matter-modem, to catch all the unclaimed pieces for further examination and categorization.

The sorters were entitled to only as many lavatory breaks as minimally consistent with the most basic needs of their species. Lunches ran for half an hour, in shifts. Payment was based on speed and accuracy of performance, with debits taken for any missed pieces. So long as standards were maintained, conversation was permitted.

Sorrel was speaking to Aurinka, a Triffid who sat diagonally across from her. They were discussing jewelry. The Triffid waved several stalks decorated with hammered brass bracelets for Sorrel's admiration, while handling her duties competently with two other limbs.

Suddenly both Aurinka and Sorrel took notice of a distant commotion near one of the shed's entrances. They strained to ascertain what was going on without slackening production. The commotion seemed to be moving through the shed, getting closer to them. At last Sorrel saw the source of the upset.

Klom and Tugger bulled their way toward her, trailing protesting supervisors. When Klom spotted Sorrel, he bellowed out her name. Then he was upon her.

Grabbing Sorrel off her stool, Klom strongarmed her out of the shed, heedless of either her protests or her struggles to escape.

Once outside, Klom released her. They stood in the lee afforded by a mud-brick pissoir, while all around them surged unemployable or underage or offshift bustee-dwellers, a motley mass of scaled and chitinous, furred and slick-skinned beings, oblate or attenuated, faces like intricate masks or nearly featureless.

Sorrel faced Klom, full of fury. "You moron! What's the matter with you? I'm going to lose half a day's wages now!"

Klom's singleminded urgency seemed to evaporate. He faced Sorrel with a look that mixed contrition and confusion.

"Sorrel, I need your help. I died today."

This last sentence, delivered matter-of-factly yet with a detectable tremor, catalyzed Sorrel's reaction from anger to a curious concern.

"What are you talking about? You're standing there as healthy as a Redskull ox."

"No, you don't understand. Here's what happened--" Klom recounted losing his arm in the matter-modem. "The last thing I remember is calling out for Tugger." The beast looked up at the sound of his name, offering a lopsided, slavering grin. "Then I blacked out. Not much time seemed to pass. Or maybe a lot. Anyway, I woke up whole."

Leerily, Sorrel regarded Tugger. "You're saying this creature was somehow responsible for regenerating your arm?"

"No, not exactly. You see, there was no blood anywhere anymore. And my sledge was empty. I had filled it with tubes, but now it was empty. Then I looked at my reader, and it said the wrong time. I was in the past."

"That makes no sense at all."

Klom whirled savagely around and punched the wall of the lavatory, sending up a puff of mortar and pulverized soil. "I know, I know! But there's something else besides. Look at my skin!"

Sorrel examined Klom's outstretched hand, bloody-knuckled from impact with the wall. "Your cruft is gone!"

"All gone! That's right! But how?"

Sorrel shook her head in bewilderment. "I--I can't explain. Maybe Airey--"

"Airey! Of course! Let's go!"

Without waiting for her agreement, Klom hustled Sorrel away.

Tugger trotted blithely along behind them.

* * * *

The fluids giving life to a typical starliner ranged from viscous hydrocarbon derivatives to thin plant-based extracts to exotically tinged protein-hormone-enzyme sera. These various liquids--some of which could be captured and sold, others of which went straight to crude disposal in the polluted swamps--invigorated a variety of mechanisms, all of which had to be drained before storage or disassembly. This task fell to the crews of the drainage pits.

Airey was right down in one of the pits, ankle deep in rainbow-sheened stenchy sludge. Unlike his downtime finery, his work uniform consisted of scarred boots and a patched brown coverall, its waterproofing peeling away in places. Employing a big spanner, he was struggling with the balky petcock of a suspended engine and cursing furiously.

"Motherless shit! Is this my reward for daring to aspire to elegance? May all the ancestors of all the mechanics who ever worked on this abomination freeze in the lowest levels of the Dimmig hells! Die, you bastard screwcap, die!"

Ranked at the edge of the pit, Airey's co-workers were enjoying his eloquent frustration. A Foraminifer was laughing so hard it kept dislocating its multiple jaws, resetting them each time with a grisly clacking of bone.

An instant cessation of the laughter caused Airey to crane his neck upward. Before he could react to the unexpected sight of Klom, he was lifted bodily from the pit.

"Come with me, Airey," Klom demanded. Airey caught Sorrel's eyes and read there the wisdom of complying. As the trio moved off for privacy, the drainman grabbed a rag to wipe his hands. Finished, he tucked it into a back pocket.

In the shadow of a belching, stinking cracking tower, Klom rehearsed his morning to Airey. Airey listened thoughtfully, his glance bouncing back and forth between Klom and Tugger. When Klom finished his account, Airey remained silent for half a minute before speaking.

"I see only one answer. Your pet can manipulate time in some fashion."

Klom's brow creased. "What? How could that be? I've never heard of such a thing being possible."

"Regardless of what we know, it's the only solution. Tugger responded to your distress by shuttling you back to the past. That explains your empty sledge and the timecheck on your reader."

"But how would that have fixed my arm? A dying time-traveler is still a dying man."

Airey stroked his negligible mustache. "This is true. The answer must be more complex then. I'll need to cogitate on this a while. But meanwhile, I think you should give Tugger anything he wants as a reward. Without him, apparently, you wouldn't be here right now. He's your guardian raksha."

"I'd gladly give him the finest meal or the thickest bed in the world. But all he seems to want is to be by my side!"

Airey hunkered down beside Tugger. He took the rag from his pocket and wiped away a line of saliva from Tugger's jowls. "There, there, good boy. What you want depends on what you are. And I guess we'll never know that. Unless--"

"Unless what?" asked Klom.

Airey straightened up, holding the rag bearing Tugger's drool before all their eyes as if it were a holy relic. "Let's send this sample to the laboratories at Radius Seven and get a genomic readout for Tugger. It will cost Klom a pretty paisa, but perhaps we'll learn more about our friend's constitution."

Sorrel said, "What could a simple lab analysis reveal that Bright Tide Rising and his majestatics overlooked?"

"I suspect that Tugger deliberately concealed his true nature from the Raisin, so that he would not be separated from Klom. Can we put anything beyond a being who can do what Tugger appears to have done for Klom?"

All three friends studied the innocuous animal with new respect. Tugger simply grinned dopily upward, then scratched behind his jaw with a rear paw, making a noise like a broom on sand.

Klom said, "Please see to it, Airey. We need to know what Tugger is so we can make sure he gets the proper treatment for his kind."

"Consider it done! And now, although *you* are suspended till after the Festival, Klom, Sorrel and I need to get back to work. Which brings me round to asking you for a small favor--"

Disdaining the spanner, Klom opened the stuck petcock with the force of his fingers alone. A torrent of purple, iron-smelling hematic coolant gouted out, splashing Klom to his knees, but he only laughed.

* * * *

Klom's crib was luxurious by bustee standards. Scabbed together out of rusty sheet metal, driftwood posts and rafters, broad swaths of cured hides from Asperna's reptilian partchrumpfs and the odd bits of scratched plastic and warped pressboard, the shack leaked only minimally during the monsoon season and retained the heat from a seacoal fire well during the mild winters. Its interior held a hammock layered with rags and a teetering set of shelves hosting Klom's few possessions, including a photo of an old woman standing in front of a hut on a lakeshore. (The unframed photo was surrounded by deva medals distributed by the marabouts during various holy days, as if it were a small shrine.) A gamecube with a fuzzed-out display and half its functions deleted by age rested on a wicker hassock. Sorrel often spent the night in Klom's crib, whether she and Klom had sex or not, preferring it to the crowded quarters she officially shared with a family of kitchen workers. The rancid oily smells her fellow tenants brought back in their clothing and hair from their shifts in the kitchen nauseated her.

This night, with Klom still unwontedly preoccupied by his earlier "death," Sorrel elected to keep company with her lover after her shift ended. Their supper, taken amidst the crowded refectory attached to Kitchen Number Twelve, had been a silent affair.

They lay quietly together now in the hammock. The Great Sun had gone down just an hour ago, and, even without any exertion, their naked bodies--one sleek and golden, one hairy and pale--were bedewed with sweat. Estuarial breezes feathered their skins.

Strung from the two biggest, most solidly anchored posts, the hammock and its ropes nonetheless creaked as Sorrel shifted her position to clamber atop Klom. She began to kiss and tease him. "Where's the nasty old cruft then, sweetling? Nothing to stop me from rubbing my boobs here now, is there?"

Most unusually, Klom did not at first respond. Sorrel persisted however, and soon the shipbreaker began to react enthusiastically. One massive hand encompassed both her breasts, while the other cupped her whole ass. Straddling Klom's hips, Sorrel looked back over her shoulder to grab his penis and guide it home. But suddenly she stopped.

"Sorrel, what's wrong?"

"I--that thing is *watching* us!"

"What thing?" Klom raised himself up on one elbow. "Oh, Tugger?" The beast sat up on its back haunches attentively, legs askew toward one side and its bifurcate horn aimed straight at the couple. If interpreted anthropomorphically, its face expressed goofy bemusement. "But he's watched us every night since I found him."

"I know! But it's different now. We don't know what he is, or what he can do, or what he wants. It shivers my bones!"

"Tugger? Never! He's just my happy little friend. Like you and Airey."

Sorrel looked incensed, and she bounced off Klom to stand on the dirt floor. "So that's all I am to you? Some kind of pet? Where's my dress?"

Klom swung his legs around to sit upright. "No, Sorrel, you're not a pet. That's not what I meant to say. Don't twist my words around. You know I can't always say things just right. I love you. Come back, please."

Standing dressed by the plank door with a hand on the latchstring, Sorrel said, "Forget it, Klom. You seem to love this --this monster more than you do me. So why don't I just leave you two to whatever obscene pleasures you can contrive!"

Klom scowled. "Now, Sorrel, you know that's not--"

"And Airey deserves more respect from you too!" she yelled, then was gone.

Klom swore. He kicked his gamecube off the hassock and banged the door open. But Sorrel was already out of sight.

Tugger continued to beam beneficently, however, and eventually Klom calmed down. Before too long, both man and beast were snoring peacefully.

* * * *

Klom's three weeks of probation were nearly over. He had spent the time increasingly frustrated by the realization that the dismantling of the *Caution Discharge Zone* was proceeding swiftly without him. For one thing, he was losing taka and paisa every day he sat idle. His dreams of quitting the Yard and retiring to Chaulk seemed to recede further each day. To conserve his meager savings --depleted drastically by the advance charges from the Radius Seven lab--Klom had taken to eating the very scraps from Kitchen Number Twelve which he had once foreseen as supplying Tugger's needs. (Luckily, that amiable companion continued, however improbably, to flourish on nothing more than air and water.) Soliciting the leftovers from the friendly but sardonic Bergamot cook named Kirsh was a chore that grew more odious to Klom each day. Kirsh's face, a pockmarked, damascene blue, would crack in a sarcastic snaggle-toothed smile as he handed over the leaky package of orts, always accompanied by some such jest as, "Here's fare fit for a fourstrand, Klom--a starving, poverty-stricken, imbecilic fourstrand, that is."

But the loss of pay and the humiliating survival tactics represented the lesser of Klom's irritations. He found himself angrier over being excluded from the more intangible aspects of dismantling the starliner, the conversion of something useless into something useful. His earlier work on the ship had begun to foster an intimate bond with the vessel, an emotional linkage he had come to relish on previous jobs. And this particular bond had been sanctified in his blood (however inexplicably counterfactual that spillage had since become). It felt as if Klom had abandoned a responsibility to tend to the corpse of a loved one, leaving the job to strangers.

Few of these feelings were cast in words, either internally or to Sorrel or Airey. Nonetheless Klom experienced deep disquiet and irritability over this exclusion.

Each day he would spend hours on the shore, gazing out at the starliner, Tugger lying patiently in the sand at his master's feet. Tugger carried about a chewed hank of rope with him, and, from time to time, by obvious gestures, would try to interest Klom in a pulling game. Klom played with his pet once in a while, but more often Tugger was ignored, left to sleep or to fret at the frayed ends of the rope with his exiguous shoulder hands.

The mountainous ship just offshore exhibited few exterior changes, and Klom was left to fantasize about the altered conditions of the interior. When the ship-to-shore ferry returned each night full of weary workers, Klom would be present at the dock to glower at Rapaille, who made certain to shelter himself amidst a knot of the brawniest breakers. But Klom never made a move on the overseer, knowing that the surest way to extend his probation would be another physical assault.

When Klom grew weary of staring out to sea, he retreated to one of the scrapheaps with his watercutter. There he would refine his already masterful carving skills by cutting up worthless old pods and wall fragments and contorted rebar with his illimitable tool, until the filthy dirt became a sea of mud. The fastidious Tugger chose to remain out of the way of the splattering, but always within easy hail.

It was at just such mindless pursuits that Sorrel found Klom this late afternoon.

"Klom! Are you mad? It's Festival Eve! The celebrations will start soon!"

The Festival of the Triple Sunset was an annual rite celebrating the conjoined westering of Great, Lesser and Least Suns. On the first night the three suns would set within several minutes of each other. On the final night the descent of the orbs would occur simultaneously, resulting in an incredible celestial display inspiring much reverence from the more devout citizens of the Yard and greater Asperna.

Klom holstered his watercutter. "I don't care about any stupid Festival."

"Oh, shut up and get over here. You've been moping for three weeks now, and enough is enough. You're going to have a good time tonight if I have to carry you on my shoulders!"

This ridiculous image amused Klom so much he laughed heartily for the first time in days. Squelching through the mud, he embraced Sorrel, causing her to squeal.

"You're filthy! Put me down!"

Klom complied. Tugger, excited, raced over and jumped up to lick Klom's face.

"Okay, let's go get drunk. Soon I'll be earning my wages again, so I'll treat tonight."

"Don't you want to change up first?"

"The hell with it. If I get drunk enough to fall down, my clothes will be dirty already."

* * * *

The twilit, odoriferous streets and alleys of the bustee already swarmed with representatives of two dozen races. Chattering, clicking, cachinnating or cawing, the impoverished breakers and sorters, stockers and drainers, matter-modem techs and vegetable slicers all seemed determined to forget their cares and woes. Interspecies camaraderie reigned. Finery of a rudimentary sort had emerged from cheap chests and cardboard closets to adorn bodies spanning the spectrum from elongated to stubby, rugose to seamless, writhing to dignified.

Vendors with small braziers sold pungent kebabs of partchrumpf flesh. Bottles of liquor circulated freely from hand to tentacle to paw. Shadowy niches half-concealed the carnal explorations of chance-met lovers.

Klom moved through the exuberant chaos easily, the crowds parting before his mass. Sorrel and Tugger slipstreamed behind him. Klom gripped a half-empty flagon of toadchunder by its neck. A smear of partchrumpf grease ringed Sorrel's mouth. Tugger's tongue hung out.

At a cross-street, the crowd refused to give way for Klom and party, and he soon saw why. They had intersected a procession of marabouts and flagellants. Spinning their prayer wheels, swinging thuribles that wafted spicy fumes, the holybeings led an elaborately carven juggernaut pulled by a score of Sphinx. Hideous and benign wooden faces of devas gazed down implacably on the onlookers.

Sorrel shouted above the banging of drums, the keening of pandits, the crack of cattails threaded with bloody metal beads, and the blowing of horns. "Airey asked us to meet him later! He's got the results from Radius Seven!"

"Where?"

"He claims we need to keep the news secret. No eavesdroppers. So he said to meet at three AM by the stockpens. No one will be in such an unlikely place at that hour."

By two-thirty in the morning, Sorrel was growing weary. Klom's vigor, unfettered from any brooding, ran unabated. Tugger dragged along gamely.

"Let's find Airey so we can get to bed, Klom."

"All right."

The stockpens housed various softly lowing food beasts for the kitchens, behind shimmering, sizzling lines of force running from stanchion to stanchion. The noisome atmosphere insured that celebrants avoided the acreage.

"Airey!" yelled Klom semi-drunkenly into the luminance-crosshatched blackness. "Here we are! Show yourself, man! Or are you too busy sucking the ten teats of a Milchmaid!"

Airey stepped from the shadows, hissing. "Quiet, you big 'rumpf! Do you want every bravo in the vicinity to come investigate your bellowings? I saw a pair of Grimjacks just a few alleys over! We're here to discuss something extremely vital."

Klom sobered up. "What have you learned about Tugger? What makes him so important?"

Airey flourished a data-palette, while Sorrel gripped Klom's arm and leaned in closer. "Your foundling is a *twelvestrand*, Klom! An incredibly powerful deva, despite his seeming lack of sapience! Perhaps the only one of his kind. But unlike all other devas, he's metastable on our ontological plane! And he might very well be the Book of Forgetting as well!"

"The Book of Forgetting? But--"

Airey gestured dismissively. "I know, I know, everyone has assumed for millennia that the Book was an artifact of some sort. But I've been doing research into the legend, and nothing in the fragments of lore is really inconsistent with the Book being a living creature. And after a little cogitation, I realized how your pet saved your life. He doesn't travel *back* in time, but *crosswise*! He forgets one universe while remembering another. And somehow he shunted the essence of your consciousness onto an alternate timetrack along with him. A timetrack that lagged just a little beyond our moment, where your accident never happened. If you wish to quibble, this universe is not the one you were born in."

The hesitant tone of Klom's speech conveyed a slowly dawning understanding. "But then, that means-- I guess Tugger is really valuable." Klom looked down at his pet. The being whose inherently recomplicated cellular structure allowed him to transcend limitations of space and time and leap across the multiverse was busy nibbling at his own hide for pests.

Airey laughed cynically. "That's understating the case a million times worse than a Neftali trader misrepresents his wares! With Tugger by your side, you can lay claim to all the riches in the Indrajal."

"I don't want so much though," said Klom. He gathered his friends to his side. "Just enough for the four of us to leave this hard place and retire to Chaulk--"

The next voice, a basso rumble, shocked them all, although only Klom recognized it. "I am afraid no one is going anywhere."

Bright Tide Rising floated above them, clouded by his majestatics. The sixstrand owner of the Asperna Yards stayed silent for a long moment--possibly regarding the quartet curiously through his mutable veil, although Klom could not say for sure--before speaking at last.

"A metastable creature with twice my own information density. No wonder I was unable to read it properly. It is hard to credit such a miracle, although I have never known the scientists at Radius Seven to be mistaken before. You will now give me that data-palette."

Airey braced his spine. "Klom paid for these tests, so they belong to him. And so does Tugger."

"Absolutely incorrect. The creature is salvage from a ship owned by me. It is mine by terms of your employment. Your co-worker will be compensated for his find. Perhaps I will give him as much as ten thousand taka."

Sorrel chimed in. "That's an insult! This animal is invaluable!"

"And you three are all too stupid and primitive to properly exploit such a treasure. But I am done arguing. With the creature's entire genome on a palette, it will be simple to rebirth him, this time without any misplaced allegiances. I have no further need of any of you."

Klom felt mentally yanked in a dozen different directions. How had this horrible situation come about, from such simple and innocent impulses? But before he could speak or act, the telecosmic corona of majestatics around Bright Tide Rising seemed to squirt four solid streams of particles, distributed along four vectors.

Klom's watercutter practically leaped into his right hand, even as he hurled himself to one side. He felt a piercing pain in his left shoulder. But the pain did not disturb his aim.

The noise that Bright Tide Rising's legs made in falling to the ground was followed in milliseconds by the accompanying mucky splash of his separate upper half.

Klom turned to his companions. All three were stretched out unmoving on the filthy ground. One by one, he searched their corpses for wounds. But the lancelike majestatics had pierced so cleanly, yet so fatally, that Klom could detect nothing. At least their deaths had been swift. There was very little blood, and in fact his own shoulder wound was invisible and unleaking.

Klom lifted first Sorrel's head from the muck, and kissed her dirty cheek. He did the same for Tugger and Airey, before turning to their killer.

Bright Tide Rising's myrmidons were attempting to put their master back together. They had already gathered up his spilled entrails and dragged his two halves into contact and were stitching golden sutures inside and out.

Klom carved the sixstrand into pieces so small that all the majestics in the Indrajal would not suffice to repair the Horseface. The he kicked shitty, hay-speckled mud atop the carrion.

* * * *

The long, harsh night was waning, with dawn a distant rumor. Klom stood, half-bewildered, in his twilit shack. In his hand he held the data-palette bearing Tugger's genome. What good was it to him? The money to reincarnate Tugger was a sum far beyond his means. And even if somehow miraculously given the fee, Klom could engineer the conception only of Tugger's mere doppelganger, a blank slate with no familiar consciousness shared with the original who had once saved Klom's life.

And now Klom was in danger of losing his own life once more. His murder of Bright Tide Rising, even in self-defense, would earn him death, under the laws of the Indrajal, which were biased against twostrands.

He knew that he must run. But where?

Klom gathered up a couple of possessions: the picture of his mother, a few deva medals handed out at religious ceremonies. But then he was overwhelmed by fatigue and despair. The lack of a certain destination left him feeling hopeless. With near-suicidal unselfconcern, he dropped into his hammock and fell asleep among his rags.

Sometime in the earliest hours of morning he awoke to a wet tongue rasping his face. He flailed his arms about, confused and slow to emerge from dreams, and encountered a familiar boulder of a head bearing a fleshy protuberance.

"Tugger?"

Something hard was spat out onto his chest, bouncing off into the hammock.

By the time Klom got his eyes ungummed and open, he was alone again.

A data-palette slimed with saliva shared the hammock with him. He dried it off on his shirt and jacked it into his reader.

The palette was a triptix in Klom's name. It registered a spendable value above the ticket price of several million taka, and listed as the bearer's ultimate destination the fabled world of Mount Sumeru.

Klom gazed around him at the familiar shabby interior of his crib.

Already it looked distant and remote. The picture of his mother on the banks of Lake Zawinul seemed to represent a stranger. Klom sensed wordlessly that he would never return to Chaulk.

Many questions and a sense of mystery suffused him. Was Tugger somehow alive? What awaited him on Mount Sumeru?

Only travel out among the worlds of the Indrajal held hope of answers.

PART 2
WORLDSHIFTER

I dropped off into a restless dream about a big room full of noise and excited faces, and a smaller room with smoke curling out past an open door, and a big tank, painted green. There was a man in a white uniform with blood on his face, and a woman, crying, and I was saying, "That's an order, damn your guts!" And then they were all backing away and I picked up the bundle in my arms and went in through the smoky door and heard behind me the sound of the woman, crying...

--*The Day Before Forever*, Keith Laumer

Waiting nervously at the gate to the starquay, Klom irritably tugged at the hem of a tight sleeve ringing his massive upper arm. His new clothes troubled him. Used to going mostly naked or raggedly clad in the semitropical climate of Asperna, he found that wearing even a snugglet was irksome. This clinging smart singlet suit in pleasingly organic patterns of taupe and ochre covered him from mid-thigh up to neck and down to biceps, leaving the rest of him bare, save for a pair of adaptive minimus peds. Klom felt the gentle enwrapment of the suit to be a constriction and a hinderance, a reminder of some heretofore hidden obligation or duty to society that he had previously managed to shirk. In truth, his range of motions was as utterly free as it had ever been while he was wresting, bare-chested, some balky component from its housing onboard a derelict starship. But the symbolism of his new attire--a metaphysical concept Klom struggled to fully formulate--conveyed only a cumbersome snaffling of his authentic nature.

But, unfortunately, he had to be conventionally clothed upon venturing into the greater galactic milieu, the Indrajal.

Should he even be so fortunate as to escape the planet after his murder of Bright Tide Rising.

When the light of day had begun to seep through the seams of his crib, Klom performed his rude ablutions. His shoulder throbbed and ached where it had been pierced, but seemed relatively uninflamed, despite the dirt of his surroundings. Such was the lucky result of the nearly surgical drilling by the deadly majestatics. He had sustained worse wounds on the job. Klom resolved to attend to it at some point.

Small quantities of dried blood from his inspection of the corpses of his three friends still flecked his skin. How could the lovely Sorrel, the whimsical Airey and the loyal Tugger possibly be dead? And if the last-named had indeed perished, despite possessing a kind of mighty power in his hypothetical role as the Book of Forgetting, who or what had visited Klom in the dark?

Such irresolvable thoughts swirled confusingly through Klom's brain—but not to such a distracting extent that he failed to focus on his escape.

The majestatics attendant on Bright Tide Rising had surely recorded Klom's crime. But here was the one element of grace: who could they report to?

Bright Tide Rising was the sole sixstrand on the planet, Asperna being his personal dominion. There was no higher authority here to receive the news of the murder and come after Klom. Lieutenants, trained to be subservient, would never take the initiative to bring their master's killer to account. And interstellar communication happened only as fast as ships bearing messages could travel—a matter of days or weeks. So if Klom could leave the planet before a response could be mounted, he might yet elude any unfair justice.

Although what risks he would face out in the Indrajal as a fugitive, he could not imagine.

First things first: a visit to the mercantile that serviced this district of the sprawling bustee.

The place was run by a Fleerowl named Alula. Highly devout, the aged avianoform kept her shelves full of animated celestial icons, portraits of famous marabouts, and touchstones that broadcast mental sensations that faintly recalled what it felt like to be in a deva's presence.

Luckily, at such an early hour there were no other customers present to wonder about Klom's sudden need for fancy new garments.

"Alula, I need some respectable clothes. But I don't want to look flashy."

Alula proffered a reader. "Have a glim at the catalogue."

Klom picked out a simple intelligent suit. Alula nodded approval. "A very good choice. But of course, I don't have your size handy. So big! No matter. I'll get it via modem."

Within half a minute, Klom's suit had been delivered through the mirror face of the mercantile's portal device. He also selected a handsome shoulder-strap satchel made of Salembier grunter leather, paid for both—from his laborer's account, not daring yet to use the mysterious data-palette bestowed on him by being or beings unknown just a few hours ago—donated a few taka to the shrine on the counter, causing its crystals to shimmer anew and eliciting a beaky grin from Alula, and then hastened to his crib.

How long did he have before Bright Tide Rising's vengeful peers came after him?

And, assuming he escaped: where was he headed, and what was his mission?

Both questions he pushed off to such time when he could feel safer.

Now, awaiting entrance to the busy industrial port where the heterogenous repurposed industrial cargo from Asperna was sent starwards, Klom felt the hot breath of pursuit on his neck, although no actual authorities had yet manifested.

Without cause or interest during his uncomplicated past, Klom had never visited the starquay before. Situated several kilometers beyond the shabby margins of the shantytown, the palisaded conglomeration of warehouses and extensive service pads for the arrival and departure of the wave-packet vehicles that circulated among the worlds of the Indrajal represented to Klom the gateway to an almost unimaginable realm. The shushed fall and rise of the ships, the scurrying of the ground crews and laborers and officials, the rapid crisscrossing of ground vehicles, wheeled and floaters, everyone wallowing under the heat of all three lofty suns, induced a kind of nervous vertigo in the giant. But then an image of Tugger, and the memory of his companion's unflappable calm, rose to steady him.

Now the line of travelers—a dozen assorted sapients of some distinction and privilege, all with legitimate business concerns, no one else a fugitive shipbreaker—began to advance. Klom shuffled forward.

The official at the gate was a fellow human, a light-skinned fellow with sandy hair, wearing what looked to be a very uncomfortable uniform for this world's climate, long sleeves and trousers patterned with corporate sigils.

When Klom drew abreast of the man, he tendered the data-palette that had been so strangely dropped into his lap.

The gatekeeper slotted it into a reader, studied the display. His eyes widened.

"This identifies you as Klom of Chaulk, a shipbreaker of indigo stripe."

"Yes." Klom awaited pronouncement of his arrest. He fantasized about briefly overpowering the official, somehow dashing onto a ship just about to depart, stowing away—

"But your documents also state that Klom of Chaulk is just a secondary identity, strictly temporary, to facilitate confidential market research. Your primary Indrajal ID is that of Brum Bravalo, flavor-water magnate from Demigrieve. You are booked all the way through several nexial transitions to—Mount Sumeru? Is this correct?"

Stunned, Klom hesitated only a moment. "Yes, of course."

"Very well, *Khun* Bravalo. All is in order. Your passage aboard the *Squall of Demons* is confirmed. Pad thirty-nine, departure in one hour."

A bevy of majestatics swarmed Klom as soon as he stepped aboard the *Squall of Demons,* and he came to a dead halt in dread. Were these killer drones, sent to enforce a mortal sentence upon him? But when they clustered only around his wounded shoulder, obviously intent on repairing it, Klom relaxed.

As fellow passengers detoured around Klom, a porter appeared at Klom's side in the spacious entryway of the ship, a short and rotund sapient of a species unknown to Klom. The being resembled one of the cheerful bristly burrowing creatures Klom knew from the forest around his native Lake Zawinul. Thoughts of the childhood refuge recalled the portrait of his mother in his satchel. Would he ever see her again in this lifetime? Klom had his doubts. Probably he was embarked on a one-way fool's errand. If only he could have taken the newfound wealth on his data-palette (were they Brum Bravalo's purloined hard-earned life savings, if such a person even existed?) and simply retired on Asperna. But his murder of the six-strand overlord had precluded that.

The little steward piped up. "The name is Lingle, *Khun* Bravalo, here to assist you during your trip. The reparative treatment on your injury is courtesy of Retta Galaxyliners, as we assess your health to ensure fellow passengers against any communicable diseases. 'Your carnal cares constitute our happy *giri.*' Have you no other luggage?"

Finished knitting up and disinfecting Klom's wound, the microworkers flew away. Klom flexed the joint and was grateful to feel nearly normal again. "No, just this satchel."

"Allow me then. I will guide you to your cabin."

Klom had the strangest sensation as Lingle conducted him through the corridors and levels of the ship. After taking apart so many obsolete and discarded starcraft, all antiques, Klom felt as if this still functioning vessel was not a contemporary artifact, but rather some ghost from the past, and he himself a time-traveling phantom, hurled backwards to another era. The reality of current-day star travel had not really registered on him while he still labored in the Shipbreakers' Yard. Stargoing vessels were always only ancient dead things.

The *Squall of Demons* was not very large—certainly no mountain like the *Caution Discharge Zone* where he had found Tugger. Klom guessed it might hold one hundred passengers, and seemed not even full today. After all, what could bring outsiders to Asperna other than commercial goals? The planet, so far as Klom knew, was no tourist destination, no center of culture, no political powerhouse. Its sole industry was shipbreaking, and these departing travelers must have all been conducting business of one kind or another with Bright Tide Rising's enterprises.

Klom wondered if they knew yet that the sixstrand was dead. And if they had heard the news, could they ever imagine that the killer resided among them?

Klom's cabin proved to be much bigger than his entire old crib. Softly glowing light panels, cushy bed, decorative artwork on the walls. Not the height of luxury, he was sure, but still more lush and pampering than any environment he had ever found himself in before.

"How many must I share this room with?"

Lingle showed professional unflappability. "A fine jest, *Khun* Bravalo. You are the sole occupant of this suite."

The porter demonstrated all the facilities, and then waited obsequiously by the door. Klom hesitated as to what was required of him, then spontaneously recalled tossing coins into a jar for the bartender at Thrash's shabeen. He sent Lingle a few taka via the ether, and the response from the hedgehog-man indicated Klom had done the right thing.

"You will find the hours for dining listed in the online directory, and of course you may have any meals brought directly to your room."

"Is this vessel going nonstop to Mount Sumeru?"

"Again, *Khun* Bravalo expresses his wit. This is only the regular shuttle between Asperna and Onza-Gora. You must change starliners there for any subsequent destinations."

Alone in his sumptuous quarters, Klom stripped off his confining singlet suit and luxuriated in his freedom. He took a long shower, marvelling at the seemingly endless hot water and fragrant soaps. How Sorrel would have loved this! Why had her life been cut so short? What evil had she ever done to merit such a sad end? Associating with Klom was her only crime. And Klom's loving possession of Tugger had been that companion's only transgression. The world was unfair and brutal. People died for no reason. If only—

Klom sat down at the desk hosting the cabin's reader. He slotted in the data-palette that verified his assumed identity and wealth, and which charted his intinerary to Mount Sumeru, far across the galaxy. What awaited him there?

He popped out that particular mysterious ultrafiche and inserted the other one he carried, obtained through Airey: the transcription of Tugger's genome. The long recomplicated scroll of twelvestrand genetic coding conveyed nothing of course to Klom's uneducated eyes, until an app in the reader produced a visualization of the genome's somatic instructions, plus-or-minus percentages of accuracy flickering alongside the image.

There on the screen showed the familiar friendly quadruped beast whom Klom had rescued from the suspensor-sac: the boulder-headed, stubby-legged, barrel-bodied, antenna-graced creature who supposedly represented a power beyond any other in the universe.

But all Klom saw was someone who loved him, had saved his life, and whom he had loved in return.

* * * *

The fifth port of call after leaving Asperna—still not a quarter of the way to Mount Sumeru—was a world named Stratcom, the oldest, most cultured, most complex, and most densely populated planet encountered so far on Klom's odd and incalculable journey through the Indrajal.

Faced with the noisy swarming warren of streets in the city of Sedge that hosted the enormous starquay where his ship had just landed, Klom felt at first utterly baffled. How to hail transportation, where to find lodgings, what kind of food was suitable for humans, how to go about locating an expert strandcrafter who could bring Tugger—or his DNA cousin—back to life— These matters and more fell beyond even his new competence gained after three weeks of travel. A changed man from the simple laborer from Lake Zawinul, Klom nonetheless remained basically what he had always been: a slow-thinking, deliberate, straightforward plodder.

Thank the devas, then, for the presence of Lingle.

That small, spiny-pelted, portly bundle of energy and efficiency had already summoned a hired car with enough storage capacity to hold the two large floater trunks that carried the belongings of the pair. Lingle's wordly goods from his years of stewardship aboard various Retta Galaxyliners had been hosted in one trunk aboard the *Squall of Demons,* while Klom's new purchases from his prior planetary stops had required the second luggage.

"You simply must have more and better clothes, *Khun* Bravalo. You can't wear that, ah, utilitarian garb under all polite circumstances. Most offputting and déclassé, I am sure. No matter how deeply you 'went native' during your investigations on Asperna, you absolutely must reengage with society on society's terms, now that you are back among your peers."

"If you say so, Ling, for you always know best."

The trip from Klom's homeworld of Asperna to Onza-Gora had taken five days. During the entire first day of the voyage, Klom had been reluctant to leave his cabin, for fear of doing something that would get him in trouble. Although what mere social infraction he could incur that would be worse than murdering a sixstrand, he could not imagine.

Paying him frequent visits during that first day to ascertain and fulfill his needs, Lingle had proven to be an essential aide, confidante, and reliable source of information. None of Klom's questions, however unsophisticated, had been met with disdain. Instead, the little Vib—the homeworld of his kind, Vibbsy, had been incinerated during a commercial war some centuries ago, leaving the scattered survivors of the species as stateless workers—showed a professional compassion and deference to the naïve Klom—an attitude which, Klom sensed, was not derived wholly from receipt of wages and tips, but also somewhat based on a native affability and empathy.

Eventually, reassured by Lingle's gentle guidance, Klom had ventured out to the various lounges, spas, gamerooms and refectories aboard the galaxyliner, and even found himself making rudimentary conversation with his fellow passengers. As he had suspected, they were assorted business types, and seemed most interested in hearing details of Klom's own beverage enterprises, his profession having been made public on the ship's virtual roster. Klom managed to fabricate some vague details that seemed to satisfy his interlocutors, who, truth be told, wanted mainly to talk about themselves. A couple of women and one man seemed interested in Klom as a bed partner, but he turned them all down, the memories of Sorrel still too painful.

Even these limited interactions and dialogues led Klom to one conclusion: the Indrajal was a complex, bewildering place, and if he were to have any success in his quest, he would need to enlist some help. By the time the ship was one day away from Onza-Gora, Klom had made up his mind about what to do.

Busy with preparations for arrival, Lingle found time to respond to Klom's call. He entered Klom's cabin with his usual professional deference. "Your summons, *Khun* Bravalo, failed to make explicit your needs."

"Sit down, will you, Lingle. I want to talk with you."

The Vib took a seat sized for Klom, a perch that left his feet dangling in mid-air.

Klom felt nervous. "Have a drink. This stuff is very smooth. Never had anything like it at Thrash's shabeen."

"Zoycean Green Mist? Smooth indeed. I will indulge in only a thimblesworth, and strictly pursuant to your command."

The liquor relaxed both Klom and the steward.

"Lingle, I want to share with you my true background."

"As you wish."

Klom disclosed his real history and recounted everything that had led to his departure from Asperna. Lingle listened with seeming imperturbability. Nonetheless, midway through the recitation the Vib felt compelled to help himself to a second, much larger drink.

Upon concluding his tale, Klom said, "So you see, Lingle, I have a long and strange road ahead of me, and I need a loyal, smart and capable companion. I think that's you. Would you ever agree to help me in my quest?"

Lingle pushed meditatively at one corner of his mouth with a forefinger that hosted a thick black clawlike nail. "You are asking me to throw over my steady and reliable employment of two decades standing, all to accompany a wanted criminal across the galaxy in search of a will-o-the-wisp?"

"I guess so. But I can pay you good. What do you make now as a steward?"

"Ten thousand taka per annum."

"I'll pay you ten times that."

"Generous indeed. But mere money is not a sufficient inducement. Tell me again about this being you named Tugger."

"Here, have a look at him." Klom caused the reader to display Tugger's conjectured portrait drawn from the genome record.

Lingle studied the image. "An unprepossessing countenance. And yet you dare to make the claim that this entity is synonymous with the Book of Forgetting? The annunciation of that being is said to herald a revolution among all the strata of the Indrajal, from devas on down. A recalibration of all relationships and values."

"Lingle, listen real close to me now. All that is beyond me. It might be true, it might not. I don't make any claims, because I don't know anything about anything. Except that I miss Tugger and want him back. That's my whole notion."

Lingle said nothing for a minute, then spoke a seeming non-sequitur. "Do you know how and why Vibbsy was destroyed?"

"No, of course not. I never heard of your birth planet till I met you. But I sure am sorry you lost your world."

"I appreciate your sympathy. The manner of its demise was such. Two sixstrands—Accidental Beauty and Damascene Indigo Feather—both wanted a monopoly on my homeworld's strangelet mines. They could not come to terms, and were too equally balanced in their powers to achieve a victory by force. So they both decided that rather than let a rival win, they would destroy the planet. Accidental Beauty planted a hardened, stellar-rated matter modem at the very center of the planet and opened it up to a hundred receivers that gushed live magma onto the surface of Vibbsy. Not to be outdone, Damascene Indigo Feather triggered a critical mass of strangelets into a planetary cascade of matter transmutation. My species had a choice between incineration and molecular decoherence."

Klom stayed silent for a spell, then said, "I guess my homeworld got off easy, then. All we had to endure under the rule of Bright Tide Rising was poverty, maiming, and dying young."

"Indeed. So as you might surmise, I harbor no love for the terabase elite who run roughshod over the galaxy. If your quadruped Book of Forgetting could bring some rebalancing of the scales of justice to the Indrajal—"

"I can't guarantee that, Lingle."

The Vib considered the situation while gnawing on a nail, then leaped from the chair. "Damn all certainty! I've spent too long in a rut of false security! I'm throwing in with you, *Khun* Bravalo, mad as you may be!"

"That is wonderful! But please, call me Klom. That's my real name."

Lingle considered. "No, I think not. Best for you to go by your assumed identity. Especially if any of the terabases are still vigilant for your reappearance."

"I never thought of that! See, your wisdom is paying off already, Ling!"

"Time will tell."

Tendering his resignation at the offices of Retta Galaxyliners on Onza-Gora (the wavepacket stewards had no long-term contract with their employers, but worked strictly on the sufferance of the corporation and subject to their own whims), Lingle announced his intention to outfit his new boss more appropriately. But first, another mission, accomplished right at the same offices, but at the transit counter: to purchase tickets for Lingle matching Klom's mystery itinerary.

When finished, Lingle studied their route silently for a time, then said, "Mount Sumeru. I never fancied I would visit that wondrous impossible place."

With any other being, Klom might have hesitated to reveal his ignorance. But already he felt fully at ease with Lingle. He had a strong intuition that only ultimate honesty between them would serve them best and promote their survival and success.

"What is Mount Sumeru, Ling? Why is it so special?"

"It is a solar system featuring one million habitable planets, that's all."

Klom pondered. "A solar system. That's one sun and all its worlds, right?"

"Concisely stated and generally accurate, but not exhaustively definitive."

"How can one sun be the mother to a million worlds?"

"Mount Sumeru is an array of three dozen suns, held in place by a supermassive black hole at the center of the matrix."

"Those words confuse me. I can't picture such a thing."

"In that you are not alone. I understand that only seeing the astronomical construction up close can even partially convey the magnitude of its reality."

"I guess I'll just have to wait then."

"As will I."

A more practical consideration popped up in Klom's mind. "If there's a million planets at Mount Sumeru, which one is our destination?"

"An excellent question, *Khun* Bravalo! Our ticket only specifies arrival at one of the many distal receiving stations that serve as gateways for out-system visitors."

"Guess it'll all work out somehow."

"Your naïve faith is infectious! Although like all infections, it requires close monitoring. Now, let's get you some decent clothes!"

After that, the pair found nothing to do but follow the pre-planned intersystem itinerary that the enigmatically bestowed ultrafiche had laid out for them. Khush, Dustbowl, and Badura were pleasant but unexceptional worlds, mere stepping stones holding no obvious answers to Klom's quest, and their prearranged bookings had the travelers leaving almost as soon as they arrived. They used the transit time to become better acquainted with each other, to make nebulous plans for the future, and to foster Klom's education.

Quizzing the big shipbreaker, Lingle found him lamentably deficient in common knowledge of the Indrajal—although he did have praise for Klom's "alley smarts." And so the little Vib commenced to tutor the man in the basics that would aid him to move without too many hinderances through the Indrajal.

Lingle maintained a non-supercilious, professorial attitude, never commenting on any amazing gap, however rudimentary, in Klom's worldview. He seemed genuinely interested in expanding Klom's horizons and dispelling his uncertainties, and for this Klom was grateful. Only once did Lingle let loose an impulsive chittering laugh.

"Tell me again," said the Vib, "exactly how you discovered your friend Tugger in his stasis pod."

"Well, it happened when we were assigned to decommission a ship named the *Caution Discharge Zone*—"

Lingle's explosive amusement could not be contained. When the little factotum finally assumed a sober look, Klom asked what had been so funny, and Lingle explained.

"You mistook a familiar warning placard for the ship's name."

Klom felt then the immense weight of his ignorance. He began to say that he had merely accepted the misinformation that his coworker Nyerephar had blithely offered. But he stopped short, acknowledging to himself that he had always before now walked through his own life with a kind of lazy acceptance of hearsay and the opinions and choices of others, rather than exert his own intelligence, however slight when compared to the norm of his fellows. But such slackness could no longer suffice. Not in a universe where all hands were raised, if not in opposition to him, then in a negligent dismissal of his worth and needs.

His feelings unhurt, Klom grinned broadly. "That was kind of dumb, wasn't it?

"Dumb, my dear student, is a relative, improvable condition which only becomes contemptible when it is cherished."

"If you say so, Ling."

By the time the unlikely pair disembarked at Sedge on Stratcom, Klom felt very much smarter than the brutish fellow who had been content to chop up ancient starliners all his life. But to his surprise, he discovered that he did not derive a sense of security or pride from his learning, but only a larger sense of how much remained outside his ken.

Within twenty minutes of their landing, Lingle had selected for them a tolerable inexpensive hotel in a slightly louche neighborhood, run by a family of fastidious, naturally talcum-scented Pinemartens, the smalles of whom resembled a ball of fur propelled by a perpetual-motion engine.

Up in their room, Lingle said, "I know you have several million taka on your fiche, but there is no telling what expenses we shall incur on this wild nildoror chase. So best to economize now. Hence our less-than-plush accomodations."

"This place is still fancier than I'm used to, Ling. It's good. Say, maybe I should check our credit balance. We did spend some extra on Badura."

"Only because you had to recompense that café owner for damages incurred to his establishment."

"But he called you a slimy water rat!"

Lingle sighed. "As an planetarily orphaned species, I am used to such slurs. Did you hear me take offense?"

"No… So that's why I had to do it for you!"

Klom slotted his palette into the portable reader that Lingle carried. He stared at the screen, then turned the reader toward Lingle. Instead of credit balance, a name, title and address showed, unprompted.

> Nomar Zabumba
> Expert Strandcrafter
> Morgay Prospect
> District of the Wells

"What does it mean, Ling?"

"It seems we are being directed towards a meeting by whoever gave you this fiche. But I swear the palette is not ensouled, and we have no outside connections on this reader. So how this new information is being planted, I cannot say. "

Klom leaped up from his seat on the edge of the bed and grabbed his companion's hand. "Who cares! We have a destination, so what're we waiting for! Let's go!"

Lingle's feet never touched another surface until they were ensconced in a tuk-tuk whose driver nodded in easy recognition at the address they named.

Whatever the ancient origin of its name, the District of Wells proved deficient in springs, fountains or watering holes, comprising several urban blocks indistinguishable from the others they had passed through: an assortment of heterogenous extruded, grown and self-assembled buildings hosting retailers, food stands, small fabs and upper-story apartments. Walls crawled with animated signage. Children racketed from a null-gee playground. The smell of some kind of fried fish vied with perfume odors spilling out of salons where fur, hair, feather, chitin and scales all received equal grooming attentions. The sidewalks hosted a plethora of different races.

The façade of Nomar Zabumba's establishment featured many screens displaying his accomplishments: cherished progeny tailored to the most minute specifications; chimeric pets assembled from impossible combinations both horrific and kawaii; industrial hybrids hard at work, digging, lifting, transporting.

Klom devoted little attention to the displays, but instead hustled through the door, followed by a scampering Lingle, hard-pressed to keep up.

The interior was a pleasantly lighted and discreet showroom with a service counter. Various small models of assorted biological creations, plus some flat static images of vats, wombs and alembics. Some multivalent seating arrangements.

Before Klom could holler out for assistance, a door at the rear of the store opened, and out skittered a midsized being who presumably must be Nomar Zabumba.

The proprietor was a Pryle. His body resembled a giant russet cereal biscuit, all thatched fibers. Parallel rows of finger-like feet on his underside offered potentially omnidirectional progress. Four tendril-like arms, ending in subtle manipulators, emerged symmetrically from the body. The Pryle's head—a globe with a ring of eyes around the equator, an iris-like mouth, and no nose—rested atop a corkscrew neck now coiled, mid-upper-body, into a supportive pile like some dockside heap of rope.

"Do you know me?" demanded Klom.

The Pryle's voice sounded rather gelatinous. "Why no, good *Khun*. Should I?"

"We were directed to you."

"By whom?"

Klom was stumped. Lingle stepped forward. "*Khun* Zabumba, I believe we have something of interest to show you. *Khun* Bravalo, please tender the genome fiche to our savant."

Klom handed over the palette containing Tugger's specs. Zabumba slotted it and studied the output for a considerable time in silence. His ring of eyes blinked in sequence several times, and his neck uncurled so that his head could bob up and down in a kind of shrug og astonishment. Finished, he reluctantly handed the fiche back.

"A genuine twelvestrand. I never thought to see such a thing. I thank you for bringing this to me. May I ask his provenance?"

Klom gave a condensed version of Tugger's life and death, omitting all of Klom's own crimes and the possibility that Tugger was the legendary Book of Forgetting. "Can you recreate him?"

"It would take every iota of skill I possess. But it would be the capstone of my career. I can but try."

"And your fee?" inquired Lingle.

"I should perhaps pay you for the privilege. But I cannot afford the commensurate amount. And my time and prowess, not to mention the cost of raw materials and reactor hours, are not negligible— Let us say, three-quarters of a million taka."

"Half that sum."

"Come now! The crafting the mitochondria alone will take me dozens of hours!"

"All right then, four hundred thousand."

"You jest with me!"

After further bargaining, a price of six-hundred-and-twenty-five thousand was agreed upon. Klom reluctantly handed over the irreplaceable genome fiche, made a partial downpayment, settled on an estimated date of delivery, then left the shop.

"I told you we had to conserve our funds, *Khun* Bravalo, and now you see why. Expenditures known and unknown lie ahead. Still, saving us a hundred-and-twenty-five thousand was a step in the right direction."

"I don't care about money. I just want to have Tugger alive again. This waiting will be hard to endure."

"We will just have to apply ourselves more diligently to your education, so that you will be a fitter companion to the Book of Forgetting when he arrives."

And indeed, despite Klom's anxiousness and impatience, the thirteen days that Nomar Zabumba had stipulated passed in a not altogether oppressive fashion. Klom's lessons were supplemented by excursions to local tourist sights, such as the Flame Falls and the extensive parklands centered on the Battlefield of the Pregnant Virgins. The pair took all their meals at an open-air stand not far from the hotel that specialized in bowls of noodle soup larded with one's choice of cubed planimal meats.

At last the promised day of Tugger's full instantiation arrived. Checking in from the hotel with the strandcrafter, Lingle verified that delivery would indeed occur at the stipulated time. Klom had them waiting at the shop in Morgay Prospect an hour ahead of their appointment. But they found the door locked, and so Klom paced anxiously while Lingle occupied himself playing some recondite boardgame with a passel of elderly Leatherheads sitting in a small park, their distinctive skulls all buffed to a high sheen.

Finally the outer door unlocked itself and the customers were allowed inside the shop.

The inner door opened as they entered, and Zabumba emerged.

Behind him trotted a fully mature Tugger, identical from antenna to paws to Klom's dear foundling.

Klom let out an exultant whoop and pushed past the Pryle gene-artisan. He fell to his knees and hugged the bulky creature. But Tugger—this avatar of him—made no sign of recognition, no gesture of joy, nor gave even an instinctive animal response by tongue or throat or tail. He seemed almost imperceptive and unprocessing of his environment: a zombie.

Klom got slowly to his feet and turned to Zabumba.

"What is the matter? Why isn't he friendly, or even really aware of me?"

Zabumba's non-human face conveyed regret and dismay as far as was possible.

"There were always two possibilities for this reincarnation. The being could emerge as a blank slate, a new entity with a natal brain-mind gestalt entirely unconnected to the life experiences of his predecessor. This would be the case if you or I were to be cloned. Baseline infantilism. But with a twelvestrand organism, I suspected—and hoped—that rebooting his carnal form would call down his soul from the deva dimensions, to fill and overlay the wetware."

"Explain further," Lingle urged.

"Well, of course you know that given your friend's ultra-dense and recomplicated genome, he should exist only in the higher deva dimensions. Instead, he's stable on our plane of reality. Nonetheless, I theorized that his soul had its basis and anchors in the deeper realities, and so that when his prior mortal form was snuffed, his severed quintessence remained intact, but outside our ken. I had hoped that reinstantiating his fleshly anchor would have served as a lure for the return of his soul. But instead there appears to be some failure to reconnect, leaving him neither inhabited nor full of naïve potential."

"This seems a sensible theory. But why did the reconnection not happen?"

"A matter beyond my expertise. For that answer, I suggest you consult a marabout. I can recommend one highly... Oh, and here is your genome fiche." The Pryle handed it over. "I must admit that I tried to copy its contents—just for academic purposes, you understand—and it self-destructed. I should have known that the boffins at Radius Seven would engineer such a protective feature. So your only source of this being's code is now the being itself."

Klom glared at Zabumba, but forebore from accusing him of duplicity. Having Tugger back, even in this partial manner, excused the strandcrafter's excess.

Discovering that the uninspired Tugger would respond to simple prodding, Klom and Lingle managed to exit the strandcrafter's shop with their new witless child. They had to summon a four-seater tuk-tuk to carry the hefty beast, who required Klom's leverage under his butt to clamber into the vehicle.

The small, colorfully painted columned temple on Windmaul Street diffused saltspray-tinged incense out its open door. Offerings from local citizens lay heaped at either side of the entrance. Klom and Lingle managed to herd Tugger inside. In the shadowy space they disturbed the marabout at an arcane ritual near the iconostasis, involving ewer, basin, hypersonic sounding rod and stochastic prayer paddles. A small water sprite danced in the bowl, yipping in an unknown tongue.

The officiant belonged to the race known as the Friment, whose genderless members resembled squat oblate cones with their sensory organs near their crowns; one multi-jointed limb splitting into two manipulators; and jaundice-colored, waffle-textured epidermis. Clad in a sigil-spattered translucent robe that covered them from narrow flattened top down to broad flexible uni-ped base, the marabout dismissed the sprite, which fell apart into molecules of the host liquid, ending its performance, and turned to the visitors.

"I am Presbyter Przl. What spiritual hunger drives you into our embrace today?"

Klom said, "We need to know where to find the soul of our friend here."

Presbyter Przl palpated Tugger's body from head to tail, evoking no response from the creature. "Yes, yes, a vitanul. His essence is elsewhere." They humped themselves to a cabinet and removed a cranial netting connected by a single cable to a detector box featuring multiple readouts. Draping the netting atop Tugger's boulder-like skull, the marabout activated the machine and began to fiddle with the controls. They studied the display intently for a full fifteen minutes, then removed the netting, tucked away the whole assemblage, and confronted Klom and Lingle.

"This is the empty shell of a deva unlike any I have ever heard of or encountered."

"We know that!" Klom said. "But we need to find his soul."

"Do you know the concept of *terma*? A hidden teaching or treasure. Insofar as I can determine, the standard three parts of your deva's soul—the *ib*, the *ka* and the *ba*—have been separated by the shock of death and taken up residence far apart as *terma*. These are not, of course, physical objects, but rather higher-dimensional matrical resonances tethered each to a particular world by synchronized lock-in of vibrational planes."

Lingle inquired, "And if we brought our friend to these special planets?"

"I believe that with expert guidance from one of my peers residing in each *terma* location, the components could be made to reinhabit his mortal frame. Upon the third world he would become once more complete."

Klom wanted to shake information out of the marabout much faster, but held back. "Where are these worlds? Which planets do we have to visit? And how can we contact the local marabouts?"

"Reaching out to my colleagues is a simple matter. I can provide you with contact specifics. But first I must make the attempt to discover the locations of the *terma*. Of course, I must risk my own sensibilities and employ rare holy resources that require frequent replenishing…"

Klom sent money to the temple's account, and Presbyter Przl immediately assembled incense, drugs, a tray of Frillgill sacrificial amphibians, and a majestic robe. With many invocations, mantras and mudras, the marabout began to scry.

Nearly an hour later, Przl emerged from their far-seeing fugue and, in a voice made raw by chanting, offered three names.

"Alnair Grus 7, Oksanax, Voyle. Here be the *terma* three."

Lingle put a small paw on Klom's wide hand. "Those names are familiar somehow… *Khun* Bravalo, let us look at your triptix."

Lingle slotted the palette into the reader and scrolled to the next three prearranged destinations, the last stops between Stratcom and Mount Sumeru.

Alnair Grus 7, Oksanax, Voyle.

And the name of the first destination was already flashing, with departure of the luxury-class wavepacket *Penhaligon* scheduled for just two hours from now.

* * * *

Returning to their hotel and assembling their belongings took nearly half the allotted time before departure, mainly due to having to wrestle with Tugger's mute inertia. But at last Klom and Lingle stood with their trunks and Tugger on the sidewalk, awaiting the hired ride to the port.

Anxious and impatient, Klom said, "What could be delaying our driver?"

Lingle looked perplexed. "I don't know... Have you noticed that the street is emptying of people?"

Klom registered that the busy citizens of this district had all retreated inside, and that vehicles had ceased flowing down the avenue. But before he could offer a guess about the phenomenon, the reason for the flight of the innocents was made plain.

From the direction of the soaring, gleaming towers that were home to Stratcom's portion of the terabase elite, a figure came floating through the sky, upborne by his swarm of majestatics. Cruising at an altitude of a dozen meters, the multistrand being, at first just a hazy dot, soon dropped to about twice the height of Klom's head and assumed recognizable configurations.

A Gorgoid by species, the entity was bipedal, reptilian, twice the size of Klom. It flaunted large ribbed membranous ears, a spike-studded tail and shell-plated back, with its soft ventral side protected by molded armor; otherwise it wore no clothing. As it came closer, it grinned to show a plethora of formidable sharp teeth.

Klom's grip went instinctively for the watercutter pistol that used to hang always at his side, with which he had dealt so effectively with Bright Tide Rising's threat. But of course his instinctive thrust was stymied.

The multistrand lordling had arrived, holding apart a few meters and floating with its bare scaly clawed feet at a level just above Klom's head.

"My name is Truth's Abstract Smile. I am here to assume possession of your twelvestrand charge."

Klom's temper flared. "Again! What right do you have to take him? Tugger's not property, he's a free creature!"

"I assert ancient provenance over The Book of Forgetting. Although long lost, he was created by my species more than a millennia ago, to ensure that our natural rule over genetically less fortunate races should never be successfully challenged. Let me be frank with you. We terabases are relatively few, you know, compared to your teeming trillions. So we needed the Book's powers of reordering reality. He is a potent weapon beyond anything you can imagine, and you and your peers are incapable of safeguarding or deploying him wisely."

"He's not a weapon, he's my friend. And you can't have him! Get rid of your cloud of killer bugs, then come down here face to face. I'll fight you for him!"

Truth's Abstract Smile grinned in a display of many sharp teeth shining in his stubby snout. "Much as I would enjoy such a frivolous and brief tussle, I decline your offer."

"Then what are you waiting for? Just kill me and Lingle, take Tugger and be gone! I'll haunt you forever! You and your greedy, ruthless kind! I killed one of you already, you know, on Asperna. And I'll do the same to you if I get a chance."

"Yes, we know about your lucky assassination of Bright Tide Rising. But, again frankly, that Horseface was an incompetent idiot. Why do you think he was assigned to your miserable world? It was the only task he was suited for, running a junkyard. You may find an assault against any other one of our kind less successful."

Klom raised a huge fist. "Do your worst then, and be damned."

The tableau persisted for aching seconds that seemed an eternity. Klom felt poor Lingle quivering against his leg, and from the corners of his vision he sensed furtive fearful movements from behind window shutters as the citizenry awaited the destruction of this big stranger who had dared to antagonize and resist one of the high multistrand caste.

Klom's consciousness was blank of ideations, just a seething ocean of fear and anger, jealousy and vindictiveness, protectiveness and rage. But then a revelation washed over him, and he laughed enormously.

"You can't take him! Something's stopping you. If you could have grabbed Tugger, you would've done it already, just drilled us without a word and made off with him. So all your threats are empty."

Truth's Abstract Smile frowned, and his self-important luster seemed to dim a fraction.

"Very bright you are, especially for a simpleton. Yes, this is correct. The Book of Forgetting seems to radiate a kind of protective noosphere around himself and you that precludes harm. Not all harm, of course. A falling boulder could still bash your head in. But intentionally malign qualia emanating from any sentience are negated. All part and parcel of the Book's multiversal phase-changing abilities. Do you understand any of this? No, of course not. What a bloody waste."

"So it's a stalemate. Fine by me! What're you going to do?"

"I could imprison the three of you, let you all rot until you decided to cooperate. I think there's a good chance that the Book's instinctive protections would not interpret such a move to incarcerate as inimical. But I believe you would rather die than surrender. And since the Book himself is still mindless and soulless and in a diminished state, he might expire as well. No, that would be a fruitless course. So I am going to let you go about your business—with this message. You will never be out of the sight of me and my peers, even if you do not see us. You will never be truly secure or safe. At any moment we might find a way to pierce your protection or separate you all from each other. You will never be sure who is a friend and who is one of our agents. So try to endure those nervewracking conditions for a while, and maybe you will change your mind and surrender the Book. And consider this, as a carrot to the stick: your instant intransigence has not yet allowed me to make you an offer for your voluntary cooperation. We can be extremely generous. A whole world can be yours, title conveyed and sealed, if you simply relinquish this dumb beast."

"Take your world and choke on it!"

"So be it. For the moment."

Truth's Abstract Smile instantly rocketed up and away, becoming a mere pinprick in the sky in seconds.

Klom felt immense relief, however conditioned. The stink of an instant flopsweat suddenly poured off him. He looked first to Tugger, who had maintained his imperturbable blank stance throughout, a thread of drool hanging from one jowl. Then he cast his gaze at Lingle.

The little Vib had collapsed to the pavement in a faint. Klom lifted him up and laid him on one of their trunks. The locals now flooded out of hiding, shouting and celebrating Klom's victory. A friendly drink vendor pressed a pod of flavored water into Klom's hand, and he got some down Lingle's throat and splashed the rest on his furry face.

Lingle came to.

"I am extremely sorry for my incapacity, *Khun* Bravalo! I promise you, it won't happen again!"

"Ling, you just beat me to the collapse. I was ready to fall all in a heap."

"Nonsense! You were a pillar of strength!"

"I would never have had the wit or courage to talk back to that bastard without your educating me, Ling."

Lingle hopped off the trunk. "Says the fellow who previously chopped up a lordling into bloody chunks. Here's our ride now. Hurry, or we'll miss our ship!"

* * * *

The *Penhaligon* was the most luxurious ship that Klom had yet voyaged on since he left Asperna, rich with sensual fabrics, woods, mosaics and other organics veneering its sophisticated technological armature. Buying passage for Lingle and Tugger had consequently chewed up a hefty portion of his monies. Some five kilometers from bow to stern, and with proportionate dimensions along its other axes, the *Penhaligon* carried ten thousand travelers in plush comfort. The passengers were heading for a variety of destinations, with Alnair Grus 7 being one of the lesser ports, some three weeks travel from Stratcom. They constituted a deep tranche of the Indrajal's many races, cultures, societies and castes, offering perplexing, alluring, disturbing customs, rituals, modes of thought and behavior, each individual journeying for reasons frivolous, ceremonial, vocational, or mystical.

Klom broke out his fanciest clothing for daily interaction with his fellows. Lingle too assumed his best outfits. Tugger remained passive in their cabin, requiring no food, just a little water, in the same metabolically enigmatic fashion that the original Tugger had manifested back on Asperna.

At first, Klom had been reluctant to get very far apart from the Book, for fear of exiting that sphere of protection which Truth's Abstract Smile had outlined. But Lingle did some research into similar phenomena—most notably among the communally bonded Crinoids of Glyphenhalle—and affirmed that such mutual dependence was not a function of proximity in four-dimensional space, but rather derived from sub-aetheric connections.

"So long as our psychic affinity bonds remain intact, we need not lie atop each other for safety. I trust my devotion to our cause protects me."

"And since I could never not love Tugger, even in his sad condition, we are all set!"

Reassured, Klom (with Lingle generally by his side, save when the little Vib attended to personal pleasures and religious duties), resolved to make the most of his expensive passage. All thoughts of what the future might bring were put aside—not actually a hard task for the stolid, close-horizoned and unanxious Klom. After dutifully blocking out several hours each day to continue his education, he exercised in the ship's gym and swam endless lengths in both the fresh- and salt-water pools, often sharing his lane with a school of sinuous cowled Ommastrephes. That is, until the family was banned from the pool when a juvenile accidently let loose a copious inky discharge.

After a life of paucity, Klom regarded the limitless cosmopolitan buffets as a personal challenge, and was willing to try anything billed as edible for humans—and some items deemed otherwise—at least once. He found many congenial table partners who expressed honest vicarious admiration for Klom's eating prowess. Many meals transitioned into boozy singalongs and table-top dancing—officially frowned on by the stewards, who were nonetheless placated by large tips.

One couple who sat apart from the common festivities intrigued Klom.

The male of the pair was human or human-adjacent and nearly as massive as Klom. Either congenitally or through some kind of infection, his entire bluish epidermis, including shaved skull, was tessellated with hard warts the size and shape of the small trapezoid biscuits Klom's mother had often baked, back at Lake Zawinul. The man's permanent expression was a belligerent scowl.

His partner, a woman, registered incontrovertibly as a chimera with human and animal components. Her white, not unattractive face was longish, with a broad flat nose and widely spaced dark eyes. Barefoot, she wore an unvarying black outfit of simple stretchy bandeau and loose trunks which revealed that her entire body was covered with a tight curly nap of cream-colored wool. Her countenance was an invariant mask of acceptance overlaid on sorrow. Or so Klom thought, having seen the identical look on many of his fellow salvage yard citizens.

After some discreet inquiries with the purser, Lingle made a report, recounting his findings in the privacy of their cabin, as Klom absentmindedly petted the unresponsive Tugger.

"The man is Ludes Kedgrigorn. He hails from Mabune, where he was until recently a foreclosure agent for a bio-camorra. Whenever a freelance member of the criminal organization became derelict in his payments for any type of augmentation, Kedgrigorn would track him down and reclaim the proprietary organ or prosthetic or enhancement. This quite often resulted in the very messy demise of the defaulter."

"What is he doing on the *Penhaligon*? Is he tracking down some runaway debtor for his false teeth?"

"Not at all. It appears that *Khun* Kedgrigorn has retired from his violent line of work. The boss of the bio-camorra was discovered recently lacking his head, and the organization's treasury had been emptied. *Khun* Kedgrigorn's surly disposition may be attributed to his entirely legitimate fears regarding pursuit and retribution. Having paid a huge amount to the security experts on the asylum world of Beschloss for a well-guarded estate, he must reach that refuge before he can breathe easy again."

"And what of the girl?"

"She is a simple off-the-shelf bondswoman named Olasia. She was one of his last purchases before leaving Mabune. There seems to be little involved in their relationship other than carnal satisfaction for Kedgrigorn."

Klom pondered this information. "He's a bad man, a criminal on the run. I don't like it. Especially him dragging that innocent girl along with him."

"Certain authorities might regard you in the same light. After all, you did kill a lordling and flee justice."

Klom jumped to his feet, anger evident in his knotted fists and rageful face. "Only in self-defense, after he had murdered three of my innocent friends!"

"Be calm! I know all that. I was just playing devil's advocate! The point I am trying to make is that we cannot set ourselves up as judge and jury in this case. Despite his crimes, Kedgrigorn has somehow obtained legal passage on this ship, and we are not representatives of any law-enforcement agency."

"Still, I will watch him closely for some chance to make things right."

"As you wish. But don't jeopardize our own mission."

The next day Klom began to shadow Kegrigorn in what he hoped was a non-obtrusive manner. The fellow generally emerged from his quarters close to eleven in the shiptime morning, just before the breakfast selections were to be cleared away. Shortly after a large meal he began drinking intoxicating beverages steadily, never to the point of debilitation though. He would occasionally play a card game called "pitch and ditch," wagering small sums with the assembled strangers and denying their attempts at conversation. For evening's entertainment he favored the lugubrious wailing of a cabaret singer from Audax, a batrachian being with enormous resonant throat pouch.

Most of the time Olasia was forced to accompany her owner. She did so meekly, but with a quiet dignity.

Kedgrigorn's liquor intake sent him on frequent trips to the lavatory, and at these times he left Olasia alone, waiting patiently in the public rooms for his return.

Klom took advantage of one such time to approach the chimera as she sat on a low stool placed next to Kedgrigorn's more comfortable lounge chair. Her posture expressed resignation and alertness for any orders.

"*Khun* Olasia."

She regarded Klom with her deep-pooled hyperteloric eyes. Her voice was soft, her articulation not precisely human. "You name me strangely. I am just Olasia. No title for my kind. How may I be of service?"

"Does he abuse you?"

"My owner? I must do whatever he wishes."

"But there are laws regarding the proper treatment of bondspeople. You are not private property, just rentals."

"I do not know about laws. I only know some behaviors are approved, and some behaviors are punished."

"This should not be. If you need help any time, just come to me."

"No one can help me."

"You are wrong." Klom looked toward the lavatories and saw Kedgrigorn emerging. "I must go. Just remember what I said."

Klom retreated across the room. Kedrigorn eyed him suspiciously, while Klom feigned a bumbling, smiling innocence. The outlaw from Mabune leaned in close to Olasia and began to question her with a low-voiced fierceness. Abruptly, he grabbed her by the arm, yanked her to her feet, and they departed the salon.

The next day Olasia appeared with the fur of one cheek barely conceal-ing a livid contusion flaring on the pink skin beneath. She looked away when she saw Klom.

Feeling awful, Klom did not know what he could do to make the girl's situation better, and feared to make it worse. For once, Lingle had no ad-vice.

For the next several days Klom maintained his interest at an unprovoc-ative distance from the pair. He had time to ponder his motives. Although nothing like the lamented Sorrel—fiery, headstrong, impestuous—Olasia conjured up similar feelings of protectiveness and affection in Klom's giant mute heart. He did not seek to source or analyze these emotions or manage them. Their simple existence provided enough justification. Klom trusted his inner guides.

But Klom's attitude of discreet watchfulness received a blow on the morning when Olasia was seen supporting a homeostatic cast on what proved to be a fractured arm. Once again, Lingle, through pumping the ship's medico assigned to their quadrant of the vast ship, learned the dirt.

"Kegrigorn's liquor consumption passed all normal bounds last night, rousing him to loud belligerence and complaints, and when Olasia tried to steer him back to their room, he lashed out at her."

Klom fumed. "This cannot stand."

"What do you propose?"

"I will batter him to a pulp!"

"And then what of our quest? Nothing will avail when you are clamped in the brig, awaiting official charges at our next port, perhaps with your true identity exposed."

Calming down, Klom said, "There must be some way to free Olasia."

"Of course, her indenture would revert to the Indrajal agency respon-sible for bondspeople if her owner died—an unlikely eventuality, for surely you don't intend to murder him."

"No, of course not!"

"Maybe you could convince the ruffian to sell her to you…"

"I'll try it!"

The next day Klom approached the ex-enforcer when the man seemed somewhat lulled by his first three drinks of the day. Olasia had, apparently, been left in their room. Anxious to attain his goal, Klom avoided all pleas-antries.

"*Khun* Kedgrigorn, I want to make a deal with you. Give me your bondmaid's lease, and I'll pay you three times what you paid. I've taken a fancy to her, that's all."

The big Mabunian studied Klom with a sober and calculating intensity tinged with ire and jealousy. "I've seen you carousing with all these swells.

You're as ugly as me, but that doesn't seem to matter. They're happy for your company. *Khun* Bravalo, the mingy juice-monger! But I'm not good enough for society. Too scary, hands too dirty, even though I'm worth more than most. You could bed any of those posh bints if you wanted. So why so interested in my little toy lamb?"

Klom could make no answer. Kegrigorn said, "Go away, and don't bother me again." He returned to his drink.

After hesitating a moment, fists bunched, Klom left.

But the affair was taken out of Klom's hands and settled the next evening, in what was perhaps an inevitable incident, given Kedgrigorn's surliness.

Klom and Lingle occupied a table in the Topaz Room with three or four spontaneous comrades. Dance music issued from a trio on stage, and servitors brisked through the room with drinks and delicious-smelling snacks. Across the salon brooded Kedgrigorn, alone save for a downcast Olasia seated by his knees on her stool. She rubbed her cast as if to solace the wound beneath. Klom bristled to see her sad discomfort.

Into the room swept a jubilant party of three Wolonines. The oversized fanged and tailed bipeds featured idiosyncratic dye jobs of their shaggy pelts, and an assortment of barbaric quasi-rhodium piercings on ears, nose and lips. Each was accompanied by a bondscreature whose main duty, it seemed, was to make sure the flagons of their masters never went dry, replenishing from leather bota bags.

One of the alien servants—they resembled Lingle if the Vib had been morphed with an awkward aquatic bird—spotted Olasia and called out a greeting in chimeric creole. Olasia perked up and actually smiled. The bouncy Wolonine servant hastened to her side.

Kedgrigorn's attention was roused from glowering over his drink. When the intruder got within range, Kedgrigorn kicked out savagely and sent the squealing bondscreature hurtling, amber liquid spraying from its bota.

The Wolonine trio came to an immediate halt. Alien countenances did not duplicate humans emotions, but their immense displeasure was nonetheless apparent. The musicians tapered off playing within seconds, and all the dancers paused as if frozen in place.

The three big bipeds moved to surround Kedgrigorn. He got hastily to his feet, realizing too late his mistake. Olasia skittered backwards on her stool.

One of the Wolonines spoke. "Deliver amends now, or prepare to fight."

Kedgrigorn manifested belligerence. "You make too much of the simple exercise of my superior rights as a free sapient. I simply kicked some trash out of my path."

"No words. Pay, grovel, or die!"

Kedgrigorn sized up the unarmed Wolonines. He seemed to reach for a fiche-reader hanging from his belt, as if to transfer funds. But then suddenly a sharpfinger leaped into his hand, and was flicked instantly alive. A thin whistling wind sounded, as air was sucked through the weapon into some distant vacuum. The cruel blade of the knife was spotted along its length with flickering mirror-shiny microscale matter-modem dots. As the blade plunged into its victim, portions of whatever it encountered would be in effect surgically removed by the on-off working of the dots, and then transported some hundreds of kilometers away. Not to any matching output modem, but rather via randomized white hole pathways—essentially into the interstellar vacuum, given the *Penhaligon*'s location. This must have been, Klom realized, the tool of the repossessor's former trade.

"Now we'll see who grovels! Or would you rather just run away!"

"Neither," growled one of the Wolonines. Fearless, the alien moved faster than Klom could apprehend, and Kedgrigorn was suddenly leaking seemingly non-fatal amounts of blood. The blue warty human looked in blank astonishment to see the sharpfinger handle protruding from his own chest. Then he collapsed to the sloppy floor, as his innards were siphoned into the void.

Screams, tumult, the crashing of overturned furniture. Lingle was nowhere to be seen, but Klom remained steadfast at his table.

When the ship's security officials eventually appeared on the run—not tardily, by any objective measure, but after a subjective eternity—Kedgrigorn was dead beyond recovery.

Klom approached the group standing around the body.

Displaying a document on his reader, one of the Wolonines said, "Diplomats, we. All relevant Indrajal courtesy and protections. Sufficient, yes?"

The head of the responders, a lanky Foambone, studied the credentials, then agreed. "Yes, fine, no legal charges. But you will have to pay for the cleanup."

"Understood."

The Wolonines left festively then, seeking to continue their celebrations in a less-messy salon. The head of the security team removed the weapon, remarkably clean, from the corpse and deactivated it. An overturned goblet trickled its contents drop by drop with surprising loudness amidst the stunned silence.

Klom spoke to the Foambone. "The bondswoman. What becomes of her?"

Her eyes wide but unfocused, Olasia sat quivering in the lee of an overturned table, her white wool dotted with some of her former master's blood.

"She will go into a suspensor-sac until we arrive at our next stop, where she will be turned over to the proper agency."

"Could I buy her lease now?"

The officer consulted with someone on the other end of his communicator. "Yes, of course, we have the power to register the transferal temporarily, until arrival."

Seemingly appearing from nowhere, Lingle now stood once more by Klom's side. "You'll excuse me, *Khun* Bravalo, but when that contretemps erupted, I felt my survival and hence my continued service would be best ensured by a swift removal to a more secure corner of the ship."

"I understand, Ling. Now, please give these folks our information so we can buy Olasia."

The transaction was concluded swiftly, and the security men helped Olasia to her feet and presented her to Klom.

"I suggest," said the Foambone, "that you bring her to the medico for a dose of calmative. We will transfer any of her luggage from *Khun* Kedrigorn's cabin to yours."

Klom gently took hold of Olasia's arm. "Come with me now, and all will be well."

The shocked chimera did not exhibit any hesitancy or eagerness, but seemed almost as will-less as the current avatar of Tugger. She allowed herself to be led away by Klom, Lingle following solicitously.

After the dispensary visit, they all returned to the cabin.

Tugger remained in his usual recumbent posture, a jowly boulder, forepaws folded beneath him, an empty shell kept going on autonomic functioning alone.

Lingle said, "Shall I have the stewards install a cot? Or do you intend for this creature to share your bed?"

Klom's face grew hot. "Her own cot, of course."

It took half an hour to get the expando-foam crib delivered and set up. Klom used that time to introduce Olasia to Tugger. Although the insensate Book of Forgetting made no overtures when Klom drew Olasia's lax hand repeatedly across his rump, the simple physical contact seemed to soothe her. By the time her bed was ready, she seemed much more composed and rational, although showing the effects of the calmative. After climbing into the crib and drawing the blankets up almost over her face, she granted Klom a look of cautious gratitude.

With lights dimmed, Klom stretched out on his own extra-large mattress. Blissful unconsciousness eluded him. He pondered the vast disjunction in his life that the past few weeks had brought. From a hovel on Asperna, with Sorrel, Airey and a sprightly Tugger, to this cabin hurtling at lightspeed through the galaxy, with a Vib, a chimera and a blank-souled twelvestrand. When the disparity of circumstances and the vector of destiny they limned became too much to contemplate, Klom finally surrendered to sleep.

When Klom awoke, Olasia's bed showed empty. (Lingle still emitted chirring snores.) Klom experienced a moment's alarm until she emerged from the bathroom, wearing her typical outfit. The specks of blood on her coat had been washed away, and her fawn-like eyes exhibited a lively curiosity. Klom took pleasure at evidence of her resilience.

"Master—"

"No, not Master. Sit. You probably don't know this, but before Kedgrigorn died, I tried to buy your contract from him. I resented the abuse he dumped on you. I've been stomped on all my life too. I thought I could make your life better. That's all. But he refused to sell you. Yet fate finally allowed me to have my way. So now you can consider yourself on vacation. And when your lease comes due again, we'll see what happens. My own future is too uncertain for me to promise more."

Olasia placed her small hand atop Klom's. "I want to be of service in any way I can. Tell me how. Say what I must do."

"Well, I'm on a mission. It involves Tugger." Klom provided a simplified history of himself and the Book of Forgetting. "If you want to come along and assist us—be an extra pair of eyes in strange places, provide some good cheer—then that would be all I ask."

"I don't understand everything. But your mission sounds honorable and important. I will do all I can to help."

Her hand warm on his, Klom gazed into Olasia's depthless eyes for what seemed a long time—until Lingle spoke.

"One prerequisite for any success in this mad quest is actually to leave the room and get some nourishment. Unless you believe you can subsist on moonbeam gazes alone."

* * * *

Kedgrigorn's body was offloaded at the very next port, far from the asylum world of Beschloss where his elite freehold offering security and protection would go untenanted—unless he had some heir who could lay claim to his dangerous legacy of stolen riches. As Klom watched the suspensor-sac concealing Kedrigorn's corpse be floated offship, he reflected on the unknowable nature of any man's future. Could the Mabunian have predicted this ignominious burial far from home? Likewise, could Klom foresee what lay around the corner of his own path? He hoped to resurrect Tugger, but then what? Would Truth's Abstract Smile and his terabase peers simply allow Klom and Tugger to live on some backwater world in peace? Not very likely. How could Klom possibly wrest control of his own destiny away from such a powerful figure? The problem seemed insoluble, and so Klom just let it go.

Four days later, the *Penhaligon* arrived at Alnair Grus 7. The ship would be leaving immediately after unloading selected passengers, and Klom and his party would continue onward later aboard the equally amenable *Varanaryan*, which had yet to arrive at Alnair Grus 7. That is, assuming they could accomplish what they needed to do first.

Alnair Grus 7 was a gas dwarf, a type of planet that resided midway between the rocky habitable worlds and gas giants without any solid cores. Its gravity rated one-point-five times the most comfortable human norm, and so any visitor who desired help with this unaccustomed burden was equipped with a personal belt-mounted floater unit with variable offset controls. Klom opted out, making the same decision for Tugger, while Lingle and Olasia gratefully accepted the aid.

The planet boasted only a single domed city, Maybloom, known far and wide across the Indrajal as a honeymoon destination. The turbulent polychromatic atmosphere of the planet, wracked by the most dramatic lightning-riven storms, afforded a constant romantic background of high emotional drama, while the hostile environment conduced otherwise towards indoor pleasures between or among partners. But Maybloom also possessed many fine restaurants, casinos and other sophisticated amusements.

On the surface the shuttlecraft bearing Klom and his friends mated with a tunnel airlock at some distance from the dome, and soon they were walking with their fellow disembarkers in gawping astonishment, separated from the swirling electric crayola skies by only a transparent tunnel roof.

Once inside the dome proper, Lingle found them a relatively inexpensive hotel within walking distance. At the reception desk, the human-adjacent clerk, a Heruka female with enormous fangs and painted claws, inquired of Klom.

"*Khun* Bravalo, we have a lovely assortment of suites ready for your enjoyment. I only need to know the type of sleeping arrangements desired."

"What do you mean?"

The veteran clerk remained nonchalant. "Would you like a bed for four? A triplet and a single? Two doubles? Or some other setup I have regretably failed to consider?"

Flustered, Klom replied, "Three singles, please. Tugger doesn't need one."

The clerk's bushy magenta eyebrow twitched almost imperceptibly. "But of course."

Up in their room, Olasia said, "I don't need my own bed either, you know. Especially if it costs extra. I can sleep on the floor next to Tugger. Or share with Lingle. He's only as big as the fuzzy Artificial Mama we used to snuggle with in the creche."

Klom laughed, and now it was the Vib's turn to be embarrassed. "Nonsense! I have restless leg syndrome and kick all night like an irate pack animal. Sleep in Klom's bed if you want to save us a few taka. I have observed that he passes the whole nocturnal period as motionless as mountain."

Olasia smiled. "That might not be the case if I slept with him."

Klom experienced an unsettling mix of emotions. "Enough of this crazy talk!" he ordered. "We need to find the marabout that Presbyter Przl named for us."

After a few necessary ablutions, the trio left the hotel room. Klom had decided not to being Tugger until they had encountered the marabout and confirmed his willingness to perform the necessary rituals to reunite the *ba* portion of Tugger's numinous body with his shell.

The temple occupied a tiny storefront wedged between a stochastic pachinko parlor and a strandcrafter specializing in "physio-harmonization for lovers." Klom and his companions entered, and discovered the place's generic resemblance to the temple on Stratcom and the millions of other dotted across the Indrajal.

Out from the private part of the building slithered a serpent-like being large enough to swallow Lingle and perhaps even Olasia at a single gulp: a member of the Sheshan race. Rearing half-ceilingward, the acolyte exhibited a flaring yellow-ribbed skin hood that folded open and shut behind its head. Without adornments, the creature was fitted with a set of prosthetic manipulators clamped around its upper body to compensate for its congenital lack of limbs.

The Sheshan's voice lacked the anticipated sibilance, and instead resembled the sound of a stick rasping across a gnurled nut. "I am Mufti Hodak. What twist of karma deposits you here today?"

Klom named Presbyter Przl and specified their mission. Hodak showed instant recognition.

"I have been anticipating your arrival. This is a most interesting phenomenon. I have been parsing the devic outfall leakage ever since I was informed of my task. Many puzzling qualia torrent upward from the implicate order. I believe that the devas of the higher dimensions deliberately sequestered the three parts of your mundane deva's soul. For what purpose I cannot say."

"Do you think they will hinder his reunion?"

"We will find out soon enough. Quickly now! Bring your friend here!"

Leaving his companions in the temple, Klom hurried to retrieve Tugger. Herding the Book of Forgetting through the crowded avenues full of unsuspecting romancers, he wondered what alterations might manifest in his friend's blank attitude if the procedure should succeed.

Mufti Hodak had arrayed all his necessary implements and a cageful of downy twitterlings as sacrifice. He reared up higher in excitement when Tugger arrived.

"Yes, yes, manifestly an empty vessel, totally bereft! We will reinsert the *ba* first, since that is the portion allocated psychically to this planetary nexus. My compeers on Oksanax and Voyle will deal with the *ka* and *ib*."

As strong fumes began to fill the temple and ineffable chants rang out, Klom, Lingle and Olasia hung back at a safe distance from Tugger and the Mufti.

Tugger stood stolidly amidst coruscations and invocations both. At last the ceremony was completed. Hodak slumped the lax upper portion of his body across a low cabinet as if utterly drained from his exertions.

"The attachment is complete. My part in this enigma is fulfilled. Go now."

Klom advanced toward Tugger—and Tugger, though still expressionless, stepped forward of his own initiative! Klom flung himself around the neck of his massive friend, expecting the old familiar slobbering kisses. None came, and Klom's heart crashed. He peered intently into the wrinkled face. Was there a slight gleam of rekindled spirit in Tugger's eyes? Any hint of recognition? Perhaps. But not yet enough.

Outside the temple, the foursome ambled toward the hotel. Tugger's newly restored facilities seemed to incline him to follow without being chivvied. The broad thronged avenue they followed featured an unbroken line of buildings on their left, but only the naked, gently curving shell of the city dome on their right, affording a spectacular vista of deadly cold and unbreathable gases.

"We have a day before we leave on the *Varanaryan*," said Klom, looking to his servant. "What can we do?"

Lingle began to answer, but stopped in mid-sentence. Klom took his eyes away from the Vib to see why.

Motionless in the air, swarmed by scintillant majestatics, Truth's Abstract Smile plainly awaited their arrival. The merciless lacertilian face of the multistrand lordling boded no good fortune.

The Gorgoid said, "You have embarked on a very unwise course. Already your attempted resurrection of the Book of Forgetting stirs currents across the whole Indrajal. And you imagine you are safe, simply because my actions cannot impinge on you directly. But that prohibition may be finessed, I have come to believe. Nothing stops me from altering your environment in some very dangerous ways. Please regard my actions now as a kindly warning not to proceed to your next destination. Merely depart this world without the Book, and all strife between us will be at an end."

Before Klom could reply, a portion of the majestatic shoal peeled off and attached themselves to the dome near the base.

Then they instantly disassembled a hole about a meter across in the protective wall.

The atmospheric pressure outside was vastly greater than that inside, so a raging river of methane and helium rushed in.

Above the atmospheric roaring came screams, scuffling, swearing, shouts.

Klom staggered against the invisible frigid assault of atmosphere, but did not fall. He saw Lingle lifted off his feet. But the Vib reacted swiftly and threw his arms around Tugger's foreleg, and held tight to that immovable bastion.

Olasia, however, was not so fortunate. The gale lifted her up, and with a wail she smashed into the high branches of an ornamental tree in its large pot. The foliage thrashed in the wind, the pot teetered, and her grip seemed destined to break. Loosened, she would slam hard against a building.

Klom ripped the floater belt off Lingle's waist and punched its simple controls. Instantly he was half his weight. He let the wind take him and he sailed also into the tree, bruising hard against its trunk. Clambering upward, he reached Olasia and snapped the buckle of her belt. Her floater mechanism dropped away, and he discarded his too. Subject to the planet's full gravity, she and he could better resist the noxious, choking gale. Klom gripped her tightly and prepared to leap down off the tree—then jumped.

Before he hit pavement, the alien wind ceased.

City repair mechanisms had clustered at the break, and applied at least a temporary seal.

Klom tried to set Olasia upon her own two feet, but she refused to loosen the grip of her arms around his neck, the clutch of her legs around his waist. Klom let her shiver out her fears. Her former master murdered before her eyes, and now the incomprehensible affairs of her current "protector" exposing her to mortal attack. It would be enough to unnerve even the most stalwart soul.

At last Olasia unclenched and climbed down. Lingle limped over, registering both his increased weight and the effects of being pummelled by the gale. Imperturbable Tugger simply awaited direction.

Truth's Abstract Smile was nowhere to be seen. Not utterly above the law, perhaps even that sovereign potentate worried about being confronted by the authorities of Maybloom and charged with terrorism.

Lingle sat down cautiously on the sidewalk. "*Khun* Bravalo, it's your decision on how to proceed."

Klom regarded the unruffled Tugger, still two-thirds unrestored. He sized up Olasia and Lingle. Both returned his inspection with frank looks of confidence and faith.

"The demands of that dirty tera-bastard mean nothing!" said Klom. "We abandon no one. Onward to Oksanax!"

* * * *

The next week's passage aboard the *Varanaryan* afforded everyone much-needed rest and recuperation—although overlain with some anxiety about how Truth's Abstract Smile would next possibly attack them. Klom did not anticipate trouble aboard the starliner, for interstellar travel was too finicky a process to permit anything but fatal interference: no simple hijacking or detours possible. What point to sabotage their wavepacket ship if it meant that the irreplaceable Tugger ended up not in the lordling's grasp, but scattered as a cloud of particles across the unforgiving supraluminal medium?

But all activity onboard was not mindless abandonment. Lingle insisted on continuing Klom's general studies, and Olasia sat in. Her caste-enforced ignorance of the Indrajal and its ways ran even deeper than Klom's, and he experienced for the first time in his life a sense of being possessed of greater sophistication than one of his companions. His days spent in complacent ignorance on Asperna seemed infinitely far away, a source of mild chagrin and bemusement. At the same time, he realized how much he continued not to comprehend. But at least he was moving in the right direction.

The chimera gradually became more at ease as one of their small posse, and unburdened herself of some of the insults to body and spirit that she had received at the hand of her old master. She spoke not vindictively, however, but matter-of-factly, and once she had shared an anecdote she never dwelled on it. Talk seemed to release any sorrow. When her cast came off her arm, she brightened even further. She was more apt to speak of her happy times as a child in the creche. "We would tumble all over each other like a pack of Rafter pups, competing for extra snacks. Look, like this!"

Olasia would then demonstrate her slithery wrestling moves on the uncooperative Tugger and then, finding his lack of response unsatisfying, turn to Klom, who provided some competitive resistance, though always calibrating his strength against her slim form. The matches usually ended in sweaty, laughing collapse. Lingle held aloof, disdaining the exertions as unseemly, although Klom thought to detect a covert desire to participate.

Often these matches left Klom with a smoldering desire to possess Olasia as a woman, taking her carefreely as he and Sorrel had once tumbled into each other's embrace. But he suppressed these urges and refrained.

By the time the ship arrived at Oksanax, Klom felt reinvigorated and ready for whatever their opponent might throw at them—assuming he had trailed them here or even anticipated their arrival, based perhaps on hacked intelligence of their triptix or even interrogation of Presbyter Przl. Maybe Tugger would exhibit some of his old formidability too, assuming the insertion of his *ka* could be achieved.

As they waited to offload from the *Varanaryan*—the *Maevelut's Pride* would carry them to Voyle three days from now—Lingle lectured on the nature of the new planet.

"Oksanax is a gaseous jovian world, and hence does not offer anything like a surface where one might set foot. Instead, a few floating city-resorts range throughout her upper atmosphere. They exist mainly to cater to the gem-hunting tourists. The atmospheric chemistry of this world promotes a steady rain of rubies and sapphires. Just as on some worlds you may with permission prospect for gold in a national park, so too here the visitor is allowed to bag his share of aerial gemstones. The process is a thrilling one. After a short virtual training session, an individual is dropped into a one-person sky sled equipped with exterior mechanical scoops. Slicing through the clouds, one spots a falling gem and then must maneuver one's craft to bag it. These approved methods are kept deliberately awkward and demanding, requiring some skill, so as not to result in industrial-level depletion of the gems. Occasionally a tourist will strike it rich by capturing an immense specimen. Occasionally, diving too deep into the atmosphere, a tourist will perish. But most just end up with thrills and a few tiny gems to show off back home."

"Oh," said Olasia, "I'd love to try it!"

"We'll see," said Klom. "Our first priority is to get Tugger's *ka* installed."

Crowded with others at the shuttle's broad panoramic window, Klom and his friends marvelled at the approach to the floating city-resort dubbed Dashaway. A huge transparent sphere with a thick interior plate at its equator, the habitat furnished antithetical gravities in each hemisphere, so that the central plate served as a floor for both sides. Half the buildings and people seemed unconcernedly upside-down to the tourists on the arriving shuttle. Although of course, once through the airlocks, the visitor would experience a natural rightside-up orientation appropriate to that hemisphere.

Again Lingle found them satisfactory quarters, where they dropped their luggage and refreshed themselves. Feeling the pressure of time and possible intervention by Truth's Abstract Smile, Klom hastened them out in search of the temple that was expecting them. At the urgings of Lingle and Olasia, he permitted a stop for a meal, albeit just a bowl of greyfriar noodles and mantis meat. Tugger, who had never eaten much back on Asperna, still showed no appetite, a feature of his twelvestrand physiology.

The modest holy building sported a decorative striped onion dome atop a blocky base. A warbling threnody issued from speakers mounted above the door.

Inside the single room, harshly and colorfully illuminated as if to mimic an alien sun, they found Saltigue Mirzo. The officiant of the temple was a Threeple: a cask-like body, unclothed and unornamented, surmounted by a hemispherical head that could rotate almost three-hundred-and-sixty degrees before resuming its default orientation. Scattered sensory elements were merely darker spots on the viridian skin. The adept's mouth resembled the intake slot on a certain model of macerator Klom had used back on Asperna to break up ceramic insulators. A pair of legs and a pair of arms could be retracted inside the Threeple's torso when not needed.

Upon the arrival of Klom and party, Saltigue Mirzo extruded his lower limbs and strode toward the visitors. Klom introduced everyone and reminded Mirzo of their mission.

The Saltigue took down some type of metaphysical probe from a shelf and examined Tugger. The hologram readout flashed arcane symbols. "Yes, yes, just as I imagined. All the theoretical parameters obtain. The *ka* can be reslotted nicely." Mirzo began fussing then with a variety of other gadgets, affixing wires to Tugger by means of clips that pinched Tugger's perdurable hide. Swiped on, the enlivened devices offered enough status lights to resemble a squad of fireflies. At last the Saltigue seemed ready to proceed.

Klom asked, "But where is the incense, the sacrifices?"

"Pah!" Mirzo replied. "The accoutrements of a superstitious past. This a branch of the Reform movement, and we do things the modern way here. Nonetheless, no layperson could channel the forces soon to be invoked. That numinous guidance requires decades of practice. Now, are you ready? Good, here we go!"

Mirzo tapped a control slate and a faint blue nimbus surrounded Tugger. The aura became host to a tangle of writhing golden threads. More and more rainbow worms invaded the space, weaving hypnotic patterns. Klom felt lost in a timeless zone. Then, with a simple pass, the array of machines was deactivated.

"Success," said Mirzo.

Klom studied Tugger intently, awaiting some new behavior that would indicate a greater autonomy and individuality.

Tugger slowly raised a forepaw into his line of vision, studied it as if it were a foreign object belonging to someone else. Then, for the first time since his rebirth, the Book of Forgetting opened his jaws in a grin and let his tongue loll out.

Klom regarded this practically infantile behavior as a minor miracle. He stroked Tugger's slab-like brow and the beast closed his mouth. Tugger's gaze, although not wholly ensouled, seemed to offer some additional facets of alertness and vivacity. Klom was pleased.

After transferring a large donation to the temple's accounts, Klom returned with his friends to the hotel.

"I intend us to hunker down here till departure time. It won't be fun, but it should be safe."

Olasia, still n her bandeau and shorts, said, "Do you think I might have some new clothes? This is my only outfit. I feel out of place in these fne quarters."

Klom felt sad and guilty that he had not considered Olasia's condition before now. New garments could have been purchased on the *Varanaryan*. "Of course. Lingle will go out with you to shop. He will know what clothes are proper."

The little Vib pretended to be put-upon, but Klom sensed some pride at his accreditation as a fashion expert.

The rest of that day and the next passed without incident. Meals and card games, naps and streamed entertainments filled the hours. From time to time Tugger would gnaw at an improbable itch, and that struck Klom as a marvelous sign.

With twenty-some hours left before departure, and no attack from Truth's Abstract Smile, Klom began to relax. Sensing this, Olasia asked, "Might we try to win some gems from the skies? It would be a little bit of real fun. We'll probably never pass this way again."

Klom considered, then asked Lingle, "What do you think?"

"It seems safe enough. Especially if I stay here with Tugger."

"All right then, let's go!"

They chose at random one of the hangers that housed the sky sled rentals that dotted the periphery of Dashaway, neither the closest nor the most distant. Klom hoped to foil anyone staking out such a place in anticipation of their arrival. Such a maneuver seemed paranoid, but they had a real enemy.

The amusement-park atmosphere of the place conjured up a gaiety that Klom had not felt in ages, if ever. Tourists of all ages prepared excitedly for their brief jaunts through the gemstone rain of Oksanax. Olasia's excitement and joy were contagious. The training session included engrammatic and proprioceptive reinforcements, and Klom felt confident at his ability to handle the simple sky sked, which in truth had a number of safety protocols embedded in it to stop amateurs from actively killing themselves. The actual controls reminded him of several semi-complex tools he had operated at the salvage yard. Olasia expressed a similar faith in her training. And communications between their sleds would be constant.

Belly down on the cushions of the coffin-sized interiors, the transparent canopies secured above them, Klom and Olasia were launched out into the planet's ruby-seeded clouds.

The propulsion units of the sky sleds were quick and powerful, the maneuvering vanes intuitive and responsive, and the grappler an arcade-worthy challenge. At the end of a long flexible piezo-muscled hollow arm was a cup with which to scoop up a falling gem. The prize was then impelled down the hollow tube into a catch-basin that could be unloaded back in the hanger.

Upon launching, Olasia immediately gunned her craft ahead of Klom's, cutting through the pastel fogs and whorls of Oksanax's upper atmosphere. The windshield of each craft featured a sizable display pane that gave an augmented reality image simulating from sensor information what might have been seen if the occluding gasses had not been present, and so Klom could keep an eye on Olasia's sled despite the reality of fluctuatingly opaque conditions.

Olasia shrieked. "I've got a stone! It's big as my pinky, I swear it!"

Klom shared Olasia's excitement and happiness. He was not even bothering to attempt to capture any drifting gems, content merely to abet Olasia's fun. "Wonderful! You can make a necklace out of them if you just get a few more."

By now they were a few kilometers away from the city sphere, with no other sleds nearby.

And thus Truth's Abstract Smile staged his appearance for them alone.

The large Gorgoid floated in the midst of the churning poisonous clouds protected by a force corona generated by his majestatics. Presumably, he could have contacted Klom through the sled's system, had he wished to bluster or threaten, but he did not deign to do so.

Instead, he simply dispatched a portion of his swarm to shear off the vanes on Olasia's sled and kill her engines.

Down her craft began to plummet.

Her piercing shrieks this time were not of joy.

Instantly Klom kicked his sled into maximum acceleration. He caught up to Olasia's craft within seconds and kept parallel with it, as close as he dared on her doomed course.

"Olasia! Stop blubbering! Do what I say! Link your grapple with mine!"

Olasia's cries ceased. Reaching out tentatively, her sinuous arm intertwined with the arm on Klom's sled, like two straws bending around each other, as Klom directed his own grapple likewise. Finally the two sleds seemed stoutly linked.

Klom attempted first to slowly halt their fall, and then to ascend, praying all the time the arms would not rupture or unlock.

Success!

They limped back to Dashaway.

Back in the hanger, Klom ignored the wild questions from the technicians and manager, just holding Olasia close. She reeked of a terror sweat that roused Klom's protectiveness and his ardor for her. But of a sudden, he started and released the chimera.

"Tugger!"

The race through the city streets seemed to take forever. But at last the hotel came into view.

Beyond a shattered door, Lingle lay unconscious with a burgeoning broad contusion on his forehead, the stippled stamp of a majestic attack that had happily stopped short of lethality.

Of the Book of Forgetting there was no sign.

* * * *

Maevelut's Pride entered Voyle's orbital plane and then began to chase the planet at a speedy clip totally consistent with all approved planetary approaches for wavepacket vessels of its size. And yet to Klom the ship seemed to be dawdling, limping along at a glacial pace solely to drive him insane with worry and fear.

Would he ever catch up to Tugger, and what would happen if he did?

His imagination (once or twice over the most recent few days, he had time to ironically consider that back on Asperna he would have said he never possessed such a thing) conjured up a hundred bad scenarios. But Klom was resolved to do his best to avoid them all.

After discovering the unconscious Lingle, Olasia and Klom had rushed him to a hospital where he was quickly diagnosed, treated and pronounced safe from any bad outcomes by a Clacker physician whose deft minuscule and majuscule claws manipulated all his instruments with a musician's grace. Leaving the Vib there still uncommunicative, Klom managed to discover through numerous inquiries the physical offices of the Dashaway agency responsible for monitoring intersystem traffic to and from the city. A bored official—a colony creature known as a Volvox, seemingly just an undifferentiated mass of viridian zooids housed in a mechanical drone body featuring a clear tank full of nourishing liquid—supplied the news Klom had feared.

The Volvox's voice issued from the drone's speaker. "Yes, a craft registered to Truth's Abstract Smile arrived and departed today, all in the space of a few hours. No destination registered."

Klom and Olasia trudged back to the hospital, and found Lingle awake.

The first words from the Vib were, "*Khun* Bravalo, I truly tried to stop that arrogant monster. Honestly, I gave my all. But he and his damn bugs were just too much for me."

"What happened, Ling? Tell me everything."

Lingle massaged the bandage on his brow thoughtfully, as if reliving the assault. "Some time after you and Olasia left, that lizard lordling simply burst into our room. He ignored me and addressed Tugger. 'Arise, World-shifter, and follow me.' And so Tugger did! That was when I hurled myself at the villain, and got myself swatted. I don't recall anything after that, till I awoke here."

Klom's puzzlement found words. "But back on Stratcom, Smile himself said he couldn't harm us, thanks to Tugger's protection. How did he manage to hurt you, and strike at Olasia? How did he get Tugger to leave with him?"

"Well," Lingle said slowly, "that promise of protection—words from the mouth of Smile himself, remember, and maybe he was lying for some reason—was extended to us before Tugger got two-thirds of his soul back. Maybe that made a difference. Was the sphere of protection broken by Tugger's new mental confusion? Who can say? But what do you mean about striking at Olasia?"

Klom explained what had happened on the sky sleds.

"It seems, *Khun* Bravalo, that Smile wanted you busy while he stole Tugger. Perhaps if you had been here, things might have gone otherwise. After all, the strongest bond is between you and the Book. Myself and the chimera—maybe we are just on the periphery of the magic."

"No, I can't believe that…"

Silent until now, Olasia spoke. "Maybe nothing has really changed. Maybe the magic is still working."

"What do you mean?"

"Maybe Tugger knew that by going with Smile, good things would happen, for him and us."

Klom mulled over that startling theory. "I don't see how that could be true. But I will hold onto it as a hope."

Sitting up more alertly, Lingle said, "It seems to me that Smile must have only one destination: the planet Voyle, where the third *terma* is to be unconvered and fused into Tugger's soul gestalt. I suggest we follow him. His ship has departed already. Ours leaves in just a few hours. He cannot increase his lead time on us, since wavepacket travel is invariant."

"What do you mean?"

"There are no faster or slower ships. The interstellar gradients allow only one velocity."

"I never knew that."

"You should have served aboard Retta Galaxyliners as I did for decades! The tediously familiar schedules would have drilled home that fact of basic physics! But in any case, we can arrive at Voyle shortly after Truth's Abstract Smile, right on his heels, and perhaps stymie him somehow, and get our friend back."

"But are you up to travel?"

Lingle swung his legs over the side of the bed. "Of course!" But then he winced and wavered. "At least I should be ready when the hour of departure arrives. Get that doctor back in here!"

Klom found the Clacker and explained. The physician updated his diagnostics, set Lingle up with some additional drugs via microneedle perfusive, and told Klom he would release his patient in an hour if he responded well.

Klom said, "Just enough time for us to clear out the hotel room. We'll be right back!"

The management at the hotel had already repaired the door to their room. Klom found all their gear intact and began assembling it for travel.

Olasia helped with a kind of abstracted solemnity unlike her usual post-Kedgrigorn vivacity. Klom noticed her mood at last and said, "What's wrong? Are you still shaken by what happened outside?"

"No. It's only that I feel I will be a burden to you, and endanger you when you arrive at Voyle. I realize now that I am trouble and a hinderance, vulnerable to the bad actions of that evil terabase because I am only a piece of property. I don't qualify for Tugger's protection because I am not really part of this—well, this family. The family of you and Ling and the Book of Forgetting. After all, as you have said, when my lease is up, then off I go, back to my agency and a new owner."

Klom grabbed Olasia by the shoulders. She averted her face, but with his pincering thumb and forefinger gentle on her chin, he brought her gaze back to his. "No, that's not true! I only mentioned your lease originally, way back on the *Penhaligon,* because I wanted you to know you had legal rights. That I would never do anything bad to you, like Kedgrigorn did. But over these weeks—Olasia, you've become so much more to me!"

"How much, Klom?"

"This much."

Klom's passionate kiss was returned in kind. When its long duration ended of mutual accord, Klom picked up Olasia's soft slight form and brought her to his bed, where they quickly shed all clothing. Klom explored her sleek furred lines, and she in turn traced his hard and scarred dimensions. He was glad he no longer wore the ugly, offputting marks of cruft from his old job.

When she swung herself eagerly atop his primed supine bulk, Klom encompassed both her breasts with one hand and used the other the cup her rear as she straddled him.

They rocketed to a bouncing climax. At the peak, Klom's mind was flung back weeks ago, to his last intercourse with poor Sorrel. How distant that era seemed! And how different this deep bond with the chimera loomed in his life, compared to the retrospectively rather shallow and superficial affair with Sorrel. Klom could not deny that he and Sorrel had solaced each other in the dire circumstances of Shipyard life; but, he saw now, it had been very much a kind of businesslike arrangement born of daily desperation.

Olasia collapsed upon Klom's chest. She whispered, "Now I truly belong to you."

"We are all together now."

Back at the hospital, Klom found Lingle waiting impatiently at the discharge station. Trained by years of stewardship to intepret the most subtle personal cues of his clients, the canny factotum instantly apprehended the changed nature of the relationship between Klom and Olasia.

"*Khun* Bravalo, I am gratified to see that you have formalized the implicit bonds between you and Olasia which only a blind and deaf man could have ignored for so long. But now, we must put aside all such carnal and emotional ceremonies and hurry to our ship!"

The subsequent days aboard *Maevelut's Pride* had consisted of a mix of angst, erotic pleasures (when Lingle very circumspectly found reasons to visit one of the ship's salons for a few hours), and planning. And now all those threads were culminating with the sight of Voyle.

Voyle was a planet boasting nearly half a billion square kilometers of varied land mass, exclusive of its gargantuan seas: over three times the habitable area of Asperna and similar worlds. And yet due to its arcane geological composition, its gravity was only slightly higher than what humans found ideal. Such an expansive territory, Lingle conveyed, fostered a comparable wealth of divergent cultures and polities, a vibrant patchwork of societies and citizens across the big planet.

The planned point of disembarkation for *Maevelut's Pride* was the Royal Sharaine starquay outside the city of Arboleda. Unfortunately, Dustar Nitch, the marabout destined to download Tugger's *ib* from the implicate order, resided in the small town of Onfroy, in the country of Navarro, almost ten thousand kilometers distant.

"How can we get there, Ling? Quickly!"

"We can take a swift plane to the borders of Navarro, three-quarters of our journey. But after that we must travel by animal-drawn carriage."

"By all the devas, why such a primitive thing?"

"Navarro is a Supressor Enclave under the aegis of a tutelary deva. Technology above a certain level is proscribed by the deva's localized manipulation of quantum events."

Klom thought a minute. "Then Truth's Abstract Smile could not have flown directly there?"

"No. He too would have to leave his starship behind at the borders of Navarro."

"So we still stand a chance of being right on his tail."

"Yes."

"Let's hurry then!"

Since his unanticipated departure from Asperna, Klom had travelled by the tidy, secure and almost boring wavepacket vessels across many lightyears, all without much excitement or consideration for the distances involved. So he did not at first imagine that a short jaunt by aircraft—a modest fifty-passenger Red Outlaw floater with the clan sigils of its owner decorating its hull--would stand out as a highlight of his journey. But to his surprise, Klom discovered that the relatively antique and small-scale enterprise of air travel aroused much more anticipation and elation than crossing from star to star. The takeoff, the dwindling of structures and people and landmarks to a tiny map, the passage through clouds—everything conduced to an almost mystical thrill. Seated beside Olasia, he clutched her hand tightly throughout the flight, calming her first-trip fears with his own virginal delight.

The transit across seventy-five hundred kilometers of Voyle occupied nearly eight hours, and offered a constantly changing variety of sights and sensations. Midway through the flight, hot meals of barbecued meat—huge cuts still sizzling on the bone—and tankards of frosty ale were matter-modemed onboard: standard Red Outlaw fare, apparently. Klom devoured his repast, but the more herbivorously inclined Lingle and Olasia had to request substitutions, ending up with cold beet soup.

The craft put down at the border town of Hottle. Led by Lingle, the trio immediately sought out conveyance to Onfroy. The wagonmaster at the bustling depot—a Warthog sporting gaily beribboned tusks—informed them that luck was in their camp: they could depart in just a few hours. They used the time to freshen up at a public spa, knowing that the two-day trip across the remaining twenty-five-hundred kilometers would not allow such niceties.

At last it came time to board the capacious, comfortably outfitted wagon (adjustable seating for all manner of rumps!), in the company of the six or seven other passengers. (Doubt remained as to the exact number of riders, since one traveler consisted of a symbiotic pairing of large host and tiny attached auxiliary being.) Their luggage was loaded, and Lingle and Olasia stepped onboard. But Klom remained outside a moment longer to admire the brace of steeds that would haul them across the mossy plains of Navarro. Two enormous mold-grey millipedes on either side of a central shaft, each one longer than the coach itself, secured with harnesses and reins. Their antennae questing, they dispersed a scent that reminded Klom of the commercial composting units used in the salvage yard refectories on Asperna.

With a shouted command from the driver on his outside perch, the wagon took off with skittering speed.

The ambiance in the coach was relaxed and friendly, but conversation among the disparate strangers, even when possible, soon petered out, as each party focused on its own idiosyncratic concerns. Lingle had laid in plentiful supplies of food in a hamper packed with dry ice, so the journey was reduced to snacking and drowsing and worrying, along with some speculation.

"Truth's Abstract Smile will be deprived of his majestatics in a Suppressor Enclave," Lingle observed. "That should make our encounter a little more balanced."

"Yes, but there must still be weapons that function here. Old-fashioned things."

"You are right, *Khun* Bravalo. I had not thought of that."

"I wish we had gotten some guns for ourselves before we left."

"Too late now. And better not to risk running afoul of any authorities in Onfroy. We must appear the aggrieved party, which we are, not the aggressors. And surely when you get close to Tugger, he will respond to you and come back to your side without a fight."

"I hope so."

Their smooth passage across leagues of pastel sphagnum conduced towards a kind of timeless drowsiness, and the three comrades all dozed. Hours later, awaking, Klom found Lingle peering abstractedly out of the window, and asked, "Ling, why do the devas ignore our mortal world? As I understand things, each deva started out as a creature of flesh and blood before they made the phase-change jump to other dimensions. Couldn't they look down and help us once in a while? Why is Tugger the only twelvestrand who stays behind?"

Lingle gnawed at a paw nail. "Vast philosophical questions, *Khun* Bravalo, for which I have no answers. Occasionally the devas do intervene. This Supressor Enclave itself is an example of such. And of course they appear when invoked by the marabouts, for ceremonial occasions. But mostly they seem content to let us poor mundane creatures struggle on our own."

"It just doesn't seem right. If I ran the universe, I'd do things different."

"So say we all."

The first night's sunset made a riot of color in the sky, and Olasia snuggled romantically into Klom's embrace to enjoy it. The dusk song of burrow-hens brought an accompanying plangent chorus. As night dropped with its suddenly chilly temperatures, her snuggling assumed a more practical purpose: staying warm in the unheated cabin. Klom thought back to his own days in the rude, merciless, harrowing salvage yards, deprived of all the modern comforts he had now come to take for granted as he moved across the Indrajal. How had he managed to experience so many happy moments nonetheless, as he labored mightily with his crewmates to break apart the starliners, and, afterwards, as he reveled in the thoughtlessly carefree company of Sorrel, Airey and other friends? Would he ever know such innocent times again? Or had his expanded horizons doomed him to a future of discontent?

Dawn brought an equally colorful celestial display. Lingle portioned out deviled eggs, slices of pressed meat flecked with olive slices, and a tart green juice served in one collapsible cup that the three had to share in turn. Across the wide cabin, the family of Lammergeiers—two parents and a child—split the seal on a box of carrion so noisome that every other passenger felt compelled to hang out of the windows until the meal was finished.

The unvarying smooth pace of the millipedes and the monotonous scenery of the plains—no settlements or stands of vegetation in sight—made for a day of frustrating boredom. Klom marveled at the way this powerful bland emotion managed to outweigh even his anxiety over Tugger's fate.

But just at dusk came an exciting change.

The coach tilted forward slightly as it began to descend a long gentle slope. After craning his head out one of the windows, Lingle explained: "We are dropping down into the ancient asteroid impact crater where Onfroy is situated. We should be there soon."

Indeed, as darkness descended Klom saw the lights of Onfroy spring alive, gas-burning fixtures on streetpoles and attached to the eccentric facades of the hundreds of low buildings that comprised the town.

When the coach finally halted outside the company depot, the cessation of motion seemed alien. Klom emerged on stiff legs that had almost forgotten how to bend. His smaller companions, more able to exercise a variety of postures in the cab, seemed less rusty.

They left their luggage at the depot, got directions to the temple of Dustar Nitch, and hurried down several blocks.

The temple was dark and silent and locked tight.

Klom grabbed a passing citizen. The town of Onfroy seemed to be inhabited predominantly by a human-adjacent type of being with copper-colored skin, whose average representatives sported a keg-like torso and extremely stubby limbs, as if formerly adapted to some high-gravity planet. Likewise, any necks were almost nonexistent, as their heads seemed to sit directly on their shoulders, obligating them to swivel their whole bodies when desirous of looking in a certain direction.

This fellow, clothed in a wide cloth-of-gold robe that made him look like a dressed-up church bell, answered Klom's question with good will.

"The inexorable Dustar is conducting some kind of baptismal ceremony in a field on the outskirts of town. He began only an hour or so ago. Just follow the Avenue of Foreshortened Ambition to its end."

"That must be the ceremony to reinstall Tugger's *ib*! We have to be there!"

Klom began to run. But after a short sprint he realized that Lingle and Olasia could not keep pace, so he dashed back, scooped them up, and raced forward again.

The margin of the town was as neatly drawn as if by an invisible fence, all buildings falling away to virgin prairie. The new unimpeded view of the starry night sky made plain that they sat at the bottom of a wide bowl. Just a few hundred meters away, a ring of torches marked the ceremony. The sound of piping wind instruments, wooden rattles and large drums floated across the distance.

Klom hurried, not even noticing the negligible weight of the friends he carried. The trodden moss disseminated a cinnamon scent.

A ring of squat Navarro spectators parted easily. Klom set his friends down on the inner edge of the circle of watchers.

In the center of the torchlight-defined space stood the naked Dustar Nitch, a typical citizen of Onfroy whose eminence was manifested by sacred armbands and a fillet, but otherwise resembling the score of similarly naked dancers who bobbed up and down with the grace of a perpetual avalanche.

Next to the Dustar stood Tugger and Truth's Abstract Smile. The terabase lordling had indeed been forced to abandon his cloak of useful and deadly techno-mites. But he still loomed large and fierce, his attention focused on the Book of Forgetting.

Tugger was swaying in time to the music and in syncopation with the dancers! Klom was startled by his four-footed friend's display of initiative and responsiveness, unprecedented since his reincarnation.

"This must be a Dervish branch of the religion," Lingle observed. "No prayers, no machines. They intend that their dancing will put themselves and Tugger into alignment with the cosmic rhythms, and thus incline his *ib* to flow naturally back into its proper mortal vessel."

"So we shouldn't interfere?"

"No. Results could be unpredictable."

"But we have to be ready to pounce to take Tugger away from Smile as soon as the dance is over. Especially if it succeeds and he is made whole."

Olasia spoke. "Look at that big patch of shadows over there. That's as close as you can get to the action. Circle around through the crowd, and I'll position myself where the lordling will be sure to see me. Once the dance is over, I'll jump out to make a scene, and you can snatch Tugger away."

"It might work," Lingle conceded.

"We don't have any other plan, so let's do it."

Klom and his little factotum headed in one direction, while Olasia crept off in the opposite. In a minute, they were all properly positioned.

The musicians suddenly picked up the pace of their playing. The celebrants hurled themselves through such wilder contortions as their stolid bodies permitted. Dustar Nitch achieved some arcing leaps that seemed impossible for such a bulky package. A quivering Tugger exhibited strange oscillations of his hide from head to tail, as if an army of ants were marching up and down his spine just under the skin.

Finally, with a loud crescendo, both music and dancing ceased. Tugger's legs folded beneath him and he went down to the ground.

Olasia leaped out into the trampled circle. "You! Devil Croc! Dirty Smiler! Look! You didn't kill me!"

The haughty Gorgoid turned his face away from Tugger, to make sense of the unexpected outcry.

Klom moved faster than he had ever moved before, launching himself directly at Tugger. He almost flew through the air, incidentally dealing Dustar Nitch a glancing blow that sent the hefty naked marabout sprawling like an upended turtle. Klom landed ultimately on his knees beside his friend and threw his arms about Tugger's broad neck.

Tugger licked Klom's face, and gave one of his old dopey grins.

But before Klom could pull Tugger upright or otherwise urge Tugger to run away with him, Truth's Abstract Smile had taken two big strides and, with a grip on Klom's shirt, lifted the shipbreaker entirely off the ground.

Klom had always been the biggest being in any group. Never one to use his size and strength to dominate, he nevertheless relied instinctively on having the physical power to best any opponent. But in the Gorgoid he had met his match—and more. Besides simply outmassing Klom, Truth's Abstract Smile, as a sixstrand, possessed a superior physiology, right down to the cellular level: muscle fibers more potent, ligaments more elastic, bones denser and better interlaced. Held in the air at arm's length, Klom could wriggle and jab punches, but to no avail, helpless as a kitten.

The Gorgoid's breath reeked of a diet of raw meat. "I am very glad you caught up with me, you witless toiler, you undeserving fool, you annoying insect. Now you will have a few seconds of terror before you attain total oblivion. I am going to use the Book of Forgetting for his original purpose. Only his going missing delayed this rightful judgment. I and my kind are the natural rulers of this universe, superior in all ways. But thousands of species of genetically inferior beings like you have bred and spread in the trillions, dominating all the planets of creation. In our lesser numbers, we multistranders have been forced to accommodate your kind, subjecting ourselves to your foolish rules, catering to your weaknesses. But no longer. For at this moment, you will all be simply wished away by my dominant will, leaving your betters to inherit an exclusive universe."

The Gorgoid hurled Klom some meters away. The soft moss cushioned his impact. With a stifled cry, Olasia rushed to his side. Klom leaped to his feet.

Truth's Abstract Smile stood by Tugger's head. He reached down with his scaly hands and grasped the two branches of the wishbone-like appendage sprouting from Tugger's brow, a feature that Klom had always considered simply decorative or vestigial.

The pressure and silence and stillness to be found only at some nighted, kilometers-deep submarine trench reigned for an unutterable span. Klom prepared himself for an instant annihilation of all he loved, a sundering so instant that he would not even be able to mourn.

But nothing happened.

Truth's Abstract Smile released Tugger's tuning-fork and stepped back with a dumbfounded look.

"Dustar! Have you not restored his soul?"

Dustar Nitch had righted himself after being bowled over by Klom. He sidled over obsequiously and, taking up one of Tugger's big paws, moved the Book's compliant limb through a series of mudras that seemed to evoke evanescent golden mandalas of light in the air.

"The *ib* is present. But there is still some metaphysical deficit. I fear that this carcass, not being the original vessel, is an insufficient and imperfect host."

The Gorgoid roared his anger and kicked Tugger solidly in his belly. "Useless abortion!" The Book of Forgetting showed no anger or pain, just a mute acceptance.

Klom thought that surely the terabase's next move would be to further savage Tugger and rip him to pieces. Klom readied himself for a futile assault on the lordling, heedless of any danger to himself.

But Truth's Abstract Smile mastered his emotions with an almost visible display of willpower. "This is ridiculous and beneath me. I have wasted too much time and energy already on this useless quest. Once that idiot Bright Tide Rising slew the original Book, all was lost. But I am not defeated. If our ancestors could make the first Book, so the savants of my generation should be able to duplicate that achievement, now that they are released from any more fantasies about an easy restoration of what was lost. Now I go. But heed my words, all of you dregs! Some day soon, you will all simply evaporate, like a nightmare from which my kind has finally awakened."

Stalking off with the ultimate arrogance that deemed them all unable to harm or stop him, the Gorgoid soon disappeared. The audience and dancers and Dustar Nitch began to disperse back home to the warrens of Onfroy.

Klom and Olasia raced to Tugger; Lingle quickly joined them. The impotent Book of Forgetting got to his feet.

Klom hugged his friend and received a slobbery kiss. He sensed an old familiar presence, for the first time since retrieving the reincarnated Tugger on Stratcom. What did he care if Tugger was powerless, so long as his individuality and sense of self were restored?

Lingle spoke. "This seems a pleasant outcome—save for one thing."

"What's that?"

"The likelihood that in the perhaps not too distant future, we shall all be rendered as if we never were, once Smile and his peers succeed in recreating their own Book of Forgetting and shifting the world we know onto another, more homogenous path."

Klom felt crestfallen. Unfair! How could his happiness be so suddenly ripped away?

"But what can we do about such a fate? We are helpless. Can't we just enjoy whatever days we have left? Maybe Smile and his buddies won't succeed."

"That is a huge gamble, *Khun* Bravalo, and not one I would care to wager on."

Olasia said, "Mount Sumeru."

Klom and Lingle could only stare at the chimera.

"Mount Sumeru. It was your original destination. The triptix you got back on Asperna pointed you there from the start. Our journey isn't over. Something awaits us on Mount Sumeru. The last part of Tugger's soul is there. Or some kind of key or answer or trigger. It must be!"

Klom felt his spirits lift. "Smile never knew about Mount Sumeru. He only learned that we planned three visits to the marabouts, and so he abandoned his greedy plot too soon. We can still win! If Tugger is restored to full powers, we can make everyone safe!"

Lingle sighed. "Assuming we can survive another two deadly days in that excruciating millipede coach!"

* * * *

The wavepacket ship that carried Klom, Tugger, Lingle and Olasia to the edge station in the Mount Sumeru system was named *What Is Your Why?*, a cognomen they took to be auspicious, since it seemed to hint at the primacy of a good motivation. The liner featured an astonishing number of luxuries, which all the quartet relished, given the abuse they had suffered and the rough travel conditions they had endured recently, and the prospect of unknown trials ahead. Lingle's head wound, mostly healed well, still gave him occasional twinges, which he soothed with long professional massages from one of the staff: a fellow Vib, a female named Zella, with whom Lingle instantly bonded, as refugees without a homeworld often will. To Klom's eyes, she looked identical to Lingle, but the factotum described her unique beauty and spirit in glowing terms which led Klom to suspect that more than simple massages were going on. He smiled and was glad, and actually refrained from teasing his companion, as he might have teased Airey back on Asperna in a similar situation.

Olasia, Tugger and Klom spent most of their free hours in one of the ship's swimming pools. So much clean water devoted only to pleasure filled Klom with awe. When wet, Olasia's short fur dispersed a lanolin perfume that Klom found enticing. Tugger raised waves that splashed over the pool's rim, and delighted all the children with rides. Klom could not believe that his inarticulate friend— discovered, seemingly an eternity ago and half a galaxy away, in a hidden suspensor-sac a thousand years old— had been revivified and restored to his natural state. Should they abandon their quest for a broader restoration, and just take whatever happy hours remained? Always Klom came back to the possibility that Truth's Abstract Smile had raised: wiping out all cosmic sapients that did not belong to the elite terabase clade. If there was some chance he could stop this, he had to take it, no matter what personal ease and happiness he had to sacrifice.

Long low conversations a-bed with Olasia, conducted after their lovemaking, confirmed this judgment and decision.

"We could never truly enjoy a moment of peace and contentment with such a fate hanging over our heads, Klom."

"Yes, you are right. But what a burden."

"A burden shared is a burden halved, Klom."

"Then with four of us together, mine is quartered!"

He scooped her up and atop his erection, and she sighed and bent down for a long kiss.

The edge station that maintained its position just outside Mount Sumeru proper hosted thousands of small ships designed to carry from one to twenty individuals down into the system itself. That fleet was impressive—especially when one learned there were thousands of identical stations spaced around Mount Sumeru. But not as impressive as the view from the observatory lounge of the station.

Klom stood at the broad, tall window and found himself wordless.

The station resided above the planetary plane, the ecliptic, and so the view was as if looking down from above onto a vast and indescribable panorama.

The nucleus of the Mount Sumeru system was a gigantic black hole with the mass of a million medium-sized suns. Its appearance was of course just a vacuity with a ring of particulate activity around it.

Arrayed in a circle around the black hole were thirty-six normally functioning stars, spaced in careful proportions.

The combined gravity of the black hole and the three dozen suns maintained their flock of planets.

Twenty-five hundred planets orbited in the innermost ring, just close enough to the suns to ensure beneficent terrestrial conditions on each world. They chased each other at a distance of a mere four hundred thousand kilometers apart. Some pairs were actually linked by space elevators.

The same was true of the next ring moving outward, also sharing the broad Goldilocks zone conducive for life.

And the next ring, and the next, and the next…

Down to Ring 400, closest to the edge station, but still within the optimal zone.

A million habitable worlds, all packed elbow to elbow, their skies hosting a constant rising and setting of their fellow orbs, at different removes and of different apparent sizes, like an endless mad parade.

Lingle broke the silence. "Somewhere down there is the last part of Tugger's ascension to the Book of Forgetting."

Klom's brain hurt. "Impossible to find."

"Let us consult an expert."

The spacious, high-ceilinged, busy offices of the Indisputable Mount Sumeru Travel Agency and Sociocultural Ephemeris was staffed by identical workers behind their desks, all of which bore a plethora of communication and information-accessing devices nearly concealing the workers. The race of each identical staff member was unknown to Klom. Each being featured a body and head seemingly composed of a stack of overlapping fleshy plates of a blue-green color, like a tree whose growths of dishlike fungus had overwhelmed it. Eyes and manipulative organs could be seen in some of the interstices of the plates. Klom decided to think of them as the Griddlecakes.

An agent beckoned to Klom and party.

"My name, eager visitors, is Susuet. How may I assist you?"

Indicating Tugger, Klom said simply, "Here is one of our party. What can you tell us about Mount Sumeru that is relevant to him?"

A tracery of colored light enwrapped Tugger. "I have digitized your party member's physical attributes. Now we conduct a quick search.... Ah, most rewarding." Susuet rotated a flatscreen so Klom could see it. "The world of Thoshubliss hosts some beings very close in nature to your companion: the Trismolians."

On the screen, a savannah of orangey grasses was dotted with dozens of quadrupeds who seemed nearly identical to Tugger—although without handy referents, their size could not be precisely gauged.

Klom exchanged glances with Olasia and Lingle. Tugger was busy chewing a hole in the office carpet. They nodded.

"We wish to go there," said Klom.

"I am in ecstasy! Faster than thought, your passage has been arranged. Departure Bay one nine two seven five. May the million hurtling spheres of Mount Sumeru shepherd your every step!"

After quickly collecting their modest possessions from temporary lockers, Klom and company hurried to the designated Departure Bay. Access to their hired pinnace was through a short enclosed walkway extending out from the station. They boarded, and the ship's outer door sealed shut, the walkway unmating.

Forward-facing, rear-facing, and side-facing windows in the hull revealed the lack of any cabin for the pilot. Klom was puzzled, until a sourceless voice spoke.

"Welcome aboard the *Zada Prior*! I am your pilot, and you may refer to me by the name of this vessel. I am entirely a kiberneticheskiy, embedded in the ship. No organic brain, not even that of a terabase, is as useful or reliable as one of my kind for guiding craft through the million-world weave. You may rest assured that the failure rate for trips such as these is as near zero as possible. Now, please take your seats and we will depart for Thoshubliss."

The *Zada Prior* detached and dropped down toward the ecliptic. Ring 400 assumed greater definition, and Klom could see the line of racing planets, a spinning necklace.

"Here in the outermost ring, one orbit about the black hole nucleus—a planetary year—is completed in just four point six standard days. A year for the planets of the innermost ring is one point six days. Your destination lies in Ring 250, and so you may enjoy calculating the exact length of year there."

So far the craft had flown above the ecliptic, but now it began to drop down, and the linearly careening worlds grew larger in their endless steeplechase. Klom felt overwhelmed and alarmed.

"I will enter the system in Ring 300 and then travel from one Ring to another, just to provide some excitement for your journey."

"No, don't!" Klom yelled.

"Oh, but I insist! You must admire my prowess! Also you will more intimately percieve the intricate and perfect construction of this system, created unknown eons ago by unknown beings."

The little ship deftly inserted itself between two full-sized planets in the chain, one as close to the other as a typical moon to its primary. They stayed in unchanging relative proximity to these two worlds only for seconds before darting forward across a broad gap and into Ring 299. Then, like a demented bee looking for the perfect flower, they raced from one Ring to the next, charting a zigzag path. Planets whizzed by at breakneck speeds, seemingly centimeters away from the ship's nose and tail.

Olasia squealed, clutching Klom's bicep with both hands so hard that it hurt. Lingle had his face buried in Tugger's chest.

Finally the hazardous course of merry-go-round planets came to an end, as Zada Prior guided them into a stable relationship with one cloud-mottled sphere.

"Here we are, the world of Thoshubliss! Shall I set you down at the main port of Grelltanser?"

"Yes, as soon as you can!"

Leaving the *Zada Prior* at the city's starquay, after uttering fervent thanks to their kibe pilot that were more of a prayer of humble worship than simple gratitude, Klom tried to imagine making the return trip, but quailed at the thought. The blue sky full of zipping rising and setting spheres of various sizes and maculations, the nearby worlds of adjacent Rings, did not contribute to his confidence.

Lingle soon discovered the name and location of the territory where Tugger's Trismolian cousins lived: a nature preserve dubbed the Serenity Protectorate. A rented floater— easily operable by Klom, thanks to his experience with heavy-duty deconstruction equipment—could get them there in just a few hours of moderate and safe speed. Their luggage remained behind in secure storage.

Once provisioned and up in the air, Klom finally felt some tension leak out of his spine.

The trip was quick and much more enjoyable than the one by millipede coach. The interval of travel passed pleasantly, with talk and food—although always at the back of Klom's mind was anxiety and wonder about what they might find. Tugger, unconcerned, rode with his massive head hanging out a window into the slipstream, tongue lolling.

Finally, adjacent to a modest sod-house reception building, the floater settled down gently to the savannah's tall grasses, bending them underneath its flat bottom. No other visitors were apparent, although Klom did note a single-person aircar bearing a governmental seal on its door.

Klom ventured inside the official outpost alone, and returned holding a gaudy printed souvenir pamphlet.

"The ranger says we can wander freely among the herd. They are gentle and friendly. Lingle, here, read this for us."

They strolled beneath the warm multiple suns toward where Tugger's cousins congregated, about half a kilometer distant. Lingle recited as they walked.

"Ranked at a qualia level that places them just below true sapience, the Trismolian quadrupeds of Serenity Protectorate constitute the last remnants of their kind anywhere in the Indrajal. Never a prolific species, the Trismolians were exploited nearly to extinction several millennia ago, when it was discovered that their unique genetic material lent itself to easy manipulation and stacking of strands. Individual members and breeding pairs from the once-extensive herds were exported in large numbers to various strandcrafter laboratories, where hopes were high for the development of autocatalytic devacentric apptitudes. But when the various lines of research proved unfruitful, and the breeding pairs refused to procreate, interest in the Trismolians waned, and their local stocks were allowed to rebound slowly to their current levels."

Halfway to the herd, Tugger grew excited and hurtled ahead. Klom dashed after him.

Tugger proved to be half again as large as his relatives. The natives crowded around their long-lost relative enthusiastically, nuzzling Tugger and making plaintive whuffling sounds. The Book of Forgetting stood proudly, like a beneficent king, home from exile and receiving his due adoration.

"So," said Klom, "millennia ago, some sly terabase genius or team of geniuses succeeded where everyone else failed. They crafted a deva—their secret weapon, the Worldshifter—who could stay stable in our dimensions, out of Tugger's ancestors. Then they kept their creation hidden from view for future use—until he went missing."

"They probably discouraged all other researchers," Lingle suggested. "To forestall a rival. Or maybe they only succeeded by a freakish stroke of luck, never to be duplicated."

Olasia spoke. "This is all very interesting. It's fascinating to know Tugger's origin and history. But how can this help us unlock all his powers?"

Klom scratched his head. "I don't know... Lingle?"

"I am at a loss."

"Well, let's go back to the floater and think about this."

Klom turned and began to walk away, but Tugger did not follow.

"Should we try to prod him to accompany us, *Khun* Bravalo?"

Klom grinned. "No, not at all. He's safe here. Let him be."

Back at their transportation they had a meal and some drinks. The ranger, a willowy Blue Aesthete wearing mere strips of artfully arrayed ribbons, came out to inform them that the reception center was now closing for the night, but they were welcome to stay.

Klom looked at the frantic sky, as illuminated as ever. He noted for the first time that some of the celestial sights were smeared, and recalled part of Lingle's lecture while they traveled. These distorted objects lived on the far side of the central black hole, and so had their images twisted by the intervening gravity lens of that omphalos.

"You say 'for the night?'"

"A mere term of convenience. The Million Worlds never know darkness. So the devas ordained. Enjoy your evening."

After the ranger departed in his little ship, Klom suddenly felt exhausted. He had traveled so far, endured so much since leaving Asperna and his old ordained way of life. And all without any real resolution so far. Still, he had Olasia and Lingle, and Tugger reborn.

"I'm going to take a nap," Klom announced. "Wake me if anything happens."

The period from dropping off to being jostled seemed both instant and forever. Klom instinctively shot up from the floater's reclined seat.

Olasia said, "Klom, there's some kind of commotion among the herd."

Klom instantly had the floater off the ground, and in seconds had closed the short gap with the herd. He and Lingle and Olasia jumped out.

Tugger had found a mate. He was energetically but silently topping one of the females, his forelegs draped over her shoulders, while all the other Trismolians raced about in circles, bellowing.

Before Klom could formulate a positive or negative thought about this surprise, perhaps a sign of Tugger's true maturation, the sky immediately overhead filled with a dozen hovering starships. Large and menacing, they resembled so many others that Klom had once cut to pieces.

One ship opened a bay, and a lone figure, corona'd with majestatics, arced downward.

Truth's Abstract Smile rested in the air just above their heads. He looked triumphant, yet resigned to a less than perfect victory.

"We arrive too late, I see, for it took us a while to pick up your trail, once we realized our error in letting you run loose after Voyle. I acknowledge my own mistakes in dropping you, and I will surely pay a high price. In fact, my peers insisted on accompanying me, as you can see, not trusting me to bring this unfortunate enterprise to a conclusion."

"Why too late?" Klom asked.

"Our instruments reveal everything. We cannot interfere directly with the Book in this foreordained moment. As he completes his *hieros gamos* ritual, the qualia emanating from the Book of Forgetting are ramping up to complete devahood. We have only minutes until his full ascension. And afterwards—well, as before, you and your puling affections have rendered him useless to us. His loyalty cannot be compromised. So we have no choice but to destroy him this instant, before his phase change. And we will not employ half-measures."

"What are you going to do?"

"We have already done it. We have radically accelerated the natural entropic decay of Mount Sumeru's black hole. It will evaporate in just a few seconds, destabilizing everything. The Million Worlds will instantly crash. A shame, really, to destroy such a brilliantly constructed astronomical treasure, but you gave us no choice. The trillions of useless creatures who must die inspire less grief. I leave now, with no regrets."

Truth's Abstract Smile rocketed up and into his ship, and the whole fleet winked out into superluminal dimensions.

Oblivious, Tugger continued his holy mating.

As the last departing black hole gravitons that had yoked Mount Sumeru together radiated out into the void, the whole world of Thoshubliss lurched, throwing Klom to the ground.

In the sky, planets began to wobble and ricochet and collide like billiard balls on an upended table. The entire glorious orrery was coming untethered, its centripetal leash snapped.

Immense roaring winds began to build. Klom fought impossibly to his feet, using the jouncing floater as a prop.

Flat on the turf, Olasia kept a grip on Lingle with one hand, while her other clutched the deep-rooted grasses. Klom strove to reach them. Eyes incredibly wide, she opened her mouth to call his name, call for help—

The ground cracked open broadly with a noise like a giant's shovel stabbed into a child's sand castle, and swallowed both Klom's friends, wailing.

Klom took a step towards the crevasse, then stopped and turned toward Tugger.

Against all circumstances, the intercourse continued, as if Tugger and his mate were stabilized by unseen forces, a nexus of solidity.

But then the soil beneath them just seemed to evanesce, as the torso of the earth split apart.

Down went Tugger and his female into the bowels of the planet.

Klom hurled himself into the canyon.

The cleft was fully illuminated, tearing open wider and deeper with every second, as the entire Mount Sumeru system flew apart in a chaotic tarantella, millions of worlds and their satellites abandoning each other. As the air whistled past his face, Klom could see Tugger finally disengage from his mate. The two Trismolians continued to plummet separately.

Some sensation caused Klom to flail about, twisting so he could look upward.

A deva had manifested at the center of its typical silvery distortion, but without help of any animal sacrifice or boom tube.

Klom saw within that whorl the same ineffable face he had seen back on Asperna, when the marabouts consecrated the beginning of work on the *Caution Discharge Zone*. He recalled the words he had said then.

"It's—it forgives everything."

And then, within his mind only, came a voice that was instantly familiar, though never before heard.

Klom, my friend...

Klom whipped around. Below him, Tugger had halted in midair. Beside him was his mate. And she looked impossibly gravid, belly ballooning out. All this Klom saw, before the female Trismolian vanished, leaving only Tugger behind.

Klom realized he too was no longer falling. Separated by a few meters, Klom could register every detail of Tugger's jowly grin and wrinkled hide.

"Tugger!"

Yes, you know me.

"Tugger, save us! Save the world, save the universe. Just like you once saved my arm!"

I will do all that, Klom. Except for one thing. I cannot save myself.

"No! You must!"

The universe is not safe with me in it. I inspire too much contention and greed. So I must remake creation without me—without the possibility of me. Goodbye, Klom. You were a kind companion, my only friend in this long life.

"Tugger, no!"

But then all was gone.

* * * *

The tall feathery lannaught trees that shaded the scattering of modest comfortable homes around the shores of Lake Zawinul rustled in the late afternoon breezes that arose each day from the amethyst lake. From one cottage, a big man stepped out onto the porch. He called back to someone inside.

"Goodbye, Mother! You'll cook what I caught today before it spoils, won't you? Do you want me to send Lingle to help? No? All right then! Until tomorrow."

The man stepped down to the grass-edged red-dirt path and walked off, humming a tune.

He was hailed at another cottage. A lazy lounger, sitting on the porch, jumped up.

"Klom, you antisocial brute! Where is our invitation to dinner at your house?"

Klom laughed. "You were there just last night, Airey. You know you need no invitation."

"Then count on seeing us tonight as well. By all the sacred spheres of Mount Sumeru, such standoffishness could make a stranger believe that we hadn't been good neighbors for ten years, ever since the salvage yards were closed down and we were all pensioned off. How I bless the coming of the Universal Reclamation of the Indrajal. No more masters, no more suffering for such as you and I. A dream come true."

As Klom nodded and began to walk away, he heard Airey yell into his house. "Sorrel! Take off your apron, my dear, we dine out again tonight!"

As he approached his own cottage, Klom felt happy. Life was as perfect as life allowed.

From his own door, two children, a boy and a girl, ran out to greet Klom. They resembled their father in size, but with more graceful faces and limbs.

"Daddy, daddy, wait till you see what momma got us from the trader who came through town while you were out fishing!"

Klom hoisted his son onto one shoulder, and his daughter onto the other, and carried them inside.

Olasia came in from the kitchen, wiping her hands dry. She smiled and gave Klom a kiss.

"The children say you bought them something."

"Oh, I hope you don't mind. It's just a little pet. The trader said it was a Trisomolian pup. Very rare. But no one else on his circuit wanted it, so I got it for just a few taka."

From the bedroom of the children waddled a roly-poly quadruped, all dewlaps and bumblefeet. Klom scooped it up.

"What shall we name it, daddy?"

Klom peered deeply into the animal's eyes. The pup licked his fish-hook-scarred thumb.

"I think I have an idea."

A CANTICLE FOR ACKERMAN

"The last installment of my series on Americans moving away from organized religion was about the sense of community as the one inarguably positive attribute of mainstream houses of worship that can be tough to replicate in the secular world. After that story ran, I heard from readers about ways they've been able to form close bonds after they'd stopped attending services... Some readers mentioned fandom as a bonding mechanism..."

--Jessica Gross, "The Church of Group Fitness,"
The New York Times, July 26, 2023.

Were the Bad Times finally coming to an end, or at least lessening? Brother Moskowitz could not be sure. There were certain encouraging signs that pointed to an upswing in the health of the planet, and a rebirth of civilization. But life continued hard for the few million people scattered around the globe who had survived the Collapse. However, Brother Moskowitz knew one thing for certain: there would have been many fewer survivors, and life would have been infinitely harder for them, if the First Church of Fandom had not existed.

This line of meditative thoughts occurred to Brother Moskowitz as he stood in the gently swaying, iron-bamboo sentry tower lifted high atop the palisade, crafted of the same hybrid plant, that surrounded the Monastery of Saint Gerrim.

The legend of Saint Gerrim, which, like all information from before the Collapse, had come down the centuries in fragmentary and confusing form, revolved around that holy personage's vast powers of invention, allied with equally large tendencies to procrastinate. And so, to honor their historo-mythical patron, the brothers of his order were apt to slide off from vigilance or labor into idle musings at the drop of a quill pen.

Brother Moskowitz had been assigned the task of watching for the arrival of the wagon train from the Nunnery of Saint T'lore. Just five or six decades past, his sentry duties would have been to monitor the surroundings for savage beasts and even more-savage human mauraders, and he would have been equipped with a fearsome crossbow. But there had not been a raid on the monastery in fifteen years—one of the hopeful signs of progress—and so Brother Moskowitz was equipped with nothing more than a large succulent purple plum-apple and his copy of the omnipresent Fandom Missal. He had been studying the prescribed rituals for Setumbre Eighth, the holy day dedicated to the first appearance of Kirken's Pock nearly one millennium ago. A Two-in-One being from the stars, half ultra-rational, half ultra-emotional, Kirken's Pock had, according to fable, launched the very notion of modern Fandom, and so their day was an important one in the liturgical year.

Having refreshed is memory with as much of the many chants and prostrations as he could, Brother Moskowitz closed the crudely printed missal—but not before pausing at the frontispiece, which exhibited in illuminated calligraphy the simple, essential credo of the First Church of Fandom, under a drawing of a beaming, homely Saint Ackerman, Defender Against Monsters and Fan Number One, the first among equals in the hagiography of the Church.

FAITHFUL FANS SHALL ABOVE ALL VENERATE THEIR CHOSEN HOLY FRANCHISE UNSTINTINGLY, DEFENDING IT AGAINST ALL DETRACTORS

FAITHFUL FANS SHALL MASTER ALL THE ARCANA OF THEIR CHOSEN HOLY FRANCHISE, EVEN UNTO THE SMALLEST OF TRIVIA

FAITHFUL FANS MAY PROSELYTIZE AND SEEK TO CONVERT UNBELIEVERS, BUT SHALL NOT DENIGRATE OR DISPARAGE THE FANS OF OTHER HOLY FRANCHISES

FAITHFUL FANS WILL HONOR THE SAINT OF THEIR CHOSEN HOLY FRANCHISE BY EMULATION OF THE SAINT'S VIRTUES AND TALENTS AND MYSTERIES, WHILST AFFIRMING THAT ALL SAINTS EXIST ON THE SAME HIGH PLANE

FAITHFUL FANS WILL SUPPORT AND AID ALL OTHER FANS, TREATING THOSE OF THEIR SHARED HOLY FRANCHISE AS BROTHERS AND SISTERS, AND THOSE OF AFFILIATED HOLY FRANCHISES AS THEIR HONORED COUSINS, SEEKING ALWAYS TO STAVE OFF THE DAY OF ULTIMATE PERIL THAT BRINGS THE WORST EPISODE EVER

And there, thought Brother Moskowitz, neither for the first nor last time, one had in a nutshell the virtues of the Church that had led it to survive and prosper amidst chaos, destruction and death: solidarity, dedication, knowledge-seeking, comity, passion, painstakingness, and diligence.

When, during the grim days of the Collapse, the un-Churched were foundering and thrashing about in a war of all against all, the acolytes of the First Church of Fandom, that glorious institution hardly yet framed nor fully born, were working together with a clear vision of what must be protected and preserved. These loyal and inventive sodalities, organized around veneration of their various idols, extended the sheltering shield of their beliefs to enclose their small communities against the harsh world outside their gates. Whether the fans had been followers of Beansay or B'lon Five; Kaypoppers or Dedders; partisans of Mc'Uer or Lukenleah; Gerrim or T'lore; Wall Terwite or Batch Loretta; Dolly Parts or Dizzy Knees; or any of a hundred other Holy Franchises, they had all shared the same attitudes and practices conducive to survival. And then after amalgamating under the unified banner of the First Church of Fandom, their powers had been magnified and synergized, until in this era the Church was the one and only global institution of any importance or might.

As Saint Ackerman himself had put it, "Having amassed such a collection, I had no fear of inviting strangers into my house."

Brother Moskowitz capped his thoughts by inscribing with his fingertip the Sign of Ackerman on his brow: the letter "E" repeated four times.

Suddenly a distant shout shifted his focus to the landscape beyond the monastery: a somewhat sere vista of sand and scrub and many contorted middling-sized trees adapted to the parched realm of the Na'lantic seaboard.

"Hola, Saint Gerrim's! The delegation from Saint T'lore's approaches!"

The formerly deserted dirt road that emerged from a copious thicket of mesquite soon hosted four covered wagons, each yoked to a shuffling pair of giant gila monsters some eighteen hands high at their shoulders. The canvas of the wagons bore the icon of Saint T'lore: a golden cardigan sweater.

Brother Moskowitz rang the alarm bell, then practically slid down the ladder from his tower, eager to greet the arrivals. Visitors to the monastery were rare enough, even in these flourishing times. But a passel of female fans was rarer still, and most welcome.

The bulk of the monastery's inhabitants were already streaming toward the iron-bamboo gates, which soon swung wide to accommodate the newcomers. In moments, introductions were being made. "Sister Trimble,

Sister Morojo, Sister Tiptree, Sister Russ, Sister Swiff, Sister Ursula…" Brother Moskowitz's head was spinning.

While the lesser acolytes mingled happily—some of the Sisters had impulsively burst into song—the head of the monastery, Brother Tucker, quickly entered into a hushed side conference with the T'lore leader, Sister Speller. Even while getting the gossip from down south and enjoying a draught of the special liquor distilled at the T'lore Nunnery, Brother Moskowitz noted the solemnity of the two leaders, and a small chill passed down his spine.

The booming voice of Brother Tucker, calling for silence, brought the spontaneous festivities to an abrupt cessation. All eyes turned to him.

"My fellow fans, I have to share with you a disturbing development, delivered to us through the good offices of Sister Speller—tidings that have the potential to undo all the centuries of progress the Church has made. For the first time since the Collapse, a rival organization has arisen, one which practices all the old ways that led in fact to the fall of civilization. Opposed to the inclusivity of the Church, they offer a kind of elite and exclusive membership in their own club, attained through much testing and trials, whilst looking down upon and casting out all those they deem inferior. They call themselves 'The Gatekeepers,' and they have already made disturbingly large inroads into our congregations, seducing our members with their poisonous philosophy. I fear we are all going to have to gird our loins and sharpen our wits for a battle we did not anticipate, but which we must win, if the world is going to continue to improve. As Saint Gerrim reminds us, 'When you play the game of thrones, you win or you die.'"

A rousing militant cheer went up from Sisters and Brothers alike. But on this bright day in this peaceful enclave, doom and troubles seemed far away, and so celebrations quickly resumed.

But even as Brother Moskowitz found himself snuggling drunkenly in the hot afternoon with a winsome dark-haired Sister named Winehouse, he could not put aside a premonition that he hoped would prove false.

It felt as if winter were coming.

NINE HUNDRED GRANDMOTHERS

The discovery of the multiverse made it really hard to be a drug addict.

I knew this fact firsthand, since I was a drug addict myself. And a seasoned one, using and maintaining now for well over a decade. A guy who speaks with the voice of much sad experience. A survivor. Lucky, I guess you could call it—from one angle. Unlucky any other way. And while I didn't generally like to complain about my self-inflicted condition or throw a pity party, I really wished that we could go back to the old days, before anyone knew the universe continually duplicated itself infinitely, *mutatis mutandis*, during every instant of time.

In that lost era when all we experienced or expected was just a unique, singular universe, being a selfish junkie was much less work. Or, at least, so it seemed to me. There were fewer impediments to your chosen lifestyle. Although I appreciated this only in hindsight. For instance: all you had was one unique iteration of your social set, one collection of family, friends and fellow users to let down, disappoint and rip off. One set of random strangers to interact casually or consequentially with. Also, your fate and destiny were a single-track journey: one foot in front of the other, from innocence to perdition—or maybe, with luck, ending up at recovery and redemption. But whatever the destination, whatever sense of choice, there was an ignorance-is-bliss feeling that the trip was linear and relatively uncomplicated. A sense of fatedness. No branches or alternatives to consider, parallel worlds always in your face.

Also, there were only limited options for drugs, limited pushers, limited numbers of antagonistic authorities, cops and such, and limited quantities of do-gooders, social workers and society matrons.

But all of this simplicity—a simplicity we did not even realize we were enjoying, until presented with the endlessly recomplicated alternatives—existed only before Doctor Bryce Finney, PhD in Temporospatial Physics from Rensselaer Polytechnic Insititute, managed to open a portal to the nearest adjacent timeline to ours. And because he was accessing, without quite knowing what he was doing, the least-divergent reality possible, he perforce opened his world-gate precisely onto his own laboratory, synced with his doppelganger or avatar, who was simultaneously opening a portal to our continuum. How the two Finneys, at first startled, then exultant, rejoiced and romped like mirrored twins at this earth-shattering moment, I leave it to you to imagine. Not that you have to actually use your imagination. The seminal moments are all on video, thanks to the lab surveillance cameras, with over one hundred billion YouTube views on my continuum alone. Curse Finney's genius soul!

And once Dr. Finney had let Schrodinger's cat out of the bag, there was no putting it back in. The whole world had to adjust to the "reality of multiple realities," the phrase that all the media commentators used when witlessly referring to the discovery.

But luckily for the world—or worlds—the adjustment went pretty well, for a number or reasons. If you stop to consider how things could have gone—well, the revelation of parallel timelines and access thereto could have totally destroyed civilization, through any number of causes. War, disease, spiritual malaise, intellectual confusion, vast population shifts… But none of that bad stuff happened, for perfectly understandable and logical reasons, all things considered.

First off came expense and cost as a limiting factor. The machine that Finney had cobbled together bulked as large as a beach cottage, and there seemed to be solid theoretical limits on how much you could miniaturize it. Plus it used a boatload of power, siphoning off the entire output of RPI's Walthousen Nuclear Research Reactor whenever it opened a portal. So there was not going to be any gadget worn on your wrist or belt that allowed an individual to jump blithely from one continuum to another, whenever he or she had a whim.

Additionally, it turned out that the multiverse had a steep cosmic gradient. Establishing a connection to our least-divergent neighbor used X amount of power, while moving further across the multiversal spectrum took more and more power as the divergence factor increased. It was as if the multiverse came with built-in barriers to discourage mingling. So the easiest continuua to visit were the ones most like your starting point, and what was the allure in that? Going someplace practically identical to your origin, just to chat with your boring and predictable doppelganger? Shit, you could do that at home!

So after all the excitement and hullaballoo died down, people began to realize that the average citizen was never going to afford or make a cross-time jaunt, and that the easily reachable destinations were not that exciting.

It was true, however, that governments and big corporations and even smaller enterprises could manage to exploit the multiverse in a highly constrained fashion. Punching through directly to a greatly divergent timeline was soon deemed not cost-effective, except in the most dire emergencies or for the most grandiose rewards. But what you could do, was mount a sequential expedition.

You sent your team to the nextdoor universe. Easy-peasy, relatively speaking. From there, using that timeline's equipment, your travelers jumped one universe further onward. From Universe Three, they moved to Universe Four, experiencing a slightly larger shift in consensus reality each time. After about a thousand jumps, you could hit some real weirdness full of interesting new stuff and people. And ideas were of course much more easily transportable than goods. But such travel took real time and physical exertion. And then you had to come back home the same laborious way.

So travel through the multiverse, regulated by a quickly established Crosstime Transit Bureau, quickly became something like the old Silk Road. A hard, dangerous, laborious trail to exotic destinations only dimly acknowledged or understood or even mundanely contemplated by the majority of stay-at-home folks. A route down which strange goods and notions might occasionally flow into your home, more often incrementally different than revolutionary.

Strange goods high in value, worthy of the efforts of securing them.

Like drugs.

* * * *

I'll pretend I'm introducing myself at some Narcotics Anonymous meeting, but I promise to keep it short and not bore you.

My name is Stafford Pinfold. Yes, of *those* Pinfolds, the family that got incredibly rich through a monopoly on practical nuclear fusion reactors. After nineteen years of respectable sobriety and general good behavior, I got hooked back in my Ivy League college days. A sports injury led to an oxy habit, which was quickly followed by experimentation with, and addiction to, a large number of other illegal substances, ranging from ecstasy, heroin, and fentanyl to krokodil, basuco and khat. Thankfully I only experimented lightly with the most heavily grievous stuff, and always returned to the vanilla drugs, which satisfied all my urges for escape from this prison called life.

My family—shocked and mourning, angry and sad—indulged me for a time, failing to cut off my allowance (easy money only led me to make more drug purchases), paying for my numerous rehab stints, staging heartfelt interventions, you know the drill. But ultimately, when I showed no signs of remorse or changing my ways, they went tough love and cut me off from all funds entirely. I was thrown right out onto the street. But even that failed to shame me or divert me from my addict's ways. I went down those all-too-familiar paths of utilitarian degradation to supply my habits, and finally became a low-level dealer, a "career" which allowed me to limp along as a maintenance case.

And then, as I hinted at the start of this sad tale, came the discovery of the multiverse.

I well recall my first experience with a trans-continuum drug, since it was what sent me seeking other such—to my eventual ruination, as you will soon see.

At that point in time, the dealer above me in the chain of supply was a tweaker gal whom everyone called "Mudball." She always dressed like some archetypical punk from the previous century, big boots and flannels and chains and ripped pants. She exhibited all the typical ravages of a meth-head, and was meaner than ten junkyard dogs. But she knew her drugs and always had access to the best stuff.

I met Mudball one night in our usual rendezvous spot, an all-night diner named Terminal Lunch. Amidst the smell of stale hotdog water and uncleaned frialator grease, she leaned in close, giving me way too intense a view of her ravaged complexion, and whispered, "I got something you're really gonna like. It's a ten-kay-divergence hit called extra-neosomaticum."

I was highly intrigued. A drug from ten thousand timelines distant. "Have you tried it yourself? What's it do?"

"Nah, it's not my thing. Plus it's too pricey. Here's the skinny. It gives you a ghost body."

"A ghost body? What's that?"

"From what my contacts tell me, you acquire a kind of invisible shell around yourself, shaped like yourself. You can sense this extra layer, whatever the fuck it's made of, and control it. It's totally malleable. Your consciousness expands into the shell. Plus, you get to see into extra dimensions."

"Sounds like pure fantasy."

"No way, it's a real phenom."

Well, I had never gone in for any of the psychedelics, even after having tried acid, psilocybin and many others, and despite Mudball's salesman protestations, this sounded like more of the same. "I don't know… It strikes me as a pretty useless high."

"What if I told you that Marfeo already tried it and was so blown away that he wanted me to sell it to him exclusively?"

Marfeo was another dealer at my level—a rival, I guess. He hated me because of my rich family, and I disliked him because of his ignorance and various loudly expressed prejudices. No way was I going to let him get a monopoly on this stuff, whatever it was.

"Okay, I'll try a hit. If it's any good, maybe I can push it to some of my more adventurous customers."

Mudball smiled, revealing the most hideous meth-decayed teeth. She reached into her tattered, safety-pinned leather jacket and came out with a ziploc bearing a single huge green pill stamped with the image of a Pac-Man ghost. It looked utterly innocuous. I paid her and we parted.

That night I took the pill and had one of the weirdest and most intense drug experiences of my whole veteran addict's life.

I was lying down on my couch when I felt the ectoplasmic shell begin to form about me. Soon I was encased toes to top in a wavery luminescent silhouette. I didn't know if anyone else could see it, but for me it shone with a pale green radiance. Then, without warning, my locus of consciousness changed. It seemed as if my brain was downloaded into the shell. And with that shift, I found I could manipulate my new form, extruding tentacles, swelling up like a balloon to fill the room. Next up, I gained something like Superman's microscopic, telescopic, X-ray vision. I could see through things and deep into sub-Planckian realms. The eleven hidden dimensions of our universe were revealed to me.

I sent one of my bodily probes through the wall and into my neighbor's apartment. A fat bus driver named, of all things, Ralph, my neighbor was sleeping. I used my pseudopod to grab a pack of his cigarettes and bring them back through the wide-open atoms of the wall. I had a smoke, and then proceeded to experiment with my new extra-corporeality.

After about three or four hours, during which I had lifted various items from my other neighbors and goosed awake the hard-working single Mom four apartments away, I could feel the new abilities and sensations began to wane and, finally, disappear. I was left feeling fagged out and confused. The trip had been fun, but towards the end, I had already been starting to get bored. Nothing I personally wanted to repeat. The drug made me feel like a Peeping Tom, which troubled my residual conscience, believe it or not, and it reminded me too much of actual physical work. Still, I could see that several of my more adventurous customers would like to try it, and that it might develop into a steady product line. So the next day I contacted Mudball and arranged for a regular supply.

I had been selling the drug for only three weeks when the cops came for me. And not just the local boys or even the Feds from my timeline. These were the enforcers from the Crosstime Transit Bureau. After this first encounter with the CTB goons, I learned that they were a kind of super SWAT team assembled from the worst bad asses of various parallel worlds. They made my homegrown police look like a suburban housewives book club.

You see now what I mean about the multiverse making everything worse and more complicated?

They busted in my door at three AM, four big heavily armed bruisers, one of whom had real fangs like a smilodon and green-tinged skin. Lord knows how many divergences separated his Earth from mine. Once I was awake, naked but able to respond somewhat intelligibly, the questioning started. Nothing physical, but they were relentless.

"Okay, kid, who sold you the X-neo?"

"I don't remember!"

"Do you know what that stuff's made from?"

"No…"

"The cerebral cortexes of Martian babies!"

"I don't believe you!"

Fang Guy laughed. "Well, you're smart not to. Harry's just jerking your chain. It's actually derived from element 125, an isotope high within the island of stability. You guys don't have it yet here. But it'll transfigure your neurons into itself if you use it long enough, and you'll end up permanently ghosted. You see why we can't let it loose on your timeline. Now, give with the names!"

I held out a little longer, but eventually caved. After all, it wasn't like Mudball and I were best friends or anything. She had palmed off heavily cut stuff on me often enough.

Amazingly, after I had ratted out Mudball, and the cops heard back from their peers that she had been successfully picked up—it was seven AM by then—I was surprised to learn that I myself wasn't about to be arrested. "Nah, you're small fry. CTB just wants the higher-ups."

After they left, I sought to compose myself with a cup of coffee brewed with shaky hands and tried to figure out what came next in my life. Unfortunately, I couldn't come up with any plan other than continuing to deal drugs to supply my own habits, while hoping not to get caught again. And practically before I could even make any moves in that direction, Fate delivered the whole package to my door. Three days later, I got a text from an unknown number. The message simply said: COME SEE ME TERMINAL LUNCH FRIDAY MIDNIGHT BONNAROO.

Even though I had never met him, I knew Bonnaroo was Mudball's supplier, so I went.

He proved to be an immensely fat guy with a shaven head, dressed in some kind of weird one-piece suit made of a sparkly synthetic that revealed every possible roll and crevice you did not desire to see. I had a sense he wasn't originally from my timeline, and his strange accent and vocabulary tended to substantiate my hunch.

He came right to the point.

"Our mutual wetch has been lubbered by the pescos."

"Huh?"

"Mudball. The seety-bees got her."

"Oh, right."

"I need to replace her to keep the drash flowing. You interested in beng my jerson on this strand?"

"Uh, sure, I guess. But won't the cops just come after me like they did her?"

"Nugatory. The lahjoa is in. I finally decided I'd pay what I had to. Hurts, but's that the cost of doing malinkey. You won't get any arazoak from them anymore. What do you say? Are you tangled?"

"I'll need a discount on the stuff I use personally."

"We're staunch!"

And so I started my new career as a midlevel dealer, the interface between Bonnaroo and the lesser runners such as I had been. It proved a lot less demanding and better paying than my old position. And there were other satisfactions. I got to sample all the new drugs, uncut, before anyone else. And also, I could boss around my old peers. The first time Marfeo had to make nice with me to get what he wanted, grovelling with a surly obsequiousness, I experienced a wonderful sensation of revenge.

I could have continued on in this role, I supposed, until either my veins collapsed, I overdosed, or there was a shakeup in the Crosstime Transit Bureau and the non-bent cops took over and staged an upright-citizen-pleasing purge of all us junkies, high and low. But alas, a different, unanticipated disaster intervened.

A year had passed, during which I sampled and sold so many crosstime drugs that I began almost to lose sense of my own self and history. Mecca Ten, blue mango, bugcrusher, ineffabilium, zogzug, cranioklept, sorolla seven… The faddish highs came and went, each one sending users in search of even greater, more esoteric kicks.

Currently, I was pushing a new one called "ent-wife." I had tried it once myself, of course, and discovered that all it seemed to do was to promote a kind of "green consciousness," so that you felt more or less like Swamp Thing, attuned to the Gaian biosphere. Not my bag, although I soon learned it appealed to many others. I think at one point I was supplying half the local chapter of Greenpeace.

But what neither I nor anyone else knew was that long-term use of ent-wife actually had the effect of rendering the user into a vegetable. Not mentally, but bodily. Blood replaced with a chlorphyll solution, cells turning to pith. Users felt compelled to leave their dwellings and find a patch of dirt, where they settled down and literally put out roots and developed bark and foliage. If found within a short time of going green, they could be saved. But otherwise, the effects were irreversible. No jolt of narcan would bring the victim around. You might as well reconcile yourself to using your loved one to provide shade for a picnic.

Naturally, the media went wild, and before too long, my name became associated with the plague, thanks to various sub-dealers narc'ing me out. But there was never enough solid proof adduced that the DA could succeed in building a case against me. Maybe some of my legal unaccountability stemmed from Bonnaroo's payoffs. But despite my staying out of jail, the well-publicized associational trail linked me to a number of the victims, and my name became an object of hate and social media banter. It really sucks, becoming a meme.

I knew I had to go to ground until all this blew over. Luckily I had stockpiled some drugs and cash. But just as I thought I had succeeded in finding a hiding place and erasing my footprints, my family stepped in.

My parents and other collateral relatives, all of them sober high-status and well-respected citizens, did not relish the name of "Pinfold" being connected in any manner with such a tragic and sordid scandal. (And come to think of it, those same "loved ones" had probably also intervened, like Bonnaroo, on my behalf with the authorities, without informing me.) Realizing that more such disgraceful public clusterfucks were likely to occur in my future if I persisted in my chosen career, and also realizing that I would probably defy any attempts at inducing me to surrender myself to professional rehab—at least at this juncture—they decided to stage another intervention, undeterred by the fact that all previous such exercises had proved futile. But this time, they were going to do things different. They brought in the big guns.

Myselves.

Avatars of Stafford Pinfold. Doppelgangers of yours truly. My cross-time twin brothers.

You remember me saying how rich my family was? Well, they could have sent for my cooperative carbon copies the long way, down the cross-time Silk Road, by dispatching emissaries in person. (Emissaries equipped with capacious wallets, I assume, since my other selves, if they held true to the template, would want to get paid for their time.) But that would have been too slow for my proactive parents. They wanted immediate action and results! Get that shithead scion straightened out now! So they paid to punch directly through to some high-divergency strands where they found acceptable and amenable versions of me that would agree to take part in their scheme. (And as I later learned, my folks had to reach out to strands that were twenty-kay or even further displaced from our home timeline. It appears that most of my nearest cousins had, disappointingly, all followed the same path I did.)

The first inkling I got of this campaign was when I was just anonymously settling in to my new quarters, a single-room-occupancy hotel in the skid row of a city not to be named. (Skid Rows in general were getting scarce, since unlimited fusion power, courtesy of the Pinfold clan, had sent the global economy into overdrive, allowing for every kind of do-gooder ameliorative social program imaginable.) I was lying down and preparing to take a hit of my new favorite drug, blammo, which caused the user to experience a wildly orgasmic condition for about three eternal hours, when a knocking sounded at the door. Before I could even tell whoever it was to go away, the door opened.

I saw myself, grinning and flourishing my room key. He said, "I told the clerk I locked myself out, and he gave me the spare. He was a little perturbed by the fact that he never saw me leave the hotel, but you have to believe your eyes."

I was momentarily croggled, just gawping, but then my temporarily undrugged mind quickly provided the most likely explanation. My duplicate's healthy tan, sedate clothing and a general sense of smug superiority provided all the clues I needed.

"My family put you up to visiting me, didn't they? You're here to 'talk some sense into me.'"

He took out a luxurious linen pocket handkerchief, unfolded it, and placed it on the bed before deigning to sit down on the stained comforter atop the spavined mattress. He crossed one leg over the other, exposing elegant stockings.

"Yes, I'm here to represent to you the wisdom of altering your ways. If only you agree wholeheartedly to give up your addictions, you could find yourself in as enviable a position as I myself occupy. Surely my simple presence is the most powerful argument."

I had been listening to this doppelganger for only about sixty seconds, and I already hated him. Hated myself.

"Part of the family business, I take it?"

"Yes, indeed. Vice-president in charge of Mars expansion."

"Big salary, beautiful wife, respect of the community?"

My double cast his eyes downward in a gesture of modesty. "All of that. And such pleasant accoutrements could be yours as well, if only—"

I didn't let him finish. I yelled, "You can take all your designer socks and Mars money and stuff them up your ass!" Before he knew what I was doing or could react, I had pinned my wimpy duplicate in a wrestling hold—his squash-racket-bolstered muscles were no match for the prowess of someone who had had often to subdue wild-eyed junkies intent on disemboweling one—and then I pushed the tab of blammo down his throat.

Well, I should have known that violence would not solve my problem. It never succeeds, except when it does. But unfortunately, this was not one of those situations. A few hours later, as my double lay drooling on the floor, four more of my avatars showed up. Hollywood Me, Rock Star Me,

Preacher Me and Scientist Me. While one of the newcomers was ministering to visitor number one, injecting him with some kind of bringdown counter-agent, the other three lashed into me with accusations, complaints, cajoling and berating.

"Staff, how could you treat one of our own avatars so disrespectfully?"

"Don't you ever want to make something good of yourself?"

"What about contributing to the cultural heritage of the species?"

"Aren't you tired of living such a miserable, grungy, dangerous, painful lifestyle?"

"Shouldn't you be leaving these juvenile practices behind?"

"Man, you are so uncool and blozarty!"

I just closed my eyes and capped my ears with my hands. Pretty soon, the room was full of about a dozen of my goody-goody selves, all haranguing me. What this all must've been costing my folks, I couldn't imagine. Just the ability to summon and transport distant avatars at the drop of a hat was mindboggling, never mind any kind of compensations they were receiving.

Finally I couldn't take anymore. Making sure I had my wallet and phone, I dashed out of the room without any of my other possessions, headed straight to the bus station, and took the first bus out to a random destination.

Surprisingly, I wasn't followed, but I soon realized that there was no need, since as soon as I used either my phone or my cards, I could be traced. So I got off ahead of where my ticket said I was going, withdrew all my money as cash, bought a burner phone, and then took a different bus to another set of anonymous lodgings.

But that only staved off discovery of my den for a week. The enormous detective resources of Pinfold Fusion Consortium eventually resulted in them tracking me down.

Into my flop came my parents. But they weren't my Mom and Dad from this continuum, they were doppelgangers of my parents. And they looked like they had been through hell and back. I knew my original folks hadn't weathered whatever these guys had gone through.

"Son," my alternate mother implored, "just look at us. Our sad state is all your fault! We're from a timeline where you became a byword for infamy. So many dead or incapacitated! All thanks to your drug dealing! A thousand times worse than the ent-wife mess. And how we suffered for your sins! Won't you spare your own parents this fate?"

My alternate father put his manly arm around his wife's shoulders. "There, there, dear, don't let yourself get worked up. I'm sure that this Stafford will benefit from the tragedy of our own son's behavior. He'll listen to reason and his sense of filial duty will prevail."

They were an affecting and pitiable sight, but I hardened myself. It wasn't me who had fucked them up so bad. Well, at least in some existential sense it wasn't, although it also was. But I resented my own folks for really playing dirty, by dragging in these pathetic losers.

"Whatever trip you two are on, I wish you'd share it. You are so far from reality, you must be halfway to Alpha Centauri."

My Mom began to weep and wail, and Dad cursed me out. They finally left, but only to be replaced by another pinch-hitting pair, employing a different tack. I ignored their arguments and logic and tirades, as well as those of the next five or six sets of doppelganger progenitors. The multiverse was really chapping my ass! Finally, after they had grown hoarse and tired and defeated, they all gave up and left me to stew in my own juices. Fine by me. That was all I had ever asked of anyone.

I was just trying to motivate myself to go on the lam again, to avoid more such encounters, when the door started to swing slowly open and I braced myself for more interference with my chosen lifestyle. But this time when the intruder appeared on the threshold, I was truly taken aback, experiencing a visceral punch to the gut.

The new interventionist was Gramma Atchison.

Abigail Atchison, my Mom's mother, had been fifty years old when I was born. She had dropped out of school as a teenager, for reasons of poverty, then raised my Mom while squeaking by as a single mother. Then my Mom had the miraculous fate-changing luck to marry into the Pinfold tribe. Gramma's life immediately turned around. All her worries and physical insecurities immediately vanished. But so did the necessity of any hard work, the practices she was accustomed to and which gave her life meaning. She foundered for a while and got morally lost, maybe even developing a drinking habit, from the whispers I heard. (Genes will tell!) Then I was born, and she had something—someone—to devote all her energies to. Sober and sensible and redeemed, she took over the raising of infant and toddler and child me, which was perfectly acceptable to my folks, who had other fish to fry.

I didn't mind either. In fact, I loved Gramma Atchison more than anyone. My childhood had been an idyl of love and joy and fun and exploration and freedom and learning. I had been prepped for a great life as a wise adult.

And then Gramma died in a car crash, when I was sixteen, three years before I turned to dope. Maybe the sports injury excuse had been just the trigger for unleashing a deeper, buried sorrow that needed the drugs as compensation or solace. Whatever.

And now here Gramma was. Amazingly, she looked hardly any older than the sixty-six years she had accumulated when she died, although nearly well over a decade had passed in our native timeline. They must have found this Gramma in a continuum that was chronologically retarded from ours. I knew she had been cynically selected especially for her familiar looks, but I still couldn't help the fact that her face struck me like a hammerblow.

"Stuffie, my baby."

Gramma often called me "Stuffie."

"Stuffie, how it pains Gramma's heart to see you like this. The stories your parents have told me! Won't you think about changing your ways? For old Atchie's sake?"

I often called her "Atchie."

But this wasn't my Gramma! My Gramma had died and deserted me, being unlucky enough to get creamed by a drunk driver blowing through a stop light. (I never did learn to drive. Wonder why…)

I hardened my heart and turned my face to the wall. "Forget it, lady! You ran out on me and those days are gone. It's just me alone against the world now."

Gramma allowed herself to weep quietly a little. Then she got a tissue out of her capacious nana purse, wiped her eyes, blew her nose, then left without another word.

I had expected more wrangling, the hard sell. But I remembered that Atchie had never believed in such coercion, and so her actions were totally consistent with her character, even across several timelines.

However, the next Gramma Atchie to show up was rather different.

This grandmother wore an eye-patch, smoked a cigar, had biceps like a stevedore's, and wore literal combat boots.

"Up on your feet, you ungrateful twerp! Do you think we ever could have beaten back the invaders from Frolix-8 if we had all been as spineless as you! You're a disgrace to the name and reputation of General Stafford Pinfold, Savior of the Jovian Battalion! In fact, you make me wanna puke!"

I skittered off the bed and into a corner of the room. "Hey now, wait just a minute! I don't know where you're coming from, but we don't have any space monsters here. Maybe I would've been different if we had, just like your Stafford was. But I'm just what my world made me."

Gramma regarded me with a steely eye, then spat in my direction. "Aw, what's the use? You can't make a tiger out of a mouse!" She stormed out in a metaphorical cloud of gunsmoke.

No sooner had she left than cyborg Gramma arrived. You really don't know creepy until the beloved face of your maternal grandmother is affixed to a combination of tank chassis and sexbot. When this Gramma spoke, she sounded just like Siri—if Siri had gargled with razor blades and barbed wire.

"Grandchild Unit! We can relieve you of all your weaknesses. Just consent to a small suite of neurosomatic modifications. Abandon the ills of the flesh!"

I shrieked like a little girl who had a dead rat dropped down her shirt. I made a superhuman leap I never imagined I could perform, right over the Gramma-borg, and was out the door.

But unlike with my doppelgangers or with my many parental visitors, the Grammas elected to pursue me. Original Gramma (returned from her temporary failure), Soldier Gramma, Cyborg Gramma, they all were hot on my heels as I raced through the grungy skid row streets, much to stunned amazement of all pedestrians and drivers and shopkeepers.

"Stafford! Come back! We love you and want to help you!"

My breath pounded hard and labored. The voices behind me grew in volume and I dared to look backwards for a moment.

There were now dozens of Gramma Atchisons chasing me! Scores in fact! More popping up every moment, until it seemed like hundreds had ported in from across the multiverse.

Stumbling, aching, snivelling, half-blinded by fear, I turned down an alley to escape them all.

Dead end at tall brick façades on three sides.

I collapsed against a rusty dumpster, amidst a pile of rotting, stinking organic debris that had spilled out in transit. My mind was disintegrating at this confrontation with my childhood bastion of safety and affection transmogrified into a hundred horrible aggressive incarnations, all clamoring for my moral and bodily reformation. I closed my eyes and waited for their vengeance.

When nothing happened for about three minutes, I opened my eyes a slit.

The Grammas filled the alley in massed ranks, extending back to the street and beyond. The frontline presented a bizarre and motley array of the woman I had childishly loved in a dozen different guises. Then the Grammas parted to let one special Gramma through.

It was Shoggoth Gramma. A giant semi-transparent gelatinous green mass that slurped as it moved, with the face of Abigail Atchison duplicated a hundred times, floating all around inside the protoplasmic bulk.

The Gramma from Ten Million Divergences Away.

When Shoggoth Gramma spoke, powdered mortar sifted out of the enclosing brick walls.

"No more half-measures! I will fix the boy!"

Before I could move or protest, I was engulfed, along with the whole dumpster, by the blob-like Gramma.

Strange matter filled my nostrils and mouth, and I couldn't breathe, so I did the only sensible thing: I passed out.

I was five years old again, sitting in Gramma's lap, and she was reading me a wonderful story that went on and on endlessly. Her familiar kind voice recounted infinite wonders and miracles, adventures and exploits, all limning my bright future. I wanted it never to end.

When I came to myself again, I lay in a familiar room. Beautiful sunlight poured through the curtain-framed windows. This had been my own bedroom during summers when I returned from college to my parents' mansion in Woodside, California, a whole continent away from that gruesome alley where I had been en-blobbed. I was dressed in clean pajamas, swathed in clean sheets, and feeling healthier and saner than I had felt in many a year. I was curious and perplexed, but not angry or resentful. The good feelings felt weird.

I got cautiously out of bed and went downstairs to the dining room, where I found my parents—my real, original parents—having breakfast.

"Have a seat, Staff," my Dad said jovially.

"It's good to have you back, son," said my Mom.

No mention was made of my intervention ordeal. We started talking about inconsequential stuff. I learned more about my various cousins' recent marriages than even the paparazzi would have wanted to know. And before I quite realized it, I was agreeing to accompany my Dad into the office, "just to lend your perspective on a few things."

It was only after a year of my new stable, happy and prosperous life had gone by that I realized I was in no danger of backsliding into my old ways. The impulse to do dope had been erased. Those druggy years seemed like a dream. Not a nightmare, precisely, but a dream of some other me. I guess I had had a multiversal experience without ever leaving my native continuum.

I never saw any of my alternate Grammas again, and the family never spoke of my intervention. But once in a while I did experience a vivid flashback to that moment in the alley, surrounded by hundreds of grandmothers and being engulfed by one special avatar.

And at those moments a small portion of my left forearm would turn a translucent green, and the face of Abigail Atchison would swim up out of my interior and wink at me both affectionately and with a certain stern remonstrative look.

THE DREAM-SCULPTOR OF A.I.P.

Sam Arkoff hated tears. Tears could not be inscribed in the fiscal ledgers of American International Pictures, and they certainly contributed nothing to the bottom line. In fact, tears held up movie-making, ate into profits, and generally could ruin a producer's day, inducing agita and nerves. Tears, Arkoff felt, should be forbidden in the industry. And yet, as his often uneasy experiences as a producer had long ago informed him, tears were a frequent concomittant of film-making. Inescapable, demanding of his time, and requiring all his savvy and soothing skills to quell.

Take, for instance, the situation right now in his office (an unimpressive, utilitarian and even somewhat dumpy space adjacent to those more-glamorous cinematic headquarters strung out along Sunset Boulevard). Before him sat one of the A.I.P. troupe of frequently employed actors and actresses, Lori Nelson, sniffling after a crying jag and dabbing at her reddened nose with a handful of tissues. A very valuable and useful resource for A.I.P. Just last year, her performance and screen sex-appeal had helped ensure that *Day the World Ended* would be a real moneymaker for 1955. Shot in nine days for sixty-five thousand dollars, the sci-fi shocker was already well on its way to earning a million in receipts. That was a box-office figure that permitted the indulgence of a few tears.

And of course, Nelson's lovely personal figure was no small inducement to management indulgence either. The leggy lass with her masses of wavy blonde hair and finely sculpted winsome features was dressed modestly today in sandals, faded-rose-colored capri pants and a white blouse whose closure involved intricate overlaps of fabric. A string of fake pearls and matching big clip-on earrings completed her ensemble. So despite her tear-stained, blotchy visage she was still a knockout. And even though her most recent A.I.P. release from a few months ago—*Hot Rod Girl*, July, 1956—had not done quite as well as *Day*, racking up only six hundred thousand gross, Arkoff still had big plans for Lori Nelson. She embodied all the qualities in his famous Arkoff formula for moviemaking success: A for Action; R for Revolution; K for Killing; O for Oratory; F for Fantasy; and F for Fornication.

Sitting back in his battered castered chair behind his messy desk while the sniffling Nelson pulled herself together, Arkoff took a moment to consider just how far his formula had taken him, in only a few short years. When he and his partner James Nicholson had formed American Releasing Corporation in 1954, no one had foreseen that the little scrappy and plucky company would soon be dominating the nation's drive-ins, providing red-hot popular culture fodder for teens and young adults. With the bold and classy name change last year to American International Pictures, their ascent had really rocketed to new levels.

Nearing fifty years of age, unprepossessing in the looks department (Arkoff knew he was moon-faced and pear-shaped), the inauspiciously fated son of Helen and Louis Arkoff, Fort Dodge, Iowa, had done pretty well for himself. He smoothed down the lapels of his grey Hart Schaffner & Marx tweed suit with a true appreciation for its quality. His clothing salesman father would have approved.

Arkoff surveyed the many framed pictures covering every square inch of the office's walls: stills and gaudy posters from his various productions, along with autographed publicity shots of many actors and actresses who had played their parts in his films. Jayne Mansfield and John Carradine; Peter Graves and Dorothy Malone; Beverly Garland and Lloyd Bridges. *Female Jungle* and *Apache Woman*; *The Beast with a Million Eyes* and *The Phantom from 10,000 Leagues*; *Girls in Prison* and *It Conquered the World*. An impressive roster of players and spectrum of films, but A.I.P. was only just gearing up. Arkoff envisioned making twenty, thirty, forty films per year, with his patented fast shooting schedule and no-frills unstaged non-studio environments. (Costumes, props, sets, locations, all on the cheap!) Imagine what *that* fabulous output of cinematic hooey would rake in!

But these hypothetical large-grossing films would not get made on time if his cast members were angry or hurt or uncooperative. And that was what he faced now with Lori Nelson.

Apparently this new writer-director he had hired—without much vetting, mainly on the say-so of his most trusted employee, the facile and fecund Roger Corman—was proving to be a bit of a bear. Arkoff did not believe in over-managing his underlings. He hired competent, talented, energetic people who subscribed to the Arkoff formula and then gave them free rein, allowing him to concentrate on financing and marketing. That was his proven recipe for success. He and his partner Nicholson could not be present at every shoot, issuing dictatorial orders that might even contradict those of his chosen directors. The creators had to have a free hand.

But according to Nelson, this tyro director of the new film (what the heck was the guy's name again?), a potential cash-minting masterpiece to be titled *The Monster of Magenta Springs,* was proving to be highly unreasonable, demanding yet imprecise—and just plain weird!

Observing that Nelson had regained control of herself, Arkoff sought to zero in on the exact nature of her somewhat vague complaints. He picked up the model of a spider-type monster from his desktop and began idly flexing its legs.

"You say this guy is demanding that you do some really bizarre stuff that don't make no sense with the script? Like what?"

Nelson's alluring voice quavered a little. "Well, gee, Sam, you know I'm no prissy tight-ass. I'm as willing as the next girl who wants to get ahead in this town to have some space alien feel me up in my bathing suit, or to do a sexy dance in front of a crowd of rowdy juvies. But the kind of wacky and perverted maneuvers this Ballard has me performing are enough to make Krafft-Ebing chew his whiskers! They just plain creep me out!"

Ballard. Jim Ballard. That was the new kid's name. Arkoff had met him several times, but never for any extensive conversations. He had relied on Corman's estimation of the lad's talents and his abilities to get the footage in the can.

"If it's not too delicate or hurtful, Lori, can you be a little more explicit, please?"

"Well, look, the story is set in the place called Magenta Springs, right? It's a kind of down-rent desert resort, full of louche playboys and their jaded dames, dope fiends and beatniks, arteestes and intellectuals. Kinda like Palm Springs crossed with Reno and Greenwich Village and Tijuana, I guess, but also with a kinda Buck Rogers look to it. Ballard's had a lot of really queer building facades put up, with some extensive interiors too."

Arkoff was not pleased to hear of any kind of possibly expensive construction beyond the barest minimum necessary. The movie was being filmed at the Vasquez Rocks Park, just forty minutes outside the city, because it was a cheap and exotic looking venue. Hollywood companies had been filming there ever since the Thirties, and Arkoff had figured there would be plenty of leftover junk on site or ready to hand as rentals, stuff that could be easily cobbled together for this production.

Nelson went on. "So anyhow, according to the script, all the unsuspecting citizens of Magenta Springs are lolling around, getting their kicks like in that new best-seller, *Peyton Place*, right?"

The Grace Metalious novel had just come out last month, September of 1956, and shot up the best-seller lists. Arkoff had momentarily contemplated seeking the screen rights, but had been swiftly outbid by Twentieth-Century Fox. He wasn't disappointed, though, because he knew he could just copy the book's most saleable and risque elements for a film or three of his own, and save the licensing fees. Maybe he'd call it something like... *Runaway Daughters* or *Naked Paradise*. Yeah, that was the ticket!

But any such exploits were in the future. Right now he had to focus on Nelson's complaints.

"So one of these rooms in Magenta Springs," the actress continued, "in a house on Stellavista Drive, has all its walls at kooky angles, like a funhouse. And the room's got no furniture in it, just like a million clocks hanging on all the walls. And I'm supposed to squirm around nude on the floor for like twenty minutes, until I like disappear into some other dimension. 'The angle between these walls will have a happy ending,' director man says."

Arkoff could not get the vivid instant image of Nelson writhing naked on the floor out of his head. "Are you really nude? That's gonna be plenty trouble with the Production Code people."

"Nah, of course not. I got a flesh-colored bodystocking on. And Fred West is behind the camera. He knows how to shoot things clean. But the whole bit is still uncomfortable. Especially since I'm more or less making out with the architecture, not with some hunky guy or even with a monster. And that leads me to another thing."

"Which is?"

"Ballard's got this sicko fascination with cars. He's got a whole fleet of them up there, rentals or some snazzy models borrowed from people. And I'm supposed to—"

Here Lori Nelson paused and blushed.

"Supposed to what?"

"I'm supposed to make love to this Austin-Healey convertible. Rub myself all over it like a cat in heat! Is that kosher or what? Can you imagine, say, Rita Hayworth or Lana Turner helping some jalopy get its rocks off? And how does this tie in with the monster anyhow? Nobody even knows what the monster looks like yet! Ballard just keeps saying, 'It derives its essence from inner space.'"

Arkoff graciously refrained from telling Nelson that Hayworth and Turner occupied a perch inaccessible to her, and that on her rung of the stardom ladder actresses had to put up with a lot of reprehensible and embarrassing stuff. But making love to a car? Even an admittedly sexy model like the Austin-Healey? Where did that fit into the Arkoff Formula? If it was Fornication, it was hardly a conventional sort. Revolution? Killing? Action? Fantasy? About all that could be ruled out definitely was Oratory. Unless maybe the script called for Nelson to make some fantastical endearments while she was buffing the exhaust pipes.

But no matter. None of this sounded like the hallmarks of an efficient and speedy film shoot of solid Grade-B material that would deliver boffo product for America's drive-ins. Something had to be done, and fast.

Arkoff tabbed his intercom. "Marie? Find Corman and tell him I need to see him right away. He's gotta drop whatever he's doing and haul his ass over here, pronto."

Turning his attention back to Nelson, Arkoff said, "Don't you worry, kiddo. Once Roger gets here, I'm sure he'll have some insights into the way his protégé is working that can explain things, and we'll straighten everything out."

"I sure hope so. I don't want this picture to turn into some goofy art-house jerk-off mess that no one sees."

"Here, while we're waiting, take a look at this script and see what you think. It's called *Voodoo Woman*, and I can see you in the lead."

"Gee, thanks, Sam."

While waiting, Arkoff lit a large stogie, then sat back and pondered a line Nelson had dropped, about the monster of Magenta Springs coming from "inner space." Something about that phrase teased Arkoff's memory… And then he had it. That sci-fi flick that had come out a few months back, *Forbidden Planet*. They had featured "monsters from the Id." Was this some new kind of trend he should look into? Psychological demons rather than physical ones? His radar for hot new fads began to ping, and he resolved to dig into the matter later.

In less than half an hour, Arkoff's office door swung open without any preamble, and in traipsed a grinning and ebullient Roger Corman.

Handsome as many a leading man, his chiseled face radiant with health, full of zest and vitality, just turned thirty years old, Corman was a powerhouse, a spark plug, a dynamo. He seemed steeped in the language of the silver screen, was fluent with the camera, beloved by his crew and actors, and undaunted by any challenges or difficulties. Arkoff knew that much of A.I.P.'s current and future success rested on Corman's broad shoulders, and he was determined to keep the director happy. That was one reason he had readily acceded to Corman's request that Ballard be given the helm of his first feature.

Corman's luxuriant quiff of dark hair was brylcreemed to perfection. He wore a baggy and fuzzy striped cardigan over a white Oxford shirt, charcoal-grey linen pants, and snazzy Thom McAn loafers—an altogether unpretentious outfit, though exuding his own style.

Corman greeted Arkoff first. "I hope this is important, chief. I was busy filming Devon as Satan for *The Undead*. What a crowd scene with all the peasants! This is gonna scare the pants off a whole generation."

Then, spotting the still-discomfited Lori Nelson, Corman shifted his attention instantly. He swooped down on her, gripped both her hands and planted a kiss on her brow. "Lori, honey, you look like hell. What's the matter?"

Regarding his boss again, Corman swiftly intuited the general nature of the difficulties. "Don't tell me there's trouble on the set of *Magenta Springs*? I would've bet that my boy Ballard would run a tight and happy ship. He's really obsessive about getting things done efficiently and bringing his vision to the screen. Why, if I hadn't had him as my assistant on *It Conquered the World*, that flick never would've become the success it was. I was having a hard time digging the psychology of our bad guy, Doctor Anderson, when Jim just laid it all out for me. 'He's a cool, unemotional personality impervious to the psychological pressures of modern life, and he thrives like an advanced species of machine in this neutral atmosphere.' Man, was he riffing the stone-cold psycho-gospel or what! That was when I knew he could sit in the director's seat himself."

Arkoff objected. "Well, your boy might have a good line of patter, but he's otherwise pretty ham-fisted with the help. Lori, tell Roger what you told me."

Lori Nelson recounted her grievances while Corman listened intently. After a few moments of contemplation, the director spoke.

"You guys have to cut Jim some slack. He didn't grow up with a wholesome normal life like we all did. He's been through some awful stuff, and it's left him with a different perspective on life. I wouldn't go so far as to call it 'warped,' but he's really out there. Sure, he's a bit of an oddball. But that's what makes him a genius."

Arkoff said, "*Pffft*, genius! That's pretty strong praise for a guy who can't think of anything better to do with his beautiful starlet than have her hump a chrome-laden chassis."

"No, listen, I'm sure he's got his reasons. Jim just sees things different from you and me. We have to give him a chance. He's had it plenty rough."

"Rougher than a kid from Fort Dodge with no education or connections?"

"Yes, Sam, even tougher than your shtick. The first thing you should know is that Jim's a Brit by birth, though he's lost most of his accent. He and his family were in Shanghai when the Japanese invaded. Father, mother, sister. They all ended up in a camp. Brutal. Only Jim survived."

"How awful!" Lori Nelson said, showing a trace of increased empathy for her nemesis.

Corman continued. "In 1945 the Allied authorities stuck him on a ship full of Displaced Peoples, the SS *Arawa*. He never made it back to England, though. Nobody was waiting for him there anyhow. He ended up here, in LA, at the Los Angeles Orphans Home, an adolescent refugee. Same place Marilyn Monroe spent some time in, in fact. He stayed there until he aged out at eighteen, three years later. Right away, he became a US citizen, which showed his heart was in the right place. The next few years he did any odd job he could find, just to stay afloat. He rode the rails up and down the West Coast before returning to LA. Then he got interested in the movies. Spent all his time hanging around the big studios, doing gopher work, being an extra. Finally, he wandered into my purview, and I took him on. He made himself so useful to me on *Apache Woman* and *Five Guns West*, I promoted him to assistant director on *It Conquered*. And that's all she wrote. I think the kid—hell, he's only four years younger'n me—has a great career ahead of him. If only we can be flexible enough to incorporate his unique methods into our system."

Nelson and Arkoff both wore less contentious expressions, as if sympathizing with the rough-and-tumble biography of Jim Ballard.

Arkoff spoke. "Okay, you made a case for him. But I still don't buy all his screwy maneuvers. They're hindering the shoot and potentially cutting into the studio's bottom line. So I want you to go up to Vasquez, Rog, and see what he's doing. Straighten him out if need be, and report back to me."

Corman pinched his chin reflectively. "It'll mean a delay in *The Undead*..."

Arkoff waved off the concern. "That's okay. I know that with you in charge, that flick'll still come in under budget and looking great. A day or two more won't matter, if it lets us get *Magenta Springs* back on an even keel."

"Well, then, of course I'll do it! I can't let my protégé down, can I? Lori, how did you get into town?"

"I got a ride back here with one of the crew who was coming in for supplies."

"Okay, you'll go back out to Vasquez with me. We'll get everyone on the same page in no time. One big happy family. We'll make sure that old Sammy here makes his next million on time."

Rising to her feet, Lori Nelson said, "I should mention one more thing. Ballard's got this pal by his side all the time. Not on the payroll, just a kibitzer. Some real Svengoolie type that Ballard picked up in his travels. Calls himself 'the Doctor.' I actually think he's weirder than Ballard."

"Not a problem. You know this guy's name? Maybe I've heard of him."

"His name's Timothy Leary. From what I can gather, he used to work at a place called the Kaiser Family Foundation in Oakland, until he got kicked out for some kinda unethical hijinks."

Corman looked puzzled. "I think that place is some kinda psychiatric research operation. Maybe Jim has brought this guy Leary onboard as a consultant for his 'monster from inner space' thing..."

Arkoff said, "I ain't paying the kinda money that shrinks charge! You get up there quick, Rog, and see what this is all about!"

After saluting with a smile, Corman turned, took Lori Nelson's arm, and escorted her out of the office, heading for his car.

Before returning to the pressing papers on his desk, Sam Arkoff picked up the spider monster model and admired it a while longer.

Monsters from inner space! Bushwa! What was wrong with the good old standbys like big bugs, giant lizards and aliens from distant galaxies!

* * * *

Vasquez Rocks could be a brutal place in the summer, with temperatures soaring well above ninety degrees. But in this temperate month of October the daytime highs seldom breached eighty, and nights could be positively chilly. Perfect weather for moviemaking, allowing the eerie and stark natural grandeur of the park to be captured easily on film, substituting for Mars, the Gobi Desert or postapocalyptic desolation.

As Corman tooled his mustard-yellow Karmann Ghia past the rustic entrance sign proclaiming VASQUEZ ROCKS NATURAL AREA—COUNTY OF LOS ANGELES, with a beautiful woman in the passnger seat and the pleasures of the brief drive from the city fresh in his mind (chatting with Lori had been very enjoyable, and might be construed to have laid the groundwork for certain other pleasures), he was already mentally rehearsing the various directions that his conversation with Jim Ballard might take. Seldom argumentative or contentious or dictatorial, Corman generally managed to get his way with sweet reason, an aura of conviction, affability, and appeals to camaraderie. Nonetheless, he was mostly implacable when the issues revolved around the best way to shoot a movie, and he had no fears about putting Ballard straight.

Following Lori's directions down a maze of sandy roads, Corman admired the flensed and essential landscape of the park under the light of the late-afternoon sun. From the sands that resembled some kind of terminal beach, jagged rock outcroppings thrust up at discordant angles in a dozen subtle shades: fawn, gold, rose, umber… The grasses of summer had dried to brown, but patches of scrub oak, manzanita, juniper, yucca and assorted succulents loaned a sparse vegetative green scrim to the sere landscape. The car's passage startled random jackrabbits, lizards and gophers, while a red-tailed hawk cut the sky.

Corman noted that the sun was well past its zenith, and he hoped that his mission could be accomplished with enough time to let him return to the city for dinner.

Finally the car rounded a bend and came upon the encampment of A.I.P. folks.

In the loose and wide embrace of some of the more sizable rock formations, a flock of sleek Airstream trailers made a settlement not unlike the primal wagon trains of the settlers. Outside a food truck, workers were setting up the evening meal on folding tables. Corman could smell hot dogs boiling, and even the vinegary tang of vats of cole slaw being stirred. His stomach rumbled, and he realized he had not eaten since breakfast. When directing, he lost all track of time. And then he had had to hustle up here on Arkoff's orders. He led an unusual, fast-paced life. But he wouldn't change it for anything. Movie-making was the only thing that mattered.

Actors and actresses hung out or sauntered by. Some young children in swimsuits—talent or family members—were roughhousing in an inflatable swimming pool. Then one boy jabbed the vinyl liner with a sharp stick and all the water drained out, to the loud consternation of his playmates.

Obviously filming was not currently underway.

Corman parked his VW and slid lithely out; Lori Nelson followed.

"Where do you think we'll find Jimmy?"

"He's probably on the set. He seldom leaves it. I think some nights he even sleeps there. It's like he's created some kind of dream paradise for himself and is always rushing towards it."

"Well, lead on."

They walked beyond the encampment. Corman offered a wave or nod or hello for everyone, and his fellows returned his gestures with genuine affability. He felt good about the atmosphere here. Surely he could resolve any difficulties quickly and get back to LA.

But when Corman and Nelson rounded the last massive flank of breccia rock that shielded the trailers from the set, the director felt all his certainties evaporate.

The natural rock formations here had been tampered with; they now all resembled alien outcroppings in a dozen different garish colors—colors that would be utterly lost in the black-and-white filming. They exhibited convoluted textures like a human brain or coral. Examining one up close, Corman realized that the natural rocks had been layered with spray-on stucco to achieve these exotic configurations.

"Holy shit! What was Jim thinking! The rangers are going to be crapping their pants when they see this. We could be in for thousands of dollars in fines for messing with Mother Nature!"

Lori Nelson said, "I told you your boy was a few Mai Tais short of a Tiki bar, didn't I?"

Corman's gaze left the violated rocks and settled on the set meant to embody the town of Magenta Springs. Astonished, he realized that Ballard had built not just a collection of false fronts, but an actual three-dimensional village of surreal houses that would have caused Salvador Dali or Dr. Seuss to rub his eyes in disbelief.

"How the hell much has he spent on this?"

"Don't ask me, not my job. So long as I get my paycheck, I don't care about the rest of the budget."

Corman picked up his pace and began calling out. "Jim! Jim Ballard! Where are you!"

An oval door swung open in a fuschia polka-dotted façade and James Graham Ballard emerged.

Twenty-six years old, he radiated an intensity of attention and concentration. Slim and graceful, he moved with a confident gait, a man with a mission. A round hearty face—flyaway hair already somewhat in retreat from a broad forehead—hosted incongrously dark and narrowed eyes and a semi-pugnacious chin. The director wore a striped buttoned shirt open at the neck, grey trousers and a scuffed brown suede jacket.

At first Ballard seemed not to recognize Corman, staring at him as if he were an apparition. But then he recovered and came forward to shake hands. Corman clasped Ballard's hand with both of his, seeking to convey his sincerity and good intentions.

"Roger! You do me the great honor of visiting my production. I had hoped you'd drop by someday, but I did not want to make further demands on your precious time. And I see that you have returned the lovely Miss Nelson to the set."

While mostly Americanized, Ballard's speech still exhibited traces of his early upbringing, as well as a certain ornate formality deriving from the dedicated self-education of an ambitious orphan of few means.

The lovely but nervous Lori Nelson sidled closer to Corman, as if for protection. Ballard took no obvious notice of her unease, but merely rolled on.

"It's all very good! Perhaps tonight, in honor of my mentor, we shall finally film a long-contemplated scene! A veritable Walpurgisnacht of creative destruction. Portraying perhaps even the final self-destruction and imbalance of an asymmetric world, the last suicidal spasm of the dextro-rotatory helix, DNA. For after all, is not the human organism an atrocity exhibition in truth?"

Corman could not register aloud his bafflement at this double-talk before Ballard swept on.

"Miss Nelson, I will call upon all your thespian powers! The future belongs to magic, and it's women who control the magic. So let the klieg lights of the midcentury illuminate the birth of what we might call the Space Age!"

Corman found his protégé's rambling talk upsetting. "Jim, I'm thrilled to be here, of course. But my visit is not entirely on my own initiative. Sam sent me up to see exactly what's going on with the filming. He's heard some upsetting stories. If I don't return a reassuring report, he's going to come down hard on you. And frankly, what I see around me has me a little doubt-ful as well. This huge set, and the illegal alterations to the cliffs…"

Ballard seemed undaunted. His speech only became more enthusiastic and fervent. "Ah, but Roger, don't you know that deserts possess a particu-lar magic, since they have exhausted their own futures, and are thus free of time? Anything erected there, a city, a pyramid, a motel, stands outside time. And these are the conditions necessary to encode my vision."

Before Corman could attempt to parse or answer this declaration, a second man emerged from the imaginary house.

Dressed entirely in a formal white suit, he owned a blocky youth-ful face under a sheaf of dark hair. Piercing eyes and a broad smile were somewhat at odds with each other. The stranger crossed the distance to the group, moving with an odd languour, almost as if swimming underwater.

"Roger, may I present Doctor Timothy Leary, my fellow 'cosmonaut,' if I may coin a descriptor. Tim has been helping me to shape and solidify my esthetic goals. He employs some useful pharmaceutical adjuncts for that purpose. You too might benefit! We met in Frisco a year or two ago, and he only recently became a free agent, so to speak, and instantly sought me out. Tim and Jim, pioneers in the subconscious!"

Corman tentatively shook Leary's hand. "Doctor Leary, I hope that along with your formal esthetic and professional advice you might be able to convince your, ah, partner that there are certain practical constraints on this operation."

Leary put his hands together palm-to-palm and made a slight bow. "Understood. But more importantly, we must acknowledge that the uni-verse is an intelligence test, and our first duty is to learn how to pass it."

This pat aphorism instantly raised Corman's hackles. He had encoun-tered enough of these Hollywood spiritual and self-improvement swami types to recognize the standard shuck-and-jive when he heard it. Whatever Ballard's innate failings or weaknesses might be, they were certainly being drawn out and exacerbated by this jerk. Any catastrophic failure here on the set of *The Monster from Magenta Springs* would be detrimental to A.I.P and to Corman's own career. He could not let things continue to spiral out of control. He decided it was time to lay down the law.

"Jim, you and I need to get a few things straight. You're forgetting ev-erything I taught you about moviemaking. I think you had better ride back to the city with me. Away from this unreal kingdom you've constructed for yourself, everything will look different, and you'll come to your senses."

Ballard only chuckled. "Roger, civilized life, you know, is based on a huge number of illusions in which we all collaborate willingly. The trouble is we forget after a while that they are illusions and we are deeply shocked when reality is torn down around us. That's your condition now. But if you just stay here a while and participate willingly, you'll soon see that in a totally sane society such as the U.S.A. is trying to impose, madness is the only freedom."

Now Corman got really angry. He grabbed Ballard's arm. "Jim, you're coming with me!"

"I think not, Mister Corman," said Leary.

Corman stared unbelievingly at the pistol in Leary's hand.

"That's not a prop, is it?"

"While reality is indeed mutable," Ballard observed, "there are some propositions that remain fixed. And death is one."

* * * *

Corman could not see Lori Nelson's face. Not only was the dark interior of Ballard's trailer unlit except by the flickering radiance derived from a large bonfire outside the trailer, but he and the actress sat, tied up, back-to-back in folding camp chairs, one emblazoned with Ballard's name, one with Leary's. But he was heartened by the plucky actress's resigned but unpanicky tone of voice.

"I'm so sorry I got you into this, Rog. If only I had let Jim go ahead with his crazy schemes, maybe he would have gotten them out of his system and returned to normality. I don't think he's truly evil. He's just a little freaky. I could've gone on making love to the Austin-Healey. What's a few kinky scenes matter in our racket anyhow? It's better than doing stag films."

"Don't recriminate yourself, Lori. You did absolutely the right thing. All this power to make his dreams come true has unbalanced the poor guy. All his old traumas resurfaced. I should have seen that tendency in him, so I'm the one to blame, if anybody. You were just trying to stop him from hurting himself and others."

"Thanks for that, Rog." Lori was silent for a few moments. Then she said, "Do you think he's going to kill us?"

"Naw, I don't. Neither he nor Leary are the murdering kind. He just doesn't want us to interfere in his mania. I figure we're actually more useful to him as witnesses. These types need an audience, or they don't feel appreciated and worshipped."

As if responding to Corman's analysis of the situation, the trailer door opened to reveal Ballard framed against the bonfire's glare. He had no gun, nor was Leary evident—factors which reassured Corman greatly.

"Roger, it's time to film the apotheosis. Can I count on you and Miss Nelson to be compliant with my desires? There's nothing you can do to stop this now. All the crew and cast are on my side. They've all experienced Tim's various sacraments, and come to appreciate my goals."

Corman contemplated his options, all too few.

"All right, Jim, we agree to stand back and not interfere."

"Wonderful! Let's drop the stick on the clapboard then, shall we!"

At the harshly illuminated Magenta Springs set, all was an ants-nest of activity. Actors in futuristic costumes were finding their places, the sound man was positioning his boom mike, and Fred West stood ready at the camera on its dolly tracks. He nodded with an acolyte's gleam in his eyes to Roger, but said nothing.

Ballard picked up a loud-hailer, and his amplified voice crackled mechanically. "All right, people! Now commences the sanctified apocalypse! Let your psyches loose!"

At this command, a recording of *Rites of Spring* blasted out through loudspeakers emplaced around the canyon, and the cast members went berserk, following no discernible script. Fighting, love-making, dancing; tears, laughter, bellows; racing to and fro, chaotic entrances and exits; perfervid perorations.

Then Leary appeared, atop one of the houses, pinned by a spotlight. The music stopped, and his mic'd voice issued from the speakers, proclaiming a text either he or Ballard must have written.

"Deep Time: one billion mega-years. They are beginning to dictate the form and dimensions of the universe. To girdle the distances which circumscribe the cosmos they have reduced their time period to one-millionth of its previous phase. The great galaxies and spiral nebulae which once seemed to live for eternity are now of such brief duration that they are no longer visible. The universe is now almost filled by the great vibrating mantle of ideation, a vast shimmering harp which has completely translated itself into pure wave form, independent of any generating source. As the universe pulses slowly, its own energy vortices flexing and dilating, all the force-fields of the ideation mantle flex and dilate in sympathy, growing like an embryo within the womb of the cosmos, a child which will soon fill and consume its parent.

"Deep Time: ten trillion mega-years. The ideation-field has now swallowed the cosmos, substituted its own dynamic, its own spatial and temporal dimensions. All primary time and energy fields have been engulfed. Time has virtually ceased to exist, the ideation-field is nearly stationary, infinitely slow eddies of sentience undulating outward across its mantles."

Roger Corman watched this incredible spectacle both aghast and impressed. This was certainly movie-making of a caliber heretofore undreamt-of. Even De Mille and his Biblical extravaganzas had never attained this pitch.

At that moment, several figures raced onto the set, each one carrying a torch lit from the bonfire. They ran from one flimsy house to another, setting them all ablaze.

Leary had vanished from his flaming perch—to safety or danger was unclear. The cast and crew began to scream and flee. Only Fred West kept to his station, filming Ballard's Hollywood dream as the flames roared higher, the young director urging him on, making certain that his first, last and only production would be captured for posterity.

Finally, when their lives seemed most in danger, Corman grabbed Lori Nelson and fled. Looking back, he saw Fred West following, while Ballard still wrestled with the stopped camera's film canisters.

The desert terrain, barren of fuel, and the rock outcroppings themselves contained the fire, sparing the trailers and the vehicles. Corman found his VW where he had left it, and he hustled a quietly weeping Lori Nelson into the passenger seat.

Just then Ballard caught up with him, sooty and reeking of smoke. He pressed the warm film canister into Corman's hands.

"Take this, Roger. See that Arkoff releases it, per our contract. It will edify humanity. The drive-ins of the world will never be the same. We live in a world ruled by fictions of every kind. It has been my task to invent reality."

Before Corman could respond, Ballard trotted off, toward a small sports car in which a dirty-white-suited figure already sat. They were out of sight before Corman quite realized he was still holding the film.

Lori Nelson, finished with her tears, said, "All those goddamn rhearsals, and my part ends up on the cutting-room floor."

* * * *

The Austin-Healey, its top down, drove east through the night, its two occupants singing loudly the tune "High Hopes," popularized by Fred Astaire last year in his film with Ginger Rogers, *The Seven Year Itch*.

> *"Just what makes that little old ant*
> *Think he'll move that rubber tree plant...!"*

Eventually they tapered off. Then Ballard said, "Timothy, I think Las Vegas is going to present us with a lot of possibilities. I would sum up my fear about the future in one word: boring. I worry that everything has happened; nothing exciting or new or interesting is ever going to happen again. The future is just going to be a vast, conforming suburb of the soul. But Las Vegas is the antithesis of all that, and we shall surely flourish within its precincts."

"Natch. If we don't crash getting there."

"Oh, but that would not be the worst thing."

And so saying, Ballard pressed down the accelerator even deeper to the floor, as if seeking the limits of physics. Leary whooped.

They were somewhere around Barstow on the edge of the desert when the drugs began to take hold.

THE STEAM HOUSE
IN INNSMOUTH

Never did I, Henri Maucler, bold Parisian globetrotter and explorer, dare to imagine that I would experience an adventure more thrilling than that which obtained when I and several stout comrades traversed the length and breadth of the Indian subcontinent in our miracle conveyance, the Steam House, whilst on the track of that rogue and scoundrel, Nana Sahib, otherwise known as Dandou Pant, instigator of the Sepoy Revolt. Those uncommon exploits, chronicled by my good friend and compatriot, the scribe Jules Verne, in his aptly but less-than-ingeniously named volume *The Steam House*, culminated in much death and destruction and parting of the ways amongst the legendary troop of comrades who had called the Steam House home for however limited a time. And so with all my brothers-in-arms scattered to the four corners of the globe, and with the miraculous modern vehicle that had enabled our travels lying in smoldering ruins, I rashly forecast that never again would this assemblage reunite and experience anything comparable. I resigned myself to having lived already, at my young age, the apex of my wondrous wanderings.

But, unlike M'sieur Verne, I proved to be no prophet. For only three years later, in 1869, much to my delighted surprise, the entire heroic troupe had miraculously reformed, albeit in a shockingly foreign and unanticipated setting, with the precipitating impulse being the creation of a newer and far grander Steam House, and the securing of an ambitious mission worthy of its instantiation. For, once assembled, our chosen enterprise proved to be even more outré, dangerous and exhilarating than even our pursuit of the Hindoo terrorist.

But prior to launching into a recounting of the rebirth of the Steam House—Steam House II, it might be dubbed—perhaps I may be allowed—very briefly, so as not to trespass overly on the hospitality and patience of my readers, new and old—to offer a précis of our earlier exploits.

Assembled in Calcutta in 1866 were as marvelous a troupe of stout and brave souls as ever graced an argosy. I will immediately discount in all due humility my own presence, for I served mainly as observer, journalist and commentator. But the others can withstand any falsely modest minimizing.

First came Captain Blake Hood, a renowned soldier recuperating on long-term wounded leave, facile with both gun and fists, and always desirous of bagging exotic prey, whether animal or human. His resourceful aide-de-camp manifested in the person of the wry and boisterous Freddy Fox.

Our accepted center of gravity was Colonel Sir Edward Munro, retired, who boasted a constitution stronger than that of many men half his age (he was a venerable forty-seven at the time) and the wisdom of a man double his years. At the outset of our exploits, his wife, Lady Beverly Munro, was among the sadly missing, but later restored to our happy company by a set of circumstances too incredible to synopsize. And of course, ever by the Colonel's side was his bluff and hearty manservant, Sergeant Jake McNeil.

There were also involved several hired men of grand proletarian character, serving as cook, coal-stoker and driver of the Steam House. But these chaps, scattered to the four corners of the globe at journey's end, were not to be found when we reconstituted ourselves, and we had to discover acceptable substitutes, as shall soon be demonstrated.

But I am reserving until this moment any mention of the final figure of our core company, the man who made our whole mission possible, and that is Josiah Banks, Mechanical Engineer par excellence. Banks it was who invented and perfected the Steam House, having accepted the challenge of fashioning a conveyance with the flexibility of a coach, the luxury accoutrements of a railroad train, the bouyancy of a ferry, and the massive indomitability of a battleship.

The main component of the Steam House was the *Behemoth*, a steam engine comparable to that of any rail company stock, but able with its more flexible undercarriage to pursue any trackless road, and also to take to the water when deploying its built-in paddlewheels. As befitted our Hindoo venue, the carapace of the engine was fashioned in the semi-realistic likeness of a mighty steel elephant, many hands high. Behind the Behemoth, securely attached to that motive engine, trailed two small palaces on wheels, in the Hindoo style, each of three stories height. Here were commodious living quarters, plenty of storage space, a well-equipped kitchen, a small but sufficient armory, and facilities for ablutions.

Thus was our party equipped to travel swiftly and in style and ease, all thanks to the technological ingenuity of Engineer Banks.

And travel we did, up and down the Indian countryside, until a mortal battle with our enemies that left our conveyance in flinders, and saw the survivors set aflight like straws in the wind, harking back to their native abodes, with only keen and vivid memories to sustain the legend of the Steam House.

It is at this point in my reminiscenses—and I beg just a few more minutes of patience from any of my readers eager to hear of Steam House II—

that I must introduce one last personage. He was not an original member of our troupe, but was encountered midway in our peregrinations and played a sizable role—a role which was only to increase in magnitude and centrality during our new forays. In fact, this fellow, along with Banks, could be said to have actually launched Steam House II into its fantastical new mission.

I refer, as my seasoned readers might have guessed, to Mathias van Guitt, former Professor of Natural History at the Rotterdam Museum, but thereafter turned supplier of exotic beasts to circuses, zoos, sideshows and exhibitory animal reserves across the planet. If I may be so lexically parsimonious as to recycle my perfected initial description of the man, I will do so now.

"Mathias van Guitt, menagerie purveyor, was a spectacled man of about fifty. His smooth face, his twinkling eyes, his turned-up nose, the perpetual stir of his whole person, his exaggerated gestures, suited to each of the sentences which issued from his wide mouth, all combined to make him a perfect type of the old provincial comedian. His language was always composed of the choicest terms, and he was sometimes rather annoying to his interlocutors if they could not keep beyond the radius of his gestures."

And so, with my friends all assembled pictorially before your gaze at last, and with some concept of the marvels of the original Steam House laid out, I can now embark on the astonishing tale of how we all reunited and to what glorious purpose.

* * * *

The precipitating telegram found me ensconced mid-morning on a fine June day in my Parisian flat on the Left Bank. For the several years that had passed since my Indian foray, I had been making my living as a journalist for *La Presse*, that penny paper whose sometimes louche ways caused much controversy. I was not overly enamored of the job nor of my lowly social status, but was not ambitious enough to throw over a decent income in favor of more speculative pursuits. And besides, the freedom afforded me as a roving reporter suited my tastes. I could spend many an hour over an appertif at Les Deux Magots or The Café de la Paix, and charge it off to research, without arousing the ire of my bosses.

Last night's alcohol-fueled *flâneurisms* had caused me to rise late today, and so I was on hand for the arrival of the messenger boy at my door. He seemed slightly in awe as he handed over the telegram to me. "It's all the way from America," he said. The first trans-Atlantic cable had been laid only three years ago, and such long-distance communications were still novel enough to provoke curiosity and interest.

Still groggy, I made no comment in return, but tipped the sallow-cheeked boy generously. Upon his departure, I tossed the communique to a side table, since I still had to deal with my post-festivities headache. When I finally felt well enough to read anything, I focused on the sparse words, and a feeling of bewilderment, anticipation, wonder and joy gradually overtook me.

HAVE RECONSTRUCTED THE STEAM HOUSE AND ES-TABLISHED A PLAN OF ACTION STOP WOULD BE GRATE-FUL FOR YOUR PARTICIPATION IN THE ENTERPRISE STOP PREPAID TICKETS TO AMERICA AWAITING YOU CU-NARD LINES LIVERPOOL STOP YOUR STOUT COMRADE, J. BANKS STOP

This news was almost too fabulous to comprehend. Apparently, Josiah Banks had somehow found the funding and motivation to reconstitute his trackless engine and its equipage, and, even more startlingly, had secured backers who had a use for the vehicle. And he was asking me to be part of the crew! How could this invitation be anything but a life-altering inducement to toss aside all my stale daily rituals? I hesitated not a moment in my decision.

I dressed hastily and went immediately to the offices of *La Presse*, where I boldly tendered my resignation. But Etienne Drouet, my editor, was not quick to accept it, instead embarking on an interrogation of my motives. After hearing my long disquistion akin to that I have placed before my reader here as a preface, he came to the decision that I should keep my position on the paper and serve as foreign correspondent for the duration of the expedition of Steam House II! This was truly the happiest of scenarios! Adventure *and* a paycheck.

Within three days I found myself stepping from the train in Liverpool, carrying only a single valise, and hiring a hansom cab to convey me to the Cunard line offices. There I discovered that the arranged tickets in my name secured me passage on the top-of-the-line Cunard vessel christened *China*—dual engines, three decks, iron construction dating from 1862, luxurious first-class accomodations—and that departure was two days hence. Chafing at the bit as I was, I nonetheless found a hotel room and set out to enjoy the night life of Liverpool until departure.

Perhaps I was a little too accomplished at drowning my impatience to leave in a welter of wine, women and song, since on the appointed day, and at nearly the appointed minute of leave-taking, I found myself rushing pell-mell to the docks and, last passenger ashore, racing up a gangplank that was in the very process of being unhinged from the ship!

But make it I did, by the skin of my teeth, and quickly repaired to my cabin, freshening up before essaying any social appearance in the eyes of my fellow passengers.

I entered one of the main saloons with its impressive eight-foot ceiling and ornate furnishings. It seemed as if most of the *China*'s two-hundred-plus first-class travelers had chosen to congregate in this dramatic space. I quickly secured a glass of champagne and, keeping an eye peeled for unmarried women desirous of companionship, began to circulate.

I was halfway into the scrum when I heard a voice at once totally familiar and utterly anticipated.

"And so there I was, halfway across the open plain, when I spotted the rhino getting ready to charge me. I turned to Fox, my man, and calmly requested him to hand me my Sharps fifty- caliber rifle. As the beast bore down on me, I took steady aim, fired, and bagged the monster at a distance of only thirty yards. His dead decelerating body plowed a trench practically to my feet."

I immediately began weaving through the crowd to verify the import of my ears. And my eyes soon attested to the aural evidence. There stood Captain Blake Hood, surrounded by appreciative listeners in all his hearty manliness. However, his costume of formal wear disconcerted me, for I had never before seen him so attired.

I dove upon him, giving him a bit of a start, and then we were embracing warmly. After some mutual surprised splutterings, I ventured to ask what his presence here betokened. He replied with a story identical to mine: the telegram from Banks, and Hood's quick assent and journey to Liverpool. It turned out that Hood had been conveniently back in London for several months, looking to clear up some military paperwork connected with his extended leave.

"And is your man Freddy Fox with you?"

"Yes, of course. He's down in second-class, doubtlessly hoisting a few tankards and swilling down platters of corned beef and cabbage."

"Wouldn't it be something if the Colonel were waiting for us in America?" I suggested. "Then we'd have the whole gang reassembled for whatever exploits await us."

Hard upon my musings came a solemn, pontifical, yet comradely voice, equally resonant with my cherished memories.

"But why should we delay our reunion until arrival on the North American continent, gentlemen, when we can enjoy eight days of pleasure here on this fine ship?"

Hood and I both swung around eagerly, and were met with the welcome sight of a smiling Colonel Sir Edward Munro, looking even more hearty than when last seen—an effect obviously derived from enjoying three years of the restoration of his charming wife, once feared lost. And by his side, there she stood, elegant and sophisticated: Lady Beverly Munro. No one seeing her chic figure now would ever believe that she had once wandered the subcontinent as a bedraggled madwoman dubbed "the Roving Flame."

Hood and I and the Munroes exchanged a flurry of greetings—Lady's Munro's dulcet tones charmed my soul—and we all agreed to retreat to one of the tables set against the saloon's walls, where we could take up our discussion in a more comfortable manner, around a small collation of drinks and food.

One of the first things we ascertained was that the Munroes had received—at their estate in South Shropshire dubbed "Little Switzerland"—a communique identical to that sent to Hood and myself. (I also was happy to learn that Sergeant Jake McNeil, loyal servant, also currently enjoyed a second-class berth in the *China*'s bowels.) We tossed out various speculations as to what awaited us at the end of our journey, but could come up with nothing conclusive. And so we tabled the matter, and set about enjoying our cruise.

The eight days till Halifax passed joyously. The subsequent short ocean transit to Boston was painless. All six of us disembarked onto the busy, bustling quay as a unified party, but were at a loss as to how to proceed. The telegrams had led us thus far and no further. I think we had all expected to see Banks awaiting us on the dock, but such was not to be.

Yet we should never have underestimated engineer Banks's planning and preparations. For we were hailed—"Munro and company?"—almost instantly by a young, round-faced and ginger-haired fellow dressed in a clean workmanlike manner. He doffed his cloth cap to us, smiled broadly to disclose a few missing teeth, and said, "The name is Wilberforce Phillips, navigator and general dogsbody aboard Steam House II. We have another small journey to make, before your reunion is complete. We'll be taking a vessel of the Fall River Line, the *Old Colony*, down to Providence, where your host awaits. I hope you have not quite lost your sea legs yet!"

Suiting his actions to his words, Phillips soon had us and our luggage aboard the *Old Colony*. The short voyage passed pleasantly—although Phillips refused to share with us any information about Banks's doings.

"The master engineer will spill all in due time."

At last our long passage from the Old World to the New was complete. We stepped onto land at India Point. And there, surrounded by a gawping crowd, stood Steam House II.

* * * *

The reader will here recall my description of the original Steam House: a massive train engine concealed under the wrought-iron camouflage of a gigantic elephant simulacrum. And behind, attached by subtle and responsive linkages, two pagoda-like domiciles on wheels. So engraved was this image on my brain cells, that I had never considered that Banks, when reconstituting the apparatus, would deviate from the old plans. And yet, strikingly, he had—and what other maneuver, in retrospect, could have been more natural? Here in the New World, brash young America, an elephant and pagodas would have seemed utterly out of place, and even perhaps be construed as an insult to the native culture. And so, Banks had contrived a most fitting appearance for Steam House II.

The engine—and I was to learn that in the past three years, many sophistications of this motive technology had come to pass, rendering Steam House II an even more powerful and formidable contrivance—was cloaked in the image of an American Bison—*Bos bison bison*, to be precise. The enormous metal torso sloped from shoulders (twenty feet high) down to rump. The shaggy and horned head represented a fusion of the arts of metalworker and furrier. The legs were folded into a couchant position, so as to conceal the engine's wheels. (As I would soon learn, this configuration imparted to the engine, when in motion, an uncanny appearance of gliding along the road.)

And what of the trailing domiciles? What else would have consorted so well with the mighty buffalo as two enormous conical teepees, or wigwams, constructed not of fabric, but cunningly bent and varnished wood? Each of them was three stories tall, and featured many windows and balconies at each level.

Plainly, this was an indigenous arrangement that would have pleased the god Manitou himself!

This unprecedented and unanticipated sight had plunged all of us into an amazed silence and fascination, so that we did not immediately spot Engineer Josiah Banks himself. But once I was able to draw my eyes away from the spectacle, I saw Banks the man, grinning broadly, with hands in his trouser pockets. I rushed to greet him, and the rest of the party followed suit.

The clever fellow was just as we had last seen him, vivacious and keen-eyed. His only newness was that he had adopted the style of abundant facial hair made famous by the Amercian General Burnside. After he had accepted our affirmations and congratulations—Fox and McNeil resorted to whistles, war-whoops and mild imprecations—and had made his own protestations of undying friendship in return, Banks explained how this situation had come to be.

"Once the original Steam House had been reduced to shards, and our mission to rescue Lady Munro was complete, I found myself tired of India and longing for my native Scotland. Thence I returned, a divagatory journey of over a year. Upon entering my apartments, I found a wealth of old mail awaiting my inspection. But among the letters was a more-recent missive from an American firm called Darling, Brown and Sharp. The owners—Samuel Darling, Joseph Brown and Lucian Sharp—had heard of of my achievements with the Steam House and been impressed. They were writing to offer me employment with their firm. What they detailed—their ultra-modern facilities, their open-minded investment in new techniques and processes, their willingness to give me free rein—was irresistible. And so I hied myself to Providence, and commenced the construction of Steam House II—a task which has filled most of the past two years. You see the result before you."

"Incredible," I said. "Such a rare and fortuitous meeting of talent and resources. The like may never happen again."

The others bestowed similar encomiums. But then the ever-practical Colonel Munro cut to the heart of the matter.

"Impressive as this monster is, Banks, it remains merely an idle toy, if it lacks any goals governing its usage. You spoke of a mission of some sort...?"

"Yes, indeed, Colonel. Not a mere excursion either, but an expedition to aquire something most rare. I will explain all when we return to the factory. Please, step aboard and make yourself at home."

Hood and his man Fox accompanied the Colonel and Lady Munro and McNeil into one of the wigwams, their luggage loaded by some idle stevedores here at this busy India Point transit site. I, however, chose to follow Banks and Phillips into the cab of the engine. Access was obtained through a door in the buffalo's flank. The artificial lighting inside the shell was subdued, and a series of periscopes and a kind of inverted camera obscura provided images of our forward path, and likewise displays to rear and sides. A clever arrangement of hoppers and chutes served to feed coal to the hungry beast. Tucked up inside the shell were the paddlewheels for aquatic travel.

With Banks at the controls and Phillips navigating, we were soon in motion.

"The factory is on South Main Street, just a short distance away."

As we trundled away from the edge of Narraganset Bay, I could admire, through the optics from our secret vantage, the astonished citizenry, the startled horses, and the quaint architecture of this city, my first brush with a New World metropolis. Whilst not a patch on the splendors of Paris, I found nonetheless a definite charm deriving from the colonial ambiance.

True to his word, Banks had us at the Darling, Brown and Sharpe establishment—a sprawling set of brick warehouses and workshops—within just fifteen minutes. I don't think we had traversed much more than a mile, thereby according the pace of a walking man to the mighty engine. As if intuiting my thoughts, Banks said, "Don't worry, Henri—on a straight road and without crowding, we can get our speed up to thirty or forty miles per hour, or above. Enough to outrun any band of brigands on horseback, such as beset the first Steam House in India."

Phillips had parked us neatly next to what seemed the main building, and the three of us left the engine, to find our comrades already disembarked from the wigwams. They formed a celebratory scrum around an unseen figure. Making my way closer, I soon discerned the person at the center of the happy melee. It was none other than Mathias van Guitt, big-game trapper extraordinaire.

The jovial, vociferous Dutchman in his colorful brocaded vest cast off his well-wishers and moved to share his bountiful camaraderie with me. When all the hearty backslapping was finally accomplished, van Guitt assumed a pontifical air, as if preparing to address a stadium of worshippers.

"My good friends, fellow seekers of adventure and glory, not to mention profits—may I announce to you that you see before you the first individual to commission the services of the new Steam House and its creator—at a very reasonable rate, influenced, I have no doubt, by longstanding ties of affection. Indeed, I, Mathias van Guitt, need this marvelous vehicle—and also am desirous of securing the skills that you all possess—to penetrate into a semi-hostile territory and return with a prize and treasure beyond compare, next to which the trapping of tigers and apes will pall into insignifcance. Let it be known amongst our select band—but not by the suspicious and ignorant hoi polloi, who might choose to misunderstand or interfere—that van Guitt the Audacious, van Guitt the Fearless, has volunteered to capture one or more of the legendary aquatic Deep Ones of New England, to be delivered to none other than that master showman, Phineas Taylor Barnum!"

* * * *

The lights in the spacious, windowless, walnut-panelled conference room of Darling, Sharp and Brown had been lowered to a mere flicker, lending the scene the air of a séance. The room's chairs had been arrayed in rows—with an aisle down their middle—to face a portable screen. On a table at the rear stood a magic lantern, making the air above it waver with the heat of its lamp. Our company had taken up seats while van Guitt fussed with the projection device, which was aimed down the middle channel at the screen. Eventually he had to give over its operation to Banks. But this surrendering of manual control only allowed him to focus more passion on his speech.

"My fellow celebrants of the Life Afield! I have prepared this small presentation as the quickest and best way of infusing the parameters of our quest into your noble craniums! So without further ado, let us commence. I have arranged the talk in what might seem a topsy-turvy fashion to you, but in a manner which suits my sense of building a foundation before erecting a superstructure. And so I will start with a look at the ultimate backer of our expedition. First slide, please, Josiah....

"Here you see the canny visage of one P. T. Barnum, hitherto known to the wide world as the great showman whose Museum in New York City featured such attractions as the Feejee Mermaid and General Tom Thumb. Next slide, please. Barnum also patronized the arts by sponsoring the tour of Jenny Lind, the Swedish Nightingale. But upon the conflagration last year—slide, please, Josiah—which claimed his Museum, Barnum was at a loss as to what venture he might next undertake. I am happy to report that the great genius of the entertainment world is now holed up productively in the midwestern state of Wisconsin with his new partner, William Cameron Coup, putting together 'P. T. Barnum's Grand Traveling Museum, Menagerie, Caravan & Hippodrome,' a roadshow guaranteed to surpass any such enterprise ever before attempted. To accomplish this miracle, however, Mister Barnum needs freaks and natural wonders never before seen. Apprehending these requisites in my ceaseless quest for clients, I began to cast about for how best to fulfill Barnum's needs. After meticulous research—conducted here at Brown University, and in nearby Massachusetts at Miskatonic University—I found just the thing to ensure the Menagerie's success, and approached Barnum with my proposition. He rapidly assented, and entered into a contract to pay me the princely sum of fifteen hundred English pounds, could I but deliver the promised goods. And that brings me now to the second part of my little lecture. Josiah, if you would be so kind..."

Onto the screen now flashed without warning or preamble a photographic image so bizarre and horrifying, even devoid of Nature's colorations, that the men involuntarily grunted as if belly-punched, and Lady Munro emitted a piercing shriek.

Depicted on the screen was an expanse of water and the rim of a stony beach, with the perspective being that of a photographer placed a bit further inshore from the marge. Standing in the shallow water, only their bare scaly upper halves exposed, were two creatures best described as fish-men. A hideous hybrid of *homo sapiens* and some be-gilled denizen of the deep, the monsters exhibited a menacing calm, as if utterly sure of their right to exist and a kind of ownership of the scene. Their huge jellied eyes and rubbery mouths contributed to a countenance expressive of an alien sentience, at once allied to mankind's, yet utterly other. One gill-man held both his arms by his side, his hands below the waterline. The other individual had one arm upraised—in greeting or admonition, who could say?—revealing a pale paw with webbed digits and talon-like nails.

It took some time for the gruesome reality of these beings to be absorbed by us the audience, and van Guitt allowed us our period of silent reckoning before continuing.

"The creatures you see on the screen represent—in the best judgment of such experts in ichthyology and paleontology as Professor Louis Agassiz, with whom I have been in constant consultation—a species of living fossil, survivors of a distant past. To display one or more of these before the public would make the reputation of any showman. And also crown with laurels the bold souls who captured the beast. And I aim for our troupe to earn that high distinction.

"This, in short, concludes my presentation. But I will certainly accept questions and comments, following which I must ask for your pledges of secrecy and commitment to the project—all contingent on a share of the fee, naturally. Of course, those who so choose may take their leave of the enterprise without prejudice."

At this point Banks extinguished the magic lantern and turned up the whale-oil lamps. I winced at the brightness, then turned my recovering gaze to my comrades.

Banks, with foreknowledge of the mission, was obviously fully onboard. After all, it was his invention that would provide the transportation and protective embrace for our party. Captain Hood and his aide-de-camp Fox were all aglow with the prospect of bagging new trophies. The Captain's quest to slaughter fifty tigers in India paled beside this novel venture. "St. Hubert be my speed!" he exclaimed. "You may count me in, van Guitt. I assume there's a colony of these creatures and that some of them might put up a fight before we capture our specimens. That's where Fox and I will shine."

"Indeed, Captain, the only known colony of these creatures exists in the bay adjacent to the small Massachusetts town of Innsmouth, near Ipswich and Rowley in Essex County. That is to be our hunting grounds. It is only some ninety miles distant from Providence—a short and easy trip for the mighty Steam House. We shall proceed north to Boston, and then aim for the coast."

Now the man we all looked up to, Colonel Munro, spoke, with somber mien. "If I am to accompany you all—and I devoutly desire to do so, for the sake of science and glory, and to add some excitement to a homebody's life that, while congenial, has grown a bit tepid of late—then Lady Munro will be my side. After our long and painful separation, we swore never to be apart again. You know her as a resourceful and brave woman—and in fact she is so self-reliant, she disdains the bevy of maids I would happily employ for her—but she is nonetheless still of the gentler sex. What kind of safety measures are in place to constrain these beasts, if we succeed in capturing them?"

"Ah, my most excellent Colonel, surely you did not think I would neglect so vital an aspect of my plan! You saw firsthand my throughness with the savage jungle denizens of India. First, the creatures will be entangled in heavy-duty netting, then cudgeled into submission and manacled. Then, they will be ensconced in their special guest quarters. The lowest level of one of the wigwams—the teepee containing the kitchen and storage rooms, not your personal quarters—features a large water tank for their pleasure, and that tank is the repository for a strong cage of iron bars which may be winched in and out. You'll see its efficacy at the proper time. So you see, nothing will endanger your lovely wife—or any of us."

Now all eyes turned to me, as the last to register my vote. I struck a mock heroic pose. "My editor dispatched me to America to supply reports of local color and human interest. He could hardly have imagined that I would be privy to the story of the century! So long as I have exclusive rights to retail the account of our expedition—when permitted by Mr. Barnum, of course—you may count me fully enrolled."

A round of applause went up then, and Banks brought out a bottle of champagne and glasses for a toast.

Finally van Guitt addressed us all. "I must now introduce the final member of our party. I have hired a local girl to act as our cook. You surely recall how greatly the skills of Monsieur Parazard enhanced our Indian trip, and we could hardly choose to fare less well in a new land. Josiah, please bring in Miss Jenny Arbutus."

Banks left the room and returned with as stunning a lass I had ever laid eyes on. Dressed in a plain gingham skirt enhanced by a fashionalble "garibaldi" blouse, our new chef was a redhead with a fiery glint in her eyes and a buxom figure. Jenny Arbutus regarded us all with no slavish false humility, but with a native New England pride and eagerness to please. Her voice was a charming contralto.

"If any of you don't like Yankee vittles, you can scrounge your fare from the countryside. Johnnycakes, cod and baked beans rank high in my repertoire, but I ain't averse to other sensible requests, such as a Delmonco steak or a tray of steaming laplanders—so long as they don't involve frogs' legs, haggis or any other culinary abominations!"

The laughter was general, and I took the occasion to bestow a gallant Gallic kiss on each of Jenny's cheeks, to which she seemed in no wise disdainful.

This trip, I anticipated, would be even more delightful than I had at first imagined.

Our excursion north to Boston proved uneventful, except for the experience of being accompanied by a daily entourage of wild urchins—and one dicey ambush of indeterminate nature. I will detail the first phenomenon lightly, merely to add some naturalistic touches to my portrait of America, but expend more detail upon the latter incident, since in retrospect it foreshadowed consequential events in Innsmouth.

Directly following Mathias van Guitt's presentation, and a fine repast at a local restaurant, all of us spent the night comfortably in our new teepee quarters. Lady and Sir Munro occupied the highest level of one wigwam, with Captain Hood and I sharing the next lower slice, and Fox and McNeil on the most spacious ground level, along with Banks and Phillips; Jenny Arbutus had her sleeping room just off the second-floor kitchen in the adjacent teepee, above the fish-men storage tank, while van Guitt had comandeered the third level of that second domicile, thus placing himself—at least physically, if not metaphorically—on the same plane as the Munroes.

In the morning, Jenny whipped up a splendid breakfast of buckwheat "flapjacks," eggs, bacon and beans, which we enjoyed communally in the teepee dining area. (I made so bold as to offer to give her lessons in making croissants, and she replied with equal verve: "Just so long as you keep your hands out of Jenny's wet dough!") A few last-minute supplies were brought onboard. Then the mighty Behemoth engine was fired up, and we departed downtown Providence, aimed at the famous Boston Post Road that would lead us north. (I chose to ride in the teepee, not in the cloistered, hot and smelly engine cab.). Whilst still within the city limits, a few citizens hailed us and wished us well. But it was only when we transitioned into the countryside and smaller burgs, where the inhabitants were less cosmopolitan, that we attracted any crowds. This was a novel sensation, since the original Steam House in India had tended to affright the natives, rather than allure.

It being the month of June, school was out of session, leaving all the children idle. And they found the Steam House to be an irresistible cynosure of their juvenile attentions. Mobs of them accumulated, whooping and dancing around our cars, only to fall away when we reached the borders of their precincts, passing the baton of attention to their identical peers to the north of their neighborhoods. Some of the little vandals even threw eggs and tomatoes at us, necessitating the closure of our windows. And so, every few hours, when sightng a lake or pond, we had to stop to slosh cleansing buckets of water over our carriages and besmirched bison engine carapace. While I suspected that English juveniles might have behaved in a similar irresponsible manner, I knew for a fact that well-bred French children never would have acted so coarsely.

In any case, we survived these harmless depredations. But with the frequent stops and the necessity to proceed cautiously, lest we squash careless little Johnny or Susie Hayseed, we made an average speed of only five miles per hour. And so we were approaching that Massachusetts landmark known as the Great Blue Hill, some thirty-five miles from our point of origin, around suppertime, making it a reasonable place to call a stop for the day.

Not wishing to impede traffic on the Post Road by our enormous parked presence, we—or, I should say, Banks and Phillips—maneuvered our caravan into a kind of spacious empty half-wild glade, conveniently reached by a short dirt track barely wide enough for our passage. In fact, I could hear the snapping of green branches that marked our progress. But eventually the Steam House was snugly parked, in what might have been some old impound for cattle, its prow aimed for easy departure, thanks to slowly circumnavigating the circumference of the glade so as to, once again, line up with the exit.

Almost immediately, delicious smells began to issue from Jenny's kitchen. Banks and Phillips repaired to the washroom to cleanse themselves of the smut of their engineering endeavors. Captain Hood, Fox and McNeil were out on the lawn, avoiding the gathering shadows whilst they played a makeshift game of croquet. I assumed van Guitt in the adjacent teepee was preoccupied with his library of abstruse and scientific books. Above me in my room, I could hear snores—presumably from Sir Munro—and a low gentle contented wordless singing—presumably from Lady Munro. It amazed me that she could have regained such a mild and sanguine character after her Hindoo ordeals.

All, in short, seemed idyllic, and I was just changing my cravat for a more lively one which, I hoped, would appeal to Miss Arbutus, when the peace was shattered by gunshots!

I knew not what was transpiring, but I had the sound instincts anyhow to grab my own pistol before rushing down the single flight of stairs that seperated me from ground level.

A most horrific sight met my astonished eyes.

Captain Hood and his man Fox stood back to back against a horde of seemingly unarmed but extremely violent invaders whose lineaments I could only half-apprehend in the confusion. Hood was using his empty pistol as a club, while Fox deployed his croquet mallet like a truncheon. Stretched out on the ground was the unconscious—I prayed, not dead!— form of Munro's man McNeil.

I let out a spontaneous battle cry that I hoped would unman the attackers, then, from the porch of the wigwam, began to plant my limited bullets where they would do the most good. I swiftly brought down the bodies of three attackers. A couple of the survivors, recognizing me as a menace, began to head my way. With my dwindling ammunition, I was on the point of despair. But then came relief!

Banks and Phillips, both naked to the waist from their ablutions, emerged with blazing rifles in hand. At the same time, I heard a window on the third level of the teepee open, accompanied by a blast from Sir Munro's ever-present Boss & Co. shotgun.

That renewed assault was enough to send the brutes loping inhumanly back into the woods from whence they had first come.

The three of us on the porch jumped down to solace those on the lawn. Our first concern was the supine form of McNeil. Much to our delight, he proved to be merely unconscious, with no evident wounds. Chafing of the wrists and application of wet cloths soon revived him. We later learned that he had gone down from a glancing roundhouse blow to the skull from one of the attackers—a blow which, we deduced, would have been fatal, had it fully connected. And in fact, McNeil suffered mildly from the effects of a concussion for days afterwards.

Hood and Fox, while sweaty and exhausted, were unharmed.

Having ascertained this good news, we turned our attention to the three corpses on the grass.

The creatures were uncanny, a chimerical mix of humans and some type of great apes. Pale as fungi, their skins were more hirsute than those of mere men, but less so than the pelts of other anthropoids. Their mouths were stuffed with sharp teeth, their long arms left their paws dangling at knee-level, and their bare feet exhibited prehensile toes. Thankfully, their intimate regions were covered with a kind of rude breechclout so familiar to us from our travels in India.

Now we were joined by Jenny and van Guitt. Our cook exhibited no trace of the female vapors, but gazed boldly on the fallen forms, her eyes lingering, I thought, a tad too long, on their nether parts. Van Guitt, it eventuated, had imbibed a few too many drafts of his potent Dutch gin, and fallen asleep before we entered the glade, waking only at the sound of gunfire. But now he forced himself to alertness, and bent down close to the creatures to scrutinize them. Just as he regained his full height, the Munroes arrived, so that our whole company was now assembled on the field of battle.

"Our foes," pronounced the Dutchman, "belong to that Congo River Basin species known as the 'white apes.' Legend has it that they were mysteriously and surrepetitiously introduced many decades ago in small numbers into England, thanks to the interventions of the Jermyn family. But I had no idea their kind had reached North America. How I would have liked to capture a living specimen for my patron, Barnum!"

Captain Hood snorted derisively. "You should have gotten down here sooner then, you old reprobate! You could have grappled hand to hand with the brutes as we did, and seen how successful you were!"

Unabashed, van Guitt tsk-tsked, then bent to finger the fur of one of the apes, as if he contemplated skinning them for profit.

Colonel Munro now comandeered the discourse. "The unanswered question is, why did these alien apes attack us? I presume it is not because we trespassed on their tribal lands. Any such enclave of oddness would surely have attracted the attention of the press and the authorities before now, and led to a campaign of extermination. No, I tend to suspect that the apes were imported here by someone tracking our expedition, someone who wished to frustrate our plans, and who then unleashed the assailants upon us."

Banks asked, "Do you think we should immediately resume our course towards Boston and safety?"

"Not at all," said the Colonel. "On the soon-benighted roads, we would make an easy target for another ambush. And even the Behemoth at full throttle could not outsprint these creatures. I suggest that we light a bonfire and keep watch overnight, then depart in the morning. We are as safe here as anywhere."

We all approved of the strategy, and our encampment fell into a smoothly oiled functioning. The white ape corpses were buried, and tables and chairs were set up outside. Guns at the ready, under the stars, we all had a pleasant meal—boiled beef, new potatoes, dandelion greens, biscuits and a dessert of shortcakes and whipped cream—foregathered around the campfire, so as not to leave the sentries—Fox and Phillips took first watch—feeling lonely. McNeil was excused from the roster due to his injuries, but the rest of the men were assigned intervals of wakefulness.

As I was helping Jenny carry dirty dishes into the wigwam, I bandied with her.

"Perhaps you'll bring me a midnight snack, and we could utilize any convenient shadows to get to know one another a little better, my dear, leaving the solo sentry duties for a short time to my comrade in arms."

"Only if you was equipped with the same man-tackle as those hairy critters," Miss Arbutus replied. "Which I can see you ain't."

Although shocked at the boldness of her reply, I was able to make a feeble riposte along the lines of: "The stature of an actor matters not when the actor knows how to perform." But Jenny merely laughed and went inside to clean up.

I could see that more than a florid cravat would be needed to charm this lass.

As we left Boston behind us, the chuffing sounds of the Behemoth by now a familiar dispason, pleasant memories solaced us all, and provided a buffer for the rigors ahead.

Our entry into the "Hub" on the day after the attack was greeted with large enthusiastic crowds blatting on horns and tossing confetti. It turned out that van Guitt, taking a page from the playbook of his patron Barnum, had publicized our arrival in advance. Without mentioning our ultimate goal of visiting Innsmouth and kidnaping some of its aquatic citizens, he had touted our trip as a display of the technological prowess of Darling, Brown and Sharpe. And so the populace received us as the latest representatives of sheer American industrial ingenuity. Banks had to address several learned societies, while the rest of us were given the keys to the city by Mayor Nathaniel B. Shurtleff. Three days passed in sheer hedonism and revelry. But then at last came the time for our departure.

Now, rolling along merrily, we were following a coastal route, the sea often being in sight and the air freshened by oceanic scents, as we headed towards our overnight stop preliminary to Innsmouth herself: Salem. Innsmouth was not much further than that fabled town, and so we could have made the whole journey in a single day. But such a push would have meant we arrived at Innsmouth after dark, and this we did not wish to do, especially after the affair of the apes.

Luckily, we had not been molested again.

Around four in the afternoon, the fabulous Steam House entered the city limits of Salem. Our reception here was allied to the one in Boston, but of a much smaller magnitude. We were all treated to a banquet at the City Hall on Washington Street, replete with stultifying speeches, but also offering a fine Continental repast. I was pleased to sample some familiar and sophisticated French cooking, for although the meals prepared by Miss Arbutus were wholesome and tasty, they did tend towards a certain colonial rudimentariness.

Not wishing to leave the Steam House unguarded, we declined the offer to take guest lodgings elsewhere, and all slept in our accustomed quarters which, by now, had come to seem like home and were in no wise deficient.

Early in the morning we were off, without so much as a single nocturnal visit from any of the town's fabled ghosts and witches.

It was a mere ten or eleven miles from Salem to Innsmouth, and van Guitt used the interval to finally brief us on his exact plan to capture his specimens. All of us—save for Banks and Phillips, who steadfastly continued to drive us forward in the Behemoth—were gathered in the room containing the water tank (still empty) with its inserted cage. The mild jouncing of the wheeled wigwam, smoothed by clever leaf-springs, gave a sense of being on some carnival ride.

"Observe," said van Guitt, while cranking a winch, "how the cage may be lifted from the water tank. When we arrive at the shore, we will remove the cage entirely, and our brawny heroes will muscle it onto a special small platform at the rear of the Behemoth. Then the Behemoth will set to sea, powering out into Innsmouth Harbor and heading towards the notorious Devil's Reef, where the gill-men are known to congregate. We shall lure two or more to the surface, subdue them, confine them behind bars, then return to land. *Et voila*! Mister Barnum will have his unique attractions, and all of us will be considerably richer."

Captain Hood had been massaging his chin in puzzlement, and now spoke. "You say you'll lure and subdue them, making it sound as easy as salting a bird's tail. But how, exactly?"

"The means of attracting the fish-men shall be revealed when we reach Innsmouth. But the trick of subduing them is right here."

Van Guitt picked up a cinched cloth sack that was obviously full of some kind of flour or powder. "This is an extract from the *akia* plant found in the Sandwich Islands. The natives use it to stupefy fish to aid in their capture. It is absolutely harmless to humans, but when sprinkled on the waters it will almost instantly render any finny creature *hors de combat*."

Hood nodded approvingly, and the rest of us assented as well to the plasuible ingenuity of the scheme. The meeting concluded, we separated to prepare for our entry to Innsmouth.

Out the windows, I could see that we were passing through a landscape of sand, sedge-grass, and stunted shrubbery, monotonous and dreary in the extreme, with the grey Atlantic off to the east.

And then, after a small ascent, we looked down on Innsmouth.

A seemingly lively and bustling town at this date, whatever its past or future held, it nonetheless seemed to hold implicit in its structures the possibility of immense decadence and decay—just as a shining young beauty may foreshadow the wizened crone she shall become. A kind of future phantom under the skin. The spires of several churches seemed a sign of wholesomeness, however—assuming they were of respectable denominations. The busy harbor area featured many wharves and schooners. Several flourishing mills obtruded, including the famous gold refinery of Captain Marsh. It was a town of wide extent and dense construction, a tangle of chimney-pots, gambrel roofs and peaked gables. There were some large square Georgian houses, too, with hipped roofs, cupolas, and railed "widow's walks."

The town was bisected by the Manuxet River, which ran west to east before dumping into the harbor. Three bridges united the two halves of the town. But I knew, from talking to Banks, that the Steam House would be confined to the southern, closest segment of the town, since the bridges would never bear the weight of the Behemoth.

Now we were among the dwellings and businesses, observing for the first time the citizenry of Innsmouth. Most appeared utterly normal, although they displayed a curious indifference to the phenomenon of a giant mechanized bison pulling two enormous teepees. But here and there, with features half-concealed, I thought to detect beings of odd physiognamy and flopping gait.

I noted by the signage that we were traversing Eliot Street, and this avenue soon debouched into a most curious plaza, formed by the conjunction of no fewer than five other avenues. This town square had the arcane dimensions of some obscure sigil. Carriages and pedestrians came and went, but paid us no heed, as if any visitors to Innsmouth could be of no import to local affairs, "foreigners" unworthy of acknowledgement or contemplation.

The Steam House came to a stop, and we all disembarked. Out of one building, as if awaiting our arrival, stepped a comely and exuberant blond lad, dressed rather dandyishly. He trotted over to us, hand outheld to be severally shaken, while he announced himself.

"Zadok Allen at your command, friends. I assume one of you is Mathias van Guitt…? Ah, very pleased to meet at last, sir. Your correspondence has been most illuminating. I'd like to discuss certain rituals of the Ponape islanders with you at greater length."

"All in due time, my boy. I assume you have the items that we need to complete our mission…?"

"Indeed. I will show you now."

And so saying, the lad took out of his coat pocket a knotted handerchief. Untying it, he revealed the contents: a dozen small stones, the *ne plus ultra* of ebony, engraven with cryptic runes.

Van Guitt grew excited. "The summoning stones of the Deep Ones, just as you promised."

"Yes, brought back by yours truly from the Caroline Islands, after my last stint aboard the fabled East Indiaman the *Narragansett*, out of Providence. I had taken on the side-task of acquiring these for Professor Shocken at Miskatonic. But alas, he did not live to receive them."

Admiring the stones, van Guitt said, "The savant's loss was our gain then. I thank you sincerely."

"Thanks are appreciated, naturally. But perhaps you might tender the payment, just as you promised."

"Half now, and half upon their demonstrated efficacy."

"But of course. I will be happy to abide with you until the return of your explorers with the prize tomorrow."

The exchange was made. Then Allen said, "As for the timbers and planks you ordered, they await you on the sands at the end of Water Street. Just follow Waite to Water, turn right, and you can't miss them."

Allen strode off, the rest of us clambered aboard the Steam House, and soon our train was in motion. A short run brought us to where Water Street petered out at the edge of the sea. There the promised lumber was heaped. Banks took over with engineering prowess.

"We must make a wooden roadbed over this short stretch of sands to allow the Behemoth to enter the sea without becoming mired on the beach."

All we males—even the fastidious van Guitt—stripped off our shirts under the July sun and got to work. Again, we received no idle attention or interference from the natives. Although I thought to detect a few observant faces framed in the windows of the nearest houses.

The simple but burdensome construction took us till supper time, and we were earnestly ready for some of Jenny's hearty fare. I fancied she looked at me more admiringly thanks to my demonstration of brute masculine prowess.

We all retired early. Since we had not abandoned our ritual of sentries inaugurated after the ape attack, I was roused at three AM for guard duty. But a subsequent return to the arms of Morpheus from six to eight left me feeling completely refreshed.

And now, after so many preliminaries and travel, it was finally time for the assault on Devil's Reef.

* * * *

Uncoupling the wigwams from the Behemoth was but the work of a minute. Lifting the cage out of the water tank and manhandling it onto the platform at the rear of the big engine took hardly any longer. It was then secured with chains. But subsequent preparations were more elaborate.

First, four special saddles were brought out of storage and emplaced with straps and buckles to the spine of the bison carapace. A ladder that was already affixed to the flank of the bison facilitated access. Van Guitt nominated the riders.

"Captain Hood, Colonel Munro, Mister McNeil and Mister Fox. You four will take up your perches and act as lookouts and snipers, if needs be. Two of you face fore, and two aft."

The marksmen did as they were bidden. I was heartened to think that we would have their protection.

Now van Guitt turned to me. "Henri, you and I will ride in the cab with Josiah and Wilber. It will be our chore to heft the stupefied gill-men out of the water, manacle them and thrust them into the cage."

Seeing Jenny and Lady Munro watching us, I clicked my heels, made an extravagant salute, and said, "Fortune favors the brave, *mon frere*, and you have found your man in me!"

I hoped for at least some batted eyelashes from Jenny, but instead received only her protruded tongue and a squint.

Truth be told, I still at this moment had little faith that this hunt would come to anything, despite van Guitt's magic-lantern lecture and associated folderol, and so I was willing to talk big.

Van Guitt and I entered the engine's cab, and Banks got the Behemoth rolling over the improvised boardwalk. When the snout of the sea-going bison overhung the water, he stopped. He and Wilberforce jumped down and effected a miraculous change in the Behemoth, like stage magicians.

First, a series of concealed overlapping plates were swung out from their niches and angled underneath the engine, forming a. kind of seaworthy hull. Then, two paddlewheels, hidden beneath the bison, were lowered into place on either side of the Behemoth, and hooked into the motive power, which was disengaged from the conventional wheels. Suddenly the Behemoth had become a sea-going craft, but more capably so than its primitive functionality in India.

With the land-wheels unpowered, the four of us had to push the Behemoth into the water. But having foreseen this eventuality, Banks had greased the boardwalk, making our task much easier. Once the bison boat was afloat, we splashed through the shallows and climbed aboard. The paddlewheels began to revolve, a rudder came into play, and we sailed off, a most astonishing sight, I am sure!

I waved to the ladies on the shore, and saw that they had been joined by Zadok Allen, who awaited his payment. I felt momentarily jealous of the gay youth's proximity to Jenny, but soon realized that my return as conquering hero would trump his bumpkin charms. I was further buoyed by their shouted good wishes for success.

As we drew further from land, we entered a moderately busy scene. Various craft came and went. But again, no one deigned to hail us with either cheer or malice.

In a relatively short time we approached the legendary Devil's Reef, discernible by a change in the ocean's hue and by unique wave configurations: a long, black line scarcely rising above the water yet carrying a suggestion of odd latent malignancy.

Banks caused the paddlewheels to cease their rotations and we dropped an anchor to afford us a stable perch.

Van Guitt called up to our snipers, elevated above us for better vantage. "Any sign of interference? No? Very good! Keep your eyes peeled though, boys!"

The Dutch big-game trapper took the mystic stones from his pocket and tossed them hither and yon into the water, murmuring unintelligible words while doing so. He next made ready the bag of *akia* powder. And then we all waited anxiously.

I have seen many paintings of Shakespeare's tragic heroine Ophelia as she lay drowned, with her face just protruding from the water, or even an inch or two below the surface. And it was this morbid image which, unbidden, sprang into my mind as I saw the first of the Deep Ones.

Obeying the magical summons, they yet chose not to emerge from the ocean. Rather, they hovered effortlessly with their horrid upturned visages just below the watery interface, drowned green gargoyle masks. The depiction of their tribe that van Guitt had shown us had failed to convey their utterly disconcerting and abnormal blend of bestial and human. We were encircled by a gallery of bizarre fluid-warped countenances, as if a troupe of mummers all in black had thrust their chalky faces out of the night. I was fascinated, horrified and thrilled. Here indeed was a prize beyond price.

Van Guitt wasted no time, but immediately began strewing the *akia* drug with broad motions.

The faces quickly disappeared, and I feared the drug had had no effect. But no! Once stricken, the monsters were only sinking momentarily before bobbing to the surface again, this time with their whole unseemly comatose lengths stretched out, limbs dangling underwater.

Producing a long-poled billhook from somewhere, van Guitt began fishing. "Henri, Wilber! Grab the ones I choose and pull them aboard! I'll assume the smaller ones are female!"

Matching deeds to words, van Guitt hooked—none too tenderly—a big brute and brought him alongside. Almost falling into the sea ourselves, Wilberforce and I sought a grip under the creature's slippery armpits. Finally we contrived to lift the insenate brute out of the water. He weighed no more than a man his size. Wilberforce quickly clapped manacles on the creature's wrists and ankles, and we dumped him through the cage door.

We repeated this procedure with a smaller, ostensibly female Deep One. Van Guitt eyed the other floating bodies with an avarice denied, then reluctantly gave the order to Banks.

"Josiah, get us to shore!"

The two gill-beings remained unconscious in a heap behind bars, and I wondered how long they would continue that way, and what they would be like when they regained awareness. I shivered, and tested the stoutness of the lock again.

As we neared the beach whence we had departed, I could see that Jenny and Lady Munro had also been busy, per the Dutchman's orders. A small hand pump and a length of hose had served to fill the holding tank with sea water. The women were just uncoupling everything when the prow of the Behemoth ground onto the sand, aligned with the boardwalk.

Van Guitt yelled up to the four marksmen. "Fellows, stay in your saddles until we get the trophies secured, just in case any belligerents should approach!"

Phillips and Banks quickly reversed all the adjustments they had done earlier to make the Behemoth seaworthy, and her wheels engaged the plank road. Within seconds, our mighty engine stood safely on terra firma.

Racing against imagined dire consequences of our actions, we quickly hooked up the wigwams to the Behemoth, then carried the heavy cage and its somnolent occupants inside and emplaced it in the sea-water tank.

I was sore, sweaty and even a bit trembly from this uncanny expedition. But when I received a congratulatory buss from Jenny (she kissed all of us) and a warm handshake from Lady Munro, I felt sufficiently rewarded.

Zadok Allen and van Guitt were concluding their financial transaction. Allen looked a trifle disconcerted.

"I never actually thought you'd bring this off, Mathias. Even though I've lived in Innsmouth all my life, I can't predict how my fellow inhabitants will react. I'd make haste to clear the neighborhood as fast as possible, if I were you."

"This is exactly our intent! All right, you sharpshooters, you may come on down!"

Sir Munro replied, "I think not, Mathias, for I see a mob approaching! Best we remain on duty up here. Now, get her under steam!"

At this mention of a mob, Allen quickly scuttled off.

The thought of a pack of angry citizens—was that their subliminal riot of voices I heard?—converging on us was sufficient spur. We all got onboard the Steam House and, after some little confusion, took what appeared to be a rutted dirt road out of town.

But the unimproved condition of the terrain did not permit the Behemoth to attain her full speed, and soon the mob was upon us. A horde of wild-eyed, howling, almost slavering maniacs, some normal-seeming, some with contorted limbs and warped countenances, they were armed with pistols, rifles, shotguns and even axes and pitchforks. Their wordless ululations struck terror into the heart, more so than any tribe of Hindoo thuggees. Bullets thwacked the wooden teepees and pinged off the engine's sides.

From atop the bison's spine, our four gallant snipers got to work. But for every Innsmouthian they felled, it seemed two sprang up.

Van Guitt and I were inside the domestic wigwam, on the first level. Without explanation, the Dutchman yelled, "Follow me!" He raced to the stairs, up to the second floor, and then to the third, where the Munros lived.

"My lad, you see that ladder on the wall. If you ascend it, and go through the trap door, you should see our salvation. I would make the climb myself, but am too old and fat. Go now!"

I did as he directed. Poking my head through the trap door, I found myself in a tiny conical room constituting the very tip of the teepee. A tiny room indeed, but big enough to host a shiny, oiled, newfangled Gatling gun.

I saw instantly that the top of the room was hinged, and secured now by a single bolt. I slammed the bolt out of its embrace, pitched back the roof, and was exposed to the open air.

They say that journalists acquire a jackdaw's nest of odd knowledge, thanks to interviewing so many diverse people. And I felt an instant gratitude for the assignment that had taken me some months ago to the training grounds of the army of France's Second Empire, where I had received a vivid lesson in the usage of such a weapon.

Canting the gun's multiple barrels towards the ground and our pursuers, I commenced firing.

The resulting slaughter was far from pretty. But it achieved its goal, allowing the Behemoth to find the easy road to Ipswich and outpace any surviving antagonists.

An hour later, once we knew we were safe from all pursuit, we stopped the Steam House, allowing our valiant snipers to descend. All of them had received grazing wounds as badges of honor, but they were quickly patched up. As for myself, I was hailed as the ultimate savior of the day, and received a plethora of kisses from Miss Arbutus, as well as a surrepetitous squeezing of my manhood. Truly, to the victor belongs the spoils!

While all of us were still exulting outside in the road at our success, van Guitt ventured into the tank room to survey his captives. But he emerged a broken, ashen-faced man.

We all rushed to his side, but he could not speak. So all of us crowded into the tank room.

The wooden tank was chest high. The taller cage stuck up out of the tank. It was assumed that the gill-creatures could crouch down fully underwater when desired, or stand upright to peer out from behind their bars. Right now, they were not visible, so they must be crouching. Dare we get close enough to peer in? Van Guitt must have done so without harm, so we all did too.

The vat of sea-water was stained with a thin kind of blood, making it hard at first to discern the condition of the captives. But eventually we saw the reality of the situation. Despite being manacled, the brutes had managed to tear out each other's throats with their savage teeth, dying in a mutual suicide pact that was obviously preferable to captivity. A kind of brutish nobility we had not anticipated.

We all went outside to commiserate with the Dutchman, and soon, through our kind words and jollying, he came around to his old boisterous, unconquerable self.

"Oh, well, perhaps it's for the best that the civilized world remains ignorant of these monsters in their midst. I suppose I could interest Phineas in some more common creature. I wonder if I could ever secure a particularly large elephant for him. That might work…"

On that note we all retired to our rooms for a well-deserved rest, prior to supper. The Steam House got underway, its gentle motion conducing to a long nap on my part.

What woke me were some unusually savory odors wafting from Jenny's kitchen. My stomach began to growl, and I was very glad when, with dusk an hour or two away, we pulled off the road and began the familiar setup of outdoor tables and chairs, linens, china, wine glasses and utensils.

All of us were seated when Jenny emerged, aided by McNeil and Fox. The three of them carried huge platters of steaming batter-coated gobbets from which issued that palate-tantalizing fragrance. The platters were ringed with fried potatoes.

"What have we here, Miss Arbutus?" inquired van Guitt. "I don't recognize this item from the larder."

"A good old New England feast of fish and chips. I've sampled it earlier of course, and will swear by its powerfully delicious flavor!"

I studied the meal in growing disbelief. I glanced left and right at the equally stunned faces of my compatriots. Then a wave of sanguine disillusionment and acceptance swept over us all, followed by gales of laughter.

And we heartily tucked in to the feast.

I, FOR ONE, WELCOME OUR NEW INSECT LITTERATEURS

"[The] flustered writer…put the infested device to the side… A week later, the flabbergasted bookworm received an email congratulating her for purchasing Isaac Asimov's science-fiction classic *Robots and Empire*. She subsequently sent Amazon an email explaining that there was a mistake."
—"Ants infest woman's Kindle—and start buying books on Amazon," Ben Cost, *The New York Post*, August 3, 2022

Generally speaking, literary agents of any repute don't have to go looking for clients. We are always getting bombarded with requests for representation. Novices, midlisters, perhaps even best-selling authors looking to ramp up with a luck-changing swap of representative—they all flood through the agent's door and inbox. That's why we here at Pawkey & Mangrum Media Cabal always have an overflowing roster of clients. In fact, we had to add three employees in the last year, just to handle metaverse rights.

But there's always an exception to any practical rule of business, and so I was only slightly surprised when I found myself moved by a literary debut to approach an unknown writer with an offer for P&MMC to act as his agent.

The book that had blown me away was titled *Switch On the Universe*, and it was a majestic space opera of epic proportions with a vivid cast of hundreds. Astonishingly, it had been self-published and put up for sale on Amazon and other platforms with absolutely zero fanfare or publicity. I happened to glom onto a copy only because I had been seeking to download some MP3s of my old favorite, *Switched-On Bach* by Wendy Carlos. Then, encountering the book, I idly delved into it via LOOK INSIDE. Before I knew it, I was hooked. This novel put *The Expanse* and works by Reynolds, Baxter, Williams, and Hamilton in the shade. I didn't put down my Kindle for the next six hours.

The authors name was Hyman O. Carebara, and he proved to be an utter enigma, with no social-media presence or civic records. Nonetheless, by employing the same detective agency that we use to vet the moral character of our authors (I think they had to illegally hack Amazon's upload protocols, but I didn't ask outright), I was finally able to get an email address for Carebara. Communications ensued. From my end, effusive praise and enticements; from Carebara's side, reluctance and demurrals. But at last I had worn him down, convincing this great new writer to drop by the offices for a talk.

On the day slated for Carebara's arrival, I cautioned all the office personnel to be on their most welcoming behavior, and not to fawn excessively over the man. The staff had also read *Switch On the Universe* and they were all equally enraptured.

The appointed hour rolled around, and I began to feel a bit nervous and exciteable—antsy, if you will. I really wanted to bag Carebara as a client. Sure, our firm would still prosper without him. But for the first time in a long jaded while, I was actually concerned with fostering a genius, making history, leaving a literary legacy, and being part of an exciting advance in the science fiction genre, rather than just toting up units sold.

When the door to my office swung inward, I shot out of my seat as if jet-propelled, so stoked was I. Our office manager Delia was ushering in our guest with all due hospitality. But beneath her smile hovered a strange, uneasy expression, and she shot me a meaningful look, as if to say, *Get ready, this is not what you expected.*

Alone with the author, I was able to size him up.

Hyman O. Carebara wore a beige trench coat from which protruded a few inches of trousers and socks. His shoes were sloppy loafers, seemingly a few sizes too big. A hipster-style bucket hat was pulled low down to his eyebrows, concealing the upper portion of his head, while a scarf hid his neck and the lower segment of his face. The result was that all I could see of his almost albino countenance was a strip of eyes and oddly shaped nose. And he sported leather gloves, although it was the month of August.

"Mister Carebara—Hyman, if I may—I'm Nigel Pawkey. May I say that I'm so pleased to meet the author of such a wonderful novel!"

I extended my hand and received his gloved one in return. His grip was flexible and somewhat squirmy. But unnatural as his handshake was, it could not prepare me for his voice. There was a breathless quality to it, and by that I meant that his utterances literally did not seem to involve breathing; his speech production involved no lungs or soft anatomical parts. Rather, his words struck me as if they were produced by modulated rasping, something sawing against something else. I flashed for a moment on Lovecraft's "The Whisperer in Darkness."

"Mister Pawkey, I am happy to be here, although I do not often go out in public. I fear my reclusiveness is a dominant part of my personality. But in a way, this is a good trait to have, since it allows me to focus all my time and energies on writing."

We had both taken our chairs. Carebara crossed one leg over the other with a kind of boneless agility. I tried not to blanch.

"Well, Hyman—and please, call me Nigel—your habits sound like those of the perfect client. You wouldn't believe how often an agent has to bail out some hard-partying writer, or rescue the reputation of an author given to social-media gaffes. Our PR staff works overtime most weeks! But of course, the primary allure in your case is not any public persona, but rather the wonderful quality of your prose and storytelling. Just incredible and unique. And by letting us handle all the boring business details of your career—and I predict a long and successful one—you'll be freed for sheer writing."

Hyman seemed to perk up at my pitch, and was about to respond—affirmatively, I hoped—when there came a knock at the door. The intruder proved to be Delia.

"Mister Pawkey, I'm so sorry to bother you, but I have a really nasty tradesman out front, and he insists on getting into your office. Says if he can't do his job today, his firm will drop us as a client. It's the exterminator—"

At that final word, the most astonishing thing happened.

Hyman O. Carebara disappeared!

Not entirely, for his empty suit of clothes remained behind, falling to the chair and carpet. But the occupant of that suit had dispersed into a million tiny skittering component parts which had swiftly swarmed across the office floor and into every crack and crevice imaginable.

I give myself retrospective credit for instantly sussing out what had happened. Not for nothing had I invested a lifetime in reading science fiction.

"Delia!" I shouted. "Out! And tell that exterminator jerk he can take his poison and shove it!"

Once the door closed, I was down on the rug, calling out gently for my guest. "Hyman…Mister Carebara…you can come out now, it's quite safe…"

There was no response for a few moments, but then all the ants began to emerge from the woodwork and shelves, from vases and ceiling tiles, from behind portraits and curtains. They flowed back into the limp clothing and reinhabited it, gradually taking on their granular, jigsaw-puzzle human shape, until at last I faced once more Hyman Carebara.

"So now you know our secret," he said. "We are not a human at all, but a unique, specialized colony of ants forming a human simulacrum. We hope this fact does not signal the end of your interest in us and our work."

I was less freaked out than I had imagined I might be, and so responded pleasantly. "Not at all, Hyman. As I said, it's the novel you created and the ones that might yet come that concern us here. Your personal life and, uh, the exact nature of your anatomy is beside the point. Nonetheless, I must admit to being a little curious. Where are your from? How did you learn to write? What makes you interested in science fiction?" A thought occurred to me. "Are you an alien species?"

"No, not at all! We are proud Terran ants. But you are somewhat on target. Our colony has been uplifted by visitors from the stars. Alien ants of great wisdom and powers."

"You're saying that Earth has been contacted by extraterrestrials already, without us knowing? Why didn't they approach humanity first?"

"Well, to be frank, our alien relatives don't think too much of humanity. They expect your species won't be around for very much longer. So they came first to us, both out of fraternal feelings and because we represent a better bet for the future."

"I see," I said mildly, silently vowing to do my best from now on to prove those alien ants wrong. "So these star visitors uplifted your colony as an act of cosmic charity."

"Exactly. But then they left us and went about their galactic mission. And we became very lonely. Talking with dumb baseline ants proved most unsatisfying. Until our altered colony is able to outbreed and replace all our formican rivals, we are the only one of our kind. Naturally, we sought communications with humans."

"But why choose the path of writing science fiction novels? Surely you could have just approached the United Nations and explained everything."

"Perhaps. But we were cautious, and a bit afraid. We know how humanity has reacted in the past to nonhuman intelligences. So we decided to reach out through our art. We had already cultivated a love of science fiction, through living in the tablets and e-readers of people and reading genre works there. It turns out we can interpret screen pixels with our antennae. So we were intimate with the conventions of the field. And besides, our benefactors had left us with the codex of all galactic history as our source material."

"Wait a minute! You're telling me that everything is *Switch on the Universe* is real?"

"Mostly. But not everything. We did invent all the characters and dialogue. Do you think we wrote some convincing humans? Sharing domestic environments as we do, we have observed your kind for so long, millennia really, that we thought we had a good grasp of your natures."

"Yes, yes, absolute verisimilitude." My mind was racing down all sorts of routes, trying to analyze how I could parlay this revelation into the best possible outcome for my client and the firm.

"Hyman, this interstellar codex—did you exhaust it by writing your first novel?"

"Oh, far from it! It chronicles over one hundred thousand years of galactic civilization. We could never completely mine it in several human lifetimes. We ourselves might come to the end of it someday, but that is only because the colony is effectively immortal."

"Okay, this is going to work out just great! Your secret is safe with the Pawkey & Mangrum Media Cabal. The only other person who knows is Delia, and she's so tight-lipped that Thomas Pynchon lets her read his diary. So you can go home—wherever that is—with absolute confidence. Or we can set you up in any kind of luxurious lodgings that appeal. In either case, you continue to churn out novels like *Switch on the Universe*, and we all become rich!"

I thought to detect something akin to a smile under Hyman's scarf. "Money does not really matter much to us, Nigel. Our art is everything. But there is one clause I would like to install in any agreement between us."

"Sure, just name it!"

"Pawkey and Mangrum are famous for the annual company picnic you throw for all your clients. Could you make sure to issue us an engraved invitation? It would be the first time our kind had ever received such an honor!"

HIVEHEAD

The queen nestled serenely in the cartiliginous valley just behind Hivehead's left ear. Her weight was a comfort, and when Hivehead tuned into her channel, the steady insectoid maternal contentment she radiated enveloped Hivehead in a bath of peace. This was a good life. He had made the right choice to become a machtiern. Leaving behind the mundane burdens of common humanity had led him to a bliss he had never before been able to obtain, back when he had been plain old Hank Bogardus, the man inadvertently responsible for the destruction of a small town and all its citizens.

Hivehead could feel the steady gentle trickle of the queen's eggs as they made a slow cascade down the side of his neck, where they were retrieved by a steady and deliberate procession of worker bees, who carried them to their appointed growth cells. The unconventional arrangement of the hive interior mandated that, unlike her baseline peers, this queen would be sessile, from annointing till death. Her traditional task of larvae emplacement had been delegated. This was just one of the many behavioral variations gengineered into this colony of some eighty thousand individuals.

The hive of course was a noisy place, what with the incessant buzzing of the many busy bees. And, given that his head was located at the center of the construct, Hivehead might have been subjected to what could have amounted to a constant sensory irritation. But Hivehead remained oblivious to the interior noises, and, unless he was channelling, to exterior ones as well, for his ears canals were sealed away behind overstuffed honeycombs.

As were his baseline eyes, offline behind slabs of wax.

But not his nostrils. Two privileged, exclusive-use tunnels led from his nose, through the hive and out to open air. And the surface openings of those passageways were perpetually staffed by delegated fan bees, serving in rotation, whose sole job was to employ their wings to waft gusts of atmosphere in and out of the breathing tubes: oxygen in, carbon dioxide out. Hivehead's breathing was easy and never labored, and he always had plenty of good freh air in his lungs.

As for his mouth— Well, that was the organ of pure delight. A trickle-feed sluice fed permanently into his lips, providing a steady dose of the colony's super-honey, his sole and sufficient delicious nourishment. The generous flow was calculated to keep his metabolism turning over at optimal rates, so that he could do his job of transporting the hive wherever it needed to be.

The weight of the colony was not a problem either, for Hivehead's bones and musculature had been bolstered in the appropriate dimensions to support the extra mass. (Likewise, his parms had been adjusted to accommodate having his head forever sharing the internal hive temperature of ninety-one degrees farenheit.) From the outside, the shell of his hive resembled a traditional "skep," looking rather like the rounded nosecone of a missile. But this skep was made of durable ivory-colored biopoly, and its lower edge was molded to Hivehead's shoulders and torso, and in fact molecularly bonded to his flesh. The only strictures that the unnatural superstructure enforced on Hivehead's mobility was the necessity of generally keeping the hive vertical—in other words, not bending over from the neck or the waist to any great degree. The bees and their internal architecture could tolerate an inclination of as much as fifteen degrees from the vertical, but became confused and alarmed at any greater deviation. Tapping into their sensory-sapience feeds at such times revealed a blend of anger, fear and retributive impulses. Better not to provoke such a reaction.

Thus, when it came time for Hivehead to sleep—in line with his commensals, he powered down from dusk to dawn—Hivehead carefully lowered his naked butt to the pleasant cushion of pillow-turf or mattress-moss beneath some supportive tree, using the trunk of the latter as a backrest during his hours of unconsciousness. This new regimen, while it certainly might have been uncomfortable or disdained by the former Hank Bogardus, suited the altered somatic parameters of Hivehead just fine.

As mentioned, Hivehead's duties all revolved around the hive that enclosed everything above his shoulders. All his individuals desires and goals had been subsumed to his symbiote. He had to protect it against any predators resident in his gretazone—a task he usually fulfilled by running away, hiding, and/or climbing a tree. But he had also been known to pick up a branch and whack some offender in search of a liquid amber treat. Luckily, his particular rewilded gretazone was a temperate place, and generally devoid of big aggressive fauna.

Hivehead's secondary duty—or rather, the raison d'etre that compelled the first imperative of protection—was to transport the hive on a circuit of fresh pastures where the pollinating skills of the winged citizens were needed.

This fecund engineered gretazone, reclaimed from desert and wastelands, featured tracts of vaccine-trees, passion-flowers, candyapple orchards, and stent-bushes, as well as myriad other species of no commercial value, but possessing intrinsic ecological utility, many of them in need of flower fertilization. If bountiful crops and sheer beauty were to be ensured, then Hivehead's commensals had to do their work all across the zone. (The harvesters of this bounty did not live inside this gretazone, which was mainly free of the settlements of civilization, but were migrating chimerae who had an arrangement with various chaebols and gongsas.)

These duties—to deliver and protect—justified Hivehead's existence, both in his own eyes and in the gaze of society. Not an overly onerous lifestyle or avocation, being a skep-bearer nonetheless took dedication and abnegation.

Of course, if matters were viewed objectively, Hivehead's very existence was a kludge, a luxury, a superfluity, or a featherbedding gig. A hive mounted on an ambulatory kibe platform running a middling-grade turingosity would have been just as efficient, perhaps moreso. Some kind of chimeric abomination could have been fabbed up: a horse with living bee saddlebags, perhaps? A pack of bee-bearing wolves, with mini-hives neatly ensconced between furry shoulder blades? Likewise, if a human had to be involved, then said human could push a hive on a cart, or carry one on her back like a knapsack or papoose. There was no rational need for this intimate bonding between insect cargo and ape carrier.

So, barring necessity, Hivehead's status and mode of being came down to only two things.

Art and penitence.

A century ago, there had been a troupe of performance artists from the extinct cull-polity known as Europe who went by the rubric of "Machtiern." They had worn inverted, gasketed, water-filled fishbowls on their heads, with live fish circulating under their drowned noses and across their watery line of vision. Like Hivehead, these "aquamen" would continue to breathe through a simple tube outlet during their englobed showtimes.

Ever since then, the fashion for expressing one's affinity with (and, sometimes, one's guilty expiation towards) nonhuman cousins through some kind of terrarium-like carapace had found a small clade of followers: the machtiern.

And so the artistry of Hivehead's existence. As a fusion of insect and man, he represented a new alliance of form and function.

As for the penitence—well, doffing his individuality, abandoning hearth and lovers, friends and conventional avocations, was merely symbolical of his remorse, not in any way able to fully compensate for what he had done. And in fact, after various civil punishments and fines had been extracted, and prison term served, none of this new lifestyle was mandated as post-parole punishment by the authorities. Nonetheless, it was the path that Hank Bogardus had taken.

Hank had been a young engineer in sole charge of a mechanical battery farm. This open-air matrix of gigantic encased spinning flywheels, each one capable of storing 50 megajoules of energy, sat at what was deemed a safe remove from the tiny hamlet of Scourfield, NU. Hank's job was to monitor performance and safety issues at the farm. He did his job diligently, even though it was exceedingly boring, except for one day. On that occasion, he succumbed to some intensive peer pressure and left work illicitly during his shift to get high and attend a sporting match (the Cascadia Super Vultures versus the Barbuda Landcrabs). He had looped into the farm's systems an off-the-shelf AI of very low turingosity to keep an eye on all indicators, and alert him if trouble arose.

Unfortunately, that was the same day that a group of terrorists, the Lanier League, decided to make a statement by sowing a drift of silicrobes at the farm. These bugs ate only carbon-glass fiber structures, which happened to be the substance from which the flywheel containment vessels were formed. They acted much too swiftly for the AI to register and report the plague.

Deprived of their casings, the flywheels entered failure mode, dispersing all their massive horde of energy as they went off-kilter and fragmented in an array of thousands of deadly shards which rocketed through the village and its inhabitants with an effect similar to the best assault any military-grade flechette cannons might have produced. In moments, there was little left of Scourfield but wet flinders.

Hank had tried living with himself in the aftermath, but all the therapy and even the finest neurotropins failed to alleviate his PTSD. Then one day he had come upon an article profiling the machtierns, and his course was settled. He had had his personality smoothed appropriately with a suite of tropes, then donned the hive, doffing all clothing at the same time in a symbolical gesture of disaffiliation from the human community.

And now, several years later, he had obtained as much happiness and contentment as he felt he deserved, in service to his bees and, down the line, to the folks who benefitted from the hive's eager exertions.

And now, as Hivehead considered today's work, consulting with his bees—the telemetry data from eighty thousand narrowcasting individuals, coordinated with a few cerebral mods in Hivehead's brain, provided him with a rich sensory input, and a deep worldview that included a kind of 360-degree visual and auditory and positional and even tactile awareness—he realized that he must migrate over the next twenty-four hours to a region of the gretazone that had not been serviced in three months, where an orchard of oxytocin-olives awaited his services.

Moving off across the soft turf, Hivehead anticipated a peaceful and quiet time among the hormone trees.

But alas, he could not foresee that the rewilding already hosted some unwelcome trespassers on a collision course with his bees.

Christopher Robin stubbed out his cigarette on the rock upon which he sat, sent the dead butt spinning with a flick of hyperarticulated fingers, and sighed.

Being a soldier in the human wing of the Cultivar Liberation Front was not the glamorous rebel existence that Christopher Robin—his *nom de guerre*—had once envisioned. His fantasy had been one of clandestine meetings, darknet or meatspace, fueled with ethnic nosh and attended by sexy mademoiselle maries, where the brilliant and inspirational leaderless planning sessions were spiced with comradely flirtations, followed by bloodless assaults during which the human and transgenic commandoes effortlessly nullified all the oppressors and freed the enslaved splices, who all acclaimed these Good Human Allies as the essence of panspecies nobility.

What his fantasy had *not* entailed was being harried across the rough nighted countryside by a posse of angry and frothing augie doggies; three-laws-null well-armed kibes; and a handful of fellow humans: cops working for the Protein Police and down-and-dirty blackwaters employed by the private security firm protecting the epcot that Christopher Robin had just raided—all while trying mightily to guard and chivvy along a dozen bumbling identical cultivars just freed from their corporate shackles.

But if such unanticipated conditions were to constitute the active fieldwork life of a principled monkeywrencher, then Christopher Robin was still determined to honor his commitment and make the most of the situation, uncomfortable and unglamorous as it might be. At least he was still free and uninjured, with the prospect of imminent rescue—which was more than his three CLF comrades could claim, poor sods, after they had been captured in the aftermath of the initial assault.

The approach to the Hundred Acre Wood epcot had come off well, under cover of an early dusk. Christopher Robin and his fellows-in-arms— Stego, Kelty and Jodee—had been all stealthed up nicely, packing the latest in gear, any lethal weaponry excluded. Looking to claim the moral highground, the CLF had no desire to leave a trail of corpses behind in their operation. But they did sport baondoliers of glue grenades and neural-disrupter sidearms.

The day was January thirty-first, Milne Day, the anniversary of the fabled creator's passing, and as always, the park was closed in his honor. It was always a slow time of the tourist year anyhow, and no great loss for the corporation to forego a day's box office.

Getting past the fence and alarm system had been a cinch. Kelty was the expert there. Heading straight to the splice dormitory, the quartet used a slap-on boot to quietly disable the lone human guard outside the quarters, then slipped inside. A warm, humid musty pong enveloped them.

Now the skills of Stego and Jodee would come into play: both were expert transgenic counselors and trainers, rated empath-plus for splice bonding. Christopher Robin's role in the whole affair was tactician and squad leader.

When the dorm lights were snapped on—unintentionally alerting the artilect that monitored the epcot, and thus eventually causing the enforcers to arrive, as Christopher Robin later deduced—all the splices came blearily awake.

The Owls started saying, "This is not the Customary Procedure, not the Thing to Do!" The Piglets began to ask, "How can I be sure of you?" The Rabbits chorused, "Honey or milk? Honey or milk?" The Eeyores plaintively wailed, "Pathetic, that's what it is. Pathetic!" The Tiggers stayed silent but began to bounce off their beds, high as the ceiling, using their myofibril-plus leg muscles.

As for the cohort of Poohs—some twelve in number, a generous ursine staff to accommodate all shifts and furnish all the prime park locations—they begin to hum: "Rum-tum-tiddle-um-tum…"

The bleating and blather immediately got on Chrisopher Robin's nerves, but he ran some calming mantra embeds and focused, with Kelty's assistance, on keeping their perimeter secure, allowing Stego and Jodee to go to work on the splices, convincing as many as they could to accompany the intruders to a better life.

Minutes passed while Christopher Robin nervously peeked out the dormitory's slit-wide-open doorway for signs of response to the invasion. (They had dragged the paralyzed guard inside, but his absence could be just as much a giveaway.) Finally Jodee approached him. She swiped a loose strand of hair back under her camo-cap, looking perturbed.

"Boss, I can't get the Piglets, the Eeyores, the Owls, or the Rabbits to agree to go with us. Their operant conditioning and leash fetishes are too strong. As for the Tiggers—well, they're just going to scatter in all directions as soon as we're outside the fence. So we can free them, but we can't take them with us for media use later."

Christopher Robin had not anticipated this reluctance to be rescued on the part of the splices. He felt the potential glory of his mission diminishing by the second. "What about the Poohs?"

"Oh, they're keen to follow us. They like our Big Boots, and say that since it's going to be an Adventure, they are Ready for Anything."

As if to prove Jodee's assessment of their enthusiasm, the ursine splices crowded around the CLF leader, chanting, "A little boy and his Bear will always be playing! Always playing, a little boy and his Bear!"

Chrisopher Robin made a swift command decision. "Okay, that'll have to do. Let's calm them down and get outta here."

The twelve identical Poohs—each as big as a baseline human child of six, with beautifully flocked sienna hide and trusting, glittering, darting eyes—were quickly formed into a herd, urged to be quiet, and led outside.

The humans and their charges had just made it through the gap in the fence en masse when the first of the Hundred Acre Wood protectors arrived.

Several three-laws-null kibes, moving like stalking praying mantises, swung around a building's corner. The lead bot bellowed, "Halt!" followed by a nigh-unintelligible hyper-recital of the standard legal disclaimers about personal injury, etc. Christopher Robin could see that their upraised arms terminated in SPECTER guns. If the projectiles from those weapons scored a hit on bare flesh, down the victim would go in a spasm of pulsed electroshock. The raiders were mostly protected by body armor, but still, SPECTER guns were nothing to trifle with.

In the open fields surrounding the epcot, Christopher Robin and Jodee were abreast of the pack of eagerly gallivanting Poohs, while Stego and Kelty had hung back. Now, as per plan, those latter two assumed defensive postures to delay pursuit. Christopher Robin yelled, "Run!" and he and Jodee raced off with their abducted bears. Luckily, the Poohs' clumsy-looking exteriors concealed good musculature designed for endurance, climbing, swimming and other customer-amusing tricks.

Distinctive shots from the SPECTER guns sounded, along with the explosions of glue grenades. Christopher Robin dared not look back. Even with sparse shrubs and occasional trees, the gully-laden terrain was tricky, despite night-vision memtax, although the Poohs seemed to be doing fine. The splices actually seemed to be enjoying the romp. After about a mile, however, the humans began to breathe hard.

"Where are we heading?" Jodee said.

"Our exfil contact will probably be sussed out by now and neutralized. So we're taking the fallback option. Into the gretazone. It's only five miles away."

The huge rewilding preserve would offer cover and refuge for a time, especially since the remit of the authorities ended at its borders.

Conceived as interference-free, unregulated autonomous biomes, their status cemented legally, the rewilded domains had something of the reputation of the old American wild west, with a kind of beneficial, non-destructive homeostasis enforced by a tension between self-appointed protectors and exploiters. While the security team from the epcot could in theory follow their quarry into the gretazone, they would find no special privilege or cooperation—and perhaps even some antagonism—from the gretazone's inhabitants.

Not hearing any close pursuers, the two humans and the Poohs relaxed to a trot, so that the humans could catch their breaths. Around them the rich-scented springtime environment of the pastures and copses exuded a quiet normalcy that was falsely soothing. Kelty and Stego must have laid down sufficient obstacles, even at the likely cost of capture, to delay the epcot defenders, small in resources and numbers. All CLF rebel glory to them!

Christopher Robin and Jodee covered almost another four miles and were, by constantly updated geolocation tags, approaching the border of the gretazone, when the far-off sound of human voices and the baying of augie-doggies reached them.

"Shit!" exclaimed Jodee. "We knew extra muscle would jetson in, but I thought we'd have more time."

The Hundred Acre Wood had been targeted for its remoteness and lack of heavy on-site security. If they had been able to rendesvous with their assigned exfil, the CLF liberators would have been long gone by now.

Christopher Robin had to make another hard decision, but it actually proved easier than he had anticipated. He handed Jodee his own neural disrupter as backup for hers.

"You stand them off as long as you can, then join us over the frontier."

The woman looked nervous, but then her training and idealism came to the forefront.

"All right, I guess. You're the one the Poohs seem to have imprinted on. I'll see you soon—I hope. Down with the Purity Laws!"

Jodee took up position behind a boulder, and Christopher Robin gathered his flock and raced forward toward safety.

Only when the geotags in his memtax signified they were fully into the gretazone did he pause and look behind, deploying visual magnification.

Jodee had gone down under a scrum of canines, as humans raced up to call the dogs off. He prayed that the dogs had deployed only immobilizing mouth-holds. But scary noises made him think otherwise.

Deeper into the gretazone Christopher Robin and the Poohs pushed, not stopping until the human was sure pursuit had ended at the border.

He found himself on the edge of a small stream with sandy sloping banks. The nearest slope held several natural cave formations. Christopher Robin found one large enough to accommodate himself and the twelve Poohs. He calibrated a module of anti-sense odor-masking spray to his signature and that of the Poohs, then sprayed the path they had taken, backwards for many yards. He lofted up a tiny drone that would watch for pursuers all night and send an alert to his memtax. Then he sent an encrypted message to CLF HQ, explaining what had happened and that he needed new exfil. No immediate answer was forthcoming.

After hustling the excited, liberated Poohs into the largest cave, he joined his troop in the gritty shelter, resigned to having done all he could do. Nothing now except to try to grab some rest till morning, or a call from HQ.

The Poohs all tried to get as close to Christopher Robin as they could. He ended up with a couple in his lap.

"This Cave is splendid. We like it very much. If only there was a sign reading 'Mister Sanders' above the door."

"Sorry. Not gonna happen."

"Oh, well. We'll just hum ourselves to sleep then."

"Very quietly!"

The almost subliminal susurrus sent Christopher Robin straight to dreamland.

When dawn arrived there was neither a message from his allies, nor any sign of the vengeful epcot squad. The Poohs had evidently spent a restorative night, for they were now tediously overactive—and hungry.

One Pooh, identical to his brethren, appeared to have been appointed, by self or peers, as representative to speak. "We need some breakfast. Marmalade over honeycomb would be very nice."

"I don't have anything like that. We didn't plan to be out this long. Can't you guys forage?"

"Certainly we can. I think. What does forage mean?"

"Go out in the woods and look for something good to eat."

"Off we go!"

The Poohs rocketed away on their stubby legs in several directions. Christopher Robin felt a little uneasy letting them out of his sight, but what else could he do? They were leash-trained to need human dominance, and would in all probability return.

Christopher Robin washed his face in the stream, drank some wild water, and chewed a meta-bar. And then the Poohs came back.

The first sign of their arrival was the galloping appearance of a panicked giant capycoypu, big as a baseline steer, with two Poohs clinging to its wet coarse fur. The other ten splices, close behind, soon arrived to bring the wild-eyed grunting herbivore down to its knees by piling on. Before Christopher Robin could really even register what was happening, never mind protest or interefere, the Poohs manifested hidden claws and teeth, and the immense water-rat had its throat ripped open. After expiring spastically, it became a raw banquet for the Poohs, who soon had their velveteeen incarnadined snouts buried deep in the carcass.

Christopher Robin watched, appalled.

The leader Pooh finished first, or took a dutiful break, and came to seek the human's approval.

"We foraged good, did we not?"

"How—how can you kill and eat another animal like that?"

"Oh, it's all in the plan, you see. We live mostly on boring old tinned stuff. But when it's time to cull an elderly worker, then the bosses say we all get a treat."

The Pooh began to lick itself clean, and, still horrified, Christopher Robin turned away from the gory spectacle.

The message from his cadre arrived soon thereafter, offering congratulations for the partial success of the mission, and condolences for the lost members of the posse. The geotags for the new exfil site were included: a grove of hormone trees, not far off, selected because the trees were due for a visit from a pollination unit, and the CLF ship could spoof its way in as an NGO team looking to monitor the operation's efficiency.

Christopher Robin waited until the Poohs were sated, then got them washed up in the stream, finally setting off for their new destination. Coming from the nearest facility, the ship would arrive an hour or so after they reached the place, and then Christopher Robin could be rid of these splices, who had proved less satisfying than the noble, tragic victims of his imagination.

* * * *

Hivehead had enjoyed his pleasant, leisurely journey of one full day across the rewilding. Walking for twenty-four hours straight, sustained by the constant drizzle of super-honey which, for a period, could supplement sleep, he had had time to wordlessly ponder life and his existence while the majority of his bee symbiotes slept. Being semi-offline from the hive while he himself remained conscious was a kind of personal mini-retreat. But there was always a small cluster of bees active whenever he was active, hovering close around the skep so as to provide Hivehead with their omnidirectional audiovisual input that allowed him to navigate meatspace.

In any case, Hivehead had used the time well, emotionally reaffirming all the wisdom of his life choices after the flywheel farm disaster, and charting out ways in which he could function even more efficiently in his given role. His lost individuality as Hank Bogardus was a distant nightmare or dream, never missed.

New insights had led Hivehead to suspect that the immense colonies of ants in the rewilding, baseline and upgraded, might offer some mutualism opportunities with his bees. There were many myrmecophyte species in the gretazone—plants that had special relationships with ants—and many of those sported flowers. Surely some kind of mutually beneficial enhancements via selective breeding of the myrmecophytes could be achieved…

As dawn surged over the horizon, Hivehead arrived at the grove of oxytocin-olive trees. Their big gnarled and knotted trunks seemed to indicate great age, although in reality the accelerated trees were just a few decades old. Their greyish-green foliage was now interspersed with the many small white clustered flowers emanating from the leaf axils. Their pungent, apricot-like scent permeated the grove. Hivehead felt a surge of happiness at the task ahead.

Admittedly a trifle fatigued from the long walk, he lowered his bare butt to a tender patch of grass beneath one tree, keeping his torso and head nice and vertical so as not to disturb his buzzy pals. As thousands of bees swarmed out of the skep, eager to fulfill the assignment, Hivehead sank into a blissful relaxed condition—not quite sleep, but not quite full awareness.

Hivehead's reverie—he found himself flying blithely through the skies, skep and all, a not uncommon fantasy derived from sharing the apian haptics—was suddenly broken by a chorus of shrill nonhuman voices. Emerging slowly from the dream, Hivehead registered the speech.

"Honey! Honey! Beautiful honey! We smell honey! We want honey!"

Tapping the bee telemetry closest to the voices, Hivehead saw the impossible: a sleuth of toy bears come alive, racing directly for him!

And then, before he could even begin to rise, the bears were upon him. Their weight toppled him flat to the ground, their bodies carpeted him and pinned him down.

The bees were furious, stinging away. But their assaults had no effects on the honey-maddened splices.

Hivehead was still receiving the angry, confused telemetry of his charges. He seemed to see the arrival of a human, who began to shout and pummel the bears, all to no avail.

Then Hivehead felt his biopoly skep being attacked! Raked by claws, bitten with sharp teeth. The skep was strong but not invulnerable. Such assaults would soon shatter it.

Hivehead frantically sent a hopeless, desperate message to his bees.

"Help! Get help! Please! Now!"

He sensed a large portion of the eighty thousand peel off from the defense and fly away. What help they could find, he had no idea.

Hivehead tried to manually dislodge some of the little powerful bears, but received only painful gashes on his arms for his troubles. He tried to squirm away, and succeeded only to the extent of rolling onto one side, while the battering continued.

The queen behind his left ear was frantic, wriggling her bulk helplessly, radiating a terror into Hivehead's consciousness that only managed to disorient him further.

Hivehead sensed minute cracks opening in the skep. Soon its intricate architecture would be exposed and pillaged, its golden plunder spilling out, the destruction rendered final.

A titanic bellowing shook the very leaves of the grove. Hivehead tried to focus on the relevant telemetry from the nearby bees, and finally tapped a coherent AV stream.

The bees that had flown off had found a reluctant ally, whom they had goaded into action, herding it to the orchard.

The creature had raced into the orchard on all fours, but now reared up on its hind legs, using its massive tail for additional support. In that stance, the megatherium stood fifteen feet tall. A formerly extinct, reintroduced species of ground sloth, big as a baseline elephant, the hairy long-snouted creature, smelling like urine and moldy hay, was plainly enraged and eager to lash out. The veil of bees around its head continued to harry it.

The first swipe of its paw sent the human stranger flying across the grove. With another bellow, it focused on the only other active opponents in sight, and began to pick up the little bears and hurl them away. The fate of one of two of their fellows proved instructive to the others, and they desisted from their attack on the skep and rushed off out of reach, and out of the grove entirely.

Seeing the success of their engineered rescue, the cowl of bees now sought to urge the sloth away from Hivehead by massing on one side of the beast and stinging uniformly. Taking its direction from this push, the sloth dropped to all fours and galloped off, making plaintive sounds in its retreat that might have been pathetically amusing if they had emerged from a smaller, unmonstrous creature.

Hivehead was too disheartned and sore and pained to do anything but lie still. He knew he should get the skep upright, but could not summon the will nor the strength. The feeder sluice for his super-honey had come dislodged, so he could not revive himself that way.

His nervous worried associates swarmed obsessively, but could offer no further help. Finally, they all reentered the tilted skep, to hunker down and await further developments.

An hour or so passed, and Hivehead heard the approach of some kind of small aircraft.

The next thing he knew, he was being lifted on a stretcher and loaded into the craft, along with the other human, who appeared to have survived the megatherium's blow.

His rescuers moved to close the hatch of the aircraft, but Hivehead stopped them by interposing one arm laxly against the door. The crew, although baffled, obeyed Hivehead's wordless demand to keep the door open.

Finally, one last bee flew in and entered the skep.

Hivehead pulled back his arm.
They could leave now.
Everyone was home.

THE VISIONARY PAGEANT ARRAYED BEFORE HER

1.

SOPHRONIA TEMPEST BEGINS HER DAY

That there should defiantly remain, in this day and age of vast scientific revelations and accomplishments, any perplexing happenings—especially instances of phenomena tinged with the occult—was to the mind of Sophronia Tempest both a large philosophical affront and a personal challenge. She regarded any notionally inexplicable doings or enigmatic incidents as blots upon her portrait of reality, a challenging, insolent glove slapped, so to speak, across the face of the human intellect.

After all, was not this year of 1886 a time of perfected marvels derived from science, concrete proof of the power of natural philosophy? Ten mighty arc lights blazed nightly in Market Square, with their power supplied from the newly launched Rhode Island Electric Lighting Company. Many homes were looking forward to that glorious day, supposedly in the next year or three, when they could acquire and install in their parlor the perfected version of one of Thomas Edison's marvelous phonographs, along with a supply of wax cylinder recordings, perhaps featuring renditions even of such popular tunes as "Two Lovely Black Eyes, Oh, What a Surprise" and "Somebody's Mother." In Germany, a fellow named Karl Benz had leaped the practical hurdles to the creation of an internal combustion engine, powered by the miracle fuel of gasoline. And as far back as 1877, had not the future-minded citizenry of Rhode Island played host to President Rutherford B. Hayes, who had placed the first presidential telephone call, speaking over a line that connected the Rocky Point Amusement Park with the City Hotel in Providence, all of fourteen miles apart! Such an instrument must soon grace every household of even moderate means.

Yes, these glittering tokens and many more marked this era as the apex of humankind's inventive prowess. Of this, Sophronia Tempest was sure.

Although only twenty years old, Sophronia was a young woman who held and frequently manifested, to the chagrin and ire of many of her unenlightened elders and her male peers, very firm beliefs and opinions about nature and the world, including the sciences and their handmaiden, technology. The reasonableness and susceptibility to understanding that God's creation exhibited was the foundation of her view of existence. She had been inculcated with this attitude at St. Mary's Seminary, that novel and progressive school located in the sprawling and repurposed Howard Mansion in Riverside, a community across Narragansett Bay from Sophronia's home in Providence, Rhode Island.

The boarding school for girls aged five through eighteen had opened in 1874, just in time to receive the eight-year-old Sophronia Tempest. The subsequent ten years there, under the broad-minded and surprisingly liberal aegis of director Sister Mary Juliana Purcell, had infused the growing girl with a love of natural philosophy, reinforcing her natal disposition towards inquisitiveness. Her holidays and summers spent away from the precincts of St. Mary's were idyls of further self-directed reading and backyard experiments.

Her father, Clarence Tempest, a vice-president at Kendall Manufacturing Company, the purveyors of the marvelous Soapine ("Soapine, the Dirt Killer! It Washes Everything!" [This motto appended to an illustration of a child scrubbing a dirty whale.]), and her mother, Minnie, happily indulged their daughter's proclivities and interests, although there had been occasional disasters and rebukes, such as the time when she was discovered in the process of sending her infant brother Oscar aloft in a basket tethered to a homemade hot-air balloon. ("But I just wanted to see how high he could go before his breathing became labored! I would have hauled him right down!")

Having graduated with honors from Saint Mary's, but with no clear vision of how best to pursue her various interests, Sophronia had embarked on a further regimen of studies at the Rhode Island Normal School, with the goal of becoming a teacher. But three semesters at the college had dissuaded her from that career. She found, in a mandated field trial among actual children, that attempting to impart her sophisticated knowledge and enthusiasm to a room full of uninterested brats was highly boring and unsatisfying. Having left the Normal School, Sophronia was at loose ends for only a few weeks, until a revelation struck her.

Although formal teaching did not appeal, and the actual practice of science seemed foreclosed to her and her sex—unless she were prepared to forsake all else in her life and endure a steady stream of contumely and harrassment (despite the success of a few rare exemplary foremothers whom she revered, such as the astronomer Maria Mitchell and the botanist Jane Colden)—there remained one route to staying abreast of current developments in the sciences and even contributing in her own way to their dissemination and furtherance. And that method was the practice of journalism.

As a newspaper scribe, Sophronia believed, she would have access to the laboratories and congresses of researchers, and to the factory floors of those titans of industry such as Edison and Westinghouse. She would be able to continue her own education and appreciation of the sciences, while simultaneously enlightening the public, serving as a handmaiden to progress.

And so Sophronia—with some admitted help from her father, who was after all responsible for the placement of a rather large number of weekly advertisements for Soapine in various publications—managed to secure a position at the state's largest newspaper, the *Manufacturers & Farmers Journal*—the *Journal*, for short. A couple of months ago, Sophronia had joined the ranks of the *Journal*'s apprentice reporters.

But, alas, her career had not proceeded exactly as she had dreamed. Very frustrating.

This misdirection or under-utilization of her talents was the very matter she intended to take up with her superior, Mack Callender, today.

But at the kitchen breakfast table on that morning of June 3, 1886, Sophronia made no mention of any vocational controversies, not wishing to hear another lecture from her father about gratitude and humility, nor endure her mother's advice about the virtues of patience. Instead, as Clarence Tempest unconsciously stroked his luxuriant tawny mustaches while studying the latest number of *Hygeia: the Soap Industry Weekly*; and eternally placid Minnie Tempest, one long curl falling unpinned alongside her red cheek, improved the unforgiving minute with some sock-darning; and twelve-year-old Oscar Tempest, a veritable freckled demon in short pants, wrestled with Clutterbuck the ginger tomcat, attempting to make the reluctant feline consume Oscar's own daily Mellin's Food Biscuit (Mother Minnie felt that Oscar was too scrawny, and needed bolstering), Sophronia broached an innocent topic in which she actually had some mild interest.

"Has anyone heard whether or not the Mayor is expected to be well enough to march in the anniversary celebrations?"

This very year marked the two-hundred-and-fiftieth anniversary of the founding of Providence by Roger Williams in 1636. Exile from censorious Massachusetts in search of "soul liberty, the bold explorer had arrived in that long-ago year at the head of Narragansett Bay, to greet the baffled yet friendly natives with the now-famous hail of "What cheer, Netop?". Williams had laid the foundation for all the subsequent glory that was to follow. Nowadays, Providence, second only in the New England region to Boston, was a small dynamic metropolis and an industrial and trade powerhouse, her ships sailing to the Far East and into whaling waters, as well as to Europe and other familiar precincts.

Naturally enough, such a proud and shining city desired and deserved a large and splendid commemoration of such a milestone anniversary, and elaborate plans had been underway for an entire year. The anticipated speeches, parades, cotillions, fireworks, compettitions, banquets, picnics, concerts and awards ceremonies would fully occupy the city—and the entire state—for two whole days, June twenty-third and twenty-fourth.

And no one had been more of a champion and inspiration for the whole shebang than Mayor Thomas Doyle, a selfless fellow of vast intellect, virtue and probity. In office on and off for nearly eighteeen years, his name was practically synonymous with the city and its reputation. If anyone deserved to bask in the glow of the festivities, to accept the accolades of the populace, it was he. But, alas, Doyle's health had been faltering of late, and his condition was on everyone's mind and lips.

Putting aside his journal, Clarence Tempest said thoughtfully, "I had lunch yesterday at the Hope Club, and old Blodget said he heard directly from Doyle's physician that the man had the constitution of an ox and would soon rebound from any temporary incapacity. I would not count him out just yet."

Now came an interruption from the region of the massive coal-fired Smith & Anthony Hub Range.

"Clear the decks! Johnnycakes for all!"

There stood young Bertha Ahlquist, maid and cook to the Tempest household. The plump and jovial seventh daughter of a family of Swedish immigrants resident in the large Scandinavian community in the adjacent town of Cranston, Bertha served the household in exemplary fashion, as she now illustrated, approaching the table with heavy skillet held effortlessly aloft. She efficiently served the steaming cornmeal cakes, then headed off to the laundry room..

Minnie Tempest picked up the thread of her husband's observation. "I surely hope the man perks up enough to enjoy all that he's wrought. He certainly deserves the rewards of his labors."

Releasing a Mellin-stuffed Clutterbuck, who scrambled out of the kitchen wildly, Oscar sauced his portion with about a pint of maple syrup, speared several sausages from the platter in the middle of the table, and commenced to devour the whole assemblage like a Fijian cannibal tucking into a serving of missionary.

"I hearily approve of Mayor Doyle," Sophronia said. "He wants to electrify the streetcars, and that's progress. I'm going to ask at the *Journal* if they've heard anything about his health."

Having devastated his breakfast, Oscar paused long enough to venture a question. "Say, Pop, how's the float for Soapine coming along? Can I get a look at it yet?"

Part of the anniversary celebrations was to be a giant Trades Procession, in which scores of retailers and wholesalers, manufacturers, importers and farmers; photographers, blacksmiths and a myriad other craftsmen would display their wares and skills, via creative arrangements atop wagons and suchlike vehicles.

Clarence Tempest chuckled. "It's going to be a whizzer, son, I can tell you that. I had not a small hand it its conception and execution myself. But I'm afraid you'll have to wait until the twenty-fourth to see it in all its glory, just like everyone else."

"Drat! What good is it having a father in high places if his son don't get no preference?"

Practically levitating off his chair and almost halfway across the kitchen, Oscar said, on the run, "Bye now! I'm off to Billy Budlong's house. We're going to go spear frogs down at the Cove!"

The remaining members of the Tempest family finished their breakfast in a quieter and less frenetic manner, and, upon wiping the last of the maple syrup from her lips, Sophronia kissed her parents goodbye and prepared to depart for the *Journal*.

"You'll be home for dinner, Soph dearest, won't you?" asked Minnie.

"Unless Mister Callender assigns me to cover President Cleveland's White House honeymoon!"

In the entryway she paused before a large mirror to check her looks. (The nearby framed Haskell and Allen lithograph of "Winter in the Country" was so familiar as to be invisible.)

A black felt derby with a white band complemented her light hair and fair skin, she affirmed. Her simple red and yellow sateen daydress looked practical yet handsome, and accentuated her fine corseted waist and modest but sufficient bosom. Common-sense cloth-topped high-buttoned shoes with a low heel allowed her excellent pedestrian mobility, a necessity for a reporter on the go. The whole rig had cost her under ten dollars at a sale at Gladding's Department Store, an economy of which she was proud.

Sophronia exited the family home, a modest manse at 380 Broadway, designed and built just two decades ago by architect Perez Mason. The house's unique third-floor dormer, resembling a lady's Easter bonnet, made the home a local landmark. The leafy neighborhood represented an elite residential part of the city, second in importance only to the East Side, the district that hosted Brown University.

Nodding to several of the many passersby, Sophronia resolved to walk to the *Journal* offices at 29 Weybosset, a pleasant stroll of fifteen minutes or so.

But when she stepped down from the porch, there on the sidewalk she saw written in chalk a sign of the inexplicable matter that had been so affronting her rational sensibilities for the past few weeks.

The legend read:

ALL THE CATS ARE GOING TO ULTHAR

2.
WHERE IS ULTHAR?

Sophronia could feel her ire rising. Realizing that one of her character defects was a tendency to respond instantly, thoughtlessly and passionately to any perceived slight against one of her particular crotchets, she deliberately throttled back her emotions. After all, should Reason not remain enthroned as Queen above the more primitive faculties? Although sometimes people's stupidity, ignorance and stubbornness did infuriate one!

This deliberately enigmatic graffito played upon a very real phenomenon, the issue that had been scandalizing Sophronia's sense of cause and effect.

For the past three months, the feline citizens of Providence had been going missing at an alarming rate, much greater than the annual statistical average for disappearing cats. From many a household each morning arose the wails and sobs of children who discovered that, overnight, poor Puss was suddenly nowhere to be found.

Now, in a scientific world such an anomalous burst of disappearances could have had any number of causes. A new disease running rampant among the cat population. A rash of cat-nappings by vivisectionists or perhaps by members of some alien racial grouping that found cats to be fodder rather than pets. An influx of predators, such as wolves. (The image of a big grey timber wolf, long extinct in New England, slinking through the clothesline-decorated backyards of the city made Sophronia smile for a moment.) These causes and others could be logically justified.

However, there was no evidence to support any of these hypotheses. No cat corpses, intact or savaged. No reports of either medical students avaricious for anatomical knowledge or indiscriminate "chop suey" chefs. No unprecedented larcenous depredations from the desperate farmers of

Rhode Island who might wish to recruit barn cats to combat some nonexistent tide of crop-nibbling rats.

And yet, cats continued to disappear.

And then, in the wake of this mystery, had come outbreaks of an infuriating slogan, scrawled hither and yon across Providence: ALL THE CATS ARE GOING TO ULTHAR.

What could it possibly mean? How could dumb animals choose a destination and then decide to flee, en masse? Where was "Ulthar?" Certainly it was no New England place; and, if very far removed from Providence, how could a cat travel there? What lure might draw cats to this unmapped region, away from comfortable homes and cosseting humans? No, the graffito was palpably the work of one or more pranksters, a rude jape intended to capitalize cruelly on the loss of beloved pets. And as such, it really "got up Soph's nose," to put it coarsely in the manner of brother Oscar.

Using the tip of one shoe, Sophronia effaced the chalked motto, and then strode resolutely off, east down Broadway, heading for the center of the city and the offices of her employer. Horse-drawn municipal trams paced her down the middle of the road, flanked on either side by rolling delivery wagons and personal conveyances. The smell of horse manure was not unpleasant, although the coming heat of August might evoke a different reaction to the piles.

The gorgeous June weather and her bold ambulations beneath the stately elms that lined the avenue soon caused her cloud of petulance to dissipate. Additionally, Sophronia had conceived of a plan to attack the enigma. First, she would consult various reference works at the office of the *Journal* in an attempt to pin down the meaning of "Ulthar." Failing to find an answer on her own, she would next consult Professor Charnley about it. Surely that savant would have an answer!

Sophronia had made the acquaintance of Professor Aurion Charnley during her enrollment at the Normal School. Although employed as a respected and elderly faculty member in the Ethnology and Anthropology Department at Brown University, the erudite, albeit somewhat scatterbrained and occasionally caustic fellow had deigned to present a course in the pedagogical techniques of other nations to the budding teachers. (The carnal reinforcements to memory utilized by the Dayaks of Borneo had been scandalous but enlightening.) Sophronia had been his star student, and had maintained an on-and-off, improbable relationship with the older man ever since. Realizing now that she had not spoken to Charnley in at least six months, Sophronia castigated herself for letting their friendship lapse just because of the demands of her new job. Surely he of anyone, with his wide knowledge of the odder corners of the globe, would be able to pin down this Ulthar! And perhaps fresh knowledge would point towards a culprit in these sidewalk and board-fence defacements. Such a "scoop," to employ the reporter's lingo, would surely get her gruff and generally implacable boss to look on her more admiringly and to grant her assignments more in accordance with her talents and interests.

Broadway descended gradually at a very slight incline, aiming for the sea-level elevation of the city's downtown. Once on the outskirts of that district, Sophronia zagged a few blocks south to pick up Weybossett, then turned east again. At number 89, she paused outside the Theatre Comique to admire the poster for their latest show: *Pepita; or, the Girl with the Glass Eyes.* Then, continuing onward, just a few doors down from the antique Arcade, an enclosed pavilion of small shops, she found the entrance to the *Journal* offices beckoning.

Inside, the cramped headquarters was a hurly-burly of noisy activity, as reporters, editors, stenographers, pressmen, copyboys, sketch artists and engravers came and went about their duties. (There was talk of hiring a photographer soon, in light of the accomplishments at the *New York Daily Graphic*, where successful reproduction of photographs was now a daily matter.) A small corps of "newsies," the raggedy, motley youths who delivered the papers to homes, hung about, although their pickup times occurred much later in the day. Most were orphans, and simply hoping to cadge a meal.

Largest contributor to the aural chaos were the active ranks of Sholes and Glidden Type-Writers, those marvelous instruments newly perfected and marketed by the Remnigton Sewing Machine Company.

Sophronia wended her way through the scrum. At one desk, she paused.

There sat her rival. At least she conceived of the fellow as such, although he probably did not regard her in the same light. But he was the reporter who most often secured the plum assignments from editor Mack Callender, the kind of stories that Sophronia dreamed of writing. And, gallingly, he was not much older than she.

Cleanshaven and ruggedly handsome, often to be discovered with an insouciant smile playing about his lips, Reuben Standeven wore a nicely tailored sack suit with houndstooth vest, a colorful foulard around his throat. Engaged in earnestly studying some papers, he idly skritched his scalp through wavy auburn hair.

Sensing Sophronia's presence, he looked up and brightened.

"What cheer, fair damsel! May I say you look most beguiling this morning. Fit to consort with the grand dames at the Art Club—but in the role of ingenue only."

Sophronia snorted. "Such is not my aim. What are you perusing there?"

"Information on the latest Corliss steam engine. I am to interview the great George Corliss himself this afternoon."

Sophronia found herself deprived of the powers of speech. This was exactly the kind of hard-edged reportorial task she herself coveted! And for which she was perfectly adapted! And yet, despite all her begging and imploring, she was relegated to covering teas and soirees, theatrical performances, school fairs, quilting bees and similar dainty and "feminine" activities.

Sophronia knew that Reuben was not bragging, nor rubbing his this peach assignment in her face. Nonetheless, she turned without a civil word and huffed off.

She did not look back, because she suspected the infuriating man would be grinning.

Pausing only briefly outside Mack Callender's office door, Sophronia knocked and entered.

The editor's office was decorated with framed lithographs from various magazines, such as *The Judge* and *Puck*. They all flaunted a satirical cast, poking savage fun at mankind's foibles, such as the depiction of a bribe-taking policemen, titled "Hush money--or money for the sewer." Additionaly, there were framed copies of front pages to which Callender had contributed.

She found her boss speaking on the telephone. That miraculous device, one of some fifty thousand now extant across the country, intrigued Sophronia no end, and she longed to take the "gadget" apart to examine its innards.

Spotting Sophronia, the editor waved her to a seat.

"Yes, yes," Callender was expostulating, "I know all that!"

Sophronia used her boss's preoccupied state to marvel anew at his formidable appearance.

Dressed in striped trousers and fawn-colored cutaway coat, Mack Callender was a bantam of a fellow, but vigorous and hard as nails. Some fifty years old, he possessed a phiz that bore many scars—and only one eye, his vacant orbit being concealed with a piratical patch. Likewise, one empty sleeve of his jacket was pinned up at the shoulder.

Callender had been a veteran reporter for the *Hartford Daily Courant* until two years ago. Covering the Tonkin War between the French and the Chinese, he had been blown up by a mine. After a long recovery, he returned to his post only to find the *Courant* shuttering shop. But he came to regard the closing as fortuitous, since it caused him to realize that his best field days were behind him, and that desk work was now his lot. The owners of the *Journal* had snapped him up as an editor as soon as they knew of his availability.

Having been a reporter himself for so long, Callender knew the desires and wiles, the deceits and demands of his staff intimately.

Callender replaced the earpiece of the telephone back on its hook and focused his fierce one-eyed glare on Sophronia like the beam from a powerful lighthouse.

"What do you want! I suppose you've discovered I'm sending Standeven to the Corliss factory instead of you! And why not? The boy is a quick study. He'll do a bang-up interview. And he won't belabor poor Corliss with a thousand dreamy questions about gasket dimensions and pipe-fitting tolerances and the future of 'steam men of the prairies,' like someone I could name. Am I correct, or am I not, Miss Tempest?"

Sophronia had to bite her tongue before replying. "Your forceful remarks display your usual vivid candor, Mister Callender."

The editor burst out into hearty laughter. "You don't back down, and you're a diplomat, girl! I predict that if you just restrain your more unnatural predilections, you'll go far in this business."

The compliment fought with her irritation, and achieved an uneasy truce. "Thank you, sir. Might I now enquire what you had on tap for me today? Another strawberry festival perhaps? The Board Meeting at the Providence Athenaeum? Maybe some heiress in Newport has a hangnail?"

Callender harumphed. "You fail to realize that such homely items draw readers to our pages in possibly even greater numbers than fantastical accounts of some crackpot inventor and his Vernean submersible. And we need readers, so as to stay fiscally afloat. And you have a knack for rendering such quotidian items interesting. However, none of your acidulous darts have quite hit the mark. I want you to attend a lecture tonight. The speaker is a woman named"—Callender rummaged through some memoranda—"named Isadora Blank. Apparently she's been making speeches here in Providence for the past several months, but it's only now that she's come to my attention, as her popularity waxes."

"What is the topic of her lectures?"

"It's some kind of self-help pap. From what I can make out, a blend of Emerson and Fourier, with a soupçon of Samuel Smiles. But in any case, she's beginning to draw crowds, and we need to render an account of her tripe."

Sophronia sighed dramatically. "I will endeavor to transcribe her wisdom accurately and objectively."

Callender's attention was already shifting to other matters. "Good, good, I knew I could count on you. Here's two tickets. Make a night of it. Take that beau of yours. What's his name? Bowtie? Arthur Bowtie?"

"Arthur Botwink," said Sophronia, feeling that familiar sense of damp and tepid amiability arise in her bosom as the image of Arthur swam into her mind's eye.

3.
LITTLE PITCHERS HAVE BIG EARS

With a tide of noontime pedestrians surging around her—in the street an ice wagon was followed by a bread wagon, which in turn was followed by a butcher's pushcart and a pack of curs—Sophronia stood outside the Hoppin Homestead Building, 287 and 289 Westminster Street, still within the downtown area and just a short walk away from the *Journal* offices. The lavish display windows of the building featured colorful ceramics and pots, dishes and platters, cups and pitchers of every style and size, all tastefully arranged on red satin-draped risers. Here was the prestigious outlet of Warren & Wood Crockery, purveyors to the carriage trade. The establishment that employed her boyfriend, Arthur Botwink, as a staff overseer.

Sophronia ransacked her brain for reasons not to enter.

She had spent a large part of the morning after leaving Callender's office in the *Journal*'s small but mighty reference library, examining the *Encyclopædia Britannica* and many other sources, such as atlases and traveler's accounts, to see if she could ascertain the meaning or location of "Ulthar." But her digging had met with no success. Reluctantly abandoning that investigation, she had been given the task of visiting the offices of the Cecilia Society to ascertain when their next chamber music concert would occur, and who the performers would be. Although Sophronia harbored a place for music in her engineer's soul, she found the bustle-wearing, matronly head of the Cecilia Society a complete snooze. She feared she had affronted the woman by letting a tremendous yawn escape during the course of the interview. Oh, well, the old harpy should be glad that any attention at all was being paid to her and her boring antique club of dry-as-dust esthetes.

After returning to the offices and writing up her inconsequential piece—the chafing figure of Reuben Standeven was nowhere to be seen—Sophronia realized it was the lunch hour, and time for her daily repast with Arthur Botwink.

And so, here she was. But while most days found her slightly anticipatory of her meeting with Arthur, in the humdrum manner of a child who had been told of the forthcoming visit of a maiden aunt who always dispensed one's least favorite candy, today Sophronia found herself positively reluctant to meet with Arthur.

What could be the matter with her? What imp of the perverse had so unsettled her today, and made her actually resent having to lunch with Arthur?

She had known Arthur since they were both five years old, and they had grown up practically side by side, save when different schools parted them. Their families had been commingled for ages, and somehow it had become a *fait accompli* that she and Arthur were practically destined to be mated someday like the only two animals of the same species in the zoo. Attending an all-girls school as she had, Sophronia had not been subjected daily to a wide variety of alternative suitors during her tender years. Nor had she really missed or sought out such male company, being preoccupied with her other interests. The adult social occasions she enjoyed these days always seemed to include Arthur at her side, thus warding off any potential rival swains. Sophronia had not resented nor even meditated on this pre-connubial condition until recently, when she had begun to experience certain fancies regarding her ideal helpmeet and romantic ideal. Nebulous images had of late begun to fill the mirror of her mind, and none of them resembled Arthur in the slightest.

And yet, she could not find it in herself to break off whatever tacit and circumspect—and dull, dull, dull!—lovers' arrangement she and Arthur implicitly shared. The fellow, she was sure, would positively collapse! And certainly he had done nothing ill-mannered or inconsiderate to merit her rebuke.

Thank the Lord that at least there had yet been no talk of setting a date for their marriage!

And so, as conflicted and irresolute as ever—an emotional and mental condition which she experienced in no other area of her life—Sophronia pushed open the doors of Warren & Wood and went in search of her dining partner.

After crossing the busy and elegant sales floor, she found Arthur standing a few steps high on a ladder, and busy overseeing the erection of a display, as two junior shopboys under his direction tried to instantiate his platonic conceptions.

"No, no, we need to see the imagery in a *panoramic* way!"

Arthur Botwink showed a medium height and the physique of some lolling adolescent on a Greek urn (a metaphorical comparison quite in keeping with his chosen trade, thought Soph). His straw-colored hair was already thinning, but even a thicker thatch would have definitely failed to conceal protuberant ears. Alas, his chin did not possess the most commanding dimensions, being rather underslung. His large blue eyes, although quite charming, did have a tendency to mist over upon any maudlin pretext, such as the coming of autumn or the recitation of "The Song of Hiawatha."

Sophronia made a quick mental comparison of Arthur's looks against that still-somewhat-unformed Adonis growing in her imagination, and sighed.

Spotting his inamorata, Arthur grinned widely, in a rather moony fashion. He climbed down, snagging one of the display items.

"Curtis, Herbert, you are dismissed until after lunch."

The boys eagerly departed.

Arthur cradled the object in his hands in the manner of a rajah holding a jewel of great price. "Look, dear, isn't this simply fabulous?"

Sophronia saw nothing unusual: a white pitcher of classical proportions, with a band of painted daisies around the rim. The belly of the object held a famous scene, rendered in exquisite detail in an umber monotone: Roger Williams standing in the prow of a small boat as it came ashore to the amazement of the local Indians. The date of 1636 showed on a banner below the portentous, city-foundational meeting.

"We commissioned these just for the anniversary celebrations. Mister Warren expects to sell a powerful grist of these." Arthur lowered his voice to a whisper. "Don't tell anyone, but our wagon in the Trades Procession is going to feature a veritable *ziggurat* of Williams pitchers!"

Sophronia made some polite sounds of approbation, and that seemed to be enough to satisfy Arthur's pride in his employer's wares.

"All this decorative work has stimulated my appetite. I'm famished! Let's head out."

Exiting the store, the pair turned their steps in a familiar direction and ended up at Wambley's Chophouse and Seafood Grotto. The spacious, echoing, rambunctious establishment was packed, but after a short wait a table was found for Sophronia and Arthur. Presented with green pasteboard menus as big as desk blotters, the pair made their choices.

Their waiter—a dissolute, middle-aged Bacchus in a dirty apron—having finally arrived, Arthur reeled off a catalogue of viands that no stranger would have associated with a fellow of his moderate size. But Sophronia knew that he could pack away quantities of food that a dock worker would have trouble ingesting—and never add weight. This was perhaps Arthur's only trait that she envied.

"I'll have lobster croquettes followed by the green turtle soup, if you please. Then the lamb chops with asparagus tips, and an oyster plant and dandelion salad too. Oh, some succotash on the side. And lastly, a wedge of gorgonzola and a Biscuit Tortoni to finish."

Arthur turned to Sophronia. "And you, my dear?"

She hesitated a moment, busy thinking of how much cooking any bride of Arthur's would have to do. "I'll take the watercress and shrimp salad. And some Champagne Wine jelly for dessert."

The waiter collected the elephant-folio menus and strode off.

Arthur's face expressed worried concern. "Soph, my love, you really should force yourself to enjoy heartier meals. Not to be coarse, but all the experts agree that a woman has to maintain her internal, ah, mechanisms with a regular and copious supply of calories if she ever hopes to fulfill her maternal function."

"I will be sure to stoke those dire engines at the appropriate season. But right now, I'm more interested in an intellectual matter. Look at these tickets I have for Friday night. I'd like you to come."

Sophronia explained her assignment. Arthur cogitated, then said, "I had wanted us to go to the San Souci or Park Gardens on Friday for some fun. I understand there's a new minstrel troupe coming to the San Souci."

Sophronia felt irritation at Arthur's unsophisticated tastes in entertainment, but did not chide him. "I'd like to see them too, Arthur. But this task is essential to my work."

"Oh, well, then,"said Arthur magnanimously, "you may count me in."

Their meals came—steaming, fragrant platters and a mingy bowl of greens—and Sophronia found that her not overly delicate consumption of her small portions was nearly outmatched by Arthur's speedy trencherman devastation of his several plates.

After a round of coffee, they left Wambley's for the Cove Promenade.

A finger of Narragansett Bay extended deep into the center of Providence, terminating in the circular Cove at the foot of Smith Hill. Despite tidal flushing and being also fed by two streams from the north and west (the Woonasquatucket and the Moshassuck), the body of water had become somewhat noisome as Providence's manufactories thrived. There was talk of some day filling it in and reclaiming the space for buildings. But for the present, a graceful railed esplanade followed the perimeter of the Cove and allowed for pleasant recreational sauntering—if the daily waxing and waning odors cooperated.

Sophronia listened patiently as Arthur spoke of retail doings at Warren & Wood Crockery involving people she barely knew. Every now and then she managed to share some of her own workplace concerns, receiving some reassuring platitudes in return.

As they reached the northernmost arc of the walk, Sophronia espied a group of ragamuffin youths ankle deep in the stinky mud beyond the railing, and recognized Oscar among them. The wildly exuberant boys were jabbing at agitated dye-sickly frogs and unseen tannery-crippled fish with improvised wooden spears. She stopped to admonish her brother.

"Oscar! Mama's going to have a fit when she sees how filthy you are!"

"Oh, don't be such a badger, sis! I'll clean up good before I go home. Anyhow, we aren't going to be here much longer, are we, fellas?"

"Why not? Where are you going next?"

"Oh, me and my chums got a line on the place where all the cats is going."

"Ulthar?"

"That's it. I reckon we can track them down and get them all home."

"Oh, don't be ridiculous! There's no such place."

"We'll see," said Oscar. "Just you wait."

4.
THE STARRY SODALITY

The next day, June fourth, was the very Friday of Sophronia's assignment, and she had been itching all throughout the day to get to the self-improvement lecture by the mysterious yet no doubt unrelievedly banal and boring Isadora Blank. Soph counted on hastening through it with jaundiced eye, (however unprofessional that might be), after which she would distill its essence into a witty screed. True, she would much rather have had the chance to attend a speech by William Stanley at Brown University about his new induction coil and the possibilities of alternating current; or been asked to bask at a salon in the presence of Kate Field, the inspirationally famous female correspondent and paragraphist and friend to Mark Twain. But those options were not open to her, and even if her story were relegated to the society column, it still stood a chance of showcasing her prose talents and perhaps convincng Mack Callender to allow her broader scope.

Sophronia spent the morning helping her mother in their kitchen garden. Sophronia had definite thoughts about new and improved scientific methods of cultivation, and lectured her placid and tolerant mother during the entire operation of weeding and hoeing, mulching and harvesting. After that, she had gone into the *Journal* offices and helped to compile the shipping news column and aided in the composition of advertisements for Burdock's Blood Bitters and Count Rumford's Baking Powder. Of course, lunch with Arthur had intervened. Today they ate less formally—albeit, on Arthur's part, with equal copiousness—enjoying liverwurst sandwiches, milk and gooseberry pie from the W. S. Sweet & Sons lunch wagon, so that Arthur could have time to visit a competitor's store and spy on their new line of merchandise for Warren & Wood.

Sophronia had returned home in the late afternoon to enjoy an early supper with family before changing her clothing and awaiting escort Arthur's arrival. During the meal Clarence Tempest reported on the Mayor's health and the progress of the Trades Procession. Minnie Tempest had to gently berate Bertha the cook for letting the brace of canvasback ducks linger in the oven too long, to the point of dryness. Oscar Tempest surreptitiously read a dime novel involving the Old Sleuth, held beneath the table. He wasn't fooling anyone about where his attention was focused, but his parents indulged him. Sophronia considered exposing her brother's infantile and fantastic scheme to discover the fabulous lands of Ulthar—what if such a pursuit involved dangerous or illicit trespasses?—but then thought better of it. There seemed to be little harm in the game. She recalled her own youthful explorations and transgressions and felt Oscar should enjoy the same liberties.

At eight PM on this balmy June night, with crickets chirruping, Arthur arrived, dressed with meticulous care in a tailcoat and top hat. He chatted politely and familiarly with Clarence and Minnie, with no evident urgency to be away, until Sophronia dragged him off. They caught the horse-drawn tram that would bring them through the center of downtown before depositing them on the eastern edge of the district, at Market Square.

On the tram, Arthur noticed that Sophronia clutched a small volume in library binding. "What's that, my dear? The latest number of *Godey's Lady's Book*, per chance? Are you assaying the latest fashions for the fall?" Arthur contorted his face in what he obviously assumed to be the coy and sly manner of a roué making an indecent remark. "Or are you intent on building up your trousseau?"

Sophronia opened the book to its title page. "These are some fairly recent proceedings from the Royal Astronomical Society. I brought them along to occupy me if this Blank woman's speech should prove to be too hideously boring. I'm most interested in this report from Albert Michelson. 'Experimental Determination of the Velocity of Light.' Arthur, have you ever considered the vastness of interstellar space, and all the myriad phenomena those reaches contain? As yet, we know only the smallest fraction of what lies beyond our atmosphere. Why, there might even be new planets relatively close by, just out beyond Neptune!"

Arthur scoffed. "Unless such remote venues hold new customers for Warren & Wood's products, I fear I'm not much interested."

Sophronia sighed, and clapped shut her book.

Under its novel electric arc lights, Market Square seemed a veritable fairyland. The civic space, dominated by the eponymous stately building that dated from before the Revolution, hosted many strollers and idlers of both sexes, including a fair number of Bohemians, obviously attracted or supported by the Rhode Island School of Design, which occupied a suite of six rooms in the same Hoppin Homestead Building that housed Warren & Wood Crockery. Not far away reared the lofty steeple of the First

Baptist Church. From this spot the land and streets sloped steeply upward to form the East Side of the city, home to many elegant houses and Brown University. Sophronia recalled her plans to visit Professor Aurion Charnley concerning the origins of Ulthar, and resolved to seek that meeting tomorrow or as soon as possible. However, at this moment she would not be ascending College Hill, but remaining at its base.

Sophronia and Arthur set out to walk the few blocks down South Main Street to their destination. South Main ran parallel to that thrust of the finger of ocean water which supplied the Cove, but it was not the street closest to the water's edge. That avenue was South Water Street, a rough district of warehouses and fish-processing plants, chandlers and coal depositories that serviced the many medium-sized ships tied up at the wharves. (Larger vessels docked at India Point, or further down the Bay.) The time-distressed buildings lining South Main Street did not present an unbroken façade, but at almost every juncture offered narrow and dark alleyways between them, connecting to South Water. Despite being only a block long, these shadowy, smelly, slimy cross-passages seemed, to Sophronia's nervous eye, to twist and turn for miles, harboring unknown and unknowable denizens. She disliked coming here at night. The uneven brick sidewalks seemed to offer pitfalls and snares. Cursing her unwonted timidity, Sophronia clung tightly to Arthur's arm as they walked along. Arthur straightened his back at the implicit compliment to his protective manliness, and cast defiant glances at whatever might lurk beyond the nimbus of the widely spaced gas lights. The foot traffic was sparse, and Sophronia imagined lascars and cutpurses lurking behind every tree trunk.

Eventually, however, they arrived without instance at the corner of Power and South Main, and the building that was to host Isadora Blank's lecture.

The Amateur Dramatic Hall was a somewhat shabby but still impressive edifice. Originally erected in 1833 as a Methodist Church, it had had a checkered career since, even serving for a time as a riding academy. Nowadays it hosted theatrical performances. Some three storeys tall, it presented its windowless but modestly ornamented brick front to South Main, at the far verge of a small plot of grass serving as front lawn, with the body of the structure running uphill along Power Street; so that although the patron would enter through the front door on the lowest level of the building, should he wish to exit from the rear, he would have to ascend to the Hall's second floor to match the rising street.

A steady stream of patrons of all sexes, ages and distinctions was converging on the entrance from every point of the compass, and Sophronia and Arthur joined them. As they drew closer to the braced-open dual doors, Sophronia registered a small signboard:

HEADQUARTERS OF THE STARRY SODALITY

ISADORA BLANK,
HIEROPHANT AND OPENER OF THE WAY
"WELCOME, ALL YE WHO DESIRE CELESTIAL PERFECTION"

Sophronia wondered aloud. "Has this unknown sect purchased the whole building? How could they have become so well established so quickly?"

Arthur assumed a mercantile and speculative mien. "I wonder if they need ewers or goblets or salvers for their ceremonies. Warren & Wood could cut a good deal for quantities of a gross or more."

Two attendants, youngish cleanshaven men, flanked the doors. There was nothing untoward or offputting about their appearance, save for the fact that they wore white belted gowns of some heavy rich fabric such as samite, and stood unshod. One of them collected the tickets proferred by Sophronia with a benign nod and the adjuration, "Reach out for the constellations, my friend, and live."

In the theater proper, facing the stage at the uphill end of the building and looking over the massed heads of a packed house, with sibilant and reverential whispers predominating, Sophronia paused to assess the audience. Arthur perforce halted as well.

The seated viewers seemed regular citizens of every stripe, rock-ribbed Yankees as well as a smattering of Negroes and Orientals and Mediterranean immigrants. Soph wondered what attraction or platform could have united such a wide spectrum of attendees. Were these all seekers after "celestial perfection?"

A familiar voice resounded from close behind the preoccupied Sophronia, making her jump.

"What's the matter, Miss Scribbler? Is there no ribbon-bedecked reserved booth for the glorious members of the press?"

Sophronia whipped around to confront a grinning Reuben Standeven. A red film of anger seemed suddenly to intervene between them.

'Why, you greedy, immoral cad! Does your professional jealousy know no bounds, that you had to follow me here to undercut my reportage? I suppose you'll rush back to the *Journal* as soon as this circus is over and file your piece before I can file mine. Well, I won't allow it! I'll—"

Reuben held up a monitory hand. "Hold on, hold on just a minute! I'm not here in a working capacity, and I have no intention of belaboring my creative faculties tonight. I've come to this chautauqua just for amusement. And it's at the behest of this fine lady, she who proposed our evening's entertainment."

Sophronia finally noticed Reuben's comrade with a start.

A blonde woman clad in expensive velvet and lace, her feet nipped in the most fashionable heels, she displayed more intoxicating curves than any seacoast road on the French Riviera. Her heavily painted face seemed an advertisement for acts of a delightfully immoral turpitude that would register no guilt or regrets. She had the temerity to leer boisterously at Sophronia and say, "Pleased to meet you, lamb's lettuce! My name's Fannie Audet. What's your handle?"

Sophronia stuttered out her name, which suddenly seemed utterly alien on her own lips.

"Fannie is a singer at the San Souci Gardens," said Reuben. "You should hear her rendition of 'Plum Pudding.' Go ahead, Fannie, regale them with a verse!"

Oblivious of the dignified circumstances, Fannie Audet commenced loudly to sing.

> "Oh! when you hear the 'whoop,' the milkman's on the stoop,
> Awaiting with his jingling can.
> Oh, never stop to chat about the pussy cat.
> Don't let him call you simple Mary Ann;
> Now when he drives away, oh, to yourself you say:
> 'When I get my Sunday out,
> I'll meet him in the park a little after dark,
> And hook him as I would a little trout!'"

A dead hush had descended in the theater during Fannie's gay song, as all heads swivelled to face the rear. But then, plainly forgetting the solemnity and reverence of their gathering, the crowd erupted in applause, hoots and catcalls. Beaming, Fannie took several bows.

Utterly mortified, Soph turned to Arthur for moral support, but found him gawping at the dancehall floozy with a fascination he had always hitherto reserved for Meissen, Delft and Wedgewood handicrafts.

Soph returned her basilisk stare to her coworker. "Mister Standeven, we will have much to thrash out at the office on Monday. But now I have to perform my duties as a reporter."

Sophronia dragged Arthur away to the nearest two empty seats, as Reuben and Fannie found their own places.

"I must say," Arthur averred, "that I don't much care for your snippy fellow reporter. He's overly blithe."

Feeling oddly defensive about Reuben Standeven, Sophronia was going to reply that this was a flaw Arthur would never embody. But she squashed her comment, for now the curtain concealing the stage was beginning to rise.

5.
SHE WHO MUST OPEN THE WAY

If Sophronia had anticipated any aspect of tonight's presentation, it had been through fostering vague notions of a lectern on a bare platform, sentryed by a spinsterish or schoolmistressly prune of a scold, who would dispense uplifting platitudes and bromides. Or, perhaps, the speaker would be some female avatar of Dr. Kellogg from the Battle Creek Sanitarium, a stern physician-type clad in Hippocratic regalia and advocating exercises with Indian clubs and jump ropes. But neither of these two conceptions could have been further from the actuality of what greeted Sophronia now.

First off, the stage was backdropped by a gaudy stellar panorama painted on canvas. Fiery comets, ringed planets, blazing stars, all cascading in a Newtonianly impossible yet impressive jumble. The next aspect that betrayed Sophronia's prejudices was a divan set center-stage and surrounded by banks of flowers whose mingled fragrances now disseminated through the hall.

Lastly, and most disturbingly, was the speaker herself.

From the left side of the stage, a magnificent, ageless woman strode forth like Boadicea marching to meet the Roman legions. Masses of Titian hair framed a classically beautiful face: noble brow, strong cheekbones, perfect mouth, dark eyes. The woman's ample charms were shockingly revealed by a clinging ivory gown of diaphanous material, unlike the stiff brocades worn by her male acolytes at the door. Her waist was limned by a gold belt in the form of a double-headed snake, while delicate sandals clasped her small but strong feet. Overall, she radiated a kind of supreme celestial confidence and power.

Reaching the divan, she turned to face the crowd. Her bare shapely arms remained comfortably by her sides. She did not smile to ingratiate herself, as any other lecturer might have done. Nonetheless her solemn yet supernal visage seemed to beam a warm and nigh-tangible message of embrace to her viewers, a loving sympathy. When she spoke, the tone and timbre of her deep and dulcet voice reeked of pure enchantment.

"Welcome, fellow voyagers among the constellations. My name is Isadora Blank, Hierophant of the Starry Sodality, and I am here tonight to guide you all to the land of your fondest dreams, a realm of languor and plenty. But before we can begin to make ourselves ready to set sail for the elysian pastures of eternity, a demanding process, we must make a tally of what we willingly leave behind.

"We leave behind all the ills that flesh is heir to.

"We leave behind all the disappointments of our friendships and loves.

"We leave behind all the necessity of earning our bread by the sweat of our brows.

"We leave behind all duties to Caesar, and all dictates of tyranny.

"We leave behind all our gold and treasures.

"We leave behind all our worries, fears and doubts, our grief and remorse.

"And what do we gain in return?"

Here Isadora Blank lifted her arms in a wide gesture that invited everyone to shelter in the harbor of her expansive and poorly concealed bosom.

"We gain peace and tranquility, ease and vigor, joy and zest, in a landscape of purest bliss, that Ultima Thule for which your soul has been ceaselessly questing since before you were born. And that is what I hope to show you now, if the Elder Gods of the Farthest Depths of Space are willing to use me as their conduit."

Despite its lack of flowery oratory—she was no John Bartholomew Gough—Isadora Blank's speech had left her audience mesmerized, their attention rapt. Even Sophronia, armed with her journalistic objectivity, her scientific precepts and her frothy, mild cynicism, felt herself struggling to remain aloof from the beguiling seduction. Looking about, she saw every face displaying pure yearning acceptance, every set of shoulders and every torso straining unconsciously towards the stage, lifting haunches half off their seats. Beside her, Arthur resembled Actaeon halfway through his transformation by Artemis into a stag, his face all mawkish.

Sophronia's gaze happened to light upon the back of Reuben Standeven's head. As if receiving a mental message, her colleague turned to regard her, and transmitted a sly wink, with all his usual irreverence. Apparently he too had not succumbed completely to the allure of Isadora Blank. Somehow this circumstance reassured Sophronia, even though she certainly retained her high dudgeon against the man.

Now Isadora Blank slowly and gracefully lowered her perfect form to the divan, first sitting upon it, then reclining fully and crossing her ankles. Her supine position seemed to release some of the tension in the audience, which let out a collective sigh and settled down in their own seats.

Acolytes lowered the gas lights to the level of an aureate dusk.

The crowd seemed to hold its breath.

Above Isadora Blank, a cloudy phosphorescent nebula with irregular borders began to take form. The hazy luminescent mass expanded to engulf the Hierophant and her couch and to fill the center volume of the stage.

Then, images began to flow across the cloud!

The successive static scenes, colorful as real life, depicted humans, nude save for tastefully placed ribbons and scarves, gambolling or lolling in alien climes, amidst fantastic foliage or in cyclopean plazas, illuminated by foreign spectra. Strange shadowy non-human beings, possessed of many queer limbs and appurtenances, were shown in several scenes, consorting with the humans in several manners subject to various interpretations.

Faster and faster the images succeeded each other across the cloud, a dizzying accelerating parade, a visionary pageant that left subliminal sensory impressions of indescribable and unspeakable vistas, ripe with ineffable meaning.

Just when Sophronia felt herself upon the verge of being overwhelmed, perhaps even of swooning, Isadora rocketed to her feet in a catlike leap, coming to a standing position atop the divan and shattering the cloud into evanescent zooming particles. The audience responded with a cataleptic jolt.

The Opener of the Way thrust her arms skyward and intoned a litany of harsh syllables which Sophronia could only register in part. The next day, attempting to render the words into print, she derived from memory phrases with these semblances:

"Ia, ia! Vulgtm hai vulgtlagln! Ilyaa uh'e wgah'n nglui ch'hupadgh! Azathoth nafln'ghft ftaghu n'ghft syha'h gotha!'"

Having completed her forceful arcane invocation, Isadora Blank stepped calmly down off the couch. "Reach out for the constellations, my friends, and live," she said, then walked slowly offstage.

No applause followed her stately exit. The assembled auditors remained transfixed and mute for a full sixty seconds, before finally bursting out into a bedlam of comments and exclamations.

Feeling curiously ennervated and drained, yet infused with a kind of eerie galvanic ichor, Sophronia got to her feet. Arthur remained seated, as if dazed, until Sophronia yanked him up. They inched their way with the shuffling crowd into the main aisle and headed toward the front entrance.

At the doors, the acolytes were pressing copies of a single-sheet broadside upon each person. Sophronia took one.

COME CLOSEST
TO THE NUMINOUS SIDEREAL REALM
WHILST YET HERE ON EARTH
BY PAYING A VISIT TO
THE COMMUNE OF
"THE BLACK GOAT OF THE WOODS
WITH A THOUSAND YOUNG"

CHOPMIST HILL
(PERMANENT DWELLERS WELCOMED)

Beneath this invitation was a drawing of a festive pastoral scene straight from the work of Pieter Bruegel, with the addition of a ghostly goat's head floating in the sky over the jolly celebrants, leering down beneficently.

Emerging into the clarifyingly crisp June night air, and halting on the grass aside from the flow of congregants, Sophronia felt her normal disposition and faculties return to her. She could analyze and better take stock of what she had just experienced. Whatever Isadora Blank was selling or preaching, the woman was no ordinary carnival barker or shill. She manifested great charisma and spellbinding potency, akin to that of a Charles Taze Russell or Henry Ward Beecher. But to what end? Surely all that talk of transaetheric migration to other spheres was just a façade for some other goal or activity? But what? There had to be some element of profit involved for the Starry Sodality. But on the basis of what venture? No one tonight had even asked for donations! Perhaps the Commune advertised on the broadside represented the financial end of the operation. Could the Sodality perhaps be drafting gullible folks into working for free, in the fields or in hypothetical manufactories at Chopmist Hill? That seemed almost too tepid and mundane a scheme for such an exotic pitch.

Whatever the rationale or hidden aspects of the Starry Sodality, Sophronia sensed that here was a much larger story than her editor had presumed. Her reporter's nose quivered with anticipation. She resolved to follow this mystery to its ultimate end.

Her whirling thoughts were suddenly halted by a confident proclamation from behind her.

"A magic lantern! That's what it had to be, plain as day. What do you think?"

Reuben Standeven, an arm insouciantly around the slim waist of Miss Fannie Audet, awaited a reaction from Sophronia, to whom he had plainly directed his query. Sophronia could feel Arthur bristling beside her, irked at Reuben's effrontery. But to her bemusement, Sophronia herself was not as put out as she might have been, since Reuben's suggestion appealed to her, and sparked off her own speculations.

"Yes!" she responded excitedly. "Mounted under the divan, perhaps, and projecting its apparitions upward through a series of mirrors. With concealed controls!"

"But what do we make of the gassy substance on which the slides cavorted, in lieu of a more conventional screen? Some kind of muslin or cheesecloth, shredded and blown apart by fans for the finale?"

"If only we could get onto that stage to search for clues!"

But already the doors to the theater had been shut and locked.

"Might I suggest," said Reuben, "An approach from the rear?"

"I'm game!"

Arthur reared backwards in shock. "Sophronia Tempest! You're not planning to sneak into that building, are you? That's highly disrespectful of the organization and the seeress that just sought to enlighten us."

"Oh, Arthur, you're not telling me you bought that bushel of codswallop Miss Chiffon Loins was selling!"

"I certainly found many aspects of her lecture enticing and provocative of thought. Who would not want to desert this vale of tears for a better home among the heavens? Life is not all crockery and cravats, you know."

Sophronia was astonished. Here was a side of Arthur she had never witnessed till now. But before she could remonstrate with him, Fannie Audet chimed in.

"I'm with this boy! That gal's a pip, a real queen! A royal Cleopatra type. She knows something we don't, and she showed us just the merest glimmering of her wisdom tonight. I know that if I didn't have to sing for my supper every night and let mashers grab at my quim, I'd be a whale happier than I am now."

Sophronia expected Arthur to express horror at Fannie's use of such a vulgar expression. But instead, he moved closer to the singer and said, "Miss Audet, I am fascinated to hear your reaction to Miss Blank's performance, which tallies with mine. It seems that we might derive additional insights by discussing our shared experience."

Reuben let go of Fannie's waist and practically thrust her upon Arthur. "It's settled then! Soph and I will endeavor to learn more here at the theater, while you you two will have a fine confab on mystical matters at Whateley's Coffee House."

Fannie smiled at Arthur, giving the impression somehow of a peckish lioness. "I ain't disinclined."

Arthur looked to Sophronia. "Soph, would you mind terribly if I did not escort you home, but instead chaperoned Miss Audet? That is, if I can safely entrust you to the aegis of this rascal, whose character you surely know more intimately than I."

To her astonishment, Sophronia found herself relishing this cavalier dismissal by her beau. "No, Arthur, I don't mind. I assume we'll see each other at lunch on Monday, when we can talk more about this affair."

"Of course."

And with that, Arthur offered his arm to Fannie, and they strolled off.

Even in the dim illumination afforded by semi-remote gas fixtures in the street, Sophronia could detect in Reuben Standeven's eyes a sparkle of excitement, pleasure, and joy at the prospect of this adventure.

And perhaps, Soph imagined, there was also showing a scintilla of eagerness, hesitation and trepidation, a smidgen of self-doubt as to how Sophronia would respond to their forced impulsive pairing? Could it be that Mister Standeven was not quite so cocksure and arrogant as she had always surmised? And that he held some regard for her sensibilities and judgments and—and her affections?

But any new respect for her coworker that might have been aborning was instantly put to flight by Reuben's words and actions.

Employing his rolled up broadside, he whapped her on the rump and said, "Quit your wool-gathering, Sappho! We've an investigation afoot!"

Sophronia prepared to let loose a rebuff as rude as Reuben's assault, when she halted herself and simply said, "Lay on, Macduff, and damn'd be him that first cries, 'Hold, enough!'"

6.
IN THE CLUTCHES OF KNYGATHIN ZHAUM

Attaining the Power Street sidewalk which led uphill from South Main, Sophronia and Reuben began to ascend alongside the theater, amidst the shadows cast by large luxuriant trees. No one else was in sight, and the cricket-filled June night seemed reserved just for them.

Sophronia suddenly realized that she was not even perturbed by Reuben inserting himself into her assignment. Somehow she did not mind his accompanying her on this mission.

"How did you become an intelligencer?" Sophronia found herself making this query almost without volition. Now why, especially at this odd juncture, should she suddenly be interested in the background of Reuben Standeven?

"An intriguing tale, one full of the most bathetic melodrama, which I shall mostly elide. As I approached my majority, I quickly discerned that journalism was the only profession open to me where I did not have to break my back and acquire a thick set of calluses, and which suited my peculiar talents. You see, I was an orphan from a very young age. My parents both died in the Great Revere Train Wreck, and no other relatives stepped forward to claim me. So by the age of eight I was living rough on the streets of Woonsocket, facilitated by charm and guile. Among a hundred petty larcenies, I carried gossip to earn my living. Utilized a facile tongue and nimble wit to escape injury and sustain myself. One day I suddenly asked myself, What better combination of talents, experience and motivations than those for a journalist? Oh, yes, and very little formal education. That's a definite plus. No book-fashioned set of blinders to obscure my perceptions of reality."

Sophronia humphed. "Your denunciation of institutional schooling is inaccurate. I myself can serve as a refutation of your premise. I am shaped by many years of formal instruction at St. Mary's Seminary, and yet I still see the lineaments of existence most clearly."

"Oh, you're pretty sharp, I grant you that. Not much escapes you, although you might not always put an accurate interpretation on matters, being too concerned with what the experts say. But we could still have a debate on your general perspicacity, at least in one area."

"And that realm would be?"

"Your boyfriend. What a nincompoop and duffer! Surely, despite his cold-fish nature, you must be blinded by passion, or you'd see him for the boring cipher he is."

Sophronia winced at this characterization of Arthur, which came all too close to several intermittent misgivings of her own. But she could hardly align herself with such a slur.

"Mister Standeven, you have seen my beau Arthur for all of five minutes, and exchanged no more than a few words with him. How could you pass such a harsh judgment from that slight acquaintance?"

"It's like I said. I've got street-savvy that you can't pick up at St. Mary's out of books. It helps me immeasureably in my job, and it's something you've got to acquire, or you'll never make the grade."

Sophronia felt that there was some truth to Reuben's assertion—outside of her romantic life, at least. "I do want more vital experiences, you know. I'm not scared or shy! I try to get Mister Callender to give me more meaty assignments. Not just the scientific beat, but rough-and-tumble stuff. But he just won't!"

"Well, I'm sure he likes you okay. But you are a female. And so you are just going to have to work twice as hard to convince him you've got what it takes."

At this moment, the pair reached the rear upper corner of the theater. A slate path led at right angles from the sidewalk to the rear door of the building, set in the middle of the windowless wall. Barely visible in the darkness, the door seemed securely shut.

Reuben put a finger to his lips, indicating silence. Taking Sophronia by the hand—a tingle of excitement accompanied his touch—and leading the way, he brought them to the door.

Sophronia reached past him to try the handle first. "Locked!" she softly exclaimed.

Reuben said nothing, but removed a large pocket-knife from his coat. Deft manipulation with its unfolded blade did the trick. In a moment, he had the door open.

"There was not a single bakery nor butcher shop in all of Woonsocket immune to my midnight incursions," he whispered, before ushering Sophronia inside.

Some faint radiance from outside perfused the interior through grimy windows. From what Sophronia could make out, this upper level of the building, above the auditorium, seemed to consist of corridors and modest rooms. Dim rubbishy shapes, as of forgotten costumes and props, lined the walls. How to descend to the stage below was a puzzle.

But then the immediacy of that task and its fulfillment was rendered secondary by the muted sound of voices. Hadn't they seen all the acolytes leave as they locked up? But could that nonetheless mean that *she* remained behind?

Sophronia instantly darted towards the exit, but was restrained by Reuben's hand on her wrist. He put his lips right next to her ear, and his warm breath made her quiver.

"You'll never reach your goal if you take flight at the first obstacle. Come on! Follow me!"

Reuben began to catfoot down the dark corridor toward the source of the ongoing conversation. Nerving herself up, Sophronia followed.

They rounded a corner and saw lamplight spilling out a partially opened office door. Reuben inched closer than Sophronia found comfortable, but she forced herself to match his boldness. Now the dialogue issuing from the unseen room could be easily interpreted.

The first voice was unmistakeably that of Isadora Blank, Hierophant of the Starry Sodality.

"I must insist, Zhaum, on you redoubling your efforts to close that trans-planar flaw. Why the rift had to be opened in the first place, I will never understand."

When it came, the voice of Blank's interlocutor was like no voice Sophronia had ever heard. Comparisons proved impossible to summon. It possessed attributes of an active gravel crusher, a wet sponge passing through a mangle, and a dog cracking a bone for its marrow.

"I needed sustenance and consultation."

"All very well. But then to let the portal drift away like that!"

"It wanders. Because of conditions at the other end."

"Yes, yes, I comprehend the astral weathers of Ulthar as well as you."

Ulthar! Sophronia could hardly believe her ears. Were these people discussing the mythical destination of lost cats as if it were real? What possible connection could there be between that plague of disappearances and the Sodality? But Isadora Blank's next words seemed to confirm the identity of one Ulthar with the other.

"All these terrestrial cats seem to have no trouble finding the rift. And their absence is arousing suspicions. Some people who know too much are putting the word about, even if only in chalked inscriptions. We need to shut this down, or it will interfere with our big day."

"Do not chide nor lecture me. I know as much as you. In fact, I know more."

"Such as what?"

"That there are two intruders just outside this room!"

And faster than Sophronia or Reuben could react, the door of the office slammed wide open and a massive bulk hurled itself out upon them like an avalanche!

Before they could even flinch, they had been snaffled. Sophronia felt herself being lifted off her feet and carried away, as her dress, gripped at the rear neckline, strained under her arms.

In the next second, squinting against the increased illumination from two wall-mounted gaslights, Sophronia found herself in the room whence the voices had issued, once more firmly planted on her feet. Reuben took a couple of staggering steps as he was set down more rudely.

Sophronia apprehended in an instant that the place was being used as a bedchamber, for an old canopied bedstead predominated, with disarrayed coverlets. At its foot was a pallet of rags, furs, raw cotton batting, straw and string, formed into a curious nest—for a dog perhaps? A wardobe with open doors revealed an array of conventional female garments.

And then Sophronia's attention was riveted by the people, one familiar, one supremely strange.

The familiar form and face belonged to Isadora Blank. Still clad in her flowing oracle's negligee, Isadora seemed slightly less glamorous than she had onstage, perhaps due to proximity and to tiredness and irritation on the part of the Hierophant. But Sophronia also had a queer notion that the woman had been caught with public pretenses relaxed, as if, prior to their arrival she had doffed some kind of mask or disguise, and only hurriedly repositioned it as the uninvited guests were dumped precipitously into her lap.

But all such speculations ceased when the second person hove into Sophronia's view from a position behind her and Reuben.

The abnormally thin fellow was nearly seven feet tall, and clad in a mustard-colored silk vest over bare chest, whilst a set of ballooning rose-colored pantaloons (bare bony and large-nailed feet poking out) concealed his lower portions, the whole outfit causing him to resemble a genie of myth. But this was no affable and boisterous, albeit mischievous spirit, as betokened by the funereal expression on his dour and elongated phiz. Utterly hairless, giving the remote and blasphemously caricatural suggestion of the shaven priest, he featured a blanched epidermis with mottled pigmentation like that of a huge boa. Mammoth hands obviously possessed enough strength to hoist Soph and Reuben simultaneously. Most startling was the manner in which he moved with an unctuous, verminous ease, exhibiting an undulant litheness and fluidity that seemed to hint at an inner structure and vertebration that were less than human—or, one might almost have said, a sub-ophidian lack of all bony framework. He seemed to slither rather than walk; and the very fashion of his jointure, the placing of knees, hips, elbows and shoulders, appeared arbitrary and factitious.

Before Sophronia could fully assimilate the inhuman creature's menacing carriage and mien, Isadora had rounded roughly on the pair.

"Who are you two? What are you doing in my temple? This space is protected by potent charms and guardians. You risk much by venturing in unbidden. What do you want? What are you seeking?"

While Sophronia was still grasping for a proper response, Reuben stepped forward—the big queer fellow sinuously shifted his posture, as if repared to stymie an assault—and made a graceful bow. Straightening, Reuben spoke blithely, as if meeting an old pal on the streetcorner.

"It's like this, Miss Blank. We are two lowly scribblers with the local rag, the *Journal*. Reuben Standeven and Sophronia Tempest. Surely an estimable, well-informed lady such as yourself takes our premier publication to stay abreast of matters, and thus you've no doubt seen our names in print. Not that I mean to stake any claim to fame, just trying to provide our bona fides. But that's neither here nor there, except as a basis of our admittedly impolite breaching of your domain. You see, we were both in attendence at your stimulating lecture tonight, and were so moved that we wish to interview you for a feature story. Your background and mission, the philosophy of the Starry Sodality, the nature of your Chopmist commune. All the usual guff. I'm sure you've fielded such questions a hundred times before. But not yet for the *Journal*! It could be most invaluable coverage in promoting your cause, and also a keen bit of fluff to delight our readers. I'm certain it would attract many new patrons to your endeavors. Now, having unanimously decided on this interview, the two of us were most excited and determined to carry it off right away, before our zest had a chance to dissipate, and while your performance was still fresh in our brainpans. We tried to make our way to see you downstairs, but the flood of people prevented us. Having been locked out by your bell-hoppers, we ventured to the rear of your establishment, where we found an open door, and made so bold as to enter. A little timorous, we hesitated just outside your door. We were just about to knock and venture inside when Gargantua here made free with our persons, without so much as a by-your-leave. And that, as the farmer's daughter said to the over-eager swain, is enough of that!"

Isadora Blank had untensed during Reuben's peroration, allowing a slight smile to brighten her lovely face, and Sophronia felt that her comrade's speech, more or less the truth, had succeeded in disarming her hostility. But the attitude of her companion was another matter.

"I don't believe them," said the giant in his ghoulishly resonant voice. "They smell of trouble. And that back door was not unlocked."

"Oh, but it was," said Reuben, and Soph could almost hear his unspoken codicil: *Once I had my way with it!*

Ignoring the giant as if he had no status, Reuben addressed Isadora alone. "Madam, I fear we have not been introduced to your compatriot. Does he speak for you?"

Isadora said, "Permit me to announce Knygathin Zhaum, my second-in-command. He bears a high rank in the Sodality, and offers much support and counsel to our endeavors. Mister Zhaum hails from the headwaters of the Nile, where his long-isolated tribe has maintained immemorial rites and precepts, long forgotten by other races, which allow communication with trans-galactic and ultramundane forces."

"An impressive, albeit archaic *curriculum vitae*, to be sure. Always glad to meet a wild foreign visitor to Columbia's shores, however uncultured they might be." Here Reuben bowed satirically to Zhaum, and received a hideous glare in exchange. "Nonetheless, Madam, I take it that you and you alone make the decisions here. So while giving all due deference to Mister Zhaum's mistaken prejudices about us, I hope to hear that you understand and perhaps even condone our forgiveable trespass, and might consent to a good long chinwag—all at your convenience, of course."

Isadora Blank pinched her lower lip with delicate forefinger and thumb and furrowed her brow in a conquettish manner that roused Sophronia's disdain. Then the Hierophant answered, "Yes, Mister Standeven, you and your partner in crime are forgiven, and I will certainly agree to an interview at some less wearisome hour. Now, if the two of you would take your departure by the way you entered, I would be most grateful, as I have had a long day."

Sophronia could hardly believe that they were escaping scot-free like this. She had been harboring vivid visions of their imminent strangulation at the hands of Knygathin Zhaum, and the disposal of their corpses into the Bay off a nearby South Water Street dock.

Reuben grabbed Sophronia by the wrist and hurried her off, calling our over his shoulder, "Reach us at the *Journal*'s offices to arrange a time, Miss Blank!"

Back out on Power Street, Sophronia felt she could breathe easily again. The whole contretemps inside the theater began to seem like an opium dream. Could there really exist such an anomalous creature as Knygathin Zhaum?

As they walked away at a good pace, Reuben said, "You accounted well for yourself back there, Soph. It took some bravery not to squeal at the sight of that monster."

"Well, yes, I suppose I did hold my ground quite steadily. But you were rather masterful yourself."

To her surprise, Reuben halted the two of them then and swept Sophronia up in his arms. He squeezed her tight for a moment, before planting a chaste kiss on her forehead and releasing her.

"Mister Standeven! I understand your sense of relief, for I share it too! But was it really necessary to express your emotion in such a peremptory fashion?"

"Ah, Soph! What a girl you could be if you did not have an astrolabe in place of your heart!"

7.
THE SAVANT OF THE STACKS

At the breakfast table Saturday morning in the warm and fragrant kitchen, Sophronia's sense of the unshakeable firmness of quotidian reality, a commonplace foundation to life that she had taken for granted during her entire two decades on the planet, had reasserted itself fully, leaving only the smallest scintilla of eerieness behind. Everything she had witnessed and undergone at the theater last night was positively explainable by scientific logic. The magic lantern gimmickry of Isadora Blank. The freakish abnormalities of that poor soul Zhaum, who, having been born in a benighted portion of the globe, had never received the proper medical care for his congenital afflictions. All things which, in the light of day, did not seem scary or inexplicable one whit, no matter how disturbing they had been in the darkness. As young Bertha fussed with muffins and fruit salad; and as her father sketched designs for improving the Kendall Manufacturing Soapine wagon meant for the much-anticipated Trades Procession; and as her mother sought to clean out Oscar's grimy ears while he squirmed and groused, Sophronia felt enveloped in blissful domestic surety.

Perhaps the most disturbing remnant of the whole expedition was the ghostly sensation of Reuben Standeven's lips on her brow. The utter audacity of that rascal! A good thing he had not made any further advances of an amorous nature, right up to the moment when he brought her back to the door of 380 Broadway—although Sophronia had been anticipating such. Had she remonstrated sternly enough with him for his bravado? Or perhaps too sternly? After all, she did not want to come across as some kind of antiquated bluenose from another generation. And what was that nasty remark about having an astrolabe for a heart? The gall! They had parted with a certain restrained and embarrassed solemnity. Oh well, there would be time to gauge his reservoir of ardor when they next met at the office, and to decide whether to stimulate or stanch it.

Along those lines, Sophronia paused to consider how Arthur and Fannie might have fared together for the rest of their Friday evening. She had a hard time picturing that tawdry chanteuse and her prim boyfriend establishing any affinities. She resolved, however, not to twit Arthur about his squiring of Miss Audet, when she and he met for lunch on Monday.

Released from his maternal toils, Oscar practically dove into his plate of food. (Today the Mellin's Biscuit had been surreptitiously chucked into the firebox of the stove.) When he surfaced for a moment, he said, "Hey, Sis, I figured out how I'm gonna find that Ulthar place. I'm just gonna set Clutterbuck loose and follow him all day. He'll lead me there!"

Sophronia experienced an instinctive shudder as she recalled Zhaum's crypt-like voice claiming he himself had impossibly been to Ulthar for "sustenance and consultation." If Oscar should run into him—

"How absolutely ridiculous! Following a cat around all day. You'd better not implement any such scheme, Oscar. You could end up someplace dangerous before you realized where you'd gotten to."

Minnie Tempest said, "Oh, Soph, let your brother be. He has to occupy himself somehow, and it sound harmless enough. Maybe Clutterbuck will lead him to the missing cats and he can claim a reward for their restoration."

"Yes!" exulted Oscar. "The Old Sleuth saves the day!"

Unable to explain the source of her worry, Sophronia remained silent.

When she had finished dining, she bade her parents goodbye, saying, "I'm off to see Professor Charnley. I'm not sure when I'll be home."

Minnie Tempest responded with only half her attention, for she was busy fishing out a scorched yet seemingly invincible biscuit from the firebox, where its repugnant smoldering smell had roused her interest.

"That's nice, dear."

Oscar had hightailed it off before any biscuit-burning accusations could be leveled.

Clarence Tempest said, "Say, isn't your Professor Charnley one of those learning-shovers who poke around in the life of the Sandwich Islanders and suchlike? Ask him if he's ever come across any queer customs relating to soap. I might be able to work a few of the more colorful bits into our float. Although the deadline is rushing at us."

Indeed, as Sophronia had witnessed in her daily duties at the *Journal*, the June twenty-third debut of the fancifully bedizened carriages of the various tradesmen, much anticipated by the public, was beginning to loom larger and larger in the consciousness of the entire state. Attendance by spectators would certainly be phenomenal, as the parade wended its way back and forth through the steets of the capital city.

"I'll do that, Papa, although I don't think Professor Charnley has necessarily paid much attention in his researches to such domestic concerns among savages. He's more interested in philosophical and religious matters."

Out on the street, Sophronia thought to open her reticule and make sure she had brought along the sheet of paper whereon she had tried to reconstruct Isadora Blank's strange invocation: *Ia, ia! Vulgtm something, something, something, uh'e wgah'n,* and so forth… Perhaps the Professor could make heads or tails of the gibberish, if indeed it was not just nonsense.

Once again, the day being fine, Sophronia set out on foot, enjoying the busy bustle of Broadway. A pleasant stroll of half an hour brought her across town to the base of College Hill: specifically, the corner of North Main and Waterman, where reared the impressive wooden-framed, high-steepled First Baptist Church. The steep and winding ascent of Waterman Street did not daunt her, and she passed several other laboring pedestrians in her youthful vigor.

At the crest of the hill, Waterman was intersected by Prospect Street. And there on the northeast corner stood her destination: Brown University's New Library.

The strikingly handsome building had been completed just eight years ago, when the University had outgrown its Manning Hall library. After all, thirty thousand volumes was an enormous set of holdings that deserved uncramped quarters. And so this brick Gothic-Venetian building had been erected, one of the most advanced bibliotheque designs in the nation. Its floorplan basically mimicked a Greek cross whose three octagonal wings lent it the semblance of a cathedral.

Here Professor Aurion Charnley was mostly to be found, when he was not engaged in actual teaching. He had an official office elsewhere, but never used it. Likewise, he must certainly possess, surmised Soph, a residence somewhere on the East Side, but probably used that only for sleeping and eating his bachelor meals. Basically, he lived in the library. Sophronia had once asked him what attracted him to these odd quarters, aside from the obvious easy access to all the school's tomes.

"It's the cruciform construction," he replied. "Very protective. Also, my aeyrie allows me to watch the horizons. Extremely valuable, you know, to have an early alert as to who or what might be visiting our fair city."

A typically eccentric response, but charming, she thought.

Sophronia glanced up at the large octagonal cupola that crowned the building, and thought to see movement behind one of its many windows.

She crossed the street and climbed the short flight of steps to the front door of the New Library. On this doorstep she invariably recalled an enigmatic comment Charnley had once made. Soph had remarked on the fact that to inaugurate the institution, Librarian Reuben Aldrich Guild had ceremoniously carried the first book into the new building, a copy of Samuel Bagster's *Polyglot Bible*. Charnley had snorted, then said, "Yes, that's the official story. But the first volume brought across the threshold was actually much older, and penned by a mad Arab." But when Sophronia inquired about the book's title, Charnley changed the subject and thereafter refused to acknowledge the matter.

Entering, Sophronia received a smile and nod from the majordomo at his station. Scattered tables and chairs occupied a capacious multi-storey rotunda that allowed access to the railed alcoves and their stacks. Six hundred gas lights ensured plenty of illumination for scholars.

Sophronia took the stairs and soon found herself on the third and penultimate level. No students or teachers were in evidence on this weekend summer day. There, bunching her skirts to achieve freedom of movement, she had to ascend an inconspicuous wall-mounted ladder to reach the cupola. At the top of the ladder she knocked on a trap door. Receiving acknowledgement to proceed, she pushed the hinged panel upward and climbed through.

Professor Charnley had his eye pressed to a small telescope aimed to the west. He continued to stare while Sophronia marveled at the wealth of papers, books and odd souvenirs of the savant's extensive travels that filled nigh to bursting the shelves and other horizontal and vertical surfaces of the relatively small space. She picked up a strangely incised box which, upon being opened, revealed only a dusty stone trapezohedron.

Charnley pulled himself away from the eyepiece. A gnomish, cherubic fellow with a monk's tonsure of fluffy white hair and a rubicund complexion, Charnley sported, as always, a tobacco-ash-stained knitted vest, woolen trousers and dingy shirt with frayed cuffs.

Seeing the box in Sophronia's hands, he said, "Please put that down gently, Miss Tempest. That artifact is, ah, somewhat liable to mutability."

Soph did as asked. Since the Professor did not allude to their six-months separation, neither did she. Truthfully, she always felt, upon seeing him, that they had only just parted.

"What were you observing, Professor?"

"Saint John's Church on Federal Hill. There have been some baffling quasi-celestial phenomena centered there of late. But for now, things seem quiet."

Soph admired the panoramic view which included a large swath of Narragansett Bay as well as the leafy city. "Well, you're certainly emplaced perfectly to catch anything that happens in your wide vista. And speaking of strange phenomena, allow me to relate what just occurred to me last night."

Soprhonia gave a detailed account of the doings at the theater. Charnley listened with growing intensity and interest.

"'Ulthar' was mentioned, you say? And coincident with this civic cat affair…. Let me see that transcription you made."

Sophronia dug out the paper with Isadora Blank's meaningless syllables.

As Charnley let his eye rove over the fragmentary words, his expression became more and more concerned. Looking up, he said, "This is a deeper affair than you might at first conceive, my dear. If you could possibly recall more of this woman's speech… No? Well then, I shall just have to proceed with what we have. I suspect my investigations will take at least a day or two. Suppose you return here on Tuesday? But meanwhile, I would advise you to steer clear of these folks. They are not necessarily whom they represent themselves to be. That Zhaum fellow in particular. Your description of him tallies more with a Hyperborean origin than any natal genesis in Ethiopia or the Sudan."

Sophronia rewarded Professor Charnley with a peck on his cheek (the innocent gesture instantly recalled to her Reuben Standeven's more daring kiss), and exited the cupola with all due care for the awkward intersection of rungs and skirts.

The rest of her Saturday Sophronia devoted to shopping, acquiring several new outfits at Edward C. Almy & Co., as well as some reagents for her basement chemistry lab, while mentally rehearsing the article she would write in fulfillment of her assignment from editor Mack Callender. There was no point in turning in an incomplete draft. She would have to delay until Charnley finished his researches into the matter, which she would incorporate into her piece, if they merited.

At home, Sophronia was half-expecting to hear from Arthur. After all, he had mentioned that he wanted to take in the new performers at the San Souci Gardens. But he never called on her, and she was not about to go running after him. Anyway, it was more pleasant to relax at home with a brand-new novel, recommended by one of her girlfriends from St. Mary's: *Atla: The Story of the Lost Island*, by Ann Eliza Smith. A little more fanciful than the lectures of Michelson, but a nice change of pace from her usual lucubrations.

Retiring to her chambers past midnight, when everyone else in the house was fast asleep, Sophronia received a horripilating scare when she glanced at her uncurtained bedroom window and thought to see a mottled white inhuman face floating outside. Instantly she thought of Knygathin Zhaum, and, heart palpitating, snatched up a heavy brass candlestick as a weapon. But upon a second look, no face was apparent. And of course, how could there be, given that her bedroom was on the third floor, with no porch or other coign of access? This could only have been a phantasm engendered by her unwonted fantastical reading.

Sunday proved a very quiet and relaxing day, with church services and visits from neighbors and friends, along with an elaborate midday feast. Oscar chafed in his fancy suit, but behaved himself for a change, until freed to roam in the afternoon.

On Monday Sophronia headed into the *Journal* offices. She had crafted an entire dialogue between herself and Reuben Standeven, with numerous alternate branchings, but it never got deployed, for he was out on an assignment. Mack Callender was so preoccupied with news emanating from the kingdom of Buganda, about the slaughter of some Christian converts, that he only half-listened to her excuses about why she was not ready yet with her article on the Starry Sodality.

"By jingo, how I wish I were in the field again! I'd wring the truth out of that weasel of a Nubian King!"

At lunchtime, with a sigh, Sophronia set out for Warren & Wood Crockery to meet with Arthur.

Upon entering the establishment, she was greeted with an inexplicable cascade of sniggers and half-suppressed jibes from Arthur's co-workers who knew her. Shrugging off the juvenile japery as simply an excess of Two Hundred and Fiftieth Anniversary high spirits, she went in search of her boyfriend. But he was nowhere to be found, and she finally had to inquire in the offices.

The secretary, a famously gruff, tight-collared fellow who nonetheless seemed to show some sympathy today, broke the news to Soph.

"Mister Botwink did not arrive to work this morning, and in fact has seen fit to tender his resignation from the firm in the form of this here mentally deviant telegram."

He handed Sophronia the paper form.

FOUND SALVATION STOP GONE TO LIVE AT THE S.S. COMMUNE STOP REACH OUT FOR THE CONSTELLATIONS AND LIVE STOP

8.
AT THE COMMUNE OF THE BLACK GOAT

Early Tuesday morning, June eighth, found a certain distinctive conveyance outbound from Providence along the Danielson Pike, its nonobvious destination the Commune of the Black Goat, in the vicinity of Chopmist Hill, Scituate. The vehicle was a standard Rockaway carriage—roofed seat for the driver, a cabin to hold six—drawn by a spirited bay stallion and painted gaudily in yellow and black and bearing the legend of *The Manufacturers and Farmers Journal* on its doors. It was in fact the official transportation utilized by Sophronia's employer for various functions and errands, and its loan had been secured with no small amount of cajolery directed at Soph's boss. In this effort she had, most gratifyingly, been aided by her coworker, Reuben Standeven. Together they had made the case to Mack Callender that the Starry Sodality deserved further investigation, since it had proven to be able to command a large following among the state's citizenry, even unto the point of establishing a cooperative agricultural enterprise. Eventually Callender had agreed, saying, "Just make sure you come back with some solid facts about their backers and credo and such. I won't be lulled into printing mere speculations."

And although Sophronia did firmly intend to dig into the reasons for the sect's popularity and their seemingly impossible plans to abandon terrestrial life for some faroff nebulous arcadian realm—mainly by quizzing Isadora Blank deeply, should she find her, as she hoped, on the sect's property—her main purpose in visiting the so-called Commune of the Black Goat was to try to discover whatever had gotten into Arthur Botwink to transform him from a sober-sided jug peddler into an irresponsible lotus eater, and, if possible, to reclaim him for sanity.

And her journalistic companion in this outing, Reuben Standeven, had much the same mixture of motives, since, in a disclosure made later that Monday, it eventuated that his ex-companion, Miss Fannie Audet, erstwhile chanteuse, had, with identical precipitousness, tossed aside her old life and also gone over to the Starry Sodality cause.

After discovering this unlikely happening, Reuben had exclaimed to Soph, "This is a woman who has to have her nightly calf's milk bath with violet-scented *sels aromatiques*! I can't picture her grubbing about among the turnips while chanting a hymn to Osiris, or whoever these Milky Way-obsessed clodpolls worship."

Sophronia replied, "And as for Arthur, I've seen him nearly reduced to tears by the proximity of an over-aggressive hornet."

Indeed, the pair of baffled reporters agreed, there must exist some powerful allure or stimulus to have attracted such unlikely recruits to the pastoral life.

Monday's lunchtime revelation of her fiance's utter abandonment of his old life had initially sent Sophronia straight home from the Crockery concern, seeking advice from her mother. To her surprise, Minnie Tempest was already consoling Charity Botwink, Arthur's plump mother, anent this very same topic, and so no further explanation of the unprecedented situation had to be made. After listening to an hour or so of repetitive maternal commiseration—"But he was always such a *good* boy!" "I know, dear, I know, but we can never tell what secret springs may be bubbling under."—Sophronia had had enough with useless weeping, and so returned to the *Journal* offices. There she had received Reuben's information about Fannie Audet.

"What are we going to do about this situation?" she demanded of Reuben.

"Plainly, we need to speak to both of our straying lambs, and convince them of the folly of their ways. I stress that I am not Fannie's caretaker, nor even her steady flame. Yet I feel some responsibility to help her. Your case is somewhat more weighty and imperative. Although why you'd actually want Arthur back—"

"Just stop it. What if we fail to persuade them?"

"I don't know. Maybe we can shanghai them both. A cosh behind the ear, and bango!"

"I would prefer not to be known as a woman who secures the attentions of her straying paramour with a 'cosh behind the ear.'"

"As you wish. Although such a reputation, I imagine, might be very useful at times. But hark, we have to get out to Scituate anyhow to accomplish anything. That's the first step. So let's brace old Mack for some help."

And so it was that Tuesday's dawn saw Reuben and Sophronia on the road.

But not alone, for two other members of the expedition had been arranged.

The first addition had been insisted on by Callender.

"I'm not entrusting the *Journal*'s exclusive carriage to a couple of youthful culverheads and gumsuckers such as you two. So you'll take a driver. Crispus Bannister is his name. You might have heard of his cousin, Edward Bannister, the famous painter."

"Yes, of course," said Reuben. "That black Barbadian who now resides here in the state."

"A Negro driver sounds fine," said Sophronia. "I've known many such wonderful men. Just so long as he won't be affrighted by anything unnatural we might encounter."

Callender laughed. "Do you recall that incident in the North Burial Grounds a few years ago, when some fellow claiming to be a wizard was digging up fresh graves? Crispus helped catch him by waiting up all night every night for a week among the lonely, looming monuments. No, he'll be quite unflappable."

The fourth member of their jaunt had enrolled himself, under the name of Professor Aurion Charnley.

Monday night found Sophronia in the kitchen, cooking up enough food for their journey. Chopmist Hill was some eighteen miles from Providence, and the ride out would occupy four or five hours, with, logically, a return trip of equal duration. Nothing else about the mission might be under her control, but she did not have to rely on chancy victuallers.

Sophronia heard the doorbell ring while she was blotting excess lard from her buttermilk fried chicken. Minnie Tempest pushed through the kitchen door almost instantly thereafter, trailed by a most unlikely figure: Professor Charnley! He looked so anomalous out of his aeyrie that Soph took a moment to fully recognize him. She had completely forgotten their appointment for the morrow.

"My dear," said the gnomish savant, "I am so glad to find you safe and sound. The things I've discovered about your Miss Blank and her crowd! Very disconcerting, very, even if I can't be one hundred percent certain about their origins and intentions. I'm here to offer my services in dealing with them. I feel I might have a few aces up my sleeve that you do not. So the next time you confront them, I'd like to accompany you."

"But this is marvelous! We go to beard them in their den tomorrow!"

After hearing the story of Arthur and Fannie, Professor Charnley said, "Perfect! I'll meet you at the appointed hour at the *Journal* offices."

And so it came to pass that at roughly eleven AM on that Tuesday, after four hours of travel down bucolic country roads—such a welcome respite from the hurly-burly of the Providence metropolis!—the black and yellow carriage could be found parked at the intersection of the Danielson Pike and Chopmist Hill Road. The spot was a shady one and featured a low stone wall on which the quartet of travellers sat, and on which was spread a checkered cloth and a large hearty collation.

Reuben and the Professor, meeting for the first time back in the city, had hit it off like old pals.

"I must say, Professor Charnley, that I was much taken with your paper on the myths of sunken cities among the Pacific islanders. It read in parts like a Nick Carter adventure."

Reuben's familiarity with any such scholarly work—even if only its dime novel aspects—raised him up in Sophronia's estimation, and she eyed him with fresh appreciation.

Before responding, Charnley hoisted into the carriage a heavy satchel whose mysterious contents he would not disclose. "Please, my boy, call me Aurion. Did you really like that little essay? I do think it represents some very original work, if I do say so myself."

As for Crispus Bannister, a burly fellow with more white than black in his close-cropped hair and beard, all three travellers felt an instant affinity with his no-nonsense aura of competence. A twinkle in his eyes somewhat belied the sternness of his dark visage.

"Mack explained to me," said Crispus after introductions, "that we all might encounter some resistance or even downright hostility from these folks we're going to meet. So I saw fit to bring along old Bessie."

From its long oiled sheath, Crispus slid partially out a rifle that seemed only slightly shorter than Sophronia herself.

"Good Lord," said Reuben, "what kind of monstrous weapon is that?"

"A Nitro Express elephant gun, imported from England. I probably would've brung it along even if we weren't planning to interrogate this pack of loonies you describe. Those Swamp Yankees out in Scituate and Foster and Chepachet are all disagreeable, ornery and touchy cusses. Look at that there Dorr Rebellion back in 'forty-two, centered right in Chepachet. Prickly about strangers, and positively anti-officialdom. Them folks just don't take to city types poking their noses into their rural doings."

After their long ride, wherein lots of pleasant chatter had further cemented the impromptu bonds among the quartet, with Crispus chiming in from his exterior seat, their picnic proved a further agreeable interlude of idle conversation. No one really wanted to speculate on what might await them at the Commune of the Black Goat, and Professor Charnley had not gone into details about his findings concerning the Starry Sodality. All he had said was, "These people, I have reason to believe, are in league with entities and forces they cannot possibly hope to control. It's a matter of not raising up things you can't put down."

Sophronia asked, "Do you mean actual supernatural beings and powers? You know I don't credit such things."

"No, not at all. Your faith in science can and should remain unshaken, my dear. I mean cosmic realities which are as much a part of the natural universe as you or I, but representative of precincts where perhaps the very laws of physics differ from what we know. Alien mentalities, a kind of cosmically cold and horrifying set of perspectives. Working through Isadora Blank and company, they mean to accomplish something. But precisely what, I cannot venture yet to say."

This nebulous declaration naturally caused Soph and Reuben to worry further about the toils in which their friends had gotten themselves enmeshed.

Eventually all of the food reserved for their first meal had been consumed with enjoyment. Reuben had remarked, "My god, this chicken could take a prize! Soph, you prove yourself not only a whiz of a scribbler, but a consumate kitchen angel. He who has you for a helpmeet someday may account himself a lucky man."

This praise caused Sophronia to blush, and she could only pooh-pooh it.

After turning onto Chopmist Hill Road the company found themselves in a district of widely separated farm houses of antique and impoverished mien, hunkered down amidst scrubby vegetation and looking more like excresences of the soil than manmade structures. The road steadily ascended, for Chopmist Hill was the highest point in the town of Scituate, and indeed one of the highest elevations in the whole state.

Before too much longer, they arrived at their destination, foreknown from inquiries made at the Scituate Town Hall.

The Commune of the Black Goat had once been, ironically, the headquarters of the Second Free Will Baptist Society, until the decades-long decay, dwindling and dissolution of that flock. An estate composed of one large hip-roofed house displaying peeling paint, and numerous straggling, shoddy outbuildings, the whole assemblage sat on the naked crown of Chopmist Hill. Seeing the place, Sophronia was struck with an anomalous sensation. Although the day was bright and mild, it seemed as if the whole place were helplessly exposed to the naked black interstellar realms lying just beyond the duplicitous blue sky.

A few tethered horses and a buggy betokened the presence of at least some persons, but no one was visible. A lone black goat, far from eldritch in its manner or behavior, cropped the weeds of its namesake territory.

Crispus parked their carriage and descended from his perch, while Soph, Reuben and the Professor disembarked—the last-named clutching his satchel. Their driver unlimbered his Nitro Express rifle and said, "I'll wait here, to watch our ride. Just holler if you need me."

Feeling somehow responsible for bringing Reuben and Professor Charnley to this unlikely camp, Sophronia strode bravely in the advance of their little party towards the house. But before she could venture inside, the sound of a familiar female voice emanating from outdoors, to the rear of the house, made her correct her course.

Behind the main building, a strange scene awaited.

A dozen acolytes of the Starry Sodality, men and women of varied sorts, all clad in plain robes, sat cross-legged on the weedy lawn. Eagerly,

Sophronia sought out Arthur's face, but found him not—nor Fannie Audet either.

Sitting likewise on a cushioned dais was Isadora Blank. Even in the light of day, the Hierophant retained the ineffable glamour she had exhibited onstage under beguiling gas light. Her russet locks lent her a leonine air, and the suggestive lineaments of her ripe body beneath gossamer fabric conveyed a lush carnal abandonment.

Imperturbable, Isadora Blank finished her address to her disciples before acknowledging the visitors.

"You must first ascend your inner chakras, before you will be qualified to ascend to the stars. Focus and concentrate! Visualize the progression of your wisdom up the column of your spine. You must transcend the merely human! Repeat to yourself these words from the *Bhagavat Geeta*: 'I am the ritual and the sacrifice. I am the womb and the eternal seed.' Now, practice your discipline until I return."

Unfolding herself gracefully, Isadora Blank stepped down from the platform—Sophronia noted it was simply a homely carpet atop some boards atop some hay bales—and gestured her visitors to follow her. Once around the corner of the house, where they would not distract the disciples, the priestess turned to them and smiled graciously.

"Miss Tempest, Mister Standeven, how good to see you again. And do my eyes detect that fabled expert on all things anthropological, Professor Charnley of Brown University?"

The professor nodded solemnly. "I claim no particular distinctions, Miss Blank. I am merely a student of human behaviors, here to assist my friends in their interrogations."

"So I am to assume that you two reporters are here to conduct that interview I promised."

Sophronia said, "Yes, of course. But we had also hoped to have a look about your establishment. Is your entire congregation busy with their, um, chakras, or are there other members present?"

"Oh, no, we have additional followers. They are busy in the fields. We alternate manual and spiritual labors here, to improve the whole person."

"Might we see them before we indulge in our dialogue?"

"Of course. Just go right over the crest of the hill. Your momentary diversion will allow me to complete the training session. Then we'll talk inside."

Sophronia and her friends left the Hierophant behind.

Reaching the high point of the property, they were presented with an unforeseen sight, formerly concealed.

An acre or two of sloping land had been furrowed and planted. But the crop bore no resemblance to any plant Sophronia knew. The dirt rows were occupied by ranks of globular fungoid masses, about shin-high, looking like black truffles or perhaps undersea brain corals.

Hoeing weeds were another dozen acolytes.

And watching over them, like some plantation overseer, was Knygath-in Zhaum. Still wearing his djinn's suit, Zhaum struck Soph like the Simon Legree of some foreign clime.

Zhaum regarded them coolly, but made no move to interfere with their visit.

Now Sophronia spotted Arthur, and beside him Fannie Audet, both berobed as disciples. She hastened over to the pair, her comrades following.

"Arthur! Wherever can have possessed you to flee to this impossible place, and put yourself under the tutelage of this—this witch! You must come back to Providence with us immediately! Your parents are beside themselves."

Arthur appeared flustered yet adamant, fully himself, albeit exhibiting different beliefs than normal, yet with no signs of being mesmerized or coerced. "Sophronia, I appreciate your concern and the efforts you have made to track me down. But my mind is made up. I have cast my lot with the Sodality, in hopes of a more glorious future life among the stars. I would like for you too to join us, but I suspect that your nature is too skeptical. So all I ask is to be left alone to pursue my destiny."

Sensing that argument would only harden her fiance's position, Soph said, "Arthur, please think carefully for the next hour or three upon your choices. We will be leaving then, and there's plenty of room in our carriage for two more. Perhaps Miss Audet could likewise be swayed to come home, if that's what's holding you here."

But Fannie Audet had been unswayed by Reuben's similar implorings. "Rube, honey, it's not that we ain't had some nanty narking together. But it's just that this here is where my soul has come to rest—and I never even knew till now that I had one!"

Soph noticed that Reuben's hand was ready to withdraw something from his pocket—possibly the aforementioned cosh—but she shook her head in the negative, rolling her eyes towards that fearsome scarecrow, Zhaum. Reuben sighed, then released his grip on the blackjack.

Reluctantly then, Soph turned aside from her beau and walked disconsolately away. Zhaum glared at them, but did not pursue or threaten.

Back at the house, Soph found the class dismissed. Venturing warily inside, the party came upon Isadora Blank ensconced on a couch in the shabbily furnished first-floor parlor, which housed what had to be the remnant chairs and tables, framed lithographs and bookcases from the Baptist heyday. Although her mind and heart were preoccupied with Arthur's condition and contrariness, Soph forced herself to assume a reportorial professionalism. With Reuben's aid, she began to conduct an interview with the priestess, although with only half her attention.

Her notes later revealed a colorful farrago of imprecise and hazy allusions to distant countries, training by secret masters, a humble apprenticeship, aspirations to spiritual transcendence, and a desire for the betterment of the whole human race. It was a beguiling fairytale that went down easily while in progress, but showed itself full of holes afterwards—at least to Soph's skeptical mind.

Finally Soph's questions and probes petered out, having broken themselves against the bland impenetrable walls of Isadora Blank's fortress of generalities.

Only then, as she looked up from her pad and pencil, did Sophronia notice that Professor Charnley was missing. She became alarmed, but tried to maintain her sangfroid.

"Well, Miss Blank, I expect we have enough information now for our piece on the Starry Sodality. Isn't that right, Mister Standeven?"

Reuben was scratching his head like a burglar stymied by an uncrackable safe. "I guess so. Can we return if we have more questions, or even see you in town?"

"Of course. I'd be delighted."

The priestess conducted them out the front entrance.

Soph's heart jumped for joy when she saw, first, Crispus Bannister vigilant by their coach, and then Professor Charnley, standing by an adjacent barn. The professor's beckoning stance plainly indicated he wished them to join him, and so they did, with Isadora seemingly unruffled.

"Miss Blank," said Charnley, "may I ask what this is?"

He swung open the barn doors.

Inside was a huge wagon, a mighty dray. It featured an outlandish simulacrum of some kind of never-neverland, a wild and tangled alien landscape scaled down to fit the bed of the wagon. Gnarled trees, grasping lianas and half-seen monsters, all fashioned of some malleable material and painted in the most eye-straining colors.

"Oh, this little thing," said Isadora lightly, "is to be our surprise entry into the Trades Procession on the twenty-third. We felt that as one of the newer enterprises in the city, we might attempt to make a paltry showing amongst the other more established concerns. I hope you won't give away our small surprise, Professor. Do you like our creation? It's meant to resemble the jungles of Abbith, a world around the star of Xoth."

"Yes, I recognized it as such. Generally regarded as a rather inhospitable place, I think."

Isadora Blank smiled. "To some, assuredly. To others, not."

The priestess saw them back to their carriage then.

Sophronia strained her gaze one final time towards the truffle fields, but was not rewarded with any last-minute appearance by Arthur or Fannie. Reluctantly, she and the others boarded the carriage, and Crispus rolled them safely away.

All disspirited and meditative, no one said anything for the length of their travel down Chopmist Hill Road. The remaining journey back to the city stretched away like a funeral. As they approached the intersection where they had enjoyed lunch—seemingly a happier eternity ago—Sophronia was about to speak—

But a sudden act of violence intervened!

As evidenced by noise and jolting, their horse must have reared up, neighing wildly and nearly upsetting the coach. Crispus's commands rang out and established some obedience over the nervous steed as they came to a juddering halt.

Sophronia stuck her head out one window. Motion drew her eye upward, and she saw the impossible.

In the sky was an enormous bat-winged wraith, a thing of grey parchment skin stretched over bizarre musculature and misarticulated bones. Its feet and hands were equipped with razored claws. But most terribly, its horned head sported *no face*, just a blank façade! Nonetheless, it seemed to have no trouble zeroing in on their vehicle.

Not wishing to be trapped, Soph impulsively tumbled out of the carriage, falling to the ground. She sensed Reuben and the professor following close behind.

Its silence more frightening than any cries, the apparition swooped down upon her. Soph could feel the buffets from its wings, smell the hot summer dirt of the road. What a catalogue of final sensations!

An enormous blast from the elephant gun erupted, and Soph saw a gaping hole open up in the thing's midriff as it recoiled from the projectile. But there came no blood or kindred fluids, merely shreds of its otherworldly substance.

And that gaping hole now knitted itself together just as swiftly as it had formed!

Reuben stood bravely above Soph, his fists raised in a defensive gesture out of all magnitude to the threat.

The creature resumed its plummet.

And then came the voice of Professor Charnley, spewing out contorted syllables akin to those Isadora Blank had used in the theater. Held aloft in the professor's hands glowed the very same trapezohedron that Soph had handled in his aeyrie, the dull stone now enlivened!

The winged being tried to retreat, but too late. Momentum carried it into the swelling nimbus radiating from the shaped stone, and the flying monster evaporated like a soap bubble.

Reuben helped Sophronia to stand. Her legs felt quavery, but she forced herself to exude calmness.

"Reuben, your risked your life for me."

"No more than Crispus or the Prof did."

"I shan't forget any of it."

Reuben grinned. "I'll hold you that, and claim my share of the reward at some future date."

Their bewildered driver was staring at the gun in his hand and shaking his head. "I ain't never seen anything stand up to old Bessie like that. What in tarnation was it?"

The Professor was calmly restoring the trapezohedron to its special box. Once the box was latched, he said, "A night-gaunt. But I was ready for just such an eventuality. You apprehend better now, I think, what we are up against."

The rest of the trip home passsed in relieved but dismal silence as Sophronia contemplated just what their fate might have been, had the professor not been so well prepared and equipped.

The path of their return to the city brought them first and most conveniently to 380 Broadway, around six PM. Uncertain about what might come next in their quest to unriddle the intentions of the Starry Sodality, Sophronia prepared to say thank you and goodbye to her comrades, and to arrange, at the very least, another meeting amongst themselves soon.

But as the carriage pulled up to Sophronia's home, her mother rushed out frantically, interrupting any attempt at planning.

"Soph, oh Soph, thank God you've returned! Your brother's gone missing since this morning. We need everyone to help find him! I can't bear to imagine him all lost and hurt!"

9.
TO ULTHAR, AND BEYOND!

Holding the Tempest family cat Clutterbuck firmly in the cradle of her arms, Sophronia paused at the spot where the ginger tom had led her, before he had paused to sit and unconcernedly lick himself. Could this be the secret means of finding her lost brother? She dared to hope so, though she found it hard to believe that such a mundane place could furnish a clue to anywhere outré.

Soph stood in front of the famous drinking fountain that graced the sidewalk boundary of the Providence Athenaeum Library on Benefit Street, halfway up College Hill in the direction of Professor Charnley's hideout. Inside a decorative pillared arch carved in the granite wall, a plain metal pipe coursed forth delicious water that fell, first, into a carven clamshell, and thence into a large trough whose drain diameter was calculated nicely to prevent overflow but always leave a full reservoir. Inscribed under the top of the arch was the legend: COME HITHER EVERY ONE THAT THIRSTETH.

Sophronia ran over once more the tangled sequence of events that had led her here on this early morning of Wednesday, June 9th.

When Minnie Tempest had feverishly accosted the returnees last night with news of Oscar's vanishing, all thoughts of the Starry Sodality had been instantly driven from her brain. And yet, as the dimensions and details of Oscar's disappearance had been revealed, Sophronia began to believe that the two were not unconnected.

For Oscar had vanished while embarked on his quixotic search for Ulthar, the same venue to which Knygathin Zhaum had once alluded.

This is what had happened, based on the collated and clarified reports from Oscar's pals who had been with him at the time of the enigmatic incident.

Yesterday morning after breakfast, while Sophronia was on the road to Scituate, Oscar had resumed his search for the passage to Ulthar, putative home of all the missing Providence cats. Failing of results, he had grown tired of following Clutterbuck about the immediate neighborhood, and so, putting the cat into a lidded pie basket (despite Oscar's sometimes rough treatment of the beast, it was generally mild and tractable, and even seemed to love the lad), Oscar had rounded up some fellows and headed down to the South Water Street docks. And there the mystery had occurred.

Setting Clutterbuck free, Oscar had followed the cat as it idled down the length of one pier, possibly trawling the scent of fish. At the end of that dock stood a small shack, no bigger than a privy. A smudged window afforded a view of the untenanted interior.

Oscar opened the door and entered with his cat.

The two had never exited.

When the other boys got tired of waiting, they opened the cabin door—the place had been under their observation the whole while—and found it empty. Baffled, they nevertheless did not think to tell the Tempest family until the lunch hour.

Upon receiving the shock, Minnie Tempest was immediately convinced that Oscar, who must have been spirited away through some impossibly concealed trapdoor in the shack, and into a waiting boat, was on his way to the white-slave markets of the Orient.

The hue and cry was raised, and six hours later, upon Sophronia's return, all the vast efforts of the searchers had revealed no more about the affair than what obtained at its inception.

Professor Charnley, Crispus and Reuben had instantly offered their services in the hunt.

"I have a certain scrying stone back at the library that might be of use," said the Professor, and departed.

"Let me return this here carriage," Crispus said, "and then I'll roust out some of the Snowtown folks to search."

"There must be a dozen of my cronies hanging out at Pickman's Ale House," said Reuben. "I'll give a cooey, and they'll come running!"

After her three friends departed, Soph realized that there was little aid she could offer in the way of physically canvassing the town, and so she took her mother's arm and ushered her inside. There the womenfolk spent a generally sleepless night, receiving reports from the various areas as they were combed, while subsisting on cookies, tea and cold ham sandwiches. (Bertha performed her extraordinary duties admirably, ceasing her continuous Nordic weeping for "poor little Oscar" at random intervals, whenever handsome young male searchers stopped in for a revivifying snack.)

Soph managed to catch a few winks here and there, so that when dawn broke she felt possessed of about a quarter of her usual energy—a miracle, especially considering the depletions wrought by the night-gaunt attack.

She ventured out onto the front stoop of 380 Broadway for a breath of fresh air. The street's normal activities went on as usual, just as if her brother were not vanished down a hole in the fabric of the universe.

Suddenly she felt something rubbing on her ankles.

Clutterbuck.

Soph snatched up the cat and rushed inside.

"Mother, Mother, look who's returned!"

Minnie Tempest was not as enthused as her daughter. "Oh, Soph, what does that matter? Of course Clutterbuck was not abducted. The white-slavers have no need for cats!"

At that moment, Clarence Tempest entered the house. He looked as if he had been dragged behind a runaway horse over six miles of gravel road.

"Papa, look, it's Clutterbuck!"

"Daughter, please, don't trouble me with inanities. I recognize our own cat, after all. I'm just back for some coffee before I go out again. We are arranging boats to drag the Cove. My God, how I wish I were dead, rather than be forced to utter that sentence with regard to my own flesh and blood! Moreover, a second calamity has struck our fair city. A universal, not personal calamity. Mayor Doyle has just died."

Even under their familial strain, Sophronia found resources within herself to sympathize with the dreadful news. The city's favorite son, beloved by all and reigning as mayor longer than any predecessor, he who had done so much to arrange the grand and glorious Two-Hundred-and-Fiftieth Anniversary celebrations, had not lived to see the joyful fruition. His predestined successor, Gilbert Robbins, was a fine man, but no paragon like Doyle. No greater tragedy since the burning of Roger Williams's settlement during King Phillip's War had ever happened! "What cheer, Netop?" now indeed!

Realizing she could not convey to her parents the significance of Clutterbuck's manifestation—if he had indeed been to Ulthar, he was the only cat ever to return—Sophronia took the pet to her chambers. There she refreshed herself and changed clothes. Twenty-four hours in the same garments had left her feeling rather "ripe." Then, without speaking to anyone, she left the house, carrying the cat in a hatbox.

Lacking any more logical starting point, Sophronia commenced her search at the dock where Oscar had vanished. But Clutterbuck showed no interest in returning to the shack. Soph recalled how Knygathin Zhaum had remarked that the entrance to Ulthar wandered. Evidently, it was no longer here.

But Clutterbuck seemed to have some idea of its new location. Like a furry arrow, he had trotted as directly as possible from South Water to South Main and thence to the foot of College Street. Uphill alongside the flank of the large courthouse, and to a stop in front of the Athenaeum Fountain.

Now Sophronia wondered what came next.

Clutterbuck showed her.

He walked unhesitatingly into the granite wall that hosted the fountain just as if it were a mirage, or a magically painted scrim of smoke, his tail disappearing last.

Closing her eyes, Sophronia practically hurled herself after the cat, all the while expecting her face and bosom to smash against the unyielding stone.

But she encountered no such commonsense barrier.

She opened her eyes.

Above her spread a velvety night sky mapped with an infinity of polychrome stars in no discernible constellations. So deep was it that for a moment Soph felt as if she were falling impossibly upward into the sidereal depths.

Something told her that it was always night here in this new dimension, that no sun ever rose and shone.

Drawing her gaze downward, Sophronia saw that she stood on the breast of a small hill, and that below her on the level ground, at no great remove, stretched a compact township, a thousand queer thatched cottages with lighted windows, with a few larger buildings interspersed along narrow and twisting cobbled roads. A somnolent snaking river bisected the town, with one distinctive elbow nearest to her, and somehow its name obtruded into Soph's brain: the Skai.

<<I must take my leave of you now.>>

She did not cognize those words as traditional verbal speech, but rather as some other form of information delivered down impalpable channels. She turned her head to view her interlocutor.

Clutterbuck stood bipedally, as large as his ex-mistress, so that he could stare eye-to-eye. His whiskers twitched as he spoke, and in some manner his muzzle conveyed a small smile.

<<I need to return to my wife and children,>> said the cat. <<Good luck finding your brother. Tell him he must eat his own vitamin biscuits from now on.>>

Clutterbuck strode manfully off, humming a gay tune.

Once she had recovered from her bewilderment, Sophronia followed down the dark grassy slope.

The cobbles of Ulthar's streets were slick with night dew. Sophronia walked carefully, lest she slip. She shared the roadways with humans—or what curiously passed for humans here in Ulthar—and of course with many human-sized cats, all perambulating proudly like Puss-in-Boots. Citizens of both these kinds acknowledged her presence politely, and yet Soph found herself reluctant to stop anyone from their busy rounds and make her queries.

Where is my brother?

What can you tell me of one Knygathin Zhaum and Isadora Blank, of the Starry Sodality and their plans?

Her wanderings up and down the byways of Ulthar seemed to go on forever. The changeless night afforded no metrics of time. She passed several taverns—or was it the same one, over and over?—which looked inviting enough and where she might have refreshed herself. But recalling the consequences for those who had wandered into Oberon's realm and eaten the food thereof, she declined any wordless invitations.

Her feet grew sore, her limbs heavy, her mind sluggish. She sat down on a horse-mounting stone outside a cobbler's. (DOUBLE PAWS OUR SPECIALTY.)

And along came two impossible creatures.

They looked like rolypoly men made of dough, as if someone had animated two obese clay Buddha statues.

<<What's this, what's this?>> said one.

<<I think it's a Thing from that world where the Yith rule.>>

<<The Yith! They've been extinct for a hundred and fifty million years!>>

<<Don't be dense or fractious! You know the place I mean, by any designation.>>

<<Oh please, sirs,>> said Soph, <<who are you? Can you help me find my brother, and learn what I need to know about some enemies?>>

<<I am Chu-bu,>> said one gingerbread man, <<and he is Sheemish.>>

<<No, not at all!>> said the other. <<I am Sheemish and he is Chu-bu!>>

<<But that's exactly what I said!>>

<<You certainly did not!>>

The pair began flailing at each other, and when their ineffectual blows landed, they left temporary dents in their doughy forms.

Sophronia got wearily up from her seat. <<If you can't help me, I must search on.>>

<<Who said we can't help you?>>

<<Well, we really can't, can we?>>

<<No, but we can take her to someone who can! Another creature from the Yith world. A clever ex-pat!>>

<<Must I remind you that the Yith no longer rule that planet? Why do you insist?>>

<<Oh, botheration! What's a hundred and fity million years one way or the other? Just ignore the perversity of Chu-bu—or is he Sheemish?—O Thing from Yith, and follow us!>>

Having no other recourse, Soph lifted her leaden feet one after the other in pursuit of the pastry men.

The open door of the house where they left her cast an oblong of light onto the street. Soph stepped inside.

No fellow human occupied the front room. Only on the table stood a foot-high metal cylinder wired up to various ancillary apparatuses, featuring lenses and sounding membranes, like some kind of infernal Edison invention. Soph faltered at the unexpected sight.

<<Yes,>> said the cylinder, <<what can I do for you?>>

<<Are you a human inside such a small can?>>

<<Just my preserved brain, actually. But once I was like you, a man named Henry Akeley, from Earth. Townshend, Vermont, to be precise.>>

<<Oh, Mister Akeley, I need your help so badly!>>

Sophronia explained her twin quests. The cylinder—Akeley—was silent for a time.

<<I believe I can easily direct you to your brother. But the other matter is less clear and of more consequence. Allow me a few minutes to communicate with the Outer Beings. They are friends to humanity, and should respond helpfully.>>

Sophronia shifted from foot to foot during the interminable period of silence. She wished for a chair, but there were none. After all, what use could a brain in a tin can have for a chair? Soph's thoughts began to whirl, as she envisioned a naked brain with legs and arms and face, sitting on a stool inside its can.

<<The Outer Beings have answered. They are perturbed. Apparently, your Starry Sodality is recruiting colonists for other planets, spheres where by treaty they are not allowed. But Blank and Zhaum believe that if they can only establish a sizable presence on these worlds, they will present a *fait accompli* to rival claimants that will allow the Sodality *de facto* permanent possession of the disputed territories, and all the riches that entails. But they need many humans, not just the few disciples they have managed so far to attract. And so they intend to open up a gate and pull through hundreds of folks, willy-nilly.>>

<<They can create a rift like the one that brought me here?>>

<<Yes, but much larger, and irresistible in its gravitation.>>

Sophronia thought a moment. Where would they open up such a portal? Not on the farm in Scituate. Not even in the Amateur Dramatic Hall. Where and when might they have access to the large crowd they needed? The Trades Procession! The Sodality float in the barn!

<<I must find my brother and return to Earth! The Sodality must be stopped!>>

<<The Outer Beings would be glad of that. Unfortunately, they are banned from interfering directly in your affairs. They *could* send you a spell to force the gate closed. But that is, only if you had the proper instrument to receive it. I doubt you do, though, for it's a very rare item. It's called the Shining Trapezohedron...>>

<<But we do have it, we do!>>

<<Ah, that gives us a chance. I will let the Outer Beings know this, and they will download the code into the Trapezohedron's RAM.>>

Soph made no sense of this gibberish, but expressed her gratitude heartily.

<<Now, Mister Akeley, if you could just help me find my brother!>>

<<I think you will discover that he is currently the feature attraction at a place known as the Ball of Yarn. Leaving my house, turn left, then your

first right, then left again, and you should find it easily. Farewell, and good luck!>>

Sophronia raced off, all weariness forgotten.

The Ball of Yarn was a tavern catering just to cats. Sophronia could smell its fishy bill of fare from a block away. She bulled in past a half dozen furry feline forms in the antechambers, and found herself in the tavern's large main room.

There on a small stage was Oscar. He was naked, save for a collar with a bell on it, and he was being made by a feline ringmaster cracking a whip to jump through hoops, mount platforms and leap off, and perform other circus tricks.

Sophronia cast about wildly for some means of distraction. Her eye fell on the tavern's bar.

They did not serve liquor, but catnip, a score of different types and grades, all neatly stored in large glass jars, as on a pharmacy's shelves.

Sophronia grabbed a broom from a kitty maid, and leaped atop the wooden bar. She smashed every jar within reach.

The released flood of intoxicating leaf drove the crowd mad! They dove for the spillage, rolling in it and fighting each other, hissing, clawing, with tails inflating like bottle-brushes.

Soph jumped down, darted onstage, grabbed a dazed Oscar by the hand, and fled.

The rift home! She had not asked Akeley where it was. Now she had gotten turned around, and could not find his house again. She would have to pray the portal had not drifted yet from where it had deposited her. Perhaps indeed it was only the Earth-anchored end of the tunnel that drifted, for it always led to Ulthar.

On the edge of town, orienting herself by the unique configuration of the Skai River, she found the hill where she had arrived—or so she hoped. Faint tracks in the grass—cat feet and human shoes—seemed to mark the earlier passage of Clutterbuck and herself.

She sped up the hill to where the tracks ended, and flung herself and Oscar into space.

Daylight hurt her eyes, and she had to squint. When she could see, she found herself in a familiar locale. In the mouth of the alley that ran alongside Gladding's Department Store.

The sidewalk was packed with an endless sea of happy eager people. Music played from several marching bands.

Sophronia grabbed the arm of a mother busily herding five peppermint-stick-sucking children out of danger in the street.

"What's going on? What day is this?"

Before replying, the woman regarded the naked and be-collared Oscar with a rueful expression that said, *Dearie, they are a handful, aren't they?*

"Why, it's June the twenty-third, my sweets, and the big Trades Procession is about to begin!"

10.

THE TRADES PROCESSION TO THE STARS

Several songs had been specifically commissioned for this epic occasion, receiving preview presentations at various concerts in advance of the big day, and Soph now recognized the one emitted by the passing military band as "City of Freedom."

> *City of beauty, favored of God and exalted in name,*
> *Foremost and fearless in patriotic duty, wearing her scars and*
> *escutcheons of fame,*
> *Struggling alone with the tempest and gloom…*

She chose to regard this allusion to her patronym as a good omen.

She was exhausted and dazed, her head filled with strange new wonders. She was saddled with a naked little brother, deprived of a couple of weeks of her mortal existence whilst under Elf Hill, and utterly famished. She had no idea of what her parents or her friends thought of her long inexplicable absence. Maybe they considered her dead, and had already finished mourning her. She had no immediate notion of how best to contact Professor Aurion Charnley and inform him of the exact nature of Blank & Zhaum's plot, along with apprising him of the new potency instilled in the Shining Trapezohedron by the Outer Beings and meant to counter those schemes. But despite all these burdens and obstacles, she felt imbued with hope and courage and a sense of possible victory. Look at what she had already endured. There was no chance in Hades that she would let the Starry Sodality pillage her city!

But first things first.

Sophronia again addressed, with some urgency, the friendly woman with her unruly brood, who stood now in her eyes as a symbol of all the goodness she was striving to protect.

"Please, ma'am, what is your name? I am Sophronia Tempest. My father is Clarence Tempest, vice-president at Kendall Manufacturing Company."

"Why, they make Soapine! 'Soapine, the Dirt Killer! It Washes Everything!' I couldn't manage my household without it! Oh, yes, I'm Clara Spink. And my children—stop that!—are Gustavus, Billy, Lucy, Wendell and Linnie."

"Clara, I must impinge upon your charity with several requests. First, tell me the hour, and exactly when the Procession commences."

"Why, it's ten AM, and the first wagons do not roll until eleven. My husband is Barton Spink, you know, of Murray, Spink and Company, Fancy Goods. They have four drays in the Procession. One features a giant cigar, one displays Tally-Ho shirts, one shows glassware in a pyramid, and the last portrays a giant American Eagle. The children can't wait to see their father pass by and cheer him on."

Gustavus—or was that Wendell?—crossed his eyes and stuck out his tongue.

An hour till the Procession took off. Surely the Starry Sodality would wait to trigger the cosmic gate until their wagon reached the place on the route with the largest concentration of people. Not the beginning, nor the end. But where would that be?

The Mayoral Reviewing Stand, planned to have been erected at the intersection of Sutton and Broadway, not far from Soph's home!

Soph returned her attention to Clara Spink, who was casting a bemused glance at this young, wild-eyed woman accompanied by a nude boy. Sophronia could only imagine what the matron was thinking.

"Clara, I must ask you to please take charge of my little brother, Oscar. I cannot send him home, for my parents are no doubt off the premises, busy with this very Procession. Nor can I take him with me, for I am about to embark on a dangerous errand. Would you do me this immense favor?"

"Why, certainly! What's one more child when you've got five? Oscar, come over here, dear."

From a capacious carpetbag, Clara Spink removed a fresh shirt.

"Billy is always spilling things on himself, so I came prepared."

She dressed Oscar in the overlarge garment that served to cover his indecency, and handed him a peppermint stick.

"Might I have one of those too, Clara? I very much need a boost."

Soph instantly bit off half the proffered candy and crunched it. It tasted heavenly.

She crouched down to Oscar's level, and removed the Ulthar collar from his neck. Inert till now, the boy seemed to be gradually regaining his normal demeanor and feisty spirit.

"Oscar, you stay with Mrs. Spink for now. If I don't return for you, just go to our home at the end of the day."

Assuming there's a house to return to, she mentally added.

"All right, Soph."

Sophronia made ready to leave, for she now had a destination in mind.

"Soph?"

"Yes?"

"You won't never tell no one about—about me on stage with the cats, will you?"

"No, never! That will be our little secret."

Clara Spink was wiping Lucy's nose—or was that Linnie's?—when Soph made her grateful adieu.

Then, rucking up her skirts, she began to run—to run as she never had, even on the playing fields of St. Mary's!

Gladding's Department Store was midtown. Brown University's New Library was many blocks away, and some of those blocks uphill at that.

Even weaving through the crowds and having to wait for gaps in the festive marchers in order to cross certain streets, Sophronia made remarkable time. Nonetheless, she felt extremely ragged and could barely draw a breath when she reached the corner of Prospect and Waterman.

There, much to her surprise, she saw the *Journal* carriage parked out front! Pausing just a moment to recover herself, she laid a hand briefly on the nose of the loyal, night-gaunt-tested bay stallion, then dashed up the library steps.

One flight, two flights, three flights, then the ladder!

Halfway emergent through the trap door and into the Professor's aeyrie, Soph paused.

The tiny room was stuffed with her friends: the Professor, Crispus Bannister, Mack Callender—and Reuben Standeven.

Grinning broadly, this last-named now said, "Murderin' Irishman, my girl! What took you so long?"

* * * *

In order to reach Broadway and Sutton, the *Journal* carriage could not take the shortest, most direct route, east to west, for all the intervening streets were filled with marchers and spectators. They had to detour by Smith Hill, making a big loop around the congested downtown. The Trades Procession would begin from Market Square and thread its way down Westminster and Jackson streets before reaching the reviewing stand on Broadway. This slow and prolonged course for the exhibitors, combined with Crispus Bannister's expert driving and navigation, should afford them enough time to beat the first display wagon there.

And, giving additional insurance, the Starry Sodality entry, a latecomer to the ranks, would be the final dray, preceding only a smattering of lesser tradesmen who followed in simple fashion, merely astride their horses or on foot.

Sophronia sat beside the Professor. In his lap rested the elaborate chest that contained the Shining Trapezohedron. Additionally, the Professor's person was encumbered with a dozen other enigmatic and esoteric charms, pinned to his vest or strung on cords around his neck. In one case, they featured as a large silver cuff studded with several gems. His normally relaxed and ruminative visage was tautened with an undeniable tension kept under firm control.

Across the way sat Reuben and Callender. Soph felt gratitude towards her boss for throwing in his lot with their ragtag bunch. But she still nursed some shreds of vexation for her co-worker. He had greeted her reappearance so blithely, and with such frivolity, that she could hardly credit him with any tender or noble feelings. This was not the way a girl liked to be received when she returned from the dead!

What a head-spinning interval she had just endured!

When Soph had recovered her wits and clambered fully into the cupola, she had been greeted with joy and warmth by the other three men. And, truth be told, even Reuben had moderated his innate flippancy to make her feel that her homecoming was special. And in short order, wasting none of their precious time, the Professor had explained to her how and why they had been awaiting her.

"You recall that on the day Oscar disappeared I left you to employ my scrying stone? Well, sure enough, after some long hours of finessing, I was able to pick up visual traces of his passage to Ulthar. And while I was trying to design the best way to convince your parents of his occult whereabouts, you showed up in the stone's purview as well!"

Reuben chimed in. "We watched your every action there! Crikey, you moved slow as molasses. We could step away for hours, and you barely shifted your pinky finger."

"Yes," affirmed Charnley, "the temporal disparities between the two continua were enormous."

Reuben said, "We couldn't *hear* a blessed thing, of course, with that damn silly stone, but over time we saw it all. That was a treble-ex job you did rescuing your brother!"

"Please, don't ever reveal you witnessed his humiliation!"

"Oh, we shan't," said the Professor. "But in any case, I was finally able to use the stone to convince your parents that you were both somewhat safe. Well, not precisely safe, but at least accounted for, and with a good prospect of returning home eventually."

"So they don't think Oscar and I are dead?"

"Oh my, no. They finally accepted your spatial displacement from the fields we know, and understood the need for secrecy. To calm the searchers, they put out the story that a relative had taken Oscar to Boston in a confusion of arrangements, and that you had gone there too, for a vacation. They are still anxious for your return, of course. When, several days ago, we saw you start to run up the hill in Ulthar and toward the rift, we calculated exactly when you would pop back out in Providence."

"But not where, of course," Reuben added. "Which is why you had no welcoming committee."

"We had to assume you'd have the wits to search me out here immediately. And so we just waited."

Sophronia hastily assimilated all this information about her missing weeks. She was glad to have this confirmation of her incredible experiences. And she felt a little proud at the compliments paid her initiative and boldness. But with a sudden shock, she realized that the clock was still ticking toward the moment when Blank & Zhaum would initiate their catastrophe.

"Professor, I must tell you what I learned from Mister Akeley, that disembodied brain! It's a most perfidious scheme!"

"Ah," exclaimed Reuben, "we wondered why you were fussing so long with that old jam jar!"

Professor Charnley and the others listened keenly to Sophronia's account. When she had finished, silence obtained, until the Professor spoke their mutual thoughts.

"This is worse than I could have imagined. A gigantic crack in space that will siphon off our citizens.... But you came back with a weapon."

He excused himself to retrieve the Shining Trapezohedron and test its new capacities.

Soph turned to her editor. "Mister Callender, I am most heartened to find you here. But how did you get involved?"

"Why, your partner in crime, Mister Standeven, saw fit to enroll me. He explained everything you had discovered about the Starry Sodality, and how you two were on the point of breaking the biggest story this town had ever seen. But more crucially, when I learned that these bastards planned to harm our fair city in some diabolical fashion, I knew I had to play a part in foiling them."

Reuben added, "I wish we could have convinced other powers that be to join in as well. But the Mayor, the police, the Governor, major businessmen, firemen, the militias, the Grange—no one would listen to us. They all said we were barmy. Actually, I think some of them were in league with Blank and company. Oh, not that they knew about her ultimate scheme, but they had been won over to her airy-fairy pipe dreams. Her personal charm was considerable, as we can attest."

"So it's just we five against them?"

Professor Charnley had finished putting the talisman through its new paces. He took the time to demonstrate for Sophronia the simple sigils which activated the device, making sure she had them pat, even guiding her hand in the patterns until the gestures became a bodily memory. Then he addressed her concern.

"Yes, it's all up to us. But we five should suffice. Our defense must of necessity be a simple one that does not require a large force. Here is what I envision. Blank and Zhaum open the gate, leading to a world of their choosing. They hope to pull through scores, if not hundreds of our fellows, and then, I believe, to follow them, leaving behind our depredated globe for their intended destination. But the instant they activate the flaw in space, I will change its attunement to a far less salubrious destination, using the Trapezohedron's new powers. We shove our two malefactors through, and then I close the whole shebang down. They shall never be able to return."

"But," reasoned Sophronia, "won't we lose at least a few innocent by-standers into the sucking void while all this is going on?"

Charnley looked grim. "I am afraid it will be unavoidable. Which is why we must move as fast as possible when the time comes. Now, as to the possible location of our defense—"

Sophronia jumped in with her logic about the reviewing stand, and found quick concord from the others. And so they hastened off.

Now in the cab of the carriage, Sophronia ceased her musings when the Professor tapped her on the arm with a small envelope.

"Miss Tempest, I'd like you to hold onto this letter for me. If all goes well, I shall reclaim it. If I suffer a misadventure, then you may read it."

"But Professor, you won't—"

"Shush! Just do as I ask, please."

Having lost her reticule somewhere in Ulthar, Soph had no recourse but to lift her skirt and tuck the folded envelope into the top of her high shoe. Callender and Charnley averted their eyes at the display, but Reuben stared and then whistled!

That boy was the absolute worst!

After making their wide circumambulation, Crispus brought them efficiently to the block of Sutton Street on Federal Hill, parallel to Broadway. They followed the cross street as far as they could before the crowds near the Broadway intersection halted their progress. They jumped out and hurried the last distance on foot.

On Broadway, they encountered the grand reviewing stand from the rear, all tricked out in colorful bunting. The platform was filled with frock-coated, top-hatted gents and their ladies in finery and ostrich-feather-plumed chapeaus. Bulling their way to the front ranks of the numerous spectators, the quintet arrived at curbside just as one of the many dignitaries—Chief Justice Durfee, in fact—was launching into a speech.

"The traveller who, after a long day's journey, reaches the summit of some high hill which overlooks the way behind him, delights to pause with backward gaze and review the scenes through which he has passed. His memory fills out the picture; until at last his whole journey, tedious sometimes in the making, lies before him, flooded with the golden evening light, a pure and perfect pleasure in the retrospect. Today the city pauses on such a high spectacular summit, and, looking backward through the vista of two hundred and fifty years, sees the long series of her historic experiences rising in visionary pageant before her...."

Within minutes of Durfee's tedious conclusion, the first float rolled up: Branden & Keep, Flour Merchants.

Sophronia at first felt a vast impatience and worry, and she shifted nervously from foot to foot, eyeing her fellow defenders with anxious imploring glances.

But then, as more and more floats came by, under the glorious June sun and to the cheers of the spectators, a curious phenomenon overtook her. The array of familiar products and plain faces, the evident exultancy and pride of the marchers, the excitement and joy of the crowd—everything conspired to instill in her a kind of placid confidence, a homely assurance that evil could not prevail against this bulwark of honest commerce, exemplary of mankind's desire to make a better world.

When the float from Murray, Spink and Company, Fancy Goods, passed, she grinned to imagine the excitement of Mrs Spink and her flock, with Oscar there too.

And when the Soapine float came by, displaying a giant whale being scrubbed by a team of Esquimaux, and she saw her father and mother smiling and waving proudly aloft, she reached a zenith of transcendant calm.

And greatly would she need all her inner resources, for finally the Starry Sodality dray was approaching! Its contorted alien jungle scene, painted in eye-jarring colors, loomed even more hideously by light of day than it had in the Scituate barn. At the rear of the wagon bed stood the immodestly alluring Isadora Blank and the uncannily repugnant Knygathin Zhaum.

And their perverted diorama was rendered even more obscene by the placement of the unsuspecting robed acolytes among the fake vegetation.

Soph saw Arthur, standing like a pompous fool. She wanted to call out a warning to him, but dared not alert Blank and Zhaum, so she bit her tongue. Would he even have responded? She was never to know.

As no other dray had done, the Sodality float came to a halt in front of the reviewing stand, causing at first mild consternation from the dignitaries and from the marchers behind, who also bumbled to a forced stop.

Isadora Blank could not resist making a taunting speech. Focused entirely on the important people, she was paying no attention to the rabble at her feet. This distraction allowed Crispus, Reuben and Callender to scuttle out into the street and merge with the marchers at the rear of the wagon, a company of lumbermen and foresters, all arrayed in their best gear. Soph remained next to the Professor, to assist as she might.

"Witless cattle!" bellowed the Hierophant. "You will now serve your only true purpose in life. To glorify the Elder Gods!"

With this, she began to chant those incomprehensible syllables, or their kin, that Soph had first heard at the lecture hall, seemingly undead eons ago.

On a plane in the air between and slightly to the forward of Blank and Zhaum, a shimmery opalescent curtain began to form. Within seconds, it had transformed to an impossible window, opening onto the alien world that had served as the model for the float! The air of Providence began to move, pulled into the portal. At first the flow was mild, just enough to snatch all the hats from the dignitaries. But soon, within seconds, it began to increase in speed and power.

The closest acolytes were snatched off their feet and sucked through the well of worlds, wailing! The other dupes began to shriek and clutch at the jungle display. But soon they too were pulled in, along with the debris.

With utter horror, Sophronia witnessed Arthur being whipped off his feet, flying away forever, to a place where no elegant crockery prevailed.

Members of the audience and the dignitaries on the stand began to feel the increasing power of the opened interstellar door. They clutched at the more secure railings or at lamp posts or each other, and for a while could resist. But as the vortex increased by the second, they would soon succumb. And who knew how strong the winds would become, how many square blocks would be devastated?

Standing to the rear of the portal and its unidirectional suction, Zhaum and Blank were safe, laughing and urging on the chaos.

Professor Charnley's fingers were inscribing those patterns he had shown Soph on the surface of the Trapezohedron.

"Now!" he shouted.

Everything seemed to happen simultaneously.

The vista in the portal changed to a roiling, burbling hellscape full of a thousand demonic yellow eyes, the intended doom for Blank and Zhaum—and, unfortunately, for anyone else who might yet be plucked.

Reuben and the one-armed Mack Callender jumped up alongside the startled Zhaum. Callender dropped to his knees and single hand in front of the tall spidery fellow, and Reuben slammed into Zhaum from behind. The combined child-like game field maneuver thrust the giant off his feet and into the maelstrom of wind. He was instantly sucked, gibbering and flailing his boneless limbs, into the churning pool of balefire, along with one or two innocents from the shrieking crowd who had lost their holds.

Crispus was struggling with Isadora. But the supposedly easy task of shoving the lightweight woman off her feet proved surprisingly hard.

For Isadora Blank now revealed her true form.

She had devolved into a writhing mass of ivory protoplasm, all human semblance lost in a nest of whipping tendrils, clattering beaks, stalked eyeballs, and suckered pseudopods, all poking through her ripped robe.

Crispus battled the snaky appendages mightily, but to no seeming avail. Enwrapped around the waist, he was losing ground fast, and faced being hurled into the vortex.

Sophronia raced out into the street, grabbed a lumberman's axe from his slack hands, and heaved it up to the valiant Negro.

With several bold strokes, he freed himself, although without appearing to inflict mortal harm on his assailant.

And the momentarily balked thing that had been Isadora Blank was no closer to the portal than before.

Sophronia found something thrust into her hands.

The Shining Trapezohedron!

"Do as I showed you!" yelled Professor Charnley. "Don't hesitate, no matter what! And do not fear! Not now, nor ever!"

For a plump, older fellow, the Professor could move adroitly. He got aboard the dray, hooking one leg and an arm around a stanchion that threatened to splinter. He ripped one of the charms from around his neck and flourished it where Isadora could see it with her multiple eyes.

It must have been a potent treasure indeed, perhaps even enough to save the day for evil. She cast forward a tentacle to snatch it.

Charnley grabbed the tentacle with both hands, released his leg hold, and cast himself into the suction, his mass serving to pull Isadora off her base and with him.

Soph witnessed a look of fulfilled serenity on the savant's face before he vanished.

Almost of their own accord, her fingers danced across the reactive surface of the Shining Trapezohedron.

The portal closed down instantly, as if it had never been.

Weeping and lamentations and groans resounded, along with the creaking of wooden structures released from the devil wind's grip.

Only when Reuben had taken her in his arms did Sophronia realize that some of the tears were hers.

* * * *

Bertha, flushed and smiling proudly, had outdone herself, with nary a culinary misstep. The feast spread out at 380 Broadway for the Fourth of July would have sufficed for a crowd of twenty. Platters were heaped with meats and vegetables and salads, rolls, pickles and olives, while puddings and sweets brought up the rear. Sparkling wine filled every glass.

But the attendees at the victory celebration and commemoration of the nation's birth were only seven in number: the four Tempests; Mack Callender; Crispus Bannister; and Reuben Standeven.

An eighth place, never to be occupied, had been set for Professor Charnley, and adorned with a wreath.

Outside in the street, cheers and the snap of firecrackers resounded.

Sophronia gazed around the table lovingly. Here were all those most dear to her, those who had gone through hell with her to preserve their fair city, and to be here today, safe and sound.

She even included in those ranks that utter unrepentant jackanapes, Reuben Standeven, whose engagement ring now graced her finger. A paltry gem, consonant with a reporter's salary, but magnificent in her eyes.

After all the toasts had been made, and at least a partial justice paid to the food, and after Minnie Tempest had updated her list of wedding guests with some afterthoughts about distant relatives, Mack Callender said, "Well, Miss Tempest, I do not suppose that you will be returning to your desk at the *Journal*, now that you have a marriage in your future."

"I shall not be. But it is no vow of wedlock that dissuades me from that. Instead, it is my legacy from the Professor."

Only when finally wearily undressing on the night of the Trades Procession disaster had Soph come upon the unremembered envelope saved in her shoe. Its contents had consisted of Professor Charnley's last will and testament, in which he bequeathed all his vast library and collections to Sophronia Tempest, to employ as she saw fit.

Before Callender could speak further, Oscar suddenly gave a yelp.

"Papa, this bad cat scratched me!"

The family's new pet—a calico named Tuppence, who had appeared from nowhere one day to attach herself to the family—sauntered out from underneath the table, wearing a particularly *knowing* look.

"Well," said Clarence Tempest, "I'm sure you were at fault in teasing her. Need I mention a certain tavern to you?"

Oscar paled, and hunched down in his seat. "No, Papa. I'll be good!"

Callender resumed the thread of his conversation. "So, Miss Tempest, you intend to pick up where Professor Charnley left off? Protecting our city from any future occult harm?"

"Yes, that is my goal. But do not use the word 'occult,' I pray you. After all, it's merely science of a different sort, in line with what I've always pursued. There's positively no magic involved."

Reuben's laughter belled out. "Why, my darling scamp, you are stuffed so full of blessed magic that it's leaking out your gorgeous little fingers!"

He took her hand in his. The stone in her ring was all aflame.

www.ingramcontent.com/pod-product-compliance
Lightning Source LLC
Chambersburg PA
CBHW010833250626
47157CB00010B/3268